Victrola

The chosen instrument
of the world's greatest artists

The instrument which plays the greatest music is the instrument you want in your home! The Victrola is supreme. Its supremacy is founded on a basis of great things actually accomplished. It is in millions of homes the world over because it takes into these homes all that is best in every branch of music and entertainment.

The artists who make records exclusively for the Victor are the greatest artists in the world. The Victrola tone is the true and faithful tone of the singer's voice and the master's instrument. It is for this reason that the Victrola is the chosen instrument of practically every artist famous in the world of opera, instrumental music, sacred music, band music, dance music, vaudeville and entertainment.

Go today to a Victor dealer's and listen to this instrument for yourself. Hear Caruso or Melba or Elman or Harry Lauder or Sousa's Band on the Victrola.

Victors and Victrolas—$10 to $400

Victor Talking Machine Co,
Camden, N. J., U. S. A.

Berliner Gramophone Co., Montreal, Canadian Distributors

Important warning. Victor Records can be safely and satisfactorily played only with *Victor Needles or Tungs-tone Stylus* on Victors or Victrolas. Victor Records cannot be safely played on machines with jeweled or other reproducing points.

To insure Victor quality, always look for the famous trademark, "His Master's Voice." It is on every Victrola and every Victor Record. It is the identifying label on all genuine Victrolas and Victor Records.

"HIS MASTER'S VOICE"
REG. U.S. PAT OFF.

New Victor Records demonstrated at all dealers on the 28th of each month

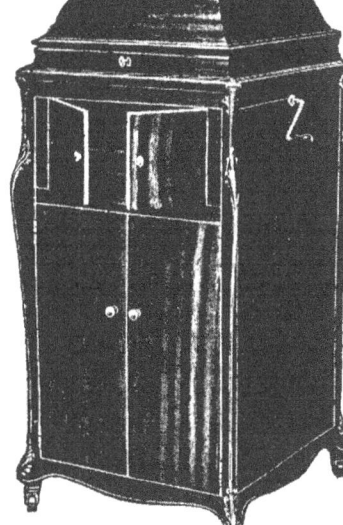

Victrola XVI, $200
Victrola XVI, electric, $250

Mahogany or oak

Richard Harding Davis said, "No lover of real stories can afford to miss reading Morgan Robertson's stories."

Booth Tarkington says, "Morgan Robertson's stories are bully! — his sea is foamy, his men have hair on their chests"

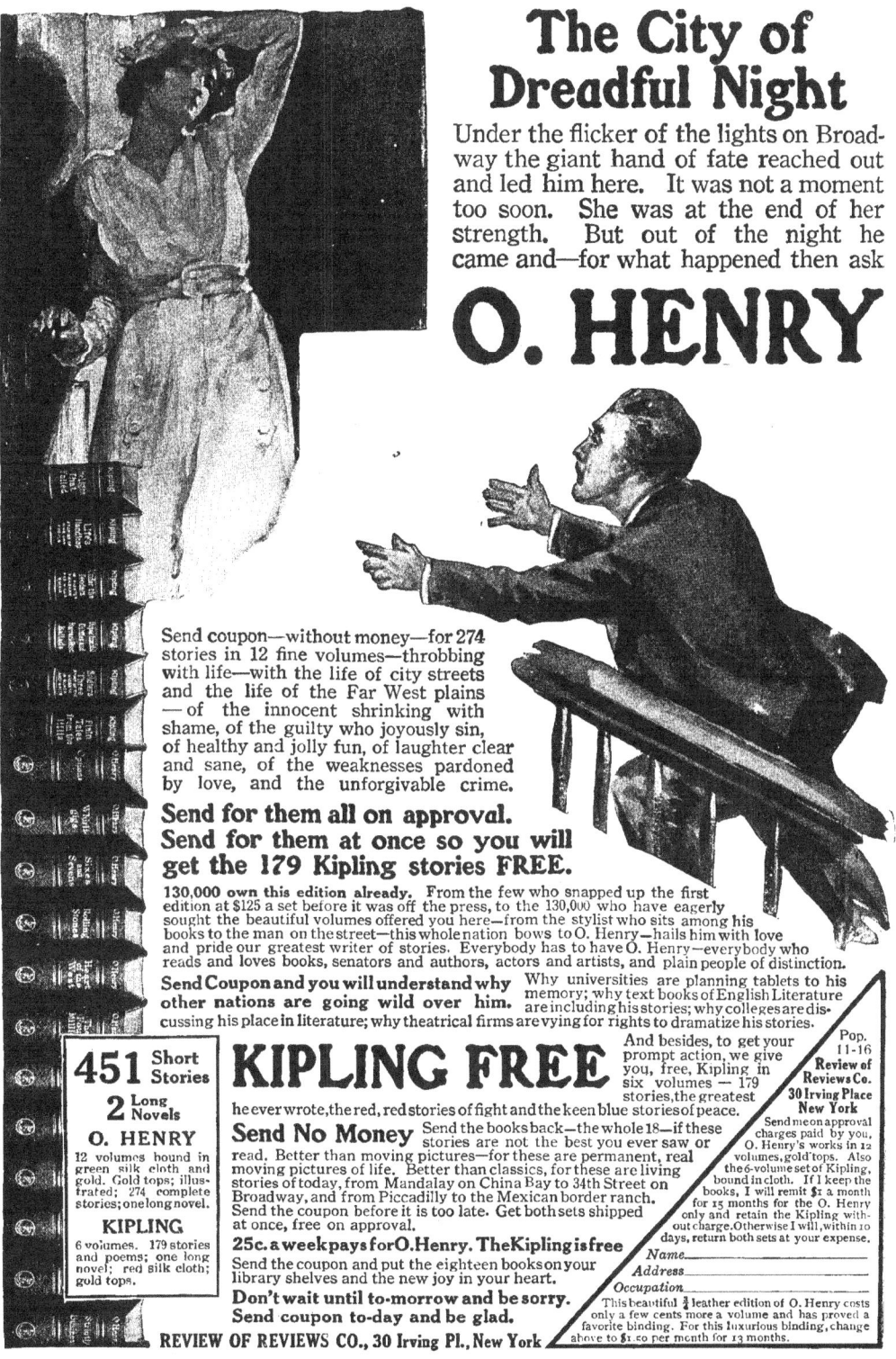

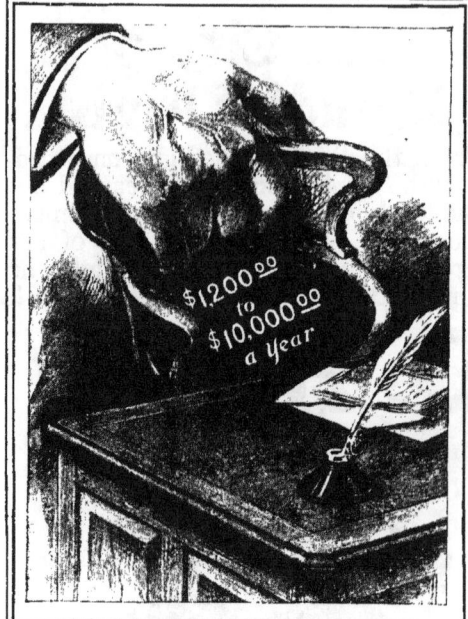

$1200.00 to $10,000.00 a Year

Trained Advertising Men Wanted to Fill Positions

NEVER in advertising history has there been so large a demand for expert ad writers. Not a demand for theoretical dabblers, the product of "lecture courses," but ad men and women who have trained imagination that interests millions of periodical readers and leads to sales.

The phenomenal increase of manufacturing industries and retail stores from coast to coast is more rapid than the increase of competent advertisers to manage their publicity departments. Brainy people, with at least a common-school education, and who are attracted to advertising as a permanent vocation, should send for my beautiful Prospectus laying bare the situation and telling how to qualify by home study in spare time.

Mr. James F. McHale, Darien, Conn., on Aug. 7, 1916, wrote: "In recognition of the invaluable, practical aid of the Powell System in properly preparing me for admittance into the great field of advertising, I cannot refrain from expressing my sincere appreciation and extending my heartiest congratulations for your genius in originating and conducting such a practical, efficient Course of Instruction. Although I have not quite finished with you, yet I have secured a position with the Phelan Ad-Sales Service—*on the merits of my lesson work.*"

The Powell System is practical ad-writing experience, and has for years had the exclusive endorsement of leading experts and publishers. Hundreds of students, like Mr. McHale, have found advertising positions before completing their study on the merits of their lesson work—the most convincing proof of worth that can be given. Send today for my free 64-page Prospectus.

George H. Powell, 65 Temple Court, New York

Please mention this magazine when answering advertisements.

BERTRAND W. SINCLAIR'S

New Novel, "LANDLUBBER'S LUCK," Complete in the November 20th Issue of POPULAR

VOLUME XLII

NUMBER 4

TWICE-A-MONTH

The Popular Magazine

CONTENTS

NOVEMBER 7th, 1916

Twice a-Month Publication Issued by STREET & SMITH, 79-89 Seventh Avenue, New York. ORMOND G. SMITH and GEORGE C. SMITH, Proprietors. Copyright, 1916, by Street & Smith, New York. Copyright, 1916, by Street & Smith, Great Britain. All Rights Reserved. Publishers everywhere are cautioned against using any of the contents of this Magazine either wholly or in part. Entered at New York Post Office as Second-class Matter, under Act of Congress of March 3, 1879. Canadian Subscription, $4.32. Foreign, $5.24.
WARNING—Do not subscribe through agents unknown to you. Complaints are daily made by persons who have been thus victimized.

IMPORTANT—Authors, agents and publishers are requested to note that this firm does not hold itself responsible for loss of unsolicited manuscripts while in this office or in transit; and that it cannot undertake to hold uncalled for manuscripts for a longer period than six months. If the return of manuscripts is expected, postage should be inclosed.

YEARLY SUBSCRIPTION $3.80

SINGLE COPIES 15 Cents

THE NEXT POPULAR ON SALE NOVEMBER 20th

THE POPULAR MAGAZINE

VOL. XLII.   NOVEMBER 7, 1916.   No. 4.

Dicky

By Henry C. Rowland

Author of "The Rubber Man," "The Film Hunters," Etc.

One of the greatest charms of the POPULAR Complete Novel is the variety presented to the reader. Perhaps you have noticed that we do not stick to any given type of story, and, as long as it is vital and interesting, we do not care whether the tale be laid in the salmon canneries, in the vast spaces of earth, or in the counting house. And this unique and fascinating novel of Rowland's proves our variety. *Dicky* is a character that will please and pique your understanding, with his utter unconventionality, his ancient Greek attitude toward life, his unlimited money for which he cares nothing, and his capacity to love. It is safe to predict that you will never forget him as long as you live. He stays in your mind as persistently as a portrait by some great master.

(A Complete Novel)

THE first time that I laid eyes on Dicky was at one of those disquieting epochs in the life of a university when the alumni and well-wishers of my Alma Mater were shaking their heads and asking one another: "What's the matter with Yale?" For several months the rival cohorts had been exulting in their sinful pride and trampling the blue in a manner to make the campus elm trees look like weeping willows.

At a considerable sacrifice of personal interests I put aside my blue prints and descended on the fostering mother to coach her baby crew. Babies they looked, too, as compared with the fierce and hairy stalwarts of my former boat, and the first time I bent my brows upon them my argus eyes fastened on Dicky, and I snorted with rage and pain. They were all pink and pretty enough, and seemed healthy and well grown for their ages, but they did not resemble the massive athletes of my own time who were wont to break training in a wild and reckless manner one day and all the oars and records and things the next.

"What is this, anyhow?" I asked the trainer, "a Yale crew or a beauty show?"

"Both, sor," he answered. "They are good lads, strong and willing. Hair on the body is no proof of the stren'th beneath."

"I hope so," I said sourly. "Have they learned yet what those long sticks with flat ends they are holding in their hands are for?"

"Not yet, sor. They are waiting for you to tell them. But you must not be hasty. Here now is a slim lad that might make good at stroke if he would work." And he ducked his head at Dicky, who was playing with his oar and making little whirlpools.

I looked Dicky over, and felt pretty tired. Not a bone in sight, nor a muscle either. He looked like a trimly built, ten-year-old boy multiplied by two. He was masculine enough, but not manly, so far as his appearance was concerned. He had a wide, boyish face, with big, gray eyes and a short, straight nose and lips rolling back a little when he grinned, which was most of the time, and he seemed to be taking the whole business, myself included, as a sort of joke.

It did not take me very long to discover Dicky's qualities. There may have been stronger men in the boat, but there was not one who had anything like his tireless endurance. He seemed, if anything, to get stronger as he went on, and when the rest of the eight would be ready to flop he was fresh and cool and smiling and making impertinent remarks on their exhaustion. The trainer had the right of it.

"The lad has great organs," said he. "His muscles rest while they work, and all there is to him is of use. Look now at his arms and legs, as smooth and soft and round as a girl's. But the muscle fiber is long and has great power of contraction."

Dicky's personal habits were also unique. He abominated fresh meat, and could not be made to touch it, though he would sometimes toy with a little corned beef or bacon, and was fond of fish. His whole diet, though, was light to the point of what would have been fasting to the others. But he was inordinately fond of fruit and nuts, and usually had a five-pound box of candy in his room. Another peculiarity was his indifference to heat and cold. He slept under a single blanket when his water pitcher skimmed with ice, and I doubt if he ever had on a sweater in his life. The contact of fresh air on his skin seemed to give him a sort of voluptuous delight. I learned from one of the chaps whose family he had visited during summer vacation that it was hard work to keep him from scandalizing the neighborhood by going around half naked whenever opportunity offered and often when it did not.

He was not very sociable nor as popular as one might have expected, appearing to enjoy his own company more than that of others, and he roomed alone with quite a menagerie of pets, principally wild things which he had tamed; birds and squirrels, and at one time he had a fox which perfumed the dormitory until he was obliged to dispose of it. But he did not appear to have any particular affection for these companions, which enjoyed perfect liberty and went in and out of the open windows as they pleased. One debauched old crow made a great nuisance of itself, but was tolerated because of its amusing habits.

Although a good enough athlete, Dicky never appeared to care particularly for sports and games, and only went in for them because strongly urged, and, even more than that, for the opportunity they gave him to spend so much of his time undressed. He was often accused of liking to show his shape, but it was not that. He was too utterly natural to be conceited, and never posed. So far as one could observe, he was at all times utterly and absolutely indifferent to popular opinion, whether favorable or the reverse.

Well, we had a corking fine crew that year and the one following, and in my opinion, as well as that of the trainer, Dicky was about the most useful man in the boat. Then he graduated, and the next I heard of him was two years later, when out in California, where I was wrestling with a big development and funding company of which I was chief engineer and a considerable stockholder, and out of which I had hopes of one day making a decent little fortune with which to start my two kids in life and give them the opportunities which their relative five and seven years of sturdy girlhood and boyhood seemed to warrant, the boy going to Yale, of course, and the girl going to a Yale man.

And if it is a girl, sir, we'll dress her up in blue
And send her down to Saltonstall to coach the freshman crew;
And if it is a boy, sir, we'll put him on the crew
And he shall wax the Hav-vards like his daddy used to do. . . .

Just at that moment the daddy was trying to wax a railroad crowd that threatened to dump the apple cart and wipe out the savings of ten hard-working years. What made it even worse, the prime pirate was a man named Maitland, the president of the road, who had been a schoolmate of mine at Andover and manager of the football team on which I played center. We were old enemies, and I'd never liked Maitland, though I had a lot of respect for his abilities. He had managed the team at a profit to everybody, himself included, and you can bet that the hotel keepers and livery stables and sporting-goods people never got any more profit than they were strictly entitled to. We were never skimped on anything, either. Maitland also was the business editor of the class book and a wonder at getting advertisements. He put that publication on a profitable basis, too, and sold typewriters and skates and transatlantic ferry tickets at reduced rates.

Most of the boys admired him a lot, and he stood well with everybody, the faculty included, because he was smart as a whip in class, though when he studied I can't imagine.

Physically, he was about the best-looking boy in school. Medium height, well built, with wide shoulders and slim hips, black hair and blue eyes, with an alert, clean-cut face and that sort of reposeful expression which seemed to patronize us overgrown kids. I made him come out on the field one day—I was captain of the football team—just to see what he had in him. He had it.

It did not surprise me a bit when I heard indirectly that Maitland had married the daughter of a well-known financier whose name I need not mention and whose affairs Maitland managed to haul out of the junk heap. Maitland married when they were both very young. He was about twenty-four and she eighteen or thereabouts. They had a daughter, Diana, who, through Maitland's excellent business ability, inherited a couple of millions from her grandmother. I had seen a picture of her, with other New York débutantes, in a Sunday newspaper, and she was very beautiful.

It was just about the time that we were having our fight for water rights with Maitland and his crowd that I got a letter from Dicky urgently asking for a job. At the moment I had about as much need of another engineer as I had of an extra leg, but our camp was way off in the backwoods, and, as it looked as though I should have to spend a good deal of the next two or three months in San Francisco fighting our case, I decided that it might be just as well to have a young chap whom I could trust to look after things in my absence and incidentally play watchdog for my motherless kiddies, the little daughter having been born in a Mexican mining camp and at the cost of my wife's life. They were at an age which required a lot of herding, and were more than a handful for their fat, sleepy, old Creole nurse, Manuela.

So I wrote to Dicky, explaining the situation and telling him that he might sign on with the outfit at seventy-five per month and found, if that interested him, with the promise of a raise to a hundred as soon as we won our suit. There was no doubt in my mind that we were sure to win eventually *if* we could raise money enough to stick it out. Dicky wired back to say that he was coming immediately. I rather wondered at his strong desire to get a job under me, first because I had never known him very well nor treated him with any great amount of gentleness, and second because I knew that he had inherited plenty of money from a male parent that nobody seemed to know much about. In fact, there was mystery and doubt as to Dicky's origin, but as it never appeared to bother him, and he being singularly free of friends or enemies, the question of his right to be alive was never questioned to my knowledge. A benevolent old gentleman with eyebrows, supposed to be his guardian, came once to New Haven in a small steam yacht in the middle of winter, and while he was there Dicky took up his quarters aboard, flatly refusing to go near the training table while she was in port. Neither did he invite any of us aboard. I stretched a point in Dicky's case, knowing how he abominated "wines, liquors, and cigars," and he went on with her to New London, whence she cleared for Nassau, Dicky returning in time for morning chapel. He never strained the college entente cordiale which should really obtain between the faculty and undergraduate body. Nor do I think that he was highly esteemed for this observance of university regulations. He had no intimacy with either faculty or students.

I must say that I rather admired Dicky's utter indifference to popularity.

He might have been so extremely popular if he had cared to be. But he never showed the slightest need of any close sympathy from a living soul. To me he seemed extremely young in spite of his resilient physique—just a grown-up little boy—and I fear that I am giving myself away in so describing him. Thinking of my own kiddies, I could never help but feel what a difference it might have made in Dicky to have crawled up on his papa's or mamma's knee and been told a story when he was very small and very tired. Though it was hard to conceive of Dicky's ever having been very tired, even when small.

Well, out he came, and I went to the station to meet him with my team of wiry little red mules. He hadn't changed the slightest particle, but was as boyishly handsome as ever and with that alert, interested way of taking in his surroundings which had about it an air of childish inquiry and eagerness. It was a hot day, and as usual he was half undressed, his coat on his arm, sleeves rolled up, and shirt open at the neck. He looked more like a schoolboy off for a vacation than a serious-minded hydraulic engineer.

"What have you been up to since I saw you last?" I asked when we had stowed his scant luggage and started off.

"Traveling, mostly," he answered. "Bicycling on the Continent and yachting in the Mediterranean last winter. All through the Greek Archipelago with some friends. Greeks mostly and relations of mine."

"I didn't know you had any Greek relations," said I.

"Oh, yes, quite a lot," he answered indifferently. "I didn't know it myself until last winter. Afterward I went to Nice and then to Paris."

"All this sounds as if you'd been having a pretty good time," I observed.

"So I have," said Dicky, looking

brightly around him as we spun along. "I always have a good time."

"How long were you in Paris?"

"A little over a month. Those mules can go, can't they?"

"Pretty well," I admitted. "What did you do with yourself in Paris?"

"Oh, I fooled around. Played tennis and golf and rode in the Bois."

"All alone?"

"No, not often. I rode with an American girl I met there, or rather I met her at Nice. I went to Paris because she was going to be there. Her name is Diana Maitland. She's here now."

"Where?" I asked, and the mules bolted. We bounced through a few ruts and roots and things before I got them quiet. Dicky pushed back his sleeves.

"Here in a sanitarium or something of the sort," he answered. "She's going to be here all summer. That's the reason I wrote to you asking for a job."

"Oh, it is, is it?" said I, reefing in the mules. "So your object in coming here is not to work for the Golden Gate Funding and Development Companies, but to be near Diana Maitland."

"Yes," said Dicky, and reached down for a peach which was in a basket between his knees. "She's going to be locked up all summer in this sanitarium place, and I promised to come out to see her."

"In that case," I told him, "it is my unpleasant duty to inform you that you are fired on the spot."

"Why?" asked Dicky, bathing his face in a large and succulent peach.

I maltreated the mules for a moment before answering. Then, once the intelligent little beasts discovered that they were to walk quietly, I said to Dicky that he was a fraud.

"But I'm not a fraud," he protested. "I'll do whatever you tell me to. You can pay me seventy-five dollars or sev-enty-five cents; I don't care. I'll make good. Just you wait and see."

"But it's foolish," said I. "If you come here as an employee of the company, that is the basis on which you are to work. Besides, this man Maitland, the father of your inamorata, is our worst enemy, barring one, and that is old Professor van Rippen."

"That nature-cure sanitarium man?"

"Yes. You can't have a foot in both camps, Dicky." I swore. "Van Rippen is even worse than Maitland. He has this big reservation just below us, and most of this railroad crowd own a lot of stock in it, though the professor has managed to hang onto the controlling interest. But he seems to be their tool more or less, and just now he's got an injunction holding us up on the riparian rights, and it looks as though we were in for no end of trouble and expense. They know that our funding the water would be of great benefit to this sanitarium plant, which is merely an advertising stunt for the land boom to come later. At this moment Van Rippen has it in his power to stall our operations for some time to come. Maitland hasn't, but he may have because he's got all sorts of money and influence back of him. All the same I'd rather take my chances with Van Rippen than Maitland."

"Why?" Dicky asked, chirping at the off mule in a peculiar way that made the little beast waggle its ears.

"Because he's a bigger man. Maitland is smart as a steel trap, but the old professor thinks all around him. Maitland stands a good chance of spoiling this scheme for all of us because he is greedy. The bird-in-the-hand thing, and then go catch another bird in some other bush. That's Maitland. He's afraid that once we get our source of water power we'll be trying to parallel his line with an electric railroad, and so we shall. We can manage it in the end if we sit tight and keep our eye on the ball, but it's going to take some doing. Meanwhile, this is an armed camp, and the sanitarium is the strategic point, so if your coming here is simply to be near Maitland's daughter, you can just consider all diplomatic relations to be closed."

"All right." Dicky looked at me a good deal as my little boy does when he feels that I'm out of patience with him. "Then I'll go away."

"Very well," said I, "but meanwhile it can't do any harm for you to visit me for a few days and call on Miss Maitland at the sanitarium."

"Thanks," said Dicky. "I'd like to visit you, but there's no use of my calling at the sanitarium. I wouldn't be let in."

"Why not?"

"Well, Maitland has set his heart on his daughter marrying a British title. He brought her over here to get her away from me."

"Oh, he did. Then how are you going to manage to see her?"

"I'll climb the fence or something," he answered cheerfully.

"You'll get yourself filled full of shot or something," I snapped. "This Van Rippen back-to-nature place is not like most such establishments. For one thing the inmates consist only of young and healthy women and girls between the ages of fourteen and thirty. He absolutely refuses to receive a person with any illness or infirmity. His particular crankism is to prepare young women physically for matrimony and future maternity, and his graduates get a diploma certifying to their capacity to produce prize specimens of their kind with the regularity of a plum tree and the unfailing accuracy of a patent multiplier. His establishment entertains at this moment about eighty fair daughters of the plutocratic class whose course of training costs three hundred dollars a month per capita, payable in advance for each term of three months.

These ladies, clad only in sandals and short tunics, range over fifty acres of park and meadow surrounded by a ten-foot wire fence patrolled on the outside by elderly gamekeepers with sour dispositions and double-barreled shotguns. Inside the inclosure there are a number of large police dogs which are trained to regard anything in pants as their particular prey. Except for certain grave and learned members of the faculty of medicine, it is probable that the only male persons admitted to the sacred premises during the past four years were the State hydraulic engineer and myself, each a *père de famille,* and we made our inspection of the brook and Diana's pool with downcast eyes and mantling color. Also we narrowly escaped being devoured by some sort of ferocious beast which looked like a cross between a spotted hyena and a Wa-Wa dog with a possible *bâton sinistre* referring to some early mésalliance between a Tasmanian wolf and a harlequin Dane."

Dicky did not look particularly impressed. He took a luscious pear from the fruit basket between his knees, and began to eat it with relish. I threw away the stump of my favorite brand of sun-kissed cigar.

"So you want to marry Diana Maitland?" I observed.

"Why, no," he said, as if surprised by the question. "I don't want to marry her. At least I don't think that I do. I don't want to marry anybody." He appeared to reflect. "I just want to see her."

"You must want to see her pretty badly to come thousands of miles and climb a wire fence to manage it," I remarked.

"Well, I guess I must," he admitted, and reached for another pear. "Why shouldn't I? She's a bully girl; about the only one I ever knew that I liked to be with."

"Does she like to be with you?"

"Of course she does. Why shouldn't she? We have a lot of fun together. We like the same things. In Paris I bought a touring car, and we used to go out to the forests of Marly and Rambouillet and spend the whole afternoon fooling around and playing with the hares and rabbits and things."

"Very amusing," said I. "Who went with you?"

"Her chaperon, the Countess de Rosoy. A nice old thing. She is English herself, and pretty hard up, I guess. When I came away I gave her the car."

"That was a kind thought. You must have inherited money, Dicky."

"I have. Is that the fence around the sanitarium?"

"Yes," I told him. "We're almost home. You'll see the lake when we turn the bend ahead. Where did you put up in Paris?" I liked to hear him talk about Paris because I had spent my own honeymoon there.

"Oh, I stopped with a chap that is sort of a relation of mine," said Dicky. "He's a secretary or something in the British embassy. That's a pretty lake. Any fish in it?"

"Some rainbow trout. All of this land will be under water when we build our projected dam. I've got a gang at work now cutting out the timber. The spillway empties into old Van Rippen's brook, Heretofore it's been nearly dry for three months of the year, and I've pointed out to him the advantage he can expect in having the flood water funded and a contract from our company to keep his mean level the same the year round. He understands it well enough. Maitland is the fly in the amber."

"What does Maitland want?" Dicky asked, as though bored.

"Oh, nothing much," I answered bitterly. "Only a controlling interest in our company, of which I happen to be the main guy at this moment. If he gets what he asks for, it means that all of my work here resolves itself into that of a rather underpaid hydraulic engineer expert. If it weren't for my kids, I'd sell out for even less to some other bandit. It's possible that I may have to do it, anyhow."

"Why?" Dicky asked.

"Through lack of funds. With another hundred thousand dollars I could stick it out, but goodness knows where I can raise it and hang onto my interest." And I reined in the mules, who were beginning to smell their alfalfa.

"Oh, don't bother about that, Tom," said Dicky. "I'll lend you the money if you like."

I fetched up my two little red devils so short that the nigh one began to kick. Dicky clucked at him, and he got docile.

"What are you trying to say?" I asked. "Have you come into a big pile or what?"

"I've always had a lot of money," Dicky answered, and stared out at the lake. "Me for a swim. I like this place." He looked at me and laughed. "Don't bother about that money question, Tom," said he.

"How can I help it?" I exclaimed. "When I show you this proposition you'll understand. There are millions in it if we can only manage to swing the business. Where did you get this money you talk so easily about?"

"I got it from my father. From my mother, too. I own quite a big island in the Mediterranean. But it isn't worth much just now. They tell me it might be some day. Is that where you live?" And Dicky looked eagerly at my little bungalow, which was on the edge of the lake and really nothing more than a rough shack.

"Yes, and the idlers we're paying to take a nature cure live in that long shanty behind. We are quite a family party here, Dicky."

"It must be nice to have a family,"

said Dicky. "I think I'd like to have one myself."

"Well," I answered, "when you marry Diana you might."

Dicky nodded. "That's so. I never thought of that."

My two kiddies discovered us about this moment, and came tearing down the trail, old Manuela sagging along in their wake. She threw away her corn-husk cigarette and developed power enough to keep Tommy from falling under the feet of the mules. They swarmed up over us, but instead of asking for the little things which I always brought them on coming back from town, they began to examine Dicky. They seemed to think that he was the big, new toy. Dicky responded to these advances graciously enough for a few minutes, but being a child himself other children did not amuse him very much. He caught sight of a cub wolf chained to a kennel, and went over to examine it, the kiddies trailing at his heels. Manuela had taught them not to go near that half-grown little devil.

"Look out!" said Tommy. "He bites."

"Does he?" Dicky looked at me. The cub was nuzzling his legs and pinching at his ankles. The little brute respected me, but others had to feed him with a stick when I happened to be away. "What if I let him loose?" Dicky asked.

"All right," I said. "That means that we've seen the last of him, but I don't care. He's a nasty little devil. Let him go."

Dicky unhitched him, and that half-grown cub proceeded to go crazy. He tore around in circles, rushed at the children, and knocked them both over, swiping their faces with his tongue, which was far out. When Manuela tried to rescue them he made a dash for her skirt, and romped off with the best part of it. Fearing that he might snap at one of the kids in his

wild exuberance, I let fly at him with a pine knot, and caught him in the ribs. He let out a snarling yelp, and I fully expected to see him start for the tall timber, and was quite willing that he should, but not a bit of it. He hovered about with a wary eye on me, and an hour later, when I came back from inspecting some gear, he was sitting on his haunches, watching Dicky disport himself in the lake. None of the rest of us could get within less than ten feet of him, but that evening he ate some scraps from Dicky's hand and permitted himself to be chained up with perfect docility, which was wise of him, as I did not propose to take any chances with his interest in my poultry once night approached.

For the next three or four days Dicky roamed about the place in knickers, bare legs, and a sleeveless shirt, sandaled and bareheaded, with my two kiddies tagging constantly at his heels and Ki-yi, the cub coyote, never far away. In the new interests of the place Dicky appeared to have forgot about Diana Maitland. He played around like a little boy, dug up the material from somewhere and built a sort of Eskimo kayak in which he disported himself on the lake to the great delight of the children and such of the hands as happened to be loitering about. He got acquainted with the men immediately, and while failing quite to make him out, they appeared to admire him and to enjoy his society. I was cutting out timber at that moment on the other side of the lake, and Dicky lent himself to this labor with great enthusiasm. Where he ever learned to handle an ax I couldn't say. The chances are that he never had learned until then. But the beautiful coördination of eye and muscle, backed by his absolute, untiring strength, quickly won the esteem of my crabbed old gang boss.

All hands regarded Dicky as a freak, but a pleasant one, and after their first reticence had worn off, which was in about an hour, they became very chummy. Too much so, I thought. He knew them all, and they called him "Dicky," and their attitude toward him was much the same as the one with which they favored Tommy and Juanita, both beloved and petted. I must say that I might have let several of them go if it hadn't been that the kids would have grieved at such a breaking up of our family party.

Then, one day when I came back from town cross and discouraged after an interview with a local attorney whom I suspected strongly of having a foot in the enemies' camp, I saw Dicky paddling up from the provisional dam which we had thrown across the gorge at the foot of the lake. He flopped out of his kayak thing, and came up dripping from his plunge, and sat down on the edge of the porch.

"Well, what have you been up to?" I asked, batting the pipe cinders off the front of my sweater. "You had better go in and rub down."

Dicky just sat and breathed hard. There was a cool north wind blowing, but he didn't seem to notice it.

"How did you get all scratched up like that?" I asked, looking at his arms and shoulders.

"In the culvert," Dicky answered. "It was choked up, but I managed to squirm through. I thought it would be easier to go that way than to try to climb the fence."

"What are you talking about?" I cried.

"I've been to see Diana," said he. "I sent her a note yesterday, asking her how to manage it. Manuela took the note for me, but there was nothing doing. She told me, though, that Diana and some of the others went to swim every afternoon in the pool just below the fence where your brook goes through the culvert underneath the trail. So I paddled down there, and

left the kayak beside the dam, then swam downstream and went through the culvert."

"You young idiot!" was all that I could say.

"It wasn't so easy as I thought," Dicky admitted. "The place was all choked up with brush. The heavy grillage that you put at the mouth of it has been ripped loose and is all over the place. But I got through. The brook widens out just beyond the fence. There is a big pool, and just below a sort of sluice. I stopped to rest in the pool, and while I was leaning there on a tree trunk an old fellow in pajamas asked me where I'd come from. He asked me in Greek; not modern Greek, but Homeric. He must have been looking at my ears, and thought that he was seeing a faun or something like that."

"What did you say?" I asked.

"I said——" And Dick rattled off something which was all Greek to me.

"That was a very good answer," said I. "And where did you learn Greek? Not at Sheff."

"I never learned it." Dicky looked out across the little lake which the night was beginning to cover up. "I just know it. Not modern Greek, of course. Well, Tom, this old chap, Van Rippen——"

"Van Rippen?" I interrupted.

"Yes. He told me his name. He was sitting there in his pajamas, eating thin slices of bread with honey smeared on 'em. He gave me some. I like honey. I don't see why you shouldn't raise some bees——"

"Never mind the bees!" I snapped. "What then?"

"Oh, nothing much. While we were talking some hens came down the bank and began to swim around——"

"What——"

"Yes. It sounds funny, but they looked just like ordinary hens; all but their feet. He told me that he had bred them with a *poule d'eau;* not the sort you see in France, but the Oriental variety. The old man's fad seems to be like Professor Burbank's principles, but applied to animals instead of plants and things. He told me all about it. The trouble is it takes so long. While we were sitting on the bank, eating our bread and honey and talking Greek— he seemed to like talking Greek—we heard the most awful racket behind us. A regular dog fight. We looked around and saw Ki-yi getting chewed, up by some sort of an animal I'd never seen. It had rings over its back and down its tail, and a lot of young ones. I rescued Ki-yi, and the young ones scuttled up and took a dive into the pouch of this beast. It was a marsupial wolf. Ki-yi had followed me through the culvert or else managed to get over the fence. He was scared and ran away. I haven't seen him since."

"I have," said I. "He is under your bed."

"Then it's all right," said Dicky, apparently relieved. "I was afraid that one of the keepers might have shot him, as I heard the sound of a gun and a yelp. Well, old Van Rippen asked me a lot of questions, and I told him that I'd come to see Diana. He laughed and told me to think of Actæon."

"All this in Homeric Greek?" I asked.

"Yes. He didn't speak it very well. Like a cockney dropping his h's, and sticking them on in the wrong places. Anyhow, I understood him. Then he asked me in English if I realized that I was trespassing and subject to prosecution and heavy fines, and I told him that I hadn't thought about it, but that no doubt it was true, but that I didn't care, as I had money enough to pay the fines. There are lots of birds in that place; mostly wood pigeons. They were all over us while we sat there. One of them snatched a piece of bread out of my hand and flew away. These

ring-tailed puppies were a nuisance, too."

"You had better go in and put on some clothes," said I. "You can tell me the rest at supper."

"I'm not cold. Besides, there isn't much more to tell." He looked up at me and laughed. "I think I've managed to do you a good turn, Tom."

"Indeed?"

"Yes," said Dicky. "It may not come to anything, but then again it might. Old Van Rippen is crazy about landscape gardening. He must have been sitting there, thinking about how he could make that brook very beautiful, when I came paddling down. He had a big portfolio under his arm, and he fished out some of his plans. They weren't any good. His idea was to dam the low places. That's Dutch thrift. But I showed him how much more beautiful the effect would be if he were to bank up the water in the high places, such as the pool where we were sitting, and drain the low ones, so as to have dry pastures. He said that would take a lot more water, and I told him that you were prepared to furnish him with all the water he needed. He's coming to see you about it."

"And Maitland?" I asked.

"He doesn't like Maitland any more than you do," Dicky answered.

"How about yourself?"

Dicky looked rather surprised.

"I've never laid eyes on him," said he.

"Well, you had better," I told him. "When a man is in love with a girl and wants to marry her it can't do any great amount of harm to make the acquaintance of her father."

"That's what Van Rippen said," Dicky replied. "He talked a good deal the way you do, Tom. I like Diana, of course. How could I help it? But I must say I can't see any sense in this marrying stuff."

"All right," I retorted. "Then somebody else has got to teach you that sort of sense one of these days. Now listen to me, Dicky, and tell me the truth. Do you want to marry this Diana girl, or do you not? Because I tell you frankly that I'm not going to have you here swimming through culverts or climbing over wire fences for the purpose of philandering. That sort of business doesn't go in this part of the country. I'm no lover of Maitland nor of Maitland's daughter, but all the same I've got some respect for modern conventions. If you want to marry the girl, go about it in a respectable manner. Tell Maitland who you are and what you've got and all the rest of the thing. But tell me first, or else keep away from Diana, as long as you are here with me. Do you get that?"

"Yes," Dicky answered, "I guess I'd better not try to see her at all."

"I guess so, too," said I, "especially if you feel that way about it. What I can't make out is why you followed her way out here unless you're really in love with her."

"I told her I'd come," said Dicky. "Maybe I am in love with her. I don't know. She's an awfully nice girl. Wait until you see her, Tom. The chances are you'll cut me out. She likes old men."

"Oh, go to the devil!" I snapped, not much caring to be put on the retired list at forty. "If she looks like the picture I saw of her in the *Sunday Magazine,* you may have your work cut out for you, my little boy. Let me tell you I've made the girls take notice in my time."

Dicky went singing off about some sort of play, Tommy and Juanita trotting after him as usual, and Ki-yi scouting on the flanks of the party. Dicky seemed to enjoy the society of the kiddies, though no more demonstrative of any particular affection for them than he had ever showed toward others. While lovable in a way, I doubted that he possessed any deep emotions of the heart. It was evident enough that he was not the least in love with Diana Maitland. The chances were, I thought, that he had greatly enjoyed her society in Paris, and, being rich and free as air, had decided to follow her to California. No doubt he had found Paris rather dull without her. It was merely the case of a child missing its playmate and resolving to go find her. He knew that I was in the same immediate locality, and, being fond of me in his immature way and rather interested in the sort of work upon which I was engaged, had made up his mind to try active occupation for a change, incidentally being near his pretty pal.

But once arrived at my camp he had found the surrounding conditions so pleasantly suited to his childish nature that he no longer felt any great need of his former playmate, and, she being particularly difficult of access, he had accepted the situation with the calm indifference of a little boy to prohibited playthings when plentifully supplied with all his juvenile interests require. Dicky had the constructive mind, and he grasped the big principles of our elaborate proposition with amazing acumen for one whose knowledge was merely theoretical. My carefully detailed plans for funding the water supply, principally torrential, and diverting it to industrial enterprises gave him the keen delight which an alert youngster might be expected to take in a mammoth toy. Incidentally he threw in several excellent suggestions which quickly proved to me that the company would lose nothing by taking him on officially as an assistant hydraulic engineer, once it cut through the jungle of legal complications.

Meanwhile, Dicky appeared to be perfectly happy, playing about the place half naked. He loved the water like an otter hound, and was usually on or about the little lake with the kiddies, with Ki-yi watching their maneuvers from the shore and occasionally dashing into the woods on business of his own. But I soon discovered that Dicky's promenades had a purposeful object.

"You can improve a whole lot on those plans of yours, Tom," said he one evening.

"Indeed!" I exclaimed, with a touch of irony in my voice.

"Yes," he went on. "The way they are now you stand to lose a lot of water in the deeper alluvials. You are counting on the torrential water from the hills to keep up the level when you build your dam in the gorge. It strikes me that it would be a lot better to divert all that muddy stuff by a big spillway, so as not to clog your reservoir with silt. Then, instead of putting your dam where you have planned, you might spend a little more money on caisson work and throw a low, masonry core dam about a mile downstream so as to control the deeper alluvial currents which are constant the year around. Better water, and no clay and stuff to clean out."

"How do you know they are there?" I demanded.

"They must be there with this formation. You don't need deep borings to know that. Most of the water runs off naturally in flood times, but an awful lot of it seeps down into the deep alluvials? Doesn't it?"

"What is the basis of your knowledge? A hazel wand?"

"No." Dicky smiled. "I never tried that. But you know why it works, don't you?"

"Probably because there is water under the ground almost everywhere."

Dicky nodded. "That's it. There's water almost everywhere. If you were to scratch a little in the Sahara Desert, you'd find water most places. Look at the people that have died of thirst in these American deserts with the water about a fathom under their feet. The Texas Panhandle, for instance; the staked plains."

"True," I said, "but your scheme has its disadvantages. The place where you propose to build this dam is in the sanitarium grounds, and we don't happen to control them."

"You might, though," suggested Dicky, and looked thoughtful.

"How?"

"Well, in the first place nobody in this country has the right to stop big schemes for development."

"They can stop them long enough to bust the developers sometimes," I said bitterly, for this was the burden of my thought at the moment.

"Sometimes," Dicky admitted. "But in your case I think you are borrowing trouble."

"No doubt," I answered dryly. "Too bad that money can't be borrowed at the same rates."

"You can borrow money, if you like," said Dicky.

"From you?"

"Yes, and from old Van Rippen."

"Are you crazy?" I asked.

"No. He told me so himself this morning."

"This morning? Where did you see him?"

"Down the brook. In the sanitarium grounds, where I saw him the other day. I saw Diana, too."

"The deuce you did!"

"Yes. It was very early. About six. I went down through the culvert again. I didn't go to see Diana, but I felt curious to see what the place was like farther down, and I thought that nobody would be about so early. Then I slid down through a sort of natural sluice into a big pool, and there were Diana and two other girls in bathing. They were frightened at first, but Diana introduced me, so it was all right."

"Quite so," I said. "How were these young ladies clad?"

"Oh, I don't know. They weren't naked, though, if that's what you mean. I apologized for butting in, and went on downstream. Coming back, I met the old man, and we had quite a talk. He was a little grouchy at first, but I explained that I hadn't expected to see anybody, and pretty soon he cheered up. We got talking about this dam thing, and I described your position in the matter."

"You mean that you told him I was hard up?"

"Not exactly. I told him that you were worried about the money end of it and the lawsuit and the lost time and all that, but there was no need of it as, rather than see the scheme fall through for lack of funds, I'd lend you all you needed myself. A couple of millions, if necessary. Pounds, I mean, not dollars. I told him how we were old friends and the same fraternity and all, and he seemed to understand. He questioned me about the plan I've been telling you for the big dam, and the end of it was he liked the idea. What seemed to please him most was that it would be an awful joke on Maitland. Just what the trouble is I don't know, but I've got an idea he's awful sore with Maitland. I'll tell you the rest of it later. Is there anything to eat? Some bread and butter and milk or something. I'm empty as a hollow log."

Naturally this information gave me food for thought. Dicky's plan for so enormously increasing the contents of our reservoir had never really occurred to me, possibly because the increased cost of such a project would have seemed prohibitive on the face of it. Besides, it meant the inundation, as closely as I could figure it, which I immediately proceeded to attempt, of about half the area of the sanitarium. It could never have entered my head that old Professor van Rippen could

have possibly been brought to discuss such a scheme.

There were a thousand and other details to consider naturally, and I was giving myself up to a sort of *folie de grandeur* in which I saw myself a millionaire and Dicky a Prince de Monte Cristo—for somehow it never occurred to me to doubt his statement in regard to his financial resources—when there came from outdoors certain sounds which fetched me up all standing. These consisted of a long, rippling peal of laughter as sweetly modulated as it is possible to imagine, followed by noises suggesting a number of smoothly running motor cars of which the engines had been set in motion at the same instant. Interspersed were guttural ejaculations in a fat voice not difficult to recognize as Van Rippen's.

I stepped to the window and beheld a curious sight. About two hundred yards away on the shore of the lake stood Dicky in his pale-green bathing suit and a measure of corn in his hand. Overhead the boughs of the trees were bent down almost to the point of breaking with a great multitude of big wood pigeons, which in later years have for some reason become so rare. He was apparently trying to coax them down by tossing handfuls of the yellow grain, while, at some distance, Tommy and Juanita were watching his maneuvers with breathless interest, and Ki-yi, near them, sitting very erect, head slightly cocked and brushy tail curled around his toes.

But it was not this Arcadian group which caught and held my attention. Just outside my door stood what seemed to me the most beautiful girl I had ever seen. It is quite impossible to describe just how she impressed me, pausing there in the late creamy sunlight, and of a cameo vividness and delicacy against the turquoise lake. She was like some exquisite goddess; a creature utterly removed from the gross, material world. Her costume, too, was singular and enhanced this effect, being the last note of simplicity, but graceful in the extreme; such a light, diaphanous, and sensitively draped tunic as seemed to caress rather than conceal the lovely form to which it clung. The long, round, dazzling arms were bare from the shoulder, and the delicious neck was exposed by an oval opening rather low between the shoulders. This shimmering, snowy gown fell nearly to the ankles, of which the nudity was modified by broad bands crossing as they rose from the open sandals incasing the small, bare, rosy feet. The profusion of very fine silvery golden hair was twisted up in a psyche knot and held by a double filet which looked like mother-of-pearl.

A few paces away stood the fat old professor, rotund and ridiculous in some sort of a costume of which the material looked like coarse homespun pongee silk, and the cut capable of claiming kin with anything from a suit of pajamas to a sentry box.

He was bareheaded, and his bald, brown pate might have been used as a heliograph. But he carried a hat in his hand, a very fine panama with a broad puggaree. His feet, very small for his enormous bulk, were beautifully shod in a curious buckskin moccasin laced up to the huge, bulging calf, and containing the lower extremities of his baggy trousers. He was armed with a stout Alpine climbing stick, and wore a pair of great, shell-rimmed, amber-tinted goggles.

The Far West "is so full of a number of things that I'm sure we should all be as happy as kings," to quote that faithful companion of my many months of loneliness, R. L. S. What with converting and diverting and perverting and animadverting at the profit or loss of all the animate or inanimate matter within reach the dweller of these parts has no reasonable excuse for be-

ing taken by surprise. All the same I was. Surprises are like floods. You can handle them when they come with some warning and not too fast and frequent, but there are limits.

While I was gaping at the goddess, with the tail of my eye on Dicky, the kids, Ki-yi, and the professor, there came another spectacle which passed in the flash of a second from the sublime to the ridiculous. I say sublime because it began by a peep through the curtain which cuts off our vision of some wonderful age which must have suggested the return of the millennium. An age when there was no war nor feelings of fear and hatred and suspicion and distrust between cognate beings high or low; when a man might have trod on an ant without meaning to do so and been forgiven by that ant's immediate family and political affiliations.

Because it became quickly evident that these migrating pigeons had no fear whatever of Dicky and desired to profit by his hospitality, but were deterred by the propinquity of others about whom they were not so sure. Perhaps it may have been Ki-yi. At any rate, they suddenly decided to take a chance, and at some sign from their flight commander the whole vast flock took wing and came crashing down like a cloudburst, and the beat of their wings was what I have already mentioned— like the whir of many motors. They deluged Dicky, and it was really a wonderful thing to see.

Then came the ridiculous, as often occurs. This violent rain of pigeons was more than Ki-yi's furtive nature could stand. He started for Dicky's room in the bungalow, voicing his name as he went. His wild stampede started a panic with the kids, but they rallied round the colors and hoofed it for Dicky, not quite sure but that he might be in danger of getting eaten with his corn. And that scared the pigeons, when there came another general movement, this time an actual rout, and they made a racket about it.

The next thing was Diana Maitland screaming with laughter and the professor blasting out remarks, and I realized that this same thing had happened before while I was poring over my plans. I should have gone out at once and welcomed my guests, but for some reason I felt upset, so instead I went in and intrenched myself behind my desk and waited for some official information that I had guests. It was not the professor nor what Dicky had told me that made me feel that way. It was something that struck through me at that last glimpse I had of Diana, up on her tiptoes and shrieking with joy and clapping her hands.

"Well," I said to myself while sitting there, "Dicky is certainly a darling of the gods." Then it occurred to me that I'd never heard any reports of his being a darling of the goddesses, and I tried to feel sorry that he was so childish and incapable of profiting by his gifts.

Nobody came to announce that I had guests, so I cursed my Chinaman in my heart, and got up to investigate. A reconnoissance from the window of the office showed all hands, barring Ki-yi, talking very happily. So I woke up Manuela and sent her to tell Chang to get tea and be quick about it. Then I went out, and found Diana being closely examined by my two kiddies and apparently enjoying their appreciation of her. I did not wait for any formal introduction from Dicky or Van Rippen, but took the small, strong hand which she offered me and welcomed her as best I could. While speaking to her I observed that the portrait which I had considered so very beautiful was actually slanderous in its shortcomings; also that she was a less ethereal creature than my first glimpse of her had led me to suppose, she being quite sufficiently palpable to withstand the

buffets of this rough world of ours and even to return them should the occasion require it.

She gave me a very intent look from her sea-green eyes, and her charming mouth, which twisted up a little at one corner, wore an amused expression.

"You don't look like the ogre I'd expected," said she.

"Who has been maligning me?" I asked.

"Dicky and the father, and Professor van Rippen. When I asked Dicky what you were like he said: 'Like the devil when he gets after a chap, and acts the part, too.' Father says that you are the only man he ever met he felt shy of having trouble with, and the professor said that in some dispute you had with them about your water power you made him feel thin. That was when you lost your temper and called him a greasy old tub of Dutch——" She looked away with a demure smile.

"Never mind," I said. "The word was inelegant and unjust. I spoke hastily."

The professor interrupted us. "This is a most informal call," said he. "Its object is neighborly. I wished to ask if you and your friend, this adolescent Pan who swims through culverts and charms wolves and pigeons and other creatures, would give me the pleasure of lunching with me to-morrow and afterward taking a stroll about the place."

"That is a very great honor," I assured him. "We should be delighted, I am sure."

"Good! At noon, then, if the hour suits your convenience. Look at him. Do you think that he is entirely human?"

"Possibly a little more than that," I answered, glancing at Dicky, who, after a brief word with Diana, had dropped down on the trunk of a tree and appeared to be looking for something inside it. His search was soon rewarded in the appearance of a "timber cat," a large chipmunk which emerged from a hole and proceeded to fill its cheeks with the kernels of grain offered it.

"Go put on some clothes," said I sternly, "and come up for tea."

"All right," said Dicky, and started for the boathouse, where he was in the habit of changing one scanty costume for another. All the luggage which he had brought consisted of a kit bag and a very large box of books, the latter a curious collection, among which were the most recent set of encyclopedia in their light bindings, a large parcel of French plays published in *feuilleton* form by *l'Illustration,* a collection of handsome colored plates of the birds of all countries of the world, some technical handbooks on different branches of my own profession, and a lot of descriptive travel books. Dicky had the same fondness for reading to be found in a schoolboy, but curiously enough, or perhaps not so curious as natural, he much preferred natural sciences to fiction. When he observed the pleasure I took in the beautiful encyclopedia he presented it to me on the spot, saying that he was tired of lugging it around.

Diana lingered with the kiddies, who insisted on her making the rounds of the place and observing their various interests. I wanted to corral them and turn them over to Manuela that they might be properly polished for tea, but both Diana and the professor requested their liberty, so I refrained, rather suspecting a conspiracy on the part of Van Rippen. Our relations having been purely antagonistic, I wondered at his having brought Diana with him, but decided, as we strolled up to the house, that the girl had forced his hand, probably being in love with Dicky and wishing to see what possible attraction our camp could hold for him if not for its propinquity to herself.

But nothing transpired to show any reason for this idea. Dicky came up

immediately, decently enough clad, and a few minutes later the children returned, chattering to Diana, and we had our tea and toast and muffins and honey and things in the most ordinary way imaginable. Then, as night approached, Diana and the professor took their departure on foot, it being scarcely a mile to the sanitarium.

We dined always at half past seven, and after dinner, while sitting on the porch, I said to Dicky:

"That suggestion of yours must have stirred up the old man a lot."

"Why shouldn't it?" Dicky asked. "It's a perfectly good idea."

"It's a pretty big idea," I answered. "You're sure that you could lay your hands on the money to back it?"

"Of course. Otherwise I would never have proposed it. When the time comes for your wanting to capitalize the business we'll write to my London bankers. They can furnish all the assurance necessary."

"Why do you want to go into it?" I asked. "There's always a certain amount of risk attached and you have money enough now."

"I like to see things like that develop," he answered, "and I'd like to have a hand in it."

I thought I understood. Here was the little boy again, playing on the beach and damming the water as the tide went out, or building miniature lakes in brooks for the fun of changing the original order of things.

"I have an idea that if we were to tackle it, we'd have a good fight on our hands with Maitland," I observed.

"What of it?" Dicky asked. "You have now, haven't you? Crowd him out if you can. That's what he'd do to you."

"How about Diana?"

"Oh, she can't suffer," said Dicky indifferently. "She's got plenty of money of her own. She once told me so."

"Even then," I ventured, "it's not

apt to help your popularity with her. Look here, Dicky, I wish you would tell me something, and tell it straight."

"I'll tell you anything I know," said Dicky, and pointed at the moon, just rising above the treetops on the other side of the lake.

"I see it." I spoke impatiently. "Very fine moon. What I want to know is, are you in love with Diana Maitland or are you not? And if not, why not? How can you help it? And if you are, why do you offer to help hand her father one in the eye? If we put through this scheme you propose, we can knock his line's local traffic galley-west and kill all his schemes for town traction and lighting companies dead as a hundred-year-old Chinese egg. It's not going to help you with Maitland, my son. With a bigger man it might; but not with him."

"Oh, he be hanged!" exclaimed Dicky. "Don't you worry about me, Tom."

"Then you must be pretty sure of yourself—and of her," I observed. "Now tell the truth. Don't you want to marry her? Did you ever meet a more lovely girl, or one whose whole nature and personality appeared to promise as much? She's a wonder!"

Dicky looked at me with an impudent, boyish grin which made me feel like giving him a back-handed slap across the mouth.

"I thought you'd fall in love with her, you old troglodyte," said he.

"Don't be an ass!" I snapped. "Here am I, a widower twice her age and with two well-grown kids. Her father and I were in the same class at Andover."

"What of it?" Dicky demanded. "Years don't count with a man of your strength."

"Good Lord!" I groaned. "To hear you talk, one might think you wanted me to marry her." ·

"So I do," he replied. "I like her

2A P

and I like you, and I don't like Maitland just from what I've heard about him. There's no use bothering about Maitland, though."

"But don't you want to marry her yourself?" I shot at him. "Yes or no. Haven't you ever thought that you wanted to marry her?"

"No," Dicky answered. "I'd rather be free to do whatever I feel like doing whenever I feel like doing it."

"A great many people feel that way at times," I commented.

"Yes," said Dicky, "but most of them feel it too late."

"Yes, most." And I was chewing this remark on the end of my pipe when there came a sound from the dark stillness all about which brought back certain memories which I had thought to be dead and buried. Dicky and I turned our heads to listen.

"Do you have nightingales here?" he asked.

"No," I answered, "but that sounds like one, doesn't it?"

"Yes," said he, and imitated it perfectly with a low whistle from the root of his tongue. There was no response. Then Ki-yi began to yelp. I had insisted on Dicky's chaining him up every night.

"We've got to get rid of that cub," said I. "He keeps everybody awake when there's a moon."

"I'll try to quiet him," said Dicky, and slipped off into the shadows.

I waited a few minutes, smoking my pipe and thinking of a good many things. Ki-yi stopped barking, but Dicky did not come back. Presently I went into my office and told Chang to make me a pot of strong coffee and then go to bed. I felt sleepless, and I was excited over this idea of Dicky's and wanted to work the business out more thoroughly before seeing Van Rippen the following day, because I was quite sure that he was thinking about it as hard as I, and that his invitation for luncheon was not based entirely on the neighborly motive which he had indicated.

So I got out my maps, and had just started to pick up the thread interrupted that afternoon when there came a rap on the door.

"Come in," I said, and looked around to see old Manuela.

"What do you want?" I growled. "Why don't you go to bed and not disturb me?" I spoke to her in Spanish, and the conversation was continued in the same tongue, Manuela's English being rather worse than my Spanish.

"I feel it my duty to tell the señor something," said she.

"Then hurry up about it."

"I have a confession to make," said Manuela. "I hope that the señor may be so kind as to forgive me. There seemed to be no harm in it, and Señor Ricardo is so very kind."

"Have you been taking any more notes to the sanitarium?" I asked.

Manuela ducked her head. "Yes. I have taken a note every day since Señor Ricardo has been here. I thought there could be no harm in it. Besides, the señorita is so much in love with him and he with her."

"True." I felt myself beginning to boil inside. "And what sort of a servant do you consider yourself, to come to me with this tittle-tattle about my guest, who has no doubt paid you very well to keep your silly old mouth shut? You make me sick. You get out of here to-morrow. Don't let me lay my eyes on you again!"

She began to gesticulate. "Oh," she wailed, "if the señor could only imagine how much they love—these two children—and how difficult it is for them——"

"Shut up your mouth and get out!" I roared.

"But, oh, señor, here am I telling you all about it——"

"I don't want to hear——" I snarled at her, and she began to weep.

A hot wave of anger and disgust swept through me. Here apparently was Dicky not only lying to me, but trying to make a fool of me into the bargain, and old Van Rippen false to his sacred charge and probably scheming to use Diana Maitland as a fulcrum to pry himself loose from her father, and here was Manuela, the *nourrice* of my little daughter, and, as I thought, a faithful and devoted servant playing the sneak—it was unbearable. I was so disgusted that for a moment I fairly saw red.

"You old pig!" I snarled at Manuela. "Is this the way you return all the kindness that you have had from me?"

She began to blubber. "Oh, señor," she wailed, "what was the harm? And she so beautiful with her great black eyes, so sorrowful——"

"Have you gone crazy?" I demanded. "Black eyes? You'll be talking next about her black hair——"

"Blacker than mine," sobbed Manuela, "and she so far from her native land with nobody who speaks her own tongue——"

"What?" I asked. "Who are you talking about, old fool?"

She bridled up. "Who should I be talking about but her excellency the princess?" she retorted. "The Princess Maria, who came from across the sea with the Señorita Maitland. And poor Don Ricardo, who is so kind and so gay——"

"All right, Manuela," I said. "Now go to bed and let me continue my work. It was very wrong of you to deceive me and carry notes from one of my guests to a person in the sanitarium. I shall demand an explanation later."

But Manuela declined to be dismissed. She hovered about, looking very much distressed.

"Well, why don't you go?" I barked.

"Oh, señor, I think that I ought to. tell you that they are out there——"

"Out where?"

"In the woods. They meet there every night——"

"All right," I interrupted. "Now go to bed, Manuela, and remind me to give Tommy a dose of castor oil to-morrow morning. Stop your silly noise and go to bed. I am very busy."

So Manuela paddled off to her room, which was next that of the kids, and I turned my mind to the effort of adjusting the information which she had cackled out to my preformed idea of things. This was not very easy, because it so upset all of my calculations, while at the same time explaining a lot that had completely puzzled me. It struck me that I had heard somewhere of Miss Maitland having arrived at the sanitarium with two or three other guests, but this fact had not impressed me. Neither was I particularly disturbed at the idea of Dicky's being out in the woods with some black-haired princess who had come to the sanitarium with Diana. He had my permission to remain in the woods with her for the rest of their lives.

I gathered some sense after a bit, and began to get a line on things. Diana was not Dicky's ladylove at all, and never had been, but was, no doubt, doing her best to help along an amorous affair between Dicky and some high-born young female person whom he had encountered in his travels and chosen to be reticent about. It made me rather sore at first to think that Dicky should have kept me in the dark and bribed Manuela to carry his messages, but I reflected that, after all, there was no great harm in that to me and mine. Neither Dicky nor I were given to heart-to-heart talks.

It struck me that, all things considered, the joke was on whoever was responsible for the discreet behavior of the black-haired princess. I got up and stepped out onto the porch. It was a soft, balmy night, the air sweet and still, and a great, mellow moon hung over the lake. I reflected that I should not care to have a daughter of mine keeping a tryst under such conditions with as handsome and self-willed a young pagan as Dicky. So far as I knew, his moral behavior had always been without reproach, but still one can never tell. Dicky had never given any indications of having principles or a code of ethics which might control the sudden sway of a strong, natural impulse, and if ever surroundings seemed rife with soft suggestions of an amorous character those silent woods, with their dark shadows and mysterious aisles, were replete with them. Moreover, Dick had acted in a furtive manner which betokened primitive stealth, and his princess must have been irresistibly attracted to him to have made her escape from the carefully guarded sanitarium and braved the unknown dangers of her lonely promenade to the edge of our clearing.

I shook my head, and, walking to where the trail entered the big timber, stood for a few moments, listening. There was not a sound, and I was about to return when a dark figure slipped across a band of moonlight some fifty yards ahead of me. I stepped back behind the trunk of a great tree and waited. A twig snapped, there was the faint rustle of a garment, and I stepped out to confront this solitary prowler. My square bulk must have loomed startling against the brilliant moonlight of the clearing. There was a smothered scream, and the figure stopped and swayed, and I caught the flash of bare white arms thrown out in terror.

"Who is that?" I asked sharply.

There was an instant's silence; then a gasping voice answered:

"It is I—Diana Maitland. Is that you, Mr. Nelson?"

"Yes," I answered. "Good Lord,

Miss Maitland, what are you doing here alone at this time of night?"

"I came to find you—to ask your help——" Her voice was low and tremulous.

"What is wrong?"

"Where is Dicky?" she asked.

"Somewhere in the woods," I told her. "We were sitting on the porch when we heard what sounded like the beginning of a nightingale's song. Dick went to investigate it, and as he did not return I walked down here to see if I could find him—or the nightingale."

She leaned back against the tree, and placed her hands against the smooth trunk.

"You know, don't you?" said she.

"I have my suspicions," I answered, "that the nightingale is some foolish bird of European species which has flown the fence of the sanitarium."

"The nightingale is——" And she told me the name of this indiscreet young person, which I immediately recognized, and whom I shall refer to as the Princess Alessandra.

"We must find them at once," Diana said. "It is all my fault because I am responsible in a way, having presented Dicky to her in Paris and afterward urging her to come here with me. Of course you know who Dicky really is, Mr. Nelson?"

"No," I told her. "I only know what he is, and that's a tricky young whelp I'd like to baste, and maybe shall. He has abused my hospitality."

"Dicky's father is of the higher British nobility," said Diana, "and his mother royalty, though not British. I can't tell you any more than that." She hesitated, then added: "Dicky's birth was—morganatic or something of that sort."

" 'Something of that sort' appears to be cropping out in Dicky," I observed. "What part have you in this clandestine affair?"

"None—at least not in Alessandra's slipping out to-night," replied Diana. "I knew that he had been coming to see her at night in the sanitarium grounds, but either her companion or I was always with her."

"How did you-all manage it?" I asked.

"He cut a hole through the fence where the rhododendron is thick. We have our apartments on the ground floor, so it wasn't hard to slip out and go down to the brook through the vineyards. There didn't seem to be any harm, because Dicky and Alessandra are such children and it was fun to know that we were fooling old Rip, who thinks himself so clever with his dogs and watchmen and things. The dogs never so much as growled at Dicky. They treated him like an old friend. But we must find them, Mr. Nelson. I can tell you all this some other time."

"Wait a minute," I said. "How did you get here to-night, and why did you come? What difference does it make whether they see each other here or in the grounds of the sanitarium? You weren't in the habit of sitting between them, were you? I must say I don't see anything to be so distressed about. Lovers usually manage to see each other in every walk of life, whether they happen to be royalty or ragpickers."

Diana let go the tree which she had been leaning against like a dryad just freed and not quite sure about the outer world. She seemed quite recovered from the shock of our meeting.

"Mr. Tom," said she, "it's not the propriety of the thing that is worrying me. All of that is their own lookout, and, after all, they are grown-up children. Dicky was to have come to-night, and when it got late and there was still no sign of him, Alessandra was wild. She was sure that something terrible had happened to him, so she went through the fence and came here to see. Lady Cardogan tried to prevent her, but it was no use, because Alessandra would not listen to her. So Lady Cardogan hurried back and told me, because Alessandra——"

"Why did Alessandra think that something terrible had happened to Dicky?" I interrupted. Diana was getting incoherent.

"Because she is sure that she is being watched by her cousin Dimitri and his servant. Alessandra came in awfully upset the other day and said that she had seen a man looking through the fence where the brook goes under the road. He limped off when he saw that she had seen him, and Dimitri's servant, Josef, limps. It must have been Josef."

"Most tramps limp," I answered, "and a good many traipse by at this season on their way south to pick oranges. But why should Dimitri want to make trouble?"

Diana waved her hands. "Oh, because he is madly in love with Alessandra and Alessandra is madly in love with Dicky, and Dicky is not madly in love with anybody, so far as I can make out."

"He tried to make me believe that he had come out here to be near you," I observed.

"Did he?" said she. "That sounds like Dicky. But what are we going to do about it all, Mr. Tom?"

"Just this, Miss Diana: I shall proceed to conduct you back to the hole in the fence, and there dismiss you with my fatherly blessing. After that I purpose to scout the premises for Dicky."

"But by that time he may be murdered," Diana objected. "They might both be murdered. Alessandra says that Dimitri is a terrible man and would stop at nothing. She came here to get away from him. He swore to kill her if she refused to marry him, and when I told her about the sanitarium she said that would be just the place. She did

not believe that Dimitri would follow her way over here."

"I don't believe he has. The sight of a lame tramp looking through a fence is not much as evidence."

"But that is not all," said she. "Alessandra had a letter from a friend not long ago saying that Dimitri had disappeared and nobody appeared to know what had become of him. He has a double reason for wanting to marry Alessandra. He's not only mad about her, but she is enormously rich, and Dimitri has gone through his fortune and is heavily in debt. Do let us try to find them, Mr. Tom." And her white face looked up at me appealingly.

"Very well," I answered, "but I must say I don't just see how we are going about it. If we start hollering through the woods, they'll hide all the closer. It wouldn't do for you to call out, and would probably bring some of the hands from the bunk house, and we don't care to have any scandal. Perhaps the best thing would be to look quietly about, stopping once in a while to listen. It's so still that sounds carry a good way."

Diana agreed to this, and, the woods being open, with scattered clumps of underbrush here and there, we started to steal quietly through the hushed darkness. Reflecting that lovers like to contemplate the moon on water, I thought it probable they might be somewhere along the shore of the lake, and so turned obliquely in that direction. Coming presently to a place where no light to speak of filtered through, I took Diana's hand, which nestled in mine most pleasantly. Every few minutes we stood for some time, straining our ears to catch the murmur of voices, but the only sound was the soft breathing of the girl beside me.

A nice situation, I thought, for a staid and sober-minded engineer and the father of a family to be stealing through the woods at night with the loveliest girl in the world and the daughter of my worst business enemy, who was at that time trying his best to ruin me, stalking a pair of lovers, one of whom was royalty, in order to warn them of possible assassination by a bloodthirsty lord of the levant! I did not for the moment have the slightest belief that this Dimitri person was within five thousand miles of the place, and was certain that were we to stumble upon Dicky and his princess they would be extremely sore. It might even cost me Dicky's friendship, and his promise of financial backing, but there was no refusing Diana's appeal.

My own pulses were by no means sluggish at the contact of her firm little hand and the faint, sweet fragrance of her when occasionally we paused, close together, listening and trying to penetrate the gloom. She had slipped a dark blue kimono over her white tunic, and her hair hung over either shoulder in two heavy braids, as she had arranged it for bed, I fancy, the hours at the sanitarium being those of small children: supper at six and their day beginning at about the same hour of the morning. Any person objecting to this régime was not required to remain. Old Van Rippen's discipline was flawless. He himself, an ex-professor of the faculty of medicine, and, as I had learned, a brilliant surgeon in his day, lived quite apart, dining well and wining well also for that matter. When with my scientific colleague I had lunched with him one day the repast had proved a delicate and delicious banquet with the rarest of food and drink. The *chef de cuisine* of the establishment was a *cordon bleu,* and no expense was spared on the table of his inmates, while yet conducted on lines of strict hygiene. The fat grew heavy on all parts of Van Rippen, excepting his clever old brain.

Weaving through the woods with Diana, I wondered what the old boy would have felt if he could have known what was going on, and the idea brought an inward chuckle which could not have been entirely suppressed, for Diana whispered in my ear to ask what amused me.

"All this folly," I whispered back, and she gave my hand a little squeeze.

"It's dear of you, anyhow," she murmured. "I knew that I could count on you."

Presently we came out on the north side of the lake, where the bank was rather precipitous. There was a fathomless silence all about. One could almost have heard a heart beat seven yards away. I had borne up in this direction because I knew that from there we could get an extended view of the shore, and, the light being now so brilliant, we could discover any object as though in broad day. And my logic proved fruitful, for as I scanned the top of the little beach I saw the gleam of some moving shapes just under the shadow of the trees. Looking closer, two dark figures became apparent, coming slowly in our direction.

"There they are," I whispered, my lips so close to Diana's ear that I could feel the tendrils of her hair against my cheek.

For some reason, probably the sense of protection it gave her, she had not withdrawn her hand from my clasp, and now I felt her fingers tighten a little as she drew back. Scarcely breathing, we watched the pair approach. The bank on which we stood was ten or twelve feet high, and they were on the beach, partly in the shadow, but occasionally emerging under the full radiance of the moon. Dicky's arm was about the girl's waist, and her head on his shoulder, their faces together. No doubt, in their rapture they forgot that they were walking at all, but felt themselves to be floating onward, borne by invisible, etheric currents.

I felt Diana quiver and heard her

breáth coming quickly. It was a beautiful, idyllic scene, these two passionate lovers drifting along on the gleaming shore of that mystic lake in the benign effulgence of the moon. Prosaic as I am, it affected me and made me forget that I was playing the part of a peeping Tom. · Diana, too, seemed spellbound and fascinated. There was something in the clinging grace of that love-drunk girl and a suggestion of Heaven-sent oblivion in the slow, gliding rhythm of their forward steps which was like an exquisite passion dance, a lovers' minuet.

I was the first to recover from the spectacle, and leaned toward Diana. This time my lips actually brushed her ear as she lifted her face to listen, her shoulder against my chest.

"We can't disturb them," I said. "It would be a crime. They'd never forgive us. We had better go away."

She seemed to hesitate. She was leaning forward, her breath coming quickly between her parted lips like a child watching the fairies.

The lovers had reached a spot where a dead and branchless tree had fallen across the beach, and here their lagging steps lingered, then paused. With Dicky's arm still about her waist, and his hand holding hers, the princess sank down on the tree trunk, drawing him beside her.

Diana's hold on my hand tightened. "Come," she whispered.

But at that second my eyes were caught by some stirring object in the shadow of the bank almost abreast of the fallen tree where our lovers were sitting. It seemed to be quadruped and with a hunched back, like a hog or hyena so far as I could outline its vague shape. But I did not waste much time in such analysis, for the creature, whatever it might be, was slinking behind the tree trunk toward the pair.

"Look out, Dicky!" I yelled, and over the brink I went, scuffling and rolling down in a small avalanche of loose earth. I heard Dicky give a sort of shout, and as I sprang up saw him scuffling with a man. Then came another assailant from the same black recess, and I took a running dive at him clean across the tree and tackled him around the knees. Good old football tactics; they are sometimes useful in later life. Over and over we went, I clawing up his body and trying to clamp his arms, and he jabbing at me with a knife. Three times I felt the bite of it in my shoulder and ribs. Then I managed to get his wrist, and, shifting my hold, I gave his arm a jujutsu wrench. He squalled like a lynx in a jaw trap, and I loosed his arm and grabbed for his throat. But he knew the game, and broke my hold, scrambling to his feet. I hopped up the same time, and for a second we stood there, panting, face to face. He had hung onto his knife and was just getting ready for another try when a thick voice behind me said:

"Stop all this or I shall shoot!" And we stopped.

In a scrimmage like that it is impossible to tell how things happen. It is like a football game when the umpire blows his whistle and all hands disentangle and get up. Here was old Van Rippen with a double-barreled shotgun, and his little spaniel was dashing around. I can't describe precisely what he said or how he said it, but it was something like this:

"Let go of that man, Dicky, and get up! Is anybody hurt? What a pack of idiots! What a scandal! How lucky that I came! What a nuisance! Stop crying, Alessandra! Diana, you have betrayed my confidence in your discretion, but it was my fault. I should have known better than to believe in the discretion of anybody. Don't dare to move, you bandits, or I shall shoot you! What a mess! Don't one of you dare to speak a word! Are any of you hurt? Answer me!"

Nobody said anything. The professor's remarks appeared to have a very soothing effect on all hands. He was quite impressive, standing there in the blaze of the moon with his shotgun. And he appeared quite to understand the strategic value of his position.

"Why don't you answer me?" he demanded.

"Because you have just told us to shut up," I made bold to answer, and sat down on the trunk of the tree. "You have the floor, professor; go ahead. The pleasure is ours."

Old Van Rippen did not waste much time about the business. I remember hearing him telling Count Dimitri that he would give him and his servant twenty-four hours to get out of the place and that if they lingered after that he would have them up on a charge of assault with intent to kill. Dimitri answered, with a bravado that I could not help but admire, that the princess was his promised wife, betrothed to him in childhood, and that he would kill any man who tried to usurp his rights; also that he would leave the country when it suited his convenience.

"Very well," said the professor. "In that case I shall march you to the jail, and the chances are that you will remain in the country permanently."

"No court in East or West would convict me for what I have done," Dimitri stated.

"You are right," answered the professor, "especially about the West. No court in this part of the country would ever get the chance to convict you. When it was learned by the local population that you had tried to assassinate a young and lovely girl, a mob would escort you from the jail to the nearest tree and there strangle you like the murderous dog you are. Come, we shall soon know. March on ahead of me! If you try to turn your head or to escape, I will shoot you as I would a wild pig in your own beech forests, and I am a very good shot."

This information rather staggered Dimitri, who had no doubt heard of Western necktie parties.

"You would not dare," he answered. "I am a prince of the blood royal."

"You will soon be of the blood coagulated," snapped the professor. "Of the many lynchings which have occurred in this region I do not believe that the star performer has ever been royalty, and the opportunity to vindicate democracy would be considered as too splendid to be neglected. As for myself, I should ask nothing better than a good excuse to get such free, world-wide advertising for my establishment."

Old Van Rippen's voice had the cold-blooded cut of the surgeon's knife. Dimitri weakened.

"Very well," he answered indifferently. "I accept your terms."

"Then go away," said the professor, "and keep on continuing to go away. Such primitive actions as yours have no place in this day and age, particularly in such a part of the world as this, where the people are peaceful and law-abiding and would break into the jail and take you out and hang you from a tree if they were to know of the crime which you have attempted. The fact of its being a *crime passionelle* would have no influence upon their judgment, because they are honest folk. Now go, or I shall be compelled to shoot my gun at you. There is nothing more to be said. Go!"

So they bowed to us and went, for while the professor's way of summing up the case may have been slightly inconsistent, the tone of his voice was very convincing.

During this brief discussion my knife cuts must have been bleeding quite freely, for I suddenly became very faint. Nobody had observed that I was wounded, nor had I thought much about it myself. But all at once the moon began to weave peculiar parabolas, and then became totally eclipsed.

When I came round a little later I found myself lying on my back, with my head in Diana's lap, and she bathing my face with cold water. Sitting on the tree trunk were the princess and the professor, conversing in low tones. I lay still, listening, and feeling none too badly. The professor got up, and, seeing my eyes wide open, nodded his big head.

"Zo!" said he. "You are feeling better? Good! What a scandal! You have three bad knife wounds, but not dangerous, especially to a man of your physique. What a business! What a scandal——"

"There needn't be any scandal about it," I interrupted. "I can lie up for a few days and give it out that I've got appendicitis or a liver attack or anything you say."

"True," said the professor. "No scandal for the ladies' sakes. That is why I let these people go. What I told them was rot, of course, but it seemed best."

"How did you happen to get here?" I asked.

"Countess Cardogan could no longer contain her anxiety, and told me what had happened. I took my gun and my little dog Rover, which is part beagle hound and has been taught to follow a trail without yelping. I put him on the scent at the hole which this precious young scoundrel, Dicky, cut in my fence, and he tracked Diana, she having been the last and also a great friend of Rover. A nice chase she led me, I must say. I arrived in the height of the struggle."

"Was Dicky hurt?" I asked.

"No. He met the attack of the servant with a kick in the hypogastric region which rendered the fellow practically *hors de combat*. The knife flew out of his hand and into the lake, which was lucky for him, as otherwise he would certainly have got a dose of his own medicine. As it was, Dicky had him nearly throttled when I arrived. The brute was all but finished. As for your own affair, that might have ended less happily but for my timely arrival."

The Princess Alessandra leaned over and shyly offered me her hand.

"Thank you for saving my life, Mr. Tom," said she, in a singularly sweet and liquid voice with a slightly foreign accent.

"I rejoice to have been of service to your royal highness," I answered, and raised her hand to my lips, whereupon, for some reason, Diana appeared to consider that my face no longer had need of her kind attentions. But she did not shift my head from its most agreeable resting place, nor did I offer to remove it.

"When Mr. Tom went over my head I thought that a tiger had leaped from the bushes," said Alessandra. "It is a wonder that Dimitri had a bone unbroken. But he is very strong."

"He is a dangerous man," growled the professor. "You will have to be very careful."

"I am not afraid," she answered. "Once I am married, it is not probable that he will continue to molest me."

I was not so sure about this, but made no remark. Personally I considered the professor to have done very wrong in dismissing two very sincere would-be assassins with his Dutch blessing. I realized, of course, that nothing would so delight the press as the trial of such a case, and that the fair fame of all concerned in it would suffer a good many hard knocks. But all the same it seemed a very poor procedure to permit such a person as Dimitri, who had taken all the trouble to come several thousand miles for the express purpose of murdering a pair of young and ardent lovers, to escape unpunished, and he promising a better job of it the next time.

The chances were, I thought, that Van Rippen had been thinking a lot less about the reputations of Diana and Alessandra than of his sanitarium. He had no desire for the particular sort of advertising to be had from such an exploitation. The old chap was not avaricious nor in any sense a fake. His establishment was his pride and joy, no doubt the fulfillment of long-cherished ideas, and he did not want it smirched. He rejoiced in this garden of paradise which he had created with all of its Adamless Eves, and no doubt he had favored Dicky's scheme of a lovely lake with a water line which should be constant, less for its commercial possibilities than because he saw that it was bound to enhance the beauties of his reservation.

These ideas were milling around in my head when Diana leaned over and asked:

"How do you feel, Mr. Tom?"

"Sleepy," I told her, "and awfully thirsty. I think I'll go down to the lake and get a drink."

"You shall drink nothing for the next few hours," said the professor. "It would only make you bleed some more. When the vessels are secured, yes. Otherwise, no. Many a wounded man has been killed by being given water too soon. The blood you have lost can do you no harm. But you must keep quiet."

Realizing that my head must be getting heavy, I started to raise it, but Diana laid her hand on my forehead and pushed it gently back. At that moment we heard the sound of oars, and presently Dicky arrived with the skiff. I managed to get aboard without fainting again, though I came pretty near it. So we said good night to the ladies, and started for camp, where Dicky got me up to the house and to bed without disturbing anybody. An hour or so later the professor arrived in his buckboard, bringing a good-sized bale

of dressings, and proceeded, with Dicky's assistance, to sew up the crease over my shoulder blade. The other two were stab wounds, inflicted with the point, so he merely inserted drains and strapped them snugly.

Though not considering my condition dangerous, the professor said that I must resign myself to at least a fortnight of bed. It did not matter particularly so far as loss of time was concerned, the engineering work being suspended until our case should be decided and such few hands as I had kept on being engaged in cutting out timber on the tract to be inundated later, and my gang boss was steady and reliable. I was supposed to have an attack of appendicitis and to be under the care of Van Rippen, who undertook to dress my wounds daily and remove the dressings in his valise.

"We shall try to make your captivity as pleasant as possible," said he. "Miss Maitland may come with me to see you, and, as soon as I decide that it is safe, the princess also. But"— he turned and shook his finger at Dicky—"there are to be no more philanderings. She has told me all about the affair and appears determined to forego her claims in order to marry you. But this cannot be managed until she comes of age, which will not be for nearly a year."

I was too much used up to have it out with Dicky that night, but I gave him a bad quarter of an hour the next morning. At least I tried to, though Dicky did not appear to be particularly repentant.

"What made you lie to me?" I asked.

"I didn't," he protested. "I never said that I was in love with Diana. I said that I wanted to be near her, which was true, because she helped me to see Alessandra."

"Then why couldn't you have said so?" I demanded.

"Because I was afraid you wouldn't

let me stay here if you had thought that I had come to carry on a love affair with a royal princess. That sort of thing always sounds so shady. My wishing to see more of a nice American girl I'd got to know in Paris was different."

"I fail to see the difference, when it comes to swimming through culverts and cutting holes in fences," I remarked crossly. "Are you very much in love with your princess?"

An indescribable look swept across Dicky's boyish face. For the first time I saw beyond that limpid, juvenile expression of childish simplicity and got a glimpse of the intense, primitively pagan nature beneath. For an instant he looked scarcely human; vital, passionate, untamed as a faun. Or perhaps it would express more accurately the impression I got to say that in that fleeting second he suggested a young demigod caught in the flame of some Olympian, supermortal impulse. There was something so hot, so vital, an incandescence that glowed up out of him, that I almost caught my breath. Then suddenly the rich, red blood suffused his face, and his eyes filled. He turned away his head.

"I beg your pardon, Dicky," I said gently. "You see, my boy, I have never really known you."

"Nobody has," he replied in a low voice. "Nobody ever could. I don't know myself. Sometimes I think there's no such person; that I'm just an idea or an element like fire or water —or a mass of senses without any soul and wrapped up in a perfect physical machine. I get horribly lonely. I have all my life. But I never noticed it particularly until I met *her*. Perhaps she is my soul. I know that my body would die if I should lose her. She's the only one that ever understood me, inside, the way birds and animals and things like that have always done. We must have been in love with each other before ever we met, because we both knew it the minute we laid eyes on each other. She's my life—all of my lives ——" And he turned suddenly and rushed out like some wild creature.

Well, here was a primordial passion but ill contained in the person of what I and others had fatuously taken to be an immature child who would probably never entirely grow up. It was such a love as poets and painters and philosophers try so vainly to explain and which perhaps musicians come nearest to suggesting remotely. A sort of an ecstasy of soul which heavy mortal senses serve rather to hamper than to interpret. A divine fire; a glory of vibrating delight—words are impossible. How describe in speech something of which one has only the vaguest appreciation of the mere existence? As well try to describe the fourth dimension, which possibly it occupies.

Van Rippen came in the afternoon, bringing Diana with him. He took my temperature, and, reading it to his satisfaction, decided not to change the dressings until the next day. Finding me rather uncommunicative—Bre'r Dimitri's cuts were giving me more pain than I cared to admit—he said that I might talk with Diana for half an hour while he smoked a cigar and drank a bottle of steam beer and conversed with Dicky, who was playing around the boathouse with the kiddies precisely as though nothing at all had happened to upset anybody.

"You are suffering, aren't you, Mr. Tom?" asked Diana, drawing a wicker chair to the side of my bed.

"Not now," I told her.

She looked at me with a curious little smile on her crooked mouth.

"Rip told me that if your bones and muscles had not been so thick and strong, we might all have been slaughtered," said she.

"Rip is an old fraud," I countered. "You wouldn't have been slaughtered at all. Dicky would have made that pair of thugs look like a canary bird caught in an electric fan. I know his work. He's as quick as a heliograph, and, at the same time, as cool as"—I hunted my mind for an apt simile—"as your father."

Diana nodded. "Perhaps Dicky is something of an unknown quantity. All the same, I'm glad that you were there, Mr. Tom." And she leaned over me and smiled. That same peculiar smile. "So is Alessandra," said she.

"You've got it all wrong," said I. "It was my being there and rushing down the bank that made Dimitri think he'd fallen into a trap. Otherwise he would have let his servant finish Dicky and then——" I stopped.

"Well," said Diana, "what then?"

"Oh, almost anything. Since it did not happen, there's no use to bother about it. I mean that Dimitri would not have tried to kill the princess if I hadn't come spilling off the top of the bank. He had it all fixed up for Sté- phan or Imri or Mohammet or what- ever his name is to do the dirty work. But when he saw me boiling down he thought it time to get busy."

"He was right," said Diana, and got up and brought me a glass of orange juice and soda. She saw that my lips and mouth were pretty dry. "Don't let's talk about it any more, Mr. Tom. Doctor's orders."

"All right. But I should like to tell you something that I learned this morn- ing from Dicky, if you care to listen."

"Tell me," said Diana.

So I told her, just as I have tried to describe it all. I told her how I had started to scold Dicky and what he had said and how it impressed me. Per- haps I exaggerated. Diana did not lis- ten very well. What I said seemed to upset her. She got up and walked around the room and then came back and stared at me.

"Do you think that love like that is possible, Mr. Tom?" she asked.

"It might be," I answered. "I don't know."

"But in your own case," she insisted, "can you imagine such love as that? Could you possibly feel it?"

"I feel it every day for my kiddies," said I. "Perhaps that may be the strongest love of all."

Diana turned and stared down at me. "I don't think there is any 'perhaps' about it, Mr. Tom," said she. "I wish that I were one of your kiddies. Not that I mean that I don't love my father now—he me. But it must be nice to be loved every minute—and close to that love. After all, love is the greatest thing in the world, isn't it, Mr. Tom? Don't you think it is? Don't you think that if there was enough love nothing very bad could ever happen? I must go now——" She looked through the window. "Here comes Rip—and Dicky looking very penitent and naked." She wheeled about. "Alessandra told me to give you her love and a kiss," said she. "Here's the kiss, Mr. Tom ——"

She dropped it on the top of my head, and went out.

Unlike most lovers, Dicky said no more to me about his state of heart, nor did he make any attempt to see Alessandra clandestinely. He went fre- quently to the sanitarium as the guest of Van Rippen, who now lent himself actively to the scheme of the big reser- voir. We decided to give Maitland the chance of coming in, though doubting that he would be satisfied with the lim- ited interest we proposed to offer him. It did not greatly matter, though, as it was certain that with Van Rippen's opposition withdrawn and the prospec- tus of the enterprise on such a grand scale to which it was now augmented nothing could hinder its progress. My own company would, I felt sure, be quick to appreciate the advantage of the new plans and lend it their support, especially as it did not necessitate the finding of more capital on our part.

This not being the history of the Sierra Funding and Development Company, I will only say that matters proceeded satisfactorily enough, the only hitch being a certain cupidity displayed on the part of the professor himself, which, however, by argument and concessions on either side, I managed to control within reasonable limits. Meanwhile, my own condition left nothing to be desired, which was to be expected in such a climate and with a man of my physique. The days passed pleasantly and busily, for there was a great deal of correspondence.

Diana came to see me almost every day, and, needless to say, I quickly realized what a barren desert the rest of my life was destined to be if obliged to traverse it without her. And yet I shrank from letting her know the depth of my feeling for her. I could not help but see that she was beginning really to care for me and seemed to ask nothing better than to be with me, but I reflected that such attractions for older men were not unusual in very young girls. It seemed to me wrong to take advantage of it. Here was Diana barely eighteen and I a widower turned forty and with two small children. It is true that she was devoted to the kiddies, and they to her, while I was a youthful man for my age, like all of my race; younger, I really believe, than most men of thirty. But still that extra ten years was always there to my debit, and Diana was possessed of such uncommon richness of soul and heart and body and estate, too, for that matter, that she was entitled to the very best life had to offer. So I tried to possess my soul in as much peace as possible, and at least to make no present attempt to win her. I should have felt unworthy and undignified in doing so. The mere fact

of her fortune did not enter into the question, as I was convinced that the venture in which I had staked all I possessed could not help but reap a golden reward.

Therefore I masked my state of heart under a direct and natural big-brother manner quite free of all gallantry and delicate attention or obvious attempts to please her. I spoke often of my early married life and ambitions for the children, and referred to myself as a man whose youthful dreams and aspirations were things of the past. This seemed always rather to irritate Diana.

"Why do you speak like that, Mr. Tom?" said she one day, drawing down her pretty brows. "Is it a pose or what? You know in your heart that you'll not be old for another thirty years, and probably not then. You haven't a gray hair in your head nor a line in your face, except the lines of character a strong man should have, and I don't believe you ever paid a dollar to a dentist! To hear you maunder along one might think you had one foot in the grave." She examined me with those limpid, multicolored eyes which, I had already discovered, held more wisdom than her years entitled. "I don't believe that you talk to other people that way," said she, with her puzzling smile, which was half tender, half mocking. "Do I make you feel as old as that? It's not very complimentary, Mr. Tom."

"Your own extreme youth is such a violent comparison," I explained.

Diana nodded. "Yes, I haven't been born very long," she admitted, "but I'm not as young as you may think. Years are as elastic as consciences or bubbles or promissory notes. They really stand terrific strains."

"Until they burst," I answered. "You can never tell when that might happen."

"Fortunately," Diana agreed. "Otherwise it would seem hardly worth while to grow up. We would all die when we were babies, and then think of all that we should miss."

"In happiness or unhappiness?" I asked.

"Both. It must be better to have been something than never to have been anything. Otherwise there would be nothing but a great empty space in nothing. Fortunately there appears always to be something in something. Like rain in the clouds and sun in the sky beyond and——"

" 'And a nightingale in the forest and hope in one's soul,' " I quoted, translating the verse.

"Precisely," said Diana. "I am glad to see that you are becoming vibrant again, Mr. Tom. The weight of years has fallen from your shoulders, and so has your bandage. Let me put it right. You have very strong shoulders for such an ancient man, Mr. Tom. Please don't wriggle or I shall pin the bandage into the outside of your earthly envelope."

She secured the loose gear over my shoulder, then sat down on the luxurious divan, of which the chassis was canned-goods boxes and the upholstering a mattress crammed with bay leaves and covered by Mohave blankets. This perfectly practical place of repose was across the room and against the windows which looked on the lake. The sun reflection, striking in, silhouetted Diana most wonderfully. She looked like a water nymph who had flitted in to mock me gently and ask what I was going to do about her domain.

She turned to the window. "There is Papa Rip sitting under a tree with his pipe, watching Dicky walk on his hands for the edification of Tommy and Juanita," said she. "Tommy is trying it, too——"

"Who is coming?" I interrupted, for I heard the rattle of a wagon.

She rested her elbows on the window

sill and looked out, then sprang to her feet.

"It's father!" she cried.

"Oh, is it? Well, run out and ask him to come in."

Diana hesitated. "I didn't know that he was coming."

"Nor I. Sorry I can't do the honors. You might tell Dicky to stop walking on his hands and act for me."

"All right, Mr. Tom," said she, and went out.

I lay there in bed, enjoying my amusement over the situation. Maitland had been advised of what was afoot, and must have been pretty well jarred by the situation, which promised to kill all of his projects for local development of the country to be penetrated by his branch lines. No doubt he had come hotfoot from San Francisco to learn more definitely what was doing, and it struck me as decidedly humorous that he should have happened to arrive at a moment to see the principal capitalizer of the scheme walking along the beach on his hands for the edification of two kids and a mongrel coyote, while the two persons who shared the controlling interest were respectively sitting on a canned-beef box smoking a porcelain pipe and reclining in a brass bedstead strewn with blue prints and entertained during the intervals of their examination by his own daughter.

However, nobody appeared to find the position embarrassing in the least. There were a few brief moments of conversation outside, and then Maitland came in with his usual brisk manner, accompanied only by Van Rippen.

Maitland was a handsome man with an active, well-knit figure and alert, clean-cut features. His eyes were gray, very intelligent, and observant. Although never in any sense a popular man, he undoubtedly possessed an unusual amount of magnetism, as he seemed always to get what he went after and to induce people to carry out his wishes. Personally I had never liked him from our school days, sensing in him always a cold, determined self-ishness, which character, backed by a quick, calculating brain, had made him a dangerous business enemy. But I had always felt that he might prove even more selfish as a business associate. However, although in hostile positions to each other, we had never quarreled, and our attitude was friendly enough.

"Hello, Tom," said he. "Sorry to find you laid up."

"Hello, John," I greeted him. "Glad to see you looking so fit yourself. Sit down. Have a smoke. Have a drink."

"Thanks," he answered, "but I just finished a cigar and scarcely ever take anything. I just ran up from town to have a little business talk with you." He turned to Van Rippen: "Sure it can't do him any harm, doctor?"

"It will do him good," the old man put in.

"Well," said Maitland, "it looks as if you had us on the go. I'd never counted on the professor's drowning us out." He said this with no hint of acrimony.

"You should have thought of it when you tried to smoke me out," observed Van Rippen, referring to Maitland's attempt to run a branch line through his reservation.

"That's so," Maitland agreed. "It's a perfectly open game. What I want to know is where I come in on the deal."

"Just as I stated in my letter," I answered.

He shook his head. "Not good enough," he answered. "Is that the best you can do, Tom?"

"'Fraid it is, John. We've got too much respect for your talents to give you room to swing a sledge in."

"You know I can knock you pretty hard from the outside," he observed.

"It would be a waste of time and money, John," I insisted. "You might have hung up the first scheme indefinitely, as you know we hadn't much money. But we've got millions back of us now."

He looked incredulous, which was to be expected, as he knew that the proposition was of very recent origin and would naturally require some time to finance. Not seeing that it could do the slightest harm to convince him, I said:

"This is no bluff, John. You can have the proof, if you like. I don't mind telling you anything you want to know. Besides what we had already and the professor's interest, we've got the sure promise of backing up to five million pounds sterling."

"Who's the goat?" he asked.

"The young gentleman whom you may have observed, half naked, walking on his hands, as you drove up," I answered. "He is an intimate friend of mine, and has great faith in this scheme. The more so as it is all his own. He is a very intelligent engineer, and he not only saw the possibilities at a glance, but managed to convince Professor van Rippen of them in about as quick a time."

Maitland glanced through the window, and, following his gaze, we saw Dicky hanging from the limb of a tree by his legs and swinging Juanita to and fro; a one-ring circus whereof the audience was composed of Diana, Tommy, and the ever-aloof Ki-yi.

"Where is his keeper?" Maitland asked.

"Here in bed at present," I answered. "He is playful, but harmless, entirely sane, and enormously rich. If it would induce you to draw in your horns and not try to butt in on our little game, I can put you in possession of full information as to his resources. The professor and I are naturally supplied with the data. You have only to say the word."

Maitland looked thoughtful. He was a keen judge of men, and believed me to be telling the truth. Besides, he was too keen a promoter and had too quick a perception of big-business possibilities not to see that we had a very magnificent proposition by the tail. I knew that he had sunk a fortune in his new and expensive branch line, and hoped to reap his harvest from local developments along its course. If we were now to parallel him with an electric system which it would cost us practically nothing to operate, and an irrigation system, he was quick to see that he would be left with a very pretty toy railroad on his hands and nothing much to carry on it. His stock was already much diluted, and the mere knowledge of what we were up to getting about would make his real-estate investments and prospective town lots and other property along the line look like a Long Island pleasure beach on New Year's Day.

But I had no idea how hard he was really hit until presently Van Rippen got up and left, saying that he was expecting some new guests by the four-o'clock train and must be getting back. He took Diana with him, as Maitland was to spend the night at the sanitarium. Diana had a friend in the arriving party whom she wished to welcome. When they were gone, Maitland lighted a cigar, and sat for a moment, smoking and looking through the open window.

"Would you consider an offer to sell you my road, Tom?" he asked presently, without looking around.

"I wouldn't take your road as a gift," I said bluntly. "It's about the worst planned and expensively built and ruinous to run of all the little lines that I ever saw. You've already had some nasty slides and washouts and lost your beautiful bridge. I don't say that the scheme might not have proved a good one but for us. Plenty of possibilities

in the country itself and all that. But wait until you see the freight rates that we'll be able to offer and the train service and the little it's going to cost We've got you stung, John."

"It looks that way," he admitted "But what makes me sore is the way I've been played for a sucker by this infernal old Dutchman. I knew, of course, that he wasn't all fat, but I thought I could count on him to play the game without fishing one out of his sleeve."

"You got his Dutch dander up when you tried to shove your branch line through the sanitarium grounds," I told him.

"That was as much to his interest as mine," said Maitland. "But he couldn't be made to see it in that light, so I tried to run over him to our joint profit. How was I to know that he was so stuck on his cussed old preserve?"

"You should have stopped to think," I retorted. "Just as a man ought to remember that he has jammed a rock under the front wheel of his car before he tries to start."

"I guess that's right," Maitland agreed. "To tell the truth, I gave in to the controlling interest he stood out for because this first funding scheme of yours had been talked about already and I thought he would be a good, useful block. So he was, too, until he saw the chance of springing a new one. It's like a game of chess. The old coot is chucking his interest in my little road because he sees the chance of getting it all back, and more besides, on this new proposition. He has swapped his knight for a bishop on the chance of a checkmate."

"Well," I countered, "isn't that playing the game?"

"Yes," said Maitland. "I can't kick about that. What jars my liver is getting beaten at my own game."

"That might do your system a lot of good," I suggested.

"It won't though," said he, "any more than it will do yours good when you find that you've been flimflammed by this old duck. Of course I don't know how you stand relatively in the deal, but I'm quite willing to bet you a thousand dollars that when it comes to the show-down you'll find that you've been done. If he'd double cross me, he will do the same for you if he gets a chance, and you bet it won't take him long to find the chance. If he can't find one, he'll make one."

Such a possibility as this had already occurred to me. I had never been a brilliant business man, though always able to see opportunities in connection with my technical work. For the financial end of it, however, it would not have taken a Morgan or a Harriman or a Hill to have outwitted me. At this moment I was not altogether pleased with Van Rippen's attitude, nor did I have any overwhelming confidence in his good faith. But in answer to Maitland's remarks I merely said:

"Oh, well, I'll have to take a chance on that, I suppose. I'll try to get things nailed down so that nobody can lift out any planks."

Maitland appeared to reflect for a moment, sitting on the edge of the window seat and swinging one leg.

"See here, Tom," said he, "why not take over our road? It would be useful in your construction work, and later on you could change the power to electricity. It needn't interfere with your building another of your own to open up the country to the south. You can have the road for a song and pay for it in stock."

"But I don't want your road at any price, John," I answered. "I don't consider it a good road. I consider it badly planned and worse constructed. If you had given me the job when I applied for it, and let me build it my-self, I'd feel differently about it. As the case stands, I'd no more think of buying it than I would a jerry-built house or a rotten ship or a salted mine. In my professional opinion, it's a bum property."

"Oh, not quite as bad as all that," he said rather lifelessly. "I'll admit, though, you've got it in your power to kick the props from under it. Once this new project of yours is announced nobody would touch it with a ten-foot pole. It will be worth about as much as an ice plant at the north pole."

He talked a little while longer, but finding me inflexible said good night, and drove back to the sanitarium, there, as I presumed, to get to work on Van Rippen. But I had no fear of his accomplishing anything in that direction. The professor disliked Maitland and distrusted him with good reason, from what he had told me. Maitland had tried to serve Van Rippen just as Van Rippen now proposed to serve Maitland, and, other interests aside, I felt confident that the old Dutchman's set and obstinate nature would effectually bar even the consideration of any of Maitland's suggestions.

I cannot say that it gave me any satisfaction to turn Maitland down so hard, and the prospect of costing him a considerable fortune was rather painful. I was never revengeful, and the fact of his being Diana's father would have been enough to make me let him in on a good basis if there had not been the interests of others at stake as well as my own. As it was, there seemed no other course to take. He had got, no doubt, the answer he really expected, and I doubted that he would try to make us any more bother. He was not vindictive, but merely a cold-blooded business man.

Consequently I was rather surprised when, the next morning at about ten, he drove up again. He looked rather badly, I thought, and like a man who

3A P

had not slept, and his manner was nervous and ill at ease. But with his usual businesslike directness he went straight at the point.

"Look here, Tom," said he, standing by the foot of my bed and with his keen, observant eyes fastened on my face, "are you in love with my daughter Diana?"

I stared at him for a moment in silence; then—— "Yes," I answered.

"Oh, you are, are you?" he snapped, and began to pace up and down. "Well, what do you expect to do about it?"

"Nothing," I answered.

He shot me a look of quick surprise. "Eh, what?"

"Nothing. She is too young and lovely a girl to throw herself away on a widower of forty with a pair of children. I don't think that it would be right for her to marry me, even in the very improbable event of her being able to care for me."

"H'mph!" he grunted. "I guess there wouldn't be much trouble about that."

"What makes you think so?" I asked.

"Because she's in love with you already," said he. "She told me so. Naturally she hardly expected me to tell you. But I don't think it would bother her much if she knew I had."

"How did she happen to tell you?" I asked, trying to keep my voice steady and natural and to control the thumping of my heart.

"I wanted to take her away from the sanitarium; to send her back East. The old man and I had rather a warm session last night, and after certain things which were said I decided to quit the ring for the present. When I told Diana to get her things packed she told me that she would rather stay where she was. Naturally I was a bit surprised, seeing as she came out here to be near me. You see, we've always been good chums; more like brother and sister than father and daughter,

so when I'd explained that my business was finished, and found her still determined to stay on I began to have suspicions. Then I thought of this young Dicky person, and it suddenly occurred to me that he might be the chap who had been hanging around her in Paris, so I asked her point-blank if she'd gone and fallen in love with somebody out here. 'I'm afraid I have,' says she. Diana is a peculiar girl in some ways. 'I was never in love before,' says she, 'so I can't be sure; but one thing is certain and that is that I don't want to go East just yet.'" He looked at me with a peculiar expression.

"Go on," said I. "What then?"

"Well, I asked her why she hadn't told me about it, and she said: 'I didn't think there was any hurry about it, especially as he has never said that he cared for me, though I've got an idea that he does care and cares a lot, but has a silly notion that just because he's so much older and has two children it's not to be thought of.' 'Good Lord,' I said, 'you don't mean to tell me it's Tom!' 'Yes,' she answered, with that twisted little smile of hers, 'it's Tom.'"

"God bless her heart!" I almost cried, raising up on my pillows, then sank back again. "But it's no use, John. Take my word, you needn't add that to your list of worries. She's too sweet and lovely a girl for an old cove like me. Tell her so, if you like, and take her back East with you."

Maitland did not answer, but stood there studying me with a curious intentness of expression that I found rather annoying.

"Well," I demanded irritably, "don't you believe me?"

"Yes," he answered, "I believe you. I know your sort. How did it happen, anyhow?"

"Oh," I said rather crossly, "Van Rippen brought her with him one day, and she seemed to like us all and enjoy seeing Dicky perform and playing with the kids. Then since I've been laid up she's come with him almost every day and stopped a while to talk to me while Dicky and the old man went over maps and things. I never so much as squeezed her hand, but we seemed to understand each other pretty well from the first. Such things happen sometimes, I suppose, though not often where there's such disparity of age. Still, as you say, Diana is an uncommon girl, and her mind is very mature for her age. However, she'll soon forget about me, once she gets away. What are you staring at me that way for? As if I were a sea serpent or something?" I demanded resentfully.

"I beg your pardon," said Maitland quietly, and glanced away. "I think you must be pretty hard hit, old chap."

" 'Fraid I am," I answered, "and the more fool I, considering my age and condition."

"Oh, I don't know," said Maitland reflectively. "You and I are the same age; both widowers, and I have a grown-up daughter, but that wouldn't prevent my marrying an eighteen-year-old girl like Diana if I happened to fall _in love with her and she with me. A man of forty is apt to make a darn sight better husband than one of twenty-four."

I looked at him in astonishment. "Heavens and earth, man, you're not in favor of it, are you?"

"Why not?" he said wearily. "I've got Diana's happiness at heart and a lot of respect for you as a man, and no end of confidence in your future success." He rested his elbows on the foot rail of the bed, and stared at me thoughtfully. "Did you know that Diana inherited a million from her mother's estate?" he asked.

"Yes, but of course that hadn't anything to do with it. She might have two million or two cents for all I'd care."

"Well," said Maitland dryly, and I noticed that his face had whitened a little, "she hasn't got even the two cents now."

I stared at him uncomprehendingly. "What do you mean?" I asked.

"Just that," he answered. "Diana's fortune is all sunk in that railroad scheme of mine." His mouth tightened.

"But how did you have the right?" I demanded.

"I didn't. That is, not the legal right. I considered at the time that I had the moral right, first because the money was of my making and got through my manipulation of a busted concern; that million and a lot besides. In the second place, I considered the railroad proposition as such a dead-sure thing that I felt justified in using Diana's fortune to slam it through. But the law would call it the misplacement of trust funds and invite me for a nice long visit at an institution which has not the luxury of Van Rippen's. That may happen yet."

"But great Jupiter!" I gasped. "Haven't you millions of your own?"

"I haven't a million cents," Maitland answered, "and I'm mortgaged up to the ears. Diana is not the only victim. There are other members of the family who are apt to want an accounting within a few months. For the last several years they have been quite well satisfied with their dividends. But two of my nieces by marriage are due to be married in the spring, and then there has got to be a show-down. I'd hoped to have everything in apple-pie order by that time, but now that you have gone and dumped the apple cart there is apt to be a corner in apples." He gave his short little laugh.

"And then what?" I asked.

"No pie," he answered, and then, with a significant gesture: "This for mine. Stripes were never becoming to me. I'd rather be measured for a suit of pine planks. But get it straight, Tom. I'm not telling you this sad story of my business career in the hope of softening your heart. I've heard 'em too many times from other people, and they never softened mine. A fellow ought to play the game without turning on water power when it comes time to cash in. Let's cut out my part of it and talk about Diana. She thinks that she's in love with you, and there's no question about your being in love with her, and I'm convinced that you would make her a darn good husband, so go ahead and don't be foolish. You are bound to make trainloads of money out of this thing if you keep your eye on the ball and don't let somebody steal your bone while you are half asleep."

"Does Diana know about this, John?" I asked.

"No—nor anybody else but you. The others will find out soon enough, but between you and me and this brass bedpost I don't give a darn about the others. They took me into the family under protest, and treated me like a poor relation at first. Then, when they discovered that I could make money, they began to get polite. I made a lot for them—scads of it—and it was 'well done, thou good and faithful servant,' and a pat on the head. I never minded much. It was the game that interested me, not the people, and, not having any money of my own, I played it with their stakes. That's a perfectly all right game when you win, but a rotten one when you lose."

"Most games are like that, John," said I.

"Yes—especially when playing with other peoples' money, even when they do give you a verbal *carte blanche*. There are worse places than the poorhouse. But to get back to Diana. The thought of her future has been the toughest thing for me in this business. Granted that she's uncommonly pretty

and talented and all the rest of it, just the same life doesn't offer much for the eighteen-year-old daughter of a busted embezzler. The family would be the first to knock her, and I have no real friends myself. Never did have, to my knowledge. The men I've helped to make fortunes know that I never did it out of love." He gave a bitter little laugh. "I know of one bunch that will probably hold a praise service when it learns that I'm down and out. So you see, Tom, you needn't hang back about marrying my daughter on her account."

He walked to the window, and stood for a moment looking out across the little lake, while I lay there with my mind in a whirl. Somehow it never occured to me to blame Maitland for his illegal actions. In my association with promoting schemes I had known of a good many such cases, and understood that often they had their mitigating circumstances. A man who has built up a big fortune out of trust funds is often apt to regard himself as privileged to use the capital as if it were his own. It's not so much the money that he wants as the use of it to further his schemes, and it is only when the crash comes that he wakes up to the fact that he is a thief in the eyes of the law.

So here we were, this former business enemy of mine and myself at the two extremities of fortune; Maitland facing ruin, disgrace, and death—for I had little doubt he would fulfill his threat of suicide rather than go to prison—and I with the only obstacle to the promise of great wealth removed and free to woo and win the girl I loved. And yet I was not conscious of any wild elation. The sight of Maitland's drawn, tired face and his quiet, manly acceptance of the situation aroused in me a sympathy which I would not have felt if he had come whining and whimpering and begging me to help him out for his daughter's sake.

"Look here, John," I said, "what can I do to help you out of this mess?"

"Nothing," he answered promptly. "If you were to take over my road and marry my daughter, it would be dishonest to your other shareholders and give you a black eye that would never clear up. Besides, Van Rippen wouldn't stand for it. As you say, the road is no good to you nor anybody else with your proposition in sight. You've got a bully scheme, Tom. I went down and looked at your site for a dam. There'll be some caisson work, but nothing enormous, and with that five-hundred-foot drop into the gorge for your flume you will have power to burn. No, there's nothing you can do, old man, thanks all the same. Well, I must be getting along. I'm starting East to-morrow on a sort of forlorn hope, and I shall leave Diana at the sanitarium. We won't say anything to her about this talk. No use to bother her until the bell rings, and I hope that by that time she'll have your strong arm to hold her up. Good-by and good luck——"

So out he went, leaving me in a regular whirlpool of conflicting ideas. For about an hour I lay there, scarcely budging, while my brain studied on the situation. But it was no use. There was no way that I could think of for tiding Maitland over his crisis. He was too deeply in the mire. As he said, I couldn't sacrifice the interests confided in me simply to save my prospective wife's father from destruction. I couldn't, and, what was more, I wouldn't if I could.

"My prospective wife!" That set off another alarm clock. It was lucky for me my wounds were about healed or I'd have probably been down with fever. Then Dicky came in, lightly clad, as was his wont, to ask if I needed anything. I did. I needed a counselor, and, knowing that Dicky would be an absolutely safe confidant, and failing to see how it could do the slightest possible harm, I told him the whole story. All about myself and Diana and Maitland's predicament; the whole business. He listened without a word, looking out the window and at times scarcely appearing to have his mind on what I was saying.

When I had finished, he looked around with his boyish expression of mild interest.

"Well, you're to be congratulated, Tom," said he. "Diana's a peach."

"Is that all you can say?" I asked impatiently. "Do you think it's a cheerful thing to marry the girl you love over her father's dead body?"

"I wish I could marry the one I love over the dead bodies of her whole blooming family," said he.

"Oh, go to the devil!" I snapped disgustedly. "This is different. Diana is really devoted to her father. Besides, she's a proud girl, and the disgrace will break her heart. She thinks, like everybody else, that he's a financial genius and a multimillionaire. Think of what it will do to her when she learns that he's a common, garden variety of everyday embezzler."

"Pretty tough," Dicky admitted, as though commenting on the breaking of a favorite meerschaum. "You had better get married before that happens."

"I don't know yet that she'll marry me when it comes right down to brass tacks."

"Then ask her and find out," he suggested, and began to look for a thorn in his knee.

"You're a darn fine spiritual adviser!" I sneered. "Supposing she does consent and we get married, it's going to be a cheerful honeymoon for me waiting every day to hear that my bride's father has blown his brains out and not knowing how she may be affected by the news. I tell you she loves her father."

Dicky found the thorn, extracted it, examined it with interest, and flicked it away.

"What do you want me to do?" he asked. "Lend him a couple of millions?"

"I want you to go to Halifax!" I said, really angry. "Why should you lend him a couple of millions? He's got no claim on you. I only told you this because you have your flashes of human intelligence at rare intervals, and I thought you might have something to suggest. If you haven't, clear out of here and go hang by your legs or stand on your head, and leave me to try to dope out the business the best I can."

Dicky looked at me pityingly. "You're getting peevish from lying so long in bed," he observed. "Old Rip says you can sit up to-morrow. Don't fret about Maitland, Tom. He's a pretty slick article, and I guess he'll be able to wriggle out of it somehow."

"Thank you so much for your kind words of comfort and cheer," I growled, and picked up a letter from the sheaf which had been brought me just before Maitland's arrival. I was pretty sore with Dicky. A couple of weeks earlier I should never have thought of taking him into my confidence at all, considering him, as I did, a mere, undeveloped, irresponsible child. But after that glimpse which I'd got at his deeper nature, I felt that I had a right to expect better things in the way of interest and sympathy.

He sat there for a few minutes, tapping his sandaled feet on the floor and humming a little tune, then slipped off the window seat, and, going to the center table, helped himself to a handful of sugared almonds, which he carried back to the divan and proceeded to munch. I had never seen him eat what one might call an actual meal, but he was always chewing at something between-times—fruit or cakes or nuts or candy, with which he took care to keep the

place supplied, feeding them also to the kiddies in spite of my injunctions to the contrary. It may have affected their appetites, though, if it did, they gave no symptoms of it. Pretty soon a flutter of wings around the window sill announced that the birds had discovered Dicky and his treasure-trove, and were demanding a hand-out. Their pipings and his crunchings interfered with my perusal of a very important mail, and I was about to tell him to clear out when he swung round and said:

"I'm going to town for a couple of days, Tom. Got to see the correspondents of my bankers. Besides, I've got to buy some clothes."

"Far be it from me to interfere with the latter errand," I said. "When are you going?"

"This afternoon. Anything I can do for you while I am there?"

If it had been any one but Dicky, I could have given him a staggering burden of commissions. As it was, I answered:

"Why, yes. You might look up Maitland to-night at the Palace and ask him for a special permit for a special at any time that we might care to look over his line. I never thought about it when he was here."

"All right," said Dicky. "I'll remember."

So off he went to town, where, instead of two days, he spent two weeks. Van Rippen and I were, of course, up to the ears in work, but I saw Diana almost every day. Maitland had told him that I had asked his permission to marry her if she would have me, and that he had given it. The professor informed me of this fact in a manner none too flattering.

"Perhaps he thinks that as your father-in-law you might manage to get him a slice in our affair," said the old fellow. "Or maybe he did not believe that she would accept you. At any rate, he knows that you will be rich one of these days."

But in spite of the open road which now lay before me, my manner toward Diana underwent no change, except perhaps for a little added tenderness which I could not help, knowing the sorrow which menaced her life. Her very joyousness cut me deeply sometimes; gave me what the French call *le cœur gros*. Often, as I listened to her gay, bantering talk and rippling laughter, I could feel my heart swell and a hot sensation about the eyes, and I would have to turn away quickly and pretend to busy myself about something in order to pull myself together. But I did not make love to her in any sense. I wished to wait a little, first in order to give her time to get over what might have been a mere transient, romantic attraction, and second to clinch the promise of our big scheme, as anything which might have arisen to thwart it would have meant financial ruin and a fresh start for me. I knew that I had still some months of leeway where Maitland's affairs were concerned, and I was hoping against hope that Dicky's suggestion that Maitland might yet find some way out of his troubles would come about.

My wounds were soon entirely healed and gave me no trouble whatever. Of course I was constantly in and about the sanitarium, and occasionally had a few words with Alessandra, whom the professor kept very close. She was certainly a very lovely and charming girl, and I did not wonder at Dicky's consuming passion for her.

Some peculiar change appeared to have been wrought in Dicky by his trip to town. He was less communicative than ever, and thoughtful and preoccupied, very. Then one day he announced that it would be necessary for him to go East and that he might be away for a couple of months, but could not be sure. His former guardian was going to be in New York, and he had a good many affairs which required his attention. So off he went, handsomely dressed in the suit with which he had supplemented his wardrobe while in town, and for some few days following he was sorely missed by Tommy and Juanita and Ki-yi and old Manuela and a few others at the camp, sundry birds and chipmunks and pigeons and things included.

So far as our work was concerned, I did not consider the lack of Dicky any great loss, and thought it far better that he should occupy himself in making sure that there be no hitch in the money supply in case of accident. It was Dicky, of course, who had struck on our present scheme and done most to make it realizable, but I was inclined to regard his suggestion for the dam as more of a lucky shot than anything else, and his conquest of old Van Rippen as the affinity between two impractical cranks. His wealth seemed to be another fortunate accident, and as I saw it our whole position was one evolved of singular luck and circumstance. I had absolutely no respect whatever for Dicky as a promoter, engineer, financier, or person of any depth of thought—though willing to concede him plenty of depth of feeling of a primitive or pagan sort. I doubted that this feeling could possibly extend beyond the limits of his own desires, any more than could that of any other pagan.

Something of this I told Diana, but she was not of my opinion.

"Nobody could love like Dicky and not have a tremendous lot of soul," said she. "That's what soul means. Love *is* soul. Mind is different."

"Don't you think they go together?" I asked.

"They ought to," she answered, "but it doesn't always happen. Sometimes one's mind is developed at the cost of soul"—she gave me a mischievous, sidelong look—"just as it may be developed at the cost of common sense," she added. "Old Rip says you have an excellent mind, Mr. Tom."

"Indeed?" I exclaimed. "That is very amiable of him. And what should you say it was developed at the cost of in this case?"

She gave me a demure look, and said, with that little smile which pushed out her delicate upper lip so charmingly: "Certainly not soul, Mr. Tom."

This was Sunday afternoon, and we had gone for a stroll around the lake and were now sitting on the same tree trunk which had been the scene of our scrimmage with Dimitri and his henchman. Van Rippen had followed with the kiddies, the trio having struck up a most intimate friendship, and they had now wandered off into the woods for an ambling lesson in natural history; not according to the Dicky school, but more academic and usually of a botanical character. It was one of those lambent days when the air seems highly charged with all the ingredients of life, so thin and fine and solvent as to have absorbed the forces of gravity themselves and one moves about with no slightest sense of weight. It would not have surprised me greatly to discover that our footsteps were leaving no traces in the sand.

Diana, however, appeared to have materialized in these latter days and become more of the mortal maid. Her costumes also were less unconventional, and she wore shoes and stockings when she left the sacred precincts of the sanitarium instead of sandals and bare ankles. But she was always lithe and supple and swaying, with her exquisite figure free and unconfined except for a high girdle, usually a band of pale green, which was her favorite color; the green of very early foliage. I have not attempted to describe her face, as that would be impossible, but its ex-

pression suggested that of a thoughtful, grown-up little girl. There was a certain wisdom in her long eyes, which were of a pale, slaty gray, with a curious amber tone in certain lights. Unlike most girls' faces, the telltale quality was not in the eyes, but in the lines about her rather wide but sensitive mouth, which was mobile in the extreme, with usually a quiver near its corners and never set in lines of prim control. Altogether it was a sensuous face, and, like all the rest of her, seemed constantly to thrill and vibrate under the perception of a multitude of impulses, whether from within or without.

Looking at her now, I turned coward again. It was inconceivable, to my mind, that so lovely and wonderfully fashioned a masterpiece of God's handiwork should be given over to the tender mercies of such an animated lump of clay as myself. Because I could not help but feel that if Diana were mine, she was bound to be very much mine; a very tremendously total quantity of mine to me. I could not imagine myself in the light of a self-obliterating, protective genius, worshiping from an adoring distance and crawling into her sacred presence on all fours after a course of fasting and prayer. No. Once Diana was married to me, I knew that she would find herself married from the bottom of her spiritual body to the top of her physical one, and I wondered how much of this she could possibly realize.

Such ideas as these were milling around my cemented depths under a surface current of trivial talk, whereof the topic was Dicky, when Diana, with one of those swift impulses which were like an overcharged induction circuit, observed:

"I know what you are thinking about, Mr. Tom."

"Of course you do," I answered. "So do I."

"Do you want me to tell you?" she asked, and leaned toward me.

"No. I'll tell you myself—when the time comes."

"In that case, I shall tell you now," said she. "It is always better to take Time by the scythe. Don't you see, Mr. Tom, that Father Time is our very best friend, and for that single reason might be our very worst enemy? Let's take away his scythe. Without his scythe he would be nothing but a harmless old bore, just as Cupid without his bow and arrows would be a harmless little love of a baby." She raised her chin, and her mouth laughed and the amber gleam came into her eyes. There was no fly in that amber.

"You might disarm Cupid first," I suggested.

"Too late," said Diana, and shook her head sadly. "His shaft is sped. I love you, Mr. Tom."

"I love you, Diana," I echoed.

"I know you do," said she. "If I hadn't, I would not have said it first. I might have, though. Will you marry me, Mr. Tom?" She dropped her hands on my shoulders, and, turning on the log, stared into my eyes. I took her hands, and, holding her at arms' length, stared back.

"Are you sure, Diana?" I asked.

She threw back her head and laughed. Some birds in the treetops answered. I did not feel like laughing myself. The chances are that if my race had been Latin, instead of Norse, I might have wept.

"Sure about your love for me?" she answered. "Of course I am, Mr. Tom. Be still. Let me have my say. I can feel love just as I can smell flowers or hear music. If I had not been sure, do you think, you silly Mr. Tom, that I would have proposed to you in this shameless way? I know what you feel before you do. Be still, Mr. Tom—and don't squeeze my wrists so hard

—that's better. Hold them, if you like, but don't hurt me. I could feel you loving me that first day when old Rip and I were watching Dicky play with the wild pigeons—and you were looking out through the window. Something began to sing in my heart, and I stood there and let it sing without looking round. I have felt it before, but never the same way—without discords and—bad sounds. I want to be loved that way, Mr. Tom. I have always wanted to be loved that way—every woman does—but no one so much as—as I do——"

"Diana!" I interrupted. "Of course I love you, and of course, you being you, you couldn't help but know it."

"All the time you were there in bed and talking to me it poured out of you like water over one of your dams——"

"But that's not the question," I interrupted again. "Are you sure of your love for me? Stop and think—or don't think. Let me do the thinking for you. Do you realize——"

"I realize *you*. You seem very real to me, Mr. Tom——"

The shadows were screening the lights in the lake when we walked back to the camp, where we found Van Rippen having tea with the kiddies. He turned his back on us when we came in, and devoted himself to Juanita, who was sleepy and spilling her chocolate. One might have thought that he dared not look at us for fear of being struck blind. Nor had he anything to say, but climbed into his buckboard when it was brought from the stable, and left me to help Diana in as best I could with his restive little broncho backing and filling and threatening to capsize the contraption. They drove off, and I stood watching them and wondering why so fat and phlegmatic a person as Van Rippen liked to drive half-trained horses. Then I started after them afoot, merely to satisfy my mind that they had arrived at the sanitarium without accident.

Van Rippen came over the next morning at about ten with a large portfolio of correspondence which required our joint attention for a couple of hours. Just as he was leaving he handed me an envelope.

"Diana asked me to give you this," said he. "The State engineer is coming to-morrow, and I shall expect you for *déjeuner* at twelve. Good-by." And he spun off down the trail.

I ripped open the envelope, and this is what I read:

Mr. Tom, you are a silly old fool, and I am a silly young fool. They say that there is no fool like an old fool, but sophistries are the excuses of lazy minds. Old fools usually know pretty well what they are about.

This is a polite way of saying that I regret what happened yesterday and of having for some weeks past cajoled you so shamelessly. But it was really pretty dull here for an eighteen-year-old girl who is a flirt by nature and accustomed to a great deal of masculine attention. You see, you were the only man available, and I wanted to keep my hand in. As to the ethics of my behavior, you must remember that I am my father's own daughter.

Please spare me the unpleasantness of reproaches, and don't try to see me again. I am leaving for the East to-morrow. A man of your age and experience ought not to be so easily taken in. Let us hope that the experience may prove of value to you. With best wishes for your future success,

DIANA MAITLAND.

I read this letter through a second time and smiled sadly to myself. Not for the fraction of a second did it deceive me. Poor girl, I thought, she must have learned by her evening's mail of her father's ruin and disgrace, and the blow to her faith and affection and pride had for the moment upset her mental balance. For her to reflect on the avowal which she had made to me and asking me to marry her, and she at that very moment the penniless daughter of a defaulter was more than

she could stand. Her heart was, no doubt, bursting with shame, and she assumed to herself the dishonor of her father's act. That phrase—"you must remember that I am my father's own daughter"—betrayed her. Of course she could not guess that I knew all about Maitland's position, and she had sent me this bitter, mocking note as the quickest and most efficient way of breaking our new relations.

I hurried to the stables, threw a saddle on my mare, and a moment later was loping along the trail for the sanitarium, to the precincts of which I was now admitted at any time without question. Tossing the reins to a servant, I walked around the house to the broad, tiled terrace on which Diana's apartment opened. I did not bother to have myself announced, knowing that she would decline to see me. It was then the luncheon hour for the guests, and there was nobody about, but I did not believe that Diana would be in the big refectory. My judgment proved to be correct, for as I stepped up to the long French blinds of her door I heard from within the sound of sobbing. I drew the butt of my riding crop down the slanting shutters, and the sobbing ceased.

"Who is there?" came a low, strangling voice. "Please go away. I am ill and do not wish to see anybody."

"It's I—Tom," I answered. "Open the blinds, dear."

There came a gasp, a rustle as though she were suddenly rising, then——

"Oh—it's you. May I ask you to be so kind as to leave me alone? Wasn't my note enough for you?"

"Open the blinds!" I commanded.

"How dare you come to my room like this?" she cried. "If you don't go away at once, I shall ring for the servants. Do you want to compromise me? Or have you merely come to strangle me——"

My answer was to shove my riding

crop into the slight opening between the door blinds, knock up the hook, and fling the blinds open. In the sudden light which flooded the place I saw Diana sitting on the side of her bed in a kimono. Her hair was disordered, and her face flushed and wet with tears. She sprang to her feet.

"Are you crazy?" she demanded furiously, and took a step toward me, her small hands clenched. "What do you mean, bursting into my room——"

"*Sh-h-h!*" I whispered. "No need to make a row. When did you learn about your father?"

The question struck her like a blow. One hand flew up to her throat, and she stared at me wildly.

"What do you know about my father?" she demanded.

"I know all about him. More than you do, I imagine. He told me himself. He is not so much to blame as you may think. What he did was done in all sincerity for the best interest of those whose affairs he had been managing. Can't you give him the benefit of the doubt? And did you think for a moment that I was such a fool as to be deceived by your silly note? Come here! Come here to me—or must I go to you?"

She stood there, staring and choking. "Come!" I said sternly, but in a low voice. For an instant she struggled to resist the force of will which I was projecting toward her. Then, with wide, frightened eyes and lagging steps, she began to move in my direction. "Come!" I repeated, holding out my arms. She paused, raised both hands in a protesting gesture, but like a person in a trance continued to approach. Almost to me, she tottered, swayed forward, and flung herself upon my chest, where I held her close, her pliant body crushed in my clasp. I kissed her hair and eyes, soothed her, petted her as I might have caressed and comforted my own baby daughter. She did not try to speak, but rested there, breathing convulsively, her bare arms twined about my neck.

I do not know how long we remained in this close embrace, but presently she grew calmer and loosed herself gently. Her hands dropped on my shoulders, and she held me at arms' length, looking into my eyes.

"Oh, Mr. Tom," she whispered, "isn't it terrible! And to think that you knew! Why didn't you tell me? Why couldn't you have prepared me in some way?"

"Because I have been hoping against hope that there might be some way out of the business," I answered. "How did you learn?"

"A letter from an aunt. Some of them grew uneasy, and they have been investigating father's affairs. He may have to go to prison. Oh, they are all so bitter—so cruel. I would rather have learned that he had been killed. I must go to him at once. Poor, poor father! I know he did not mean to be dishonest. I must go to him and tell him so. I am leaving to-night."

"Then I'll go with you," I said.

"But how can you?"

"I can, and will. That's all. What's more, if you feel that you really must go, you shall go as my wife."

She shook her head. "That is not to be thought of any longer, Mr. Tom."

"Not much longer," said I. "Just long enough to get the knot tied. Tied good and hard, too, my darling."

She shook her drooping head, and I took her in my arms again. At the same moment there came a sharp rap at the door. Diana sprang back.

"Who is there?" she called.

"A telegram for you, Miss Maitland," came a woman's voice.

I stepped out upon the terrace and drew the blind in front of me. Diana crossed the room, took the telegram from the maid, then closed and locked her door. She came to the window, the message in her hand, her face as white as chalk. My own could not have held much more color, as I fully expected the wire to announce Maitland's death, not stopping to reflect that such ill tidings would probably have been addressed to the professor. Diana held out the telegram with a trembling hand.

"See what it says, Mr. Tom," she faltered, and leaned against the window casement. I ripped it open, glanced it through, then looked at her with a smile and the sweat breaking out on my forehead.

"Good news," I said, and, stepping inside, I put my arm around her shoulders and drew her to me as I read:

Don't be disturbed by rumors or letters of bad news. Matters clearing up and nothing to fear. Best love. FATHER.

"Thank God!" I murmured, and kissed her bright hair as her head fell on my shoulder. She twisted about, slipped her arms about my neck, and crushed her wet face against mine.

"I adore you, Mr. Tom," she whispered. "You *do* love me, don't you?"

Back I rode to camp, feeling rather limp, but with a singing heart. It had turned hot again, and I was sitting at my desk, busily filling my waste-paper basket with torn-up, unfinished letters, when there came the rattle of a loose-jointed trap—all of this was before the time of motor cars—and I looked out and saw Dicky disentangling a wad of bills to present one to the driver. He gathered his loose clothes under one arm and came in.

"Hello, Tom," said he. "Everything all right? How are the kids?"

"Fine and dandy," I answered. "Why didn't you let me know that you were coming?"

"Oh, I thought I'd go straight through to Frisco, but it was so hot on the train I decided to get off and have a swim. Besides, I wanted to relieve your mind about Maitland."

"That was kind of you," I said rather ironically. "When did you see Maitland?"

"In New York." Dicky was divesting himself of his negligee shirt and trousers. Refreshingly costumed in abbreviated underclothes, he seated himself on the divan, and looked at me with a grin. "I've bought his blooming railroad," said he.

"You have—excuse me—what?" I exclaimed.

"I've bought his road." He slipped off the window seat, and, going to the fruit basket which the Chinaman had brought in with his other scant effects, selected a luscious peach in which he proceeded to bathe.

"That is very interesting," I observed. "Tell me about it."

"Well," said Dicky, his mouth full of peach, "when I went to Frisco that last time I looked up Maitland and asked him to show me his property. He didn't seem to think it worth while at first, but I told him that if I could see my way clear to buy it without too great a loss there might be something doing. He asked me why I wanted to buy it at all, and I told him that it was on your account."

"Why on my account?" I asked.

"Because he is Diana's father, of course, and you want to marry Diana," he answered. "You explained all that. No use going all over it again. But from what I had heard about the property I got sort of an idea that it might be just my business. So it was, too, as it turned out——"

"Wait a minute," I interrupted. "Tell me why his being Diana's father and my wanting to marry Diana should have made you consider the purchase of an absolutely worthless property and one which your interests here were bound to push even deeper into the soup."

Dicky threw away what was left of his peach. He turned his square, boyish face toward me, and I caught another of those flashes which were like the flame from a short-circuited high-tension wire. Just for a second, though.

"You saved Alessandra's life," he explained.

I said nothing. Dicky looked out across the lake, and continued talking. His voice sounded strained for a moment or two, but soon returned to its usual boyish tone.

"I told Maitland that I thought his road was punk, from all I'd heard about it," said he, "but that if I could see the possibilities for a scheme I had in mind I might buy it, first on your account, as I've said——"

"What did he say about that?" I asked.

"Oh, he wanted to know where you came in, and I told him that you were in love with his daughter and would like to feel that you hadn't busted up her father's pet scheme, and that I felt that I owed you a lot for certain things that you had done for me. He didn't seem to take much stock in all that, but he changed his mind and stopped over to take me out to see the property. It turned out to be just what I wanted, and when I had told him why he was like a kid with a new toy."

"What was the why, if it's not a secret?"

"It might be better to say nothing about it outside just yet," Dicky answered, "but, you see, Tom, my scheme is this: I propose to transplant about a thousand families of Greek peasants —small farmers—and stake 'em out along that line on the tracts which it controls. You know I told you once that I inherited a good-sized island in the Greek Archipelago? Well, I'm the hereditary lord of that pile of dirt, and so I naturally feel sort of responsible for the good of the people that live there. They have a pretty tough time of it to get along, I guess, but they are a thrifty, industrious bunch, and really a mighty decent lot, taking 'em all around. So far the dam' place hasn't paid me anything at all to speak of. On the contrary, I've had to help 'em out from time to time. But the people are really good people, hard-working and well behaved and all that. Once they get a fair chance they'll make things hum. You wait and see."

For a moment I sat and stared at this nearly naked youth with feelings impossible to describe. Dicky helped himself to another peach.

"Why not have staked them out on our own prospective grants?" I asked.

"Oh, stop and think a minute, Tom. You know as well as I do that it would have put all the surrounding country on the bum. These Greeks of mine are all right, but any big immigrant colony knocks the value of surrounding real estate. That is, it does at first, until they get Americanized, and it usually takes the second generation to do that. Since Maitland's road was a dead issue, and as it struck me that the country thereabouts would be just the meat for my Greeks, I thought I could see a way of killing two birds with one stone—or three maybe. In the first place, my buying the road saves Maitland from disaster. Second, it may prove a land of Canaan for my starving crowd. Third, I stand to make a lot out of it in the end when they get well rooted. Maitland thinks so, and so does my former guardian, and so does Dimitri——"

"So does—Dimitri!" I gasped. "Hold on, Dicky! Don't fling it in too fast and frequent or you'll have me sitting on the floor playing with paper dolls!" I mopped my brow. It seemed to me as though I had already stood as many shocks that day as was good for a white man. "Dimitri? *My* friend?"

"Yes," Dicky answered, flinging his peach pit through the window. The birds had already discovered his return, and were fluttering all about. Fortunately the children had not returned from the district school. "Dimitri is a sort of cousin of mine. I knew where to find him in Frisco. I've been keeping tabs on him through a detective agency ever since he tried to get gay. I felt sort of sorry for Dimitri because —oh, for a lot of reasons. All the same, that wouldn't have kept me from sticking a knife into his throat if I got a good chance. Dimitri's kick wasn't so much jealousy through love as it was being sore at seeing a rank outsider and what he thought to be just an ordinary, everyday American fellow come along and cut him out of his girl and no end of money. When I went to see him this last time, and proved to him who I was it gave him no end of a jolt. He turned green, and Stefan nearly had a fit. Got down and groveled."

"Did you go to see them alone?" I asked.

"Yes," he answered. "I knew that there was no danger. They were flat broke and living in the attic of a rotten sailors' boarding house. You must have given his arm a darn good wrench, as he still had it in a sling. Well, I told Dimitri that while he didn't deserve it I was willing to put him in a way to make a fortune if he'd behave himself and stick to business. Then I explained my scheme, and he was keen about it and promised to be good." Dicky clapped his hands, and Chang came in. "Look in my valise and bring me that big box of candy."

I leaned back in my chair and stared at him with wonder. Chang brought the candy, and Dicky began to munch nougat, feeding the birds little morsels which they pecked from his fingers. It seemed to me that there was a sort of radiance about him which was brighter than the sunlight streaming in.

"Go on," I said in a subdued voice. "What then?"

"Oh, I took them up over the prop-erty and showed them all the possibilities of the business, and then we went to New York, where we met Maitland and worked the proposition out in detail. Maitland was really in the devil of a mess, but I got him out of that by advancing him money on his shares. We formed a syndicate, of which I am president with a controlling interest. Maitland is to run the railroad and land business, and Dimitri will have charge of the colonists and all that part of it. We are going to charter a ship to fetch these people out, and Dimitri is going over on her to round up the bunch."

"You are sure they'll come?" I asked.

"You bet they'll come. They'd go to the north pole on my say-so. Besides, Dimitri has a lot of influence, and so has my former guardian, Mr. Constant. He's in the syndicate, too, and he's going out with Dimitri. Maitland is coming here in about a fortnight and he's going to look after this end of it. Here come the kids——" And Dicky ran out just as he was to greet them.

"Chang!" I shouted. "Saddle Nelly and bring her up—and be quick about it!"

"It allee same lunch time——"

"Do what I say, and get a move on you!" I bellowed, and, five minutes later, was tearing back over the road to the sanitarium.

The rest of the tale is quickly told; that is, as much as requires the telling. Diana and I were married a month later, and left for the East, where there was much business to transact.

Dicky and Alessandra were married about a year later, and finally settled on their palatial estate in California, there to rear an interesting family. We are all rich people now, but when I contemplate my golden goddess and our sturdy flock I feel myself to be the richest of them all.

For Brodie's Benefit

By Charles E. Van Loan

Author of "A Job for the Pitcher," "The Crab," Etc.

This joyous tale, filled with the well-known Van Loan brand of rough humor, opens with a spirited scrap between a boxer and the portrait of the next heavyweight champion The aftermath of the unequal contest will get you up on your toes. Van Loan knows the fight game, and—as the POPULAR'S six years' acquaintance with him has demonstrated—he knows how to tell a good story. This is one.

BIG TOM O'CONNOR strolled into Shaughnessy's place about ten minutes after the proprietor finished decorating the west wall of the establishment with his most recently acquired work of art, the same being a full-length, life-size portrait of Robert Emmet Brodie, heavyweight, done in oils and also to a turn. That the artist had never seen his victim might possibly be regarded in the light of a mitigating circumstance; at any rate, he had drawn Brodie's classic outlines from a half tone in a pink illustrated weekly, and his inspiration from a quart bottle kindly furnished by Shaughnessy. The result of these two drawings caused Tom O'Connor to gasp and pass his hand before his eyes.

"And me off the hard stuff for a week!" said Big Tom. "What have you there, Denny? Is it a fighter or is it a Spanish omelet?"

"Have yer joke, Tom," responded Shaughnessy, with a nervous grin, for Big Tom's jokes were often akin to violence. "Have yer joke, lad. Ye will, annyhow, but I take it hard ye do not recognize Bob Brodie when ye see him on the wall."

"Bob Brodie!" howled O'Connor. "Brodie? And what right has *he* got to be hangin' on a wall, I'd like to know? Brodie! A great, big four-flushin' piece of cheese like him! Who did he ever lick?"

"He put away a lot of them boys in the East," said Shaughnessy. "Have a drink, Tom?"

O'Connor waved away this friendly invitation.

"Yeh, he put away a lot of dubs," growled Big Tom, eying the work of art truculently. "Dubs, all dubs. Brodie never licked a good man in his life, and you know it. Why, he can't even lick *me!*"

"Ah, well," said Shaughnessy, wisely avoiding the personal note in the argument, "maybe it ain't so much what he *has* done as what he's *goin'* to do."

"You're whistlin'!" remarked O'Connor shortly. "And I'm the lad can tell you what he's goin' to do. He's comin' down off that wall. He's comin' down if I have to pull him down!"

"Now, Tom, don't be gettin' rough," pleaded Shaughnessy, who was a small man, and informed of his weak heart.

"Don't be startin' anything in here, there's a good——"

"He's comin' down, I tell you!" repeated O'Connor, in tones which reached the street. "Only a champion of the world has got a right to be in a gold frame, with a brass plate under him. Will you take him down yourself, or——"

Shaughnessy squeaked and made a dash for the street door to summon assistance, but Big Tom executed a surprisingly swift flank movement and cut him off, herding the terrified proprietor to the rear of the saloon, where he took refuge among the empty beer kegs. This little matter attended to, the censor of art turned his attention to the offending portrait. He dragged it from the wall and balanced it against a table.

Plainly O'Connor's first impulse was to kick several holes in the canvas, but as he stood facing the life-size and shrimp-pink prize representation of a fighter, a change came over his mood, and his lip curled in scornful amusement. With mocking deliberation Big Tom copied the painted pose, left hand advanced, right arm drawn back, a thunderbolt in reserve. He feinted and skipped and side-stepped, now creeping up on the portrait, now retreating as from an attack, and his clumsy left jabs grazed Brodie's pink nose. While thus employed, he addressed the portrait, as follows:

"Huh! Think you're a whale of a feller, eh? Think you're a *fighter*, don't you? Been talkin' about fightin' the heavyweight champ, ain't you, hey? You—make—me—sick! They tell me you're clever with your mitts—but I'm givin' you a tip. Lay off of me, Brodie! Yes, lay off of me, you big bum—because if I ever git you in a barroom, an' nobody to yell 'Foul' or call time, I'll beat you to death! Yes, that's what I said—to death! I'll lick you the same as I used to lick you when we was kids in school. Maybe I

couldn't do it in a *ring*—but in a barroom! Why, listen to me, you ugly man's dog—in a barroom—I'd murder you alive! Think not, hey? Well, smell of this, once!"

Having talked himself into a state of mind demanding more physical expression than may be found in futile left jabs, Big Tom feinted twice in rapid succession, and, stepping in, let fly with the heavy artillery. His right fist shot forward, with two hundred pounds of O'Connor behind it, full into the painted countenance of Robert Emmet Brodie. There followed a dull thump, a splitting, tearing crash, a wail from the wretched Shaughnessy, dodging among the empty beer kegs, and Big Tom O'Connor strode out into the street, blowing upon his knuckles. The canvas had been reënforced with a backing of pine boards.

Shaughnessy's next customer found him mourning over the life-size portrait of a fighter without a face.

"Save us from harm!" ejaculated Mr. Casey, peering at the ruin. "Has the Germans been usin' that thing for a target, or what? An' whose picture was it before the bombardment come off?"

"It was Bob Brodie's," replied Shaughnessy.

Mr. Casey sucked in his breath with a clucking noise.

"An' a grand likeness!" said he. "The legs is done fine. You could almost tell 'em annywhere. Who busted him?"

"Tom O'Connor took a punch at it just for meanness," said Shaughnessy bitterly. "He was showin' me how he could lick Brodie—in a barroom."

Mr. Casey brightened visibly.

"Has Tom got a spite agin' Brodie?" he asked.

"Look at what he done to the oil paintin' an' ask me that!"

"But what for?" persisted Casey.

"How should I know? By what I

could make out, he used to lick Brodie when they was kids in school."

"Ah, he did that!" chuckled Mr. Casey. "An' like as not, he's sore because he can't lick him now. It makes him mad to be stickin' in the gas house when Brodie's gone up in the world! What you goin' to do about it?"

"I was thinkin' I might have him pinched," said Shaughnessy thoughtfully, as he surveyed the headless gladiator.

"No," said Casey, "don't do that. They would only let him go with a small fine, an' then some night when he's got a skate on he'll come in here an' move the saloon out into the alley. There's a better way."

"Tell it to me."

"Put the picture in the back room, just as it is. Jerry Brodie has had a letter from Bob, an' he's comin' home for a visit. When he gets here, we'll show him the insult that has been done on him. He'll go out——"

"An' knock the face off the big bully!" chirped Shaughnessy. "Oho, but that'll be better than havin' him pinched, an' when they come together —may I be there to see!"

"I'm wonderin'," mused the crafty Casey, "I'm wonderin' if there ain't a way to fix it so's we can all be there."

II.

The prophet, we are told on the very best of authority, has no honor in his own country, and frequently the artist finds that the same rule applies in his case. The actor, returning from metropolitan triumphs, sometimes encounters a black frost in the town which remembers him only as Old Man Jones' boy Willie; the prima donna has trouble in pleasing the critics who sang with her in the old church choir; the author—oh, well, an author gets no credit anywhere and pays cash or goes without—but the home-coming gladiator, ah, here we

4A P

have one hero who is sure of an admiring populace!

For two days Robert Emmet Brodie did little else but shake warm, kindly hands and listen to words of praise. He was a large, overdressed, bejeweled, lop-eared young man with a deep dent where the bridge of his nose should have been, and he spoke briefly, if at all, out of the extreme corner of his mouth. Somewhere on his travels he had acquired the art of listening without visible embarrassment to middle-aged men who wished to tell him how much he reminded them of the great and only John Lawrence Sullivan in his prime. It is only fair to Brodie to state that he usually dissented from this opinion, in manner as follows:

"Listen to me, guy. You're way off there—way off. I seen a picture of John L. when I was a kid, an' he had a mustache. You don't see no mustache on me, do you? And that ain't the only difference, either. From what they tell me, Sullivan was a rough, knock-'em-dead slugger—no science, no fancy stuff, no cleverness, nothin' but the big wallop in the belly or on the jawr, an' good night. I don't see where you git that stuff 'bout me bein' like him. Now, I ain't that kind of a fighter at all. I box 'em, I do; I jab the faces off of 'em, an' then—wham!"

From Robert Emmet's unwillingness to be compared with John L. Sullivan the reader will deduce at least one deduction—at least, we hope so. It will save us the trouble of saying that under no circumstances would Robert Emmet ever become extremely bored with himself. He lorded it over the young men of his home town, and, in conversation with his manager, referred to them as "hicks" and "jaspers." The young men enjoyed his patronizing manner and continued to feed his vanity until Mr. Brodie came near the bursting point.

On the evening of the second day it

suited him to favor Denny Shaughnessy's saloon with a visit. Robert Emmet brought his Greek chorus with him, and the silver dollar which he slammed on the bar bounded at least two feet into the air.

"See what everybody'll have to take!" ordered Brodie. "Let 'em all in on it, Denny, an' git in yourself."

Now, one of those who was let in on it was Casey, who edged his way to Brodie's side.

"We got something in the back room to show you, Bob," said he, with an ingratiating smile. "An oil painting, ain't we, Denny?"

"We have so," answered the proprietor.

Robert Emmet yawned ostentatiously, openly, as openly as the end of the Hoosac Tunnel.

"I seen a lot of them things when I was East," said he. "Oil paintings is old stuff to me."

"Come over here a minute," said Casey, tugging at Robert Emmet's sleeve. "Come over here an' listen. This ain't the kind of an oil paintin' ye think it is at all." He lowered his voice to a whisper. "It's a paintin' of *you*, Bob!"

"Eh! What?" exclaimed Brodie, beginning to show signs of interest. "Who done it?"

"Ye mean who painted it?" asked Casey, and Robert Emmet nodded.

"It ain't so much a question of who done it," explained Casey, "as who done something *to* it. A dirty, black shame an' a disgrace. Come on an' I'll show it to ye. No, never mind callin' the gang, Bob. 'Tis a private exhibition— for reasons we got."

His curiosity roused, Robert Emmet entered a back room, and the language which burst from his lips when he beheld the desecration of art was all that Casey had hoped for—and more.

"Accident?" chirped Shaughnessy, from the doorway. "Ye can bet your

sweet life it wasn't an accident! It was done a-purpose. A friend of yours come in here one day, just after I hung it on the wall, an' he put a right swing through it—if ye call that an accident!"

"Who was it?" demanded Brodie. "Tell me his name, an' I'll beat him to a pulp! I'll lick him within an inch of his life!"

"It was Thomas O'Connor—Big Tom," said Casey. "An' what was it he said about Bob when he done it, Shaughnessy?"

"He said ye never licked a good man, an' never will. He said he used to make ye quit when he was a kid an' he could do it anny time. He said ye always had a streak as wide as the Mississippi River, an'——"

"He said enough," interrupted Robert Emmet, from the extreme corner of his mouth. "He said a-plenty. Big Tom, hey? So he done that to me picture? Humph! I ain't seen him yet. Where does he keep himself?"

"Oh, he's round about somewheres," answered Casey.

"Likely stayin' out of yer way," supplemented Shaughnessy.

"But where does he hang out? Where can I find the big bum?"

"Well, this was the way we figured it all out," explained the diplomatic Casey. "Suppose ye ketch him in a saloon an' tear his block off. The bartender will have a treat, but the rest of us'll miss it. Suppose ye pile into him on the street. Only them that happens to be takin' a walk will see the show. Now, what ought to happen to Tom O'Connor is a public lickin'—the more public the better. Now, this is what we was thinkin' of: next Friday night the boys is goin' to pull off a benefit for ye down to Freeman's Hall."

"Yeh," growled Brodie shortly. "I know. Go on."

"We was goin' to have some boxin' on the program," continued Casey, "an' we thought it would be just the ticket to rib O'Connor up to go on an' spar four rounds with ye."

"Make it six!" interrupted Brodie, an eager sparkle in his eye. "Gimme time to cut him up till his own mother wouldn't know him. I'll jab his face to ribbons an' then knock him out!"

"Well, then, six rounds. Ye can act friendly when ye meet him, an' he'll never suspect there's annything doin' in the way of a job. Then, with the whole town lookin' on, ye can play even for this here outrage."

"Yes," said Shaughnessy, "give him a lovely trimmin' an' let him guess why."

"It listens good enough," said Robert Emmet, with deep corrugations on his brow, which, had he the gray material necessary, would have indicated thought. "It *sounds* all right, but how do you know this big bum will fall for it? Chances are he ain't lookin' for even a friendly bout with a real scrapper."

"Don't be worryin' on that score," said Shaughnessy. "The joke of it is, Bob, O'Connor really thinks he can lick ye."

Brodie laughed uproariously.

"Plenty more of 'em have had the same notion!" said he. "I knocked it out of their fool heads in jig time. Now, here's the frame-up. I'll meet Tom and I won't let on that I'm sore. I'll even let him bluff me a little if he wants to. Then, Casey, you go to him an' tell him you can fix it for him to get on with me at the benefit. Tell him I'm all out of trainin' an' he'll have to promise not to tear into me rough. He'll eat that up, and when I get him into the ring—well, say!" Robert Emmet completed the sentence with a very effective bit of pantomime, consisting of three left jabs and an annihilating right cross which, placed in the right spot, would have jarred the entire O'Connor family for generations.

The next day Casey, the fixer, called at the gas works and found Big Tom O'Connor raking coke out of the furnace.

"Your pal Bob Brodie is back in town," said Casey, after remarking on the state of the weather.

"So I've just heard," said O'Connor gruffly.

"I was wonderin' if I could git ye to do something for him."

Big Tom rose, wiped his grimy hands on his stiff shock of hair, and essayed a bit of shadow boxing, mostly composed of giant swings. When satisfied that his right arm was in working trim, he tried his right leg, and went through the motions of "putting the boots" to a fallen foe.

"Will I *do* something for him?" he repeated, breathing hard from his exertions. "With all the pleasure in life! Where is the big bum keepin' himself?"

Casey seemed astonished.

"Why, I thought you boys was friends!" said he.

Big Tom tossed his forelock out of his eyes and his lower lip protruded.

"If I'm a friend to that stiff, he better pray never to have an enemy," said he.

"But couldn't you forget that for a while?" asked Casey.

"When I'm down among the daisies, maybe. Not till then."

"Too bad," said Casey, sighing. "We all thought you'd be just the man."

"The man for what?"

"Why, the boys are givin' Brodie a benefit next Friday night at Freeman's Hall——"

"The big bum don't need no benefit," interrupted O'Connor. "He's big enough to work."

"Well, be that as it may, Tom, we want a man to go on an' spar with him. Six rounds."

"*Yeh?*"

"A man that won't be too rough."

"What's the idea?"

"Well, to tell ye the trut', Bob ain't in trainin'" an' he's kind of soft—no wind to speak of. He'd want to go kind o' easy. Now, if ye could forget this ill will, ye'd be doin' Bob a favor, an' the committee a favor, an' everybody a favor."

"I'd rather have it out with him in a barroom," said Tom.

"Man, ye can do that *afterward!*" cried Casey.

"You're sure he ain't just wantin' to show me up?"

"I tell ye, he don't want to show anybody up! He ain't able."

"That's different again," said Big Tom thoughtfully. "I'll take a chance."

"Remember now," said Casey, as he took his leave, "no rough stuff. It's a benefit."

"Yeh," said Big Tom. But to himself he said: "I'll *benefit* him, the big bum! I'll benefit him till he hollers for the police!"

And when Robert Emmet Brodie heard that the despoiler of art was willing to crawl through the ropes with him, he smiled a smile which threatened to engulf his lopped ears, and advised all his friends to secure front seats.

III.

The Brodie Benefit, judging by the attendance, promised to be a brilliant success, for Freeman's Hall was crowded long before the opening number on the program, the overture from "William Tell," was executed in cold blood by the local orchestra. Fully half the spectators were women, and the star of the evening grinned as he looked through the peephole in the curtain.

"So much the better," said Brodie to Isaac Marx, his manager.

"Better leave the tea-lead out of the bandages then," advised Isaac. "Women don't like the sight of blood, and when you start cutting him up

with that left hand they'll make trouble."

"They got no business here, then," said Brodie. "The tea-lead goes, and I only wish I could slip a horseshoe in the right mitt!"

"You're bloodthirsty to-night," said Isaac.

"This big tramp thinks he can lick me," said Robert Emmet, "an' I'm goin' to change his notions if I have to kill him to do it."

An outsider with knowledge of ring-craft would have been amazed could he have peeped into two dressing rooms and seen the preparations being made for this friendly, six-round sparring bout for points. He might even have thought that mutilation and murder were among the points desired, for in one dressing room Isaac Marx was binding adhesive tape about Brodie's left hand, and putting a strip of tea-lead under each wrapping. Now, a left jab, reënforced by a sufficient amount of tea-lead, will gash the human countenance even through a heavy boxing glove—and it was Brodie's intention to wear the lightest gloves permitted by law. In another dressing room "Red Eddie" O'Day, retired bantamweight boxer and bosom friend of the ponderous O'Connor, was also busy with bandages, but he scorned anything as coarse and brutal as tea-lead—oh, my, yes! He dipped inch-wide strips of cloth into a bowl containing a pasty, white substance, and bound them about O'Connor's hands. The soft, wet covering thus secured looked innocent enough, and would remain innocent until the plaster of Paris had time to harden, when the soft bandage would become a deadly weapon. Needless to say, the only witnesses to these activities have been mentioned.

The gladiators met in the wings shortly before going on the stage. They did not shake hands, probably because of the boxing gloves, but Robert Emmet smiled in a very friendly fashion.

"You're lookin' fit, big feller," said he, his glance taking in the massive details of O'Connor's undraped figure.

"Ah-r-r!" growled Tom, wishing he had a turkey-red bath robe like Brodie's.

"Don't be scared of the crowd," continued Robert Emmet patronizingly. "Don't pay no 'tention to the audience at all."

"Huh!" snorted Big Tom, tossing his heavy forelock.

"And whatever you do, don't get mad an' start roughin' it."

It was at this point that Tom grinned, and five minutes later he was blinking at the footlights and hearing himself mentioned by Casey, the official announcer, as "Big Tom O'Connor, the pride of the gas house." There was a thin sputter of applause, for Tom was no public idol, and he allowed Red Eddie to lead him to his corner, where he sat down to wait for Brodie.

Robert Emmet had a fair sense of the fitness of things. He knew that a certain amount of delay whets the public appetite; too much delay leads to impatient demonstrations. He timed his entrance to the exact second and marched upon the stage with a flourish of the tail of his turkey-red bath robe. The house rose at him, and he bowed three times, but refused to respond to the loud yells for a speech. Casey introduced him as the man who needed no introduction—the next heavyweight champion of the world, and Big Tom snorted in his corner.

Brodie tossed off his bath robe and skipped lightly about the ring, pivoting on his toes and shooting tentative left jabs into the air. Big Tom watched this display of agility with a curling lip.

"Pipe the big stiff showin' off!" he whispered to O'Day.

"He ain't showin' off," answered O'Day. "He's testin' the floor."

"He'll test it with his head when I git a smash at his jaw," said Big Tom.

Butch Dillon, the referee, motioned the men to the middle of the ring and delivered his instructions, with a special clause for O'Connor. Butch had not been let in on the secret.

"You wanna box nice now, Tom," said he warningly. "Remember, they's ladies present."

"Sure!" grunted O'Connor, rolling his eyes toward the footlights. "Sure, Butch!"

Dillon then took the referee's privilege and made the final announcement, dwelling at length upon the friendliness of the bout and mentioning the Marquis of Queensberry in complimentary terms. Big Tom listened to this in his corner, gloves on his hips. Red Eddie whispered in his ear:

"Right off the reel now, big guy! Right off the reel! Beat him to the punch an' you've got him!"

As the gong clanged Big Tom walked slowly to the middle of the ring, his right hand carried carelessly at his side. Now, according to custom, all friendly bouts for points, and many bouts which are not friendly, begin with a handshake, but as Robert Emmet advanced he noted the position of O'Connor's right hand and read violence in his eyes.

"He thinks he can sneak one over, the big stiff!" thought Robert Emmet. "If that's his notion——"

Thus it happened that the friendly bout for points began with two terrific right-hand blows, delivered simultaneously. Robert Emmet's uppercut crashed against O'Connor's chin, but Robert Emmet did not duck his head soon enough to avoid the plaster of Paris entirely, and Big Tom's sturdy haymaker landed full on Brodie's ear. If it had found a spot only two inches lower the entertainment would have been jolted to an abrupt close; as it was, the first five seconds of this friendly bout found both principals on the floor

—Brodie on his face near the ropes, and O'Connor on his haunches in the middle of the ring, slightly puzzled as to how he got there.

Butch Dillon did not know how to meet such an emergency or which man to favor with the count, and, in his excitement, he made a serious error. He rushed over to O'Connor and shook his fist at him.

"That ain't boxin' for points!" he yelled. "What you tryin' to do—kill somebody?"

Now, no man should argue with an Irishman named O'Connor who has been knocked down by a trick which he hoped to practice himself. Big Tom rose to his feet and cuffed Dillon soundly with his open glove, knocking him flat. A tremendous uproar came from the audience, and there was no note of commendation in it. Tom started for the ropes with a hazy idea of explaining his position, but on the way he encountered a wild-eyed human thunderbolt, which in sane moments passed for Robert Emmet Brodie. The tea-leaded left caught him fairly on the bridge of his nose, and Big Tom began to fight.

Some who were in the front of the house remember that women fainted and strong men raced up and down the aisles, whooping deliriously. A very few recall that Butch Dillon found his feet and tried to force his way between the infuriated gladiators, and Butch's memories of the evening ended abruptly at that point. None can tell who fathered the cruel stroke which knocked him headfirst through the ropes and out into the orchestra pit, where he put his right shoulder through the bull fiddle. Above the shrill screams of hysterical women and the shouts of excited men, Big Tom heard one voice—that of his second and adviser, Red Eddie O'Day:

"Tear into um, boy! Don't let um get set! On toppa him alla time, Tom! Thassa stuff!"

And in the midst of all this riot and turmoil and clamor Robert Emmet Brodie and Thomas Martin O'Connor devoted themselves each to the other with an increasing devotion. There had been a referee, there had been certain rules of combat, perhaps even ethics, but these they cast into the discard. There was still a gong, which clanged wildly under the trembling hand of Isaac Marx, but they paid not the slightest attention to it. They had forgotten the signal to cease firing.

It is a fact that when fighters lose their heads they forget the left hand and the science its use demands, employing it, if at all, as a flail. Brodie and O'Connor stood toe to toe in the middle of the ring and battered each other with wild swings. Once the plaster of paris connected solidly with the chin and Brodie dropped to the floor, but was up again before O'Connor could kick him in the face. Once Big Tom went reeling to the ropes, but when Robert Emmet rushed after him, he stepped squarely into a pile-driving right swing which had no particular aim, and for that reason caught Brodie in the pit of the stomach and made him very sick for a few seconds.

"Downstairs, Tom! The belly! The belly!" shrieked O'Day, but O'Connor was past advice, past everything but the red desire for slaughter, so, instead of following up an advantage, he plastered Robert Emmet heavily about the head until he ducked his jaws below his shoulders and so weathered the storm.

Big Tom's face suffered terribly, but he fought doggedly on with his left eye closed to a blue slit, and Brodie was unable to find a vulnerable spot, though he found all the others and left his autograph upon them.

Nobody knows how long that first round lasted; upon that subject the official timekeeper is dumb. To Robert Emmet it seemed an eternity; he was used to three minutes of fighting and one minute of rest. Tom O'Connor was hardened to barroom brawls with no call of "Time!" but he found this encounter quite long enough for his liking. Robert Emmet began to give ground; O'Connor crowded him to the ropes and Brodie clinched. O'Connor lowered his head and drove short rights and lefts crashing into unprotected territory below the breastbone. He literally hammered Brodie out of the clinch, and for a second the men stood facing each other, each with the right hand poised. It was the last shot in Robert Emmet's locker, and he knew it. As his eye caught the first movement of O'Connor's fist, he threw every remaining ounce of vitality into an attempt to beat him to the punch. So intent was he on sending his own blow home that he made not the slightest attempt to protect himself in the exchange.

Six seconds later Tom O'Connor awoke from a troubled dream and lifted his battered face from the canvas. As if from a great distance, he heard men yelling and women screaming. Blinking his one undamaged eye, he looked about for Brodie and discovered a human leg tangled with his arms. His first impression was that the leg belonged to him. Slowly he turned his head, and there, beside him on the canvas, a thousand fathoms deep in merciful oblivion, was Robert Emmet Brodie, the next heavyweight champion of the world, for the present unavoidably delayed.

Big Tom O'Connor hoisted himself to his feet and stood erect, swaying unsteadily. He looked at Brodie again, oddly enough without any desire to kick him. For once in his life Tom O'Connor had had all the fighting he wanted —perhaps more than he really needed. His face felt that way, at least. He helped several men to carry the unconscious Brodie to his corner, and then heaved himself through the ropes and disappeared.

While Red Eddie was ministering to his battler the door of the dressing room opened and Isaac Marx looked in.

"I'll make you a business proposition," said he, with commendable brevity. "Let me be your manager, and I'll get you more coin that you ever saw. You can fill the dates I had fixed up for Brodie."

"Let Brodie fill his own dates," mumbled Big Tom through his swollen lips.

"He can't," said Marx. "That last punch you took at him busted his jaw like an eggshell. Maybe he won't never be no good again."

Big Tom O'Connor stared at Marx for several seconds. Then he began to laugh, rocking himself back and forth in his chair.

"Ho, ho!" he chuckled. "I guess I done what I started out to do, at that! Ho, ho!"

"And what did you start out to do?" asked Marx.

"I wanted to fix this big bum so he'd *need* a benefit, and I guess I done it!"

"Correct as hell!" said Marx. "But how about this proposition I made you?"

"Forget it!" said O'Connor. "I got a steady job down to the gas house!"

THE OLD-TIMER'S TIP

J. B. OKIE, a sheepman, of Lost Cabin, Wyoming, who lives in the midst of his acres like a feudal baron, tells of an old-timer who gave the following advice to his only son when he was starting out to make his fortune.

"Bill," said the wise father, "don't steal unless you have to. But if yuh must steal, steal from a feller that's so rich he won't miss it, or from one that's so poor he can't foller ye."

Rimrock Jones

By Dane Coolidge

Author of "Pecos Dalhart, Rustler," "Hidden Water," Etc.

This fierce, ungovernable desert man will command your interest. He is the man with the vision, the big man of a big country, the man whose touch brings forth gold. An honest man, but the law is against him, for Rimrock Jones prospects in a country—the only one in the world—where a mining claim doesn't go straight down. That left the way open for the lawyer sharps to jump his mine when he had begun to make money. It soured him, and made him suspicious even of a girl who was willing to help. It's a strong story, stronger than "Pecos Dalhart," and if you will think back a few years you will remember how fine a novel that was.

(A Five-Part Story—Part One)

CHAPTER I.

THE MAN WITH A GUN.

THE peace of midday lay upon Gunsight, broken only by the distant *chang, chang!* of bells as a ten-mule ore team came toiling in from the mines. In the cool depths of the umbrella tree in front of the company's office, a Mexican ground dove crooned endlessly his ancient song of love, but Gunsight took no notice. Its thoughts were not of love, but of money.

The dusty team of mules passed down the street, dragging their double-trees reluctantly, and took their cursing meekly as they made the turn at the tracks. A switch engine bumped along the sidings, snaking ore cars down to the bins and bunting them up to the chutes, but except for its bangings and clamor the town was still. An aged Mexican, armed with a long bunch of willow brush, swept idly at the sprin-kled street, and Old Hassayamp Hicks, the proprietor of the Alamo Saloon, leaned back in his rawhide chair and watched him with good-natured contempt.

The town was dead, after a manner of speaking, and yet it was not dead. In the Gunsight Hotel, where the officials of the company left their women-folks to idle and fret and gossip, there was a restless flash of white from the upper veranda; and in the office below, Andrew McBain, the aggressive president of the Gunsight Mining and Development Company, paced nervously to and fro as he dictated letters to a typist. He paused, and as the clacking stopped, a woman who had been reading a novel on the veranda rose up noiselessly and listened over the railing. The new typist was really quite deaf—one could hear every word that was said. She was pretty, too, and—well, she dressed too well, for one thing.

But McBain was not making love to his typist. He had stopped with a word on his lips, and stood gazing out the window. The new typist had learned to read faces, and she followed his glance with a start. Who was this man that Andrew McBain was afraid of? He came riding in from the desert, a young man, burly and masterful, mounted on a buckskin horse and with a pistol slung low on his leg. McBain turned white, his stern lips drew tighter, and he stood where he had stopped in his stride like a wolf that has seen a fierce dog; then suddenly he swung forward again, and his voice rang out harsh and defiant. The new typist took the words down at haphazard, for her thoughts were not on her work. She was thinking of the man with a gun. He had gone by without a glance, and yet McBain was afraid of him.

A couple of card players came out of the Alamo and stopped to talk with Hassayamp.

"Well, bless my soul," exclaimed the watchful Hassayamp, as he suddenly brought his chair down with a bump, "if hyer don't come that locoed scoundrel, Rimrock! Say, that boy's crazy, don't you know he is?—jest look at that big sack of rocks!"

He rose up heavily and stepped out into the street, shading his eyes from the glare of the sun.

"Hello, thar, Rimmy!" he rumbled bluffly, as the horseman waved his hand. "Whar you been so long, and nothin' heard of you? There's been a woman hyer, inquirin' for you, 'most every day for a month now."

"'S that so?" responded Rimrock guardedly. "Well, say, boys, I've struck it rich!"

He leaned back to untie a sack of ore, but Old Hassayamp was not to be deterred.

"Yes, sir," he went on, opening up his eyes triumphantly, "a widde' woman —says you owe her two bits for some bread!"

He laughed uproariously at this pointed jest and clambered back to the plank sidewalk, where he sat down, convulsed, in his chair.

"Aw, you make me tired!" said Rimrock shortly. "You know I don't owe no woman."

"You owe every one else, though," came back Hassayamp, with a Texas yupe. "I got you there, boy. You shore cain't git around that."

"Huh!" grunted Rimrock, as he swung lightly to the ground. "Two bits, maybe! Four bits! A couple of dollars! What's that to talk about, when a man is out after millions? Is my credit good for the drinks? Well, come on in, then, boys, and I'll show you something good."

He led the way through the swinging doors, and Hassayamp followed ponderously. The card players followed also, and several cowboys, appearing as if by miracle, lined up along with the rest. Old Hassayamp looked them over grimly, breathed hard, and spread out the glasses.

"Well, all right, Rim," he observed, "between friends—but don't bid in the whole town."

"When I drink, my friends drink," answered Rimrock, and tossed off his first drink in a month. "Now" he went on, fetching out his sack. "I'll show you something good!"

He poured out a pile of blue-gray sand and stood away from it admiringly.

Old Hassayamp drew out his glasses and balanced them on his nose, then he gazed at the pile of sand.

"Well," he said, "what is it, anyway?"

"It's copper, by grab, mighty nigh ten per cent copper, and you can scoop it up with a shovel. There's worlds of it, Hassayamp—a whole dog-goned mountain! That's the trouble—there's almost too much! I can't handle it, man; it'll take millions to do it; but, believe me, the millions are there. All I need is a stake now; just a couple of thousand dollars——"

"Huh!" grunted Hassayamp, looking up over his glasses. "You don't reckon I've got that much, do you, to sink in a pile of *sand?*"

"If not you, then somebody else," replied Rimrock confidently. "Some feller that's out looking for sand. I heard about a sport over in London that tried on a bet to sell five-pound notes for a shilling. That's like me offering to sell you twenty-five dollars for the English equivalent of two bits. And d'ye think he could get any one to take 'em? He stood up on a soap box and waved those notes in the air, but d'ye think he could get anybody to buy?"

He paused with a cynical smile and looked Hassayamp in the eye.

"Well—no," conceded Hassayamp weakly.

"You bet your life he could!" snapped back Rimrock. "A guy came along that knowed. He took one look at those five-pound notes and handed up fifty cents.

"'I'll take two of 'em,' he says, and walks off with fifty dollars."

Rimrock scooped up his despised sand and poured it back into the bag, after which he turned on his heel. As the doors swung to behind him, Old Hassayamp looked at his customers and shook his head impressively. From the street outside Rimrock could be heard telling a Mexican in Spanish to take his horse to the corrals. He was master of Gunsight yet, though all his money had vanished and his credit would buy nothing but the drinks.

"Well, what d'ye know about that?" observed Hassayamp meditatively. "By George, sometimes I almost think that boy is right!"

He cleared his throat and hobbled toward the door, and the crowd took the hint to disperse.

On the edge of the shady sidewalk, Rimrock Jones, the follower after big dreams, sat silent, balancing the sack of ore in a bronzed and rock-scarred hand. He was a powerful man, with the broad, square-set shoulders that come from much swinging of a double jack or cranking at a windlass. The curling beard of youth half covered his hard-bitten face, and his head was unconsciously thrust forward, as if he still glimpsed his vision and was eager to follow it farther. The crowd settled down and gazed at him curiously, for they knew he had a story to tell, and at last the great Rimrock sighed and looked at his work-worn hands.

"Hard going," he said, glancing up at Hassayamp. "I've got a ten-foot hole to sink on twenty different claims, no powder, and nothing but Mexicans for help. But I sure turned up some good ore—she gets richer the deeper you go."

"Any gold?" inquired Hassayamp hopefully.

"Yes, but pockety. I leave all that chloriding to the Mexicans while I do my discovery work. They've got some picked rock on the dump."

"Why don't you quit that dead work and do a little chloriding yourself? Pound out a little gold—that's the way to get a stake!"

Old Hassayamp spat the words out impatiently, but Rimrock seemed hardly to hear.

"Nope," he said, "no pocket mining for me. There's copper there, millions of tons of it. I'll make my winning yet."

"Huh!" grunted Hassayamp, and Rimrock came out of his trance.

"You don't think so, hey?" he challenged, and then his face softened to a slow, reminiscent smile.

"Say, Hassayamp," he said, "did you ever hear about that prospector that found a thousand pounds of gold in one chunk? He was lost on the desert, plumb out of water, and forty miles from nowhere. He couldn't take the chunk along with him, and if he left it there the sand would cover it up. Now, what was that poor feller to do?"

"Well, what did he do?" inquired Hassayamp cautiously.

"He couldn't make up his mind," answered Rimrock, "so he stayed there till he starved to death."

"You're plumb full of these sayings and parables, ain't you?" remarked Hassayamp sarcastically. "What's that got to do with the case?"

"Well," began Rimrock, sitting down on the edge of the sidewalk and looking absently up the street, "take me, for instance. I go out across the desert to the Tecolotes and find a whole mountain of copper. You don't have to chop it out with chisels, like that native copper around the Great Lakes; and you don't have to go underground and do timbering like they do around Bisbee and Cananea. All you have to do is to shoot it down and scoop it up with a steam shovel. Now, I've located the whole danged mountain and done most of my discovery work, but if some feller don't give me a boost, like taking that prospector a canteen of water, I've either got to lose my mine or sit down and starve to death. If I'd never done anything, it'd be different, but you know that I *made* the Gunsight."

He leaned forward and fixed the saloon keeper with his earnest eyes, and Old Hassayamp held up both hands.

"Yes, yes, boy, I know!" he broke out hurriedly. "Don't talk to me—I'm convinced. But, by George, Rim, you can spend more money and have less to show for it than any man I know. What's the use? That's what we all say. What's the use of staking you when you'll turn right around in front of us and throw the money away?

Ain't I staked you? Ain't L. W. staked you?"

"Yes, and he broke me, too!" answered Rimrock, raising his voice to a defiant boom. "Here he comes now, the blue-faced old dastard!"

He thrust out his jaw and glared up the street where L. W. Lockhart, the local banker, came stumping down the sidewalk. L. W. was tall and rangy, with a bulldog jaw clamped down on a black cigar and an air of absolute detachment from his surroundings.

"Yes, I mean you!" shouted Rimrock insultingly, as L. W. went grimly past. "You claim to be a white man, and then stand in with that lawyer to beat me out of my mine. I made you, you old nickel pincher, and now you go by me and don't even say: 'Have a drink.' "

"You're drunk!" retorted Lockhart, looking back over his shoulder, and Rimrock jumped to his feet.

"I'll show you!" he cried, starting angrily after him, and L. W. turned swiftly to meet him.

"You'll show me *what?*" he demanded coldly, as Rimrock put his hand to his gun.

"Never mind!" answered Rimrock. "You know you jobbed me. I let you in on a good thing, and you sold me out to McBain. I want some money, and if you don't give it to me I'll—I'll go over and collect from him."

"Oh, you want some money, hey?" repeated Lockhart. "I thought you was going to *show* me something!"

The banker scowled as he rolled his cigar, but there was a twinkle far back in his eyes. "You're bad now, ain't you?" he continued tauntingly. "You're just feeling awful! You're going to jump on Lon Lockhart and stomp him into the ground! Huh!"

"Aw, shut your mouth!" answered Rimrock defiantly. "I never said a word about fight."

"Uhhr!" grunted L. W., and put his

hand in his pocket, at which Rimrock became suddenly expectant.

"Henry Jones," began the banker, "I knowed your father, and he was an honorable, hard-working man. You're nothing but a bum, and you're getting worse. Why don't you go and put up that gun?"

"I don't have to!" retorted Rimrock, but he moved up closer, and there was a wheedling turn to his voice. "Just two thousand dollars, Lon—that's all I ask of you—and I'll give you a share in my mine. Didn't I come to you first, when I discovered the Gunsight, and give you the very best claim? And you ditched me, L. W., dad-burn you, you know it; you sold me out to Mc-Bain. But I've got something now that runs up into millions! All it needs is a little more work."

"Yes, and forty miles of railroad," put in L. W. intolerantly. "I wouldn't take the whole works for a gift!"

"No, but, Lon, I'm lucky—you know that yourself—I can go East and sell the old mine."

"Oh, you're lucky, are you?" interrupted L. W. "Well, how come, then, that you're standing here, broke? But here, I've got business; I'll give you ten dollars—and, remember, it's the last that you get!"

He drew out a bill, but Rimrock stood looking at him with a slow and contemptuous smile.

"Yes, you dog-goned old screw," he answered ungraciously, "what good will ten dollars do?"

"You can get just as drunk on that," replied L. W. pointedly, "as you could on a hundred thousand."

A change came over Rimrock's face, the swift mirroring of some great idea, and he reached out for the money.

"Where you going?" demanded L. W., as he started across the street.

"None of your business," answered Rimrock curtly, but he headed straight for the Mint.

CHAPTER II.

WHEN RICHES FLY.

The Mint was Gunsight's only gambling house. It had a bar, of course, and a Mexican string band that played from eight o'clock on; besides a roulette wheel, a crap table, two faro layouts, and monte for the Mexicans. But the afternoon was dull, and the faro dealer was idly shuffling a double stack of chips when Rimrock brushed in through the door. Half an hour afterward, the place was crowded, and all the games were running big. Such is the force of example—especially when you win.

Rimrock threw his bill on the table, bought a stack of white chips, placed it on the queen, and told the dealer to turn 'em. The queen won, and Rimrock took his chips and played as the spirit moved. He won more, for the house was unlucky from the start, and soon others began to ride his bets. If he bet on the seven, eager hands reached over his shoulder and placed more chips on the seven. Petty winners drifted off to try their luck at monte; the sports took a flyer at roulette; and as the gambling spirit, so subtly fed, began to rise to a fever, Rimrock Jones, the cause of all this heat, bet more and more—and still won.

It was at the height of the excitement when, with half the checks in the rack in front of him, Rimrock was losing and winning by turns, that the bull-like rumble of L. W. Lockhart came drifting in to him above the clamor of the crowd.

"Why don't you quit, you fool?" the deep voice demanded. "Cash in and quit—you've got your stake!"

Rimrock made a gesture of absent-minded impatience and watched the slow turn of the cards. Not even the dealer or the hawk-eyed lookout was more intently absorbed in the game. He knew every card that had been played, and he bet where the odds were best. Every so often a long, yellow hand reached past him and laid a bet by his stake. It was the hand of a Chinaman, those most passionate of faro players; and at such times, seeing it follow his luck, the face of Rimrock lightened up with the semblance of a smile. He called the last turn, and they paused for the drinks, while the dealer mopped his brow.

"Where's Ike?" he demanded. "Well, somebody call him—he's hiding out, asleep, upstairs."

"Yes, wake him up!" shouted Rimrock boastfully. "Tell him Rimrock Jones is here."

"Aw, pull out, you sucker!" blared L. W. in his ear, but Rimrock only shoved out his bets.

"Ten on the ace," droned the anxious dealer; "the jack is coppered. All down?"

He held up his hand, and as the betting ceased he slowly pushed out the two cards.

"Trey loses, ace wins!" he announced, and Rimrock won again.

Then he straightened up purposefully and looked about as he sorted his winnings into piles.

"The whole works on the queen," he said to the dealer, and a hush fell upon the crowd.

"Where's Ike?" shrilled the dealer, but the boss was not to be found, and he dealt unwillingly for a queen. But the fear was on him, and his thin hands trembled; for Ike Bray was not the type of your frozen-faced gambler—he expected his dealers to win. The dealer shoved them out, and an oath slipped past his lips.

"Queen wins," he quavered. "The bank is broke." And he turned the box on its side.

A shout went up—the glad yell of the multitude—and Rimrock rose up, grinning.

"Who said to pull out?" he demanded arrogantly, looking about for the glowering L. W. "Huh, huh!" he chuckled. "Quit your luck when you're winning? Quit your luck, and your luck will quit you—the drinks for the house, barkeep!"

He was standing at the bar, stuffing money into his pockets, when Ike Bray, the proprietor, appeared. Rimrock turned, all smiles, as he heard his voice on the stairs, and lolled back against the bar. More than once in the past Bray had taken his roll, but now it was his turn to laugh.

"Lemme see," he remarked, as he felt Bray's eyes upon him, "I wonder how much I win."

He drew out the bills from his faded overalls and began laboriously to count them out into his hat.

Ike Bray stopped and looked at him, a little, twisted man with his hair still rumpled from the bed.

"Where's that dealer?" he shrilled, in his high, complaining voice. "I'll kill the danged piker—that bank ain't broke yet—I got a big roll right here!"

He waved it in the air and came limping forward until he stood facing Rimrock Jones.

"You think you broke me, do you?" he demanded insolently, as Rimrock looked up from his count.

"You can see for yourself," answered Rimrock contentedly, and held out his well-filled hat.

"You're a piker!" yelled Bray. "You don't dare to come back at me. I'll play you one turn, win or lose—for your pile!"

A hundred voices rang out at once, giving Rimrock all kinds of advice, but L. W.'s rose above them all.

"Don't you do it!" he roared. "He'll clean you for a certainty!" But Rimrock's blue eyes were aflame.

"All right, Mr. Man," he answered on the instant, and went over and sat down in his chair. "But bring a new pack and shuffle 'em clean, and I'll do the cutting myself."

"Ahhr!" snarled Bray, who was in villainous humor, as he hurled himself into his place. "Y' needn't make no cracks—I'm on the square, and I'll take no lip from anybody!"

"Well, shuffle 'em up, then," answered Rimrock quietly, "and when I feel like it I'll make my bet."

It was the middle of the night, as Bray's days were divided, and even yet he was hardly awake; but he shuffled the cards until Rimrock was satisfied, and then locked them into the box. The case keeper sat opposite to keep track of the cards, and a lookout on the stand at one end, and while a mob of surging onlookers fought at their backs they watched the slow turning of the cards.

"Why don't you bet?" snapped Bray; but Rimrock jerked his head and beckoned him to go on.

"Yes, and lose half on splits," he answered grimly. "I'll bet when it comes the last turn."

The deal went on till only three cards remained in the bottom of the box. By the record of the case keeper they were the deuce and the jack—the top card, already shown, did not count.

"The jack," said Rimrock, and piled up his money on the enameled card on the board.

"You lose!" rasped out Bray, without waiting for the turn, and then drew off the upper card. The jack lay, a loser, in the box below, and as he shoved it slowly out the deuce appeared underneath.

"How'd you know?" flashed back Rimrock, as Bray reached for his money; but the gambler laughed in his face.

"I outlucked you, you yap!" he answered harshly. "That dealer—he wasn't worth hell room!"

"Gimme a fiver to eat on!" demanded Rimrock, as Bray banked the money, but he flipped him fifty cents. It was the customary stake, the sop thrown by the gambler to the man who has lost his last cent, and Bray sloughed it without losing his count.

"Go on, now," he said, still keeping to the formula; "go back and polish a drill!"

It was the form of dismissal for the hard-rock miners whose earnings he was wont to take, but Rimrock was not particular.

"All right, Ike," he said, and as he drifted out the door, his prosperity friends disappeared. Only L. W. remained, a scornful twist to his lips, and the sight of him left Rimrock sick.

"Yes, rub it in!" he said defiantly, and L. W., too, walked away.

In his sober moments—when he was out on the desert or slugging away underground—Rimrock Jones was neither childish nor a fool. He was a serious man, with great hopes before him and a past, not ignoble, behind. But after months of solitude, of hard, yegging work and hopes deferred, the town set his nerves all atingle—even Gunsight, a mere dot on the map—and he was drunk before he took his first drink— drunk with mischief and spontaneous laughter, drunk with good stories untold, new ideas, great thoughts, high ambitions. But now he had had his fling.

With fifty cents to eat on, and one more faro game behind him, Rimrock stood thoughtfully on the corner and asked the old question: "What next?" He had won, and he had lost. He had made the stake that would have taken him far toward his destiny, and then he had dropped it foolishly by playing another man's game. He could see it now; but then we all can—the question was: What next?

"Well, I'll eat," he said at last, and went across the street to Woo Chong's. "The American Restaurant," was the way the sign read, but Americans don't run restaurants in Arizona. They don't know how. Woo Chong had fed forty miners when he ran the cookhouse for Rimrock for half what a white man could; and when Rimrock had lost his mine, at the end of a long lawsuit, Woo Chong had followed him to town. There was a long tally on the wall, the longest of all, which told how many meals Rimrock owed him for; but Rimrock knew he was welcome. Adversity had its uses, and he had learned, among other things, that his best friends were now Chinamen and Mexicans. To them, at least, he was still El Patron—the Boss!

"Hello, there, Woo!" he shouted at the doorway, and a rapid fire of Chinese ceased. The dining room was deserted, but from the kitchen in the rear he could hear the shuffling slippers of Woo.

"Howdy-do, Misse' Jones!" exclaimed Woo, in great excitement, as he came hurrying out to meet him. "I see you—few minutes ago—ove' Ike Blay's place! You blakum falo bank, no?"

"No, I lose," answered Rimrock honestly. "Ike Bray, he gave me this to eat on."

He showed the fifty-cent piece and sat down at a table, whereat Woo Chong began to giggle hysterically.

"Aww! Allee time foolee me," he grinned facetiously. "You no see me the'? Me playum, too. Win ten dolla' you bet!"

"Well, all right, Woo," said Rimrock. "Just give me something to eat—we won't quarrel about who won."

He leaned back in his chair, and Woo Chong said no more till he appeared again with a T-bone steak.

"You ketchum mine, pletty soon?" he questioned anxiously. "All lite, me come back and cook."

Rimrock sighed and went to eating, and Woo remembered the coffee, but somehow even that failed to cheer.

A shadow of doubt came across Woo's watchful face, and he hurried away for more bread.

"You no blakum bank?" he inquired at last, and Rimrock shook his head.

"No, Woo," he said; "Ike Bray, he came down and win all my money back."

"Aw, too bad!" breathed Woo Chong and slipped quietly away; but after a while he came back.

"Too bad!" he repeated. "You my fliend, Misse' Jones." And he laid five dollars by his hand.

"Ah, no, no!" protested Rimrock, rising up from his place as if he had suffered a blow. "No money, Woo. You give me my grub, and that's enough—I haven't got down to that!"

Woo Chong went away—he knew how to make gifts easy—and Rimrock stood looking at the gold. Then he picked it up slowly, and as slowly walked out and stood leaning against a post.

There is one street in Gunsight, running grandly down to the station; but the rest is mostly vacant lots and scattered adobe houses, creeping out into the infinitude of the desert. At noon, when he had come to town, the street was deserted, but now it was coming to life. Wild-eyed Mexican boys, mounted on barebacked ponies, came galloping up from the corrals; freight wagons drifted past, hauling supplies to distant mining camps; and at last, as he stood there thinking, the women began to come out of the hotel.

All day they stayed there, idle, useless, on the shaded veranda above the street; and then, when the sun was low, they came forth like indolent butterflies to float up and down the street. They sauntered by in pairs, half hidden beneath silk parasols, and their skirts swished softly as they passed. Rimrock eyed them sullenly, for a black mood was on him—he was thinking of his lost mine. Their faces were powdered to an unnatural whiteness, and their hair was elaborately coiffed; their dresses, too, were white and filmy, and their high heels clacked as they walked. But who was keeping these women, these wives of officials and superintendents and mining engineers? Did they glance at the man who had discovered their mine and built up the town where they lived? Well, probably they did, but not so as he could notice it and take off his battered old hat.

Rimrock looked up the road, and, far out across the desert, he could see his own pack train coming in. There was money to be got to buy powder and grub, but who would trust Rimrock Jones now? Not the Gunsight crowd, not McBain and his hirelings—they needed the money for their women! He gazed at them, scowling as they went pacing by him, with their eyes fixed demurely on space; and all too well he knew that beneath their lashes they watched him and knew him well. Yes, and spoke to each other, when they were off up the street, of what a bum he had become. That was women —he knew it—the idle kind—they judged a man by his roll.

The pack train strung by, each burro with his sawhorse saddle, and old Juan and his boy behind.

"El corral!" directed Rimrock, as they looked at him expectantly—and then he remembered something.

"Oyez, Juan!" he beckoned, calling his manservant up to him. "Here's five dollars—go buy some beans and flour. It is nothing, Juanito; I'll have more pretty soon—and here's four bits; you can buy you a drink."

He smiled benevolently, and Juan touched his hat and went sidling off like a crab; and then once more the black devil came back to plague him, hissing: Money, *money*, MONEY! He looked up the street, and a plan, long formless, took sudden shape in his brain. There was yet McBain, the horse leech of a lawyer who had beaten

him out of his claim. More than once, in black moments, he had threatened to kill him; but now he was glad he had not. Men even raised skunks, when the bounty on them was high enough, and took the pay out of their hides. It was the same with McBain. If he didn't come through—— Rimrock shook up his six-shooter and stalked resolutely off up the street.

The office of the company was on the ground floor of the hotel—the corner room, with a rented office beyond— and as Rimrock came toward it, he saw a small sign, jutting out from the farther door:

MARY ROGET FORTUNE. TYPEWRITING.

He glanced at it absently, for strange emotions came over him as he peered in through that plate-glass window. It had been his office, this same expensive room; and he had been robbed of it under cover of the law. He shaded his eyes from the glare of the street and looked in at the mahogany desk. It was vacant—the whole place was vacant— and silently he tried the door. That was locked. McBain had seen him and slipped away till he should get out of town.

"The sneaking cur!" muttered Rimrock, in a fury, and a passing woman drew away and half screamed. He ignored her, pondering darkly, and then to his ears there came a familiar voice. He listened intently and raised his head, then tiptoed along the wall. That voice, and he knew it, belonged to Andrew McBain, the man that stole mines for a living. He paused at the door where Mary Fortune had her sign, then suddenly forced his way in.

Without thinking, impulsively he had moved toward that voice as a man follows some irresistible call. He opened the door and stood blinking in the doorway, his hand on the pistol at his side. Then he blinked again, for in the gloom of the back office there was nothing but a desk and a girl. She wore a harness over her head, like a telephone operator, and rose up to meet him tremulously.

"Is there anything you wish?" she asked him quietly, and Rimrock fumbled and took off his hat.

"Yes—I was looking for a man," he said at last. "I thought I heard him—just now."

He came down toward her, still looking about him, and there was a stir from behind the desk.

"No, I think you're mistaken," she answered bravely, but he could see the telltale fear in her eyes.

"You know who I mean!" he broke out roughly. "And I guess you know why I've come!"

"No, I don't," she answered; "but—but this is my office, and I hope you won't make any trouble."

The words came with a rush, once she found her courage, but the appeal was lost upon Rimrock.

"He's here, then!" he said. "Well, you tell him to come out. I'd like to talk with him on business—alone!"

He took a step forward, and then suddenly from behind the desk a shadow rose up and fled. It was Andrew McBain, and as he dashed for the rear door the girl valiantly covered his retreat. There was a quick slap of the latch, a scuffle behind her, and the door came shut with a bang.

"Oho!" said Rimrock, as she faced him, panting. "He must be a friend of yourn."

"No, he isn't," she answered instantly, and then a smile crept into her eyes. "But he's—well, he's my principal customer."

"Oh!" said Rimrock grimly. "Well, I'll let him live, then. Good-by."

He turned away, still intent on his purpose, but at the door she called him back.

"What's that?" he asked, as if awak-

5A P

ened from a dream. "Why, yes, if you don't mind, I will."

CHAPTER III.
MISS FORTUNE.

It was very informal, to say the least, for Mary Fortune to invite him to stay. To be sure, she knew him—he was the man with the gun, the man of whom McBain was afraid—but that was all the more reason, to a reasoning woman, why she should keep silent and let him depart. But there was a businesslike brevity about him, a single-minded directness, that struck her as really unique. Quite apart from the fact that it might save McBain, she wanted him to stay there and talk. At least, so she explained it, the evening afterward, to her censorious other self. What she did was spontaneous, on the impulse of the moment, and without any reason whatever.

"Oh, won't you sit down a moment?" she had murmured politely; and the savage, fascinating Westerner, after one long look, had with equal politeness accepted.

"Yes, indeed," he answered, when he had got his wits together, "you're very kind to ask me, I'm sure."

He came back, then, a huge, brown, ragged animal, and sat down very carefully in her spare chair. Why he did so when his business, not to mention a just revenge, was urgently calling him thence, was a question never raised by Rimrock Jones. Perhaps he was surprised beyond the point of resistance; but it is still more likely that, without his knowing it, he was hungry to hear a woman's voice. His black mood left him; he forgot what he had come there for, and sat down to wonder and admire.

He looked at her curiously, and his eyes for one brief moment took in the details of the headband over her ear; then he smiled to himself in his masterful way, as if the sight of her pleased him well. There was nothing about her to remind him of those women who stalked up and down the street; she was tall and slim, with swift, capable hands, and every line of her spoke subtly of style. Nor was she lacking in those qualities of beauty which we have come to associate with her craft. She had quiet, brown eyes that lit up when she smiled, a high nose, and masses of hair. But across that brown hair that a duchess might have envied lay the metal clip of her ear phone, and in her dark eyes, bright and steady as they were, was that anxious look of the deaf.

"I hope I wasn't rude," she stammered nervously, as she sat down and met his glance.

"Oh, no," he said, with the same carefree directness, "it was me, I reckon, that was rude. I certainly didn't count on meeting a lady when I came in here looking for—well, McBain. He won't be back, I reckon. Kind of interferes with business, don't it?"

He paused and glanced at the rear door, and the typist smiled discreetly.

"Oh, no," she said. And then, lowering her voice: "Have you had trouble with Mr. McBain?"

"Yes, I have," he answered. "You may have heard of me—my name is Henry Jones."

"Oh—*Rimrock* Jones?"

Her eyes brightened instantly as he slowly nodded his head.

"That's me," he said. "I used to run this whole town—I'm the man that discovered the mines."

"What—the Gunsight mines? Why, I thought Mr. McBain——"

"McBain *what?*"

"Why, I thought *he* discovered the mines."

Rimrock straightened up angrily, then he sat back in his chair and shook his head at her cynically.

"He didn't need to," he answered. 'All he had to do was to discover an error in the way I laid out my claim. Then he went before a judge that was as crooked as he was, and the rest you can see for yourself."

He thrust his thumb scornfully through a hole in his shirt and waved a hand in the direction of the office.

"No, he cleaned me out, using a friend of mine, and now I'm down to nothing. What do you think of a law that will take away a man's mine because it apexes on another man's claim? I discovered this mine, and I formed the company, keeping fifty-one per cent of the stock. I opened her up, and she was paying big, when Andy McBain comes along. A shyster lawyer—that's the best you can say for him—but he cleaned me, down to a cent."

"I don't understand," she said at last, as he seemed to expect some reply. "About these apexes—what are they, anyway? I've only been West a few months."

"Well, I've been West all my life, and I've hired some smart lawyers, and I don't know what an apex is yet. But in a general way it's the high point of an ore body—the highest place where it shows above ground. But the law works out like this: Every time a man finds a mine and opens it up till it pays, these apex sharps locate the high ground above him and contest the title to his claim. You can't do that in Mexico, nor in Canada, nor in China—this is the only country in the world where a mining claim don't go straight down. But under the law, when you locate a lode, you can follow that vein, within an extension of your headlines, under anybody's ground. *Anybody's!*"

He shifted his chair a little closer and fixed her with his fighting blue eyes.

"Now, just to show you how it works," he went on, "take me, for instance. I was just an ordinary ranch kid, brought up so far back in the mountains that the boys all called me Rimrock, and I found a rich ledge of rock. I staked out a claim for myself, and the rest for my folks and my friends, and then we organized the Gunsight Mining Company. That's the way we all do out here—one man don't hog it all; he does something for his friends. Well, the mine paid big, and if I didn't manage it just right I certainly never meant any harm. Of course I spent lots of money—some objected to that—but I made the old Gunsight pay.

"Then"—he raised his finger and held it up impressively as he marked the moment of his downfall—"then this McBain came along and edged into the company, and right from that day I lose. He took on as attorney, but it wasn't but a minute till he was trying to be the whole show. You can't stop that man short of killing him dead, and I haven't got around to that yet. But he bucked me from the start, and set everybody against me, and finally he cut out Lon Lockhart. There was a man, by Joe, that I'd stake my life on it he'd never go back on a friend; but he threw in with this lawyer and brought a suit against me, and just naturally took—away—my—mine!"

Rimrock's breast was heaving with an excitement so powerful that the girl instinctively drew away; but he went on, scarcely noticing, and with a fixed glare in his eyes that was akin to the stare of a madman.

"Yes, took it away; and here's how they did it," he went on, suddenly striving to be calm: "The first man I staked for, after my father and kinfolks, was L. W. Lockhart, over here. He was a cowman then, and he had some money, and I figured on bidding him in. So I staked him a good claim, above mine on the mountain, and, sure enough, he came into the company. He financed me from the start; but he kept this claim for himself without putting it in with the rest. Well, as luck would have it, when we sank on the ledge, it turned at right angles up the hill. Up and down she went—it was the main lode of quartz, and we'd been following in on a stringer. And rich? Oh, my, it was rotten!"

He paused and smiled wanly, then his eyes became fixed again, and he hurried on with his tale:

"I was standing out in front of my office one day when Tuck Edwards, the boy I had in charge of the mine, came riding up and says:

"'Rim, they've jumped you!'

"'Who's jumped me?' I says.

"'Andrew McBain and L. W.!' he says, and I thought at first he was crazy.

"'Jumped our mine?' I says. 'How can they jump it, when it's part their own already?'

"'They've jumped it all,' he says. 'They had a mining expert out there for a week, and he's made a report that the lode apexes on L. W.'s claim.'

"I couldn't believe it. L. W.? I'd made him. He used to be nothing but a cowman; and here he was in town, a banker. No, I couldn't believe it; and when I did, it was too late. They'd taken possession of the property, and had a court order restraining me from going onto the grounds. Not only did they claim the mine, but every dollar it had produced—the mill, the hotel, everything! And the judge backed them up in it. What kind of a law is that?"

He leaned forward and looked her in the eyes, and Mary Fortune realized that she was being addressed not as a woman, but impersonally as a human being.

"What kind of a law is that?" he demanded sternly, and took the answer for granted.

"That cured me," he said. "After this, here's the only law I know."

He tapped his pistol and leaned back in his chair, smiling grimly as she gazed at him, aghast.

"Yes, I know," he went on, "it don't sound very good, but it's that or lay down to McBain. The judges are no better—they're just promoted lawyers——"

He checked himself, for she had risen from her chair and her eyes were no longer scared.

"Excuse me," she said, "my father was a judge." And Rimrock reached for his hat.

"Whereabouts?" he asked, groping for a chance to square himself.

"Oh—back East," she said evasively, and Rimrock heaved a sigh of relief.

"Aw, that's different," he answered. "I was just talking about the Territory. Well, say, I'll be moving along."

He rose up quickly, but as he started for the door a rifle cartridge fell from his torn pocket. It rolled in a circle, and as he stooped swiftly to catch it the bullet came out like a cork and let spill a thin, yellow line.

"What's that?" she asked, as he dropped to his knees. And he answered briefly:

"Gold."

"What—real gold?" she cried rapturously. "Gold from a mine? Oh, I'd like——"

She stopped short, and Rimrock chuckled as he scooped up the elusive dust.

"All right," he said, as he rose to his feet, "I'll make you a present of it, then." And he held out the cartridge of gold.

"Oh, I couldn't!" she thrilled, but he only smiled encouragingly and poured out the gold in her hand.

"It's nothing," he said; "just the clean-up from a pocket. I run across a little once in a while."

A panic came over her as she felt the telltale weight of it, and she hastily poured it back.

"I can't take it, of course," she said, with dignity, "but it was awful good of you to offer it, I'm sure."

"Aw, what do we care?" he protested lightly. But she handed the corked cartridge back. Then she stood off and looked at him, and the huge man in overalls became suddenly a Crœsus in her eyes.

"Is that from your mine?" she asked at last, and of a sudden his bronzed face lighted up.

"You bet it is—but look at this!" And he fetched a polished rock from his pocket. "That's azurite," he said—"nearly forty per cent copper! I'm not telling everybody, but I find big chunks of that, and I've got a whole mountain of low grade. What's a gold mine compared to that?"

He gave her the rich rock, with its peacock-blue coloring, and plunged forthwith into a description of his find. Now at last he was himself, and to his natural enthusiasm was added the stimulus of her spellbound, wondering eyes. He talked on and on, giving all the details, and she listened like one entranced. He told of his long trips across the desert, his discovery of the neglected mountain of low-grade copper ore, and then of his enthusiasm when, in making a cut, he encountered a pocket of the precious, peacock-blue azurite. And then of his scheming and hiring American-born Mexicans to locate the whole body of ore, after which he engaged them to do the discovery work, and later transfer the claims to him. And now, half finished, with no money to pay them, and not even food to keep them content, the Mexicans had quit work, and unless he brought back provisions all his claims would go by default.

"I've got a chance," he went on fiercely, "to make millions, if I can only get title to those claims! And now, by grab, after all I've done for 'em, these pikers won't advance me a cent!"

"How much would it cost?" she asked him quickly, "to finish the work and pay off the men?"

"Two thousand dollars," he answered wearily. "But it might as well be a million."

"Would—would four hundred dollars help you?".

She asked it eagerly, impulsively, almost in his ear, and he turned .as if he had been struck.

"Don't speak so loud," she implored him nervously. "These women in the hotel—they're listening to everything you say. I can hear all right if you only whisper. Would four hundred dollars help you out?"

"Not of your money!" answered Rimrock hoarsely. "No—I'll never come to that!"

He started away, but she caught him by the arm and held him back till he stopped.

"But I want to do it!" she persisted. "It's a good thing—I believe in it—and I've got the money!"

He stopped and looked at her, almost tempted by her offer; then he shook his great head like a bull.

"No!" he said, talking half to himself. "I won't do it—I've sunk low enough. But a woman? Nope, I won't do it."

"Oh, quit your foolishness!" she burst out impatiently. "I guess I know my own mind. I came out to this country to try and recoup myself, and I want to get in on this mine. No sentiment, understand me; I'm talking straight business; and I've got the money—right here!"

"Well, what do you want for it?" he demanded roughly. "If that's the deal, what's your cut? I never saw you before, nor you me. How much do you want—if we win?"

"I want a share in the mine," she answered instantly. "I don't care— whatever you say!"

"Well, I'll go you," he said. "Now give me the money, and I'll try to make both of us rich."

His voice was trembling, and he followed every movement as she stepped behind her desk.

"Just look out the window," she said, as he waited; and Rimrock turned his head. There was a rustle of skirts, and a moment later she laid a roll of bills in his hand.

"Just give me a share," she said again, and suddenly he met her eyes.

"How about fifty-fifty—an undivided half?" he asked, with a dizzy smile.

"Too much," she said. "I'm talking business."

"All right," he said. "But so am I."

CHAPTER IV.

AS A LOAN.

Rimrock Jones left town with four burroloads of powder, some provisions, and a cargo of tools. He paid cash for his purchases, and answered no questions beyond saying that he knew his own business. No one knew or could guess where he had got his money—except Miss Fortune, and she would not tell. From the very first she had told herself that the loan was nothing to hide, and yet she was too much of a woman not to have read aright the beacon in Rimrock's eyes. He had spoken impulsively, and so had she; and they had parted, as it turned out, for months.

The dove that had crooned so long in the umbrella tree built a nest there and cooed on to his mate. The clear, rainless winter gave place to spring, and the giant cactus burst into flower. It rained, short and hard, and the desert floor took on suddenly a fine mat of green, and still he did not come. He was like the rain, this wild man of the desert—swift and fierce, then gone and forgotten. Once she saw his Mexican, the old, bearded Juan, with his string of shaggy burros at the store; but he brought her no word and went off the next day with more powder and provisions in his packs.

It was all new to Mary Fortune, this stern and barren country; and its people were new to her, too. The women, for some reason, had regarded her with suspicion, and her answer was a patrician aloofness and reserve. When the day's work was done, she took off her headband and sat reading in the lobby, alone. As for the men of the hotel, the susceptible young mining men who passed to and fro from Gunsight, they found her pleasant, but not quite what they had expected—not quite what Dame Rumor had painted her. They watched her from the distance, for she was undeniably good looking—and so did the women upstairs. They watched and they listened, which was not the least of the reasons why Mary Fortune laid her ear phone aside. No person can enjoy the intimacies of life when they are shouted ill-advisedly to the world.

But if, when she first came to town, worn and tired from her journey, she had seemed more deaf than she was, Mary Fortune had learned, as her hearing improved, to artfully conceal the fact. There was a certain advantage, in that unfriendly atmosphere, in being able to overhear chance remarks. But no permanent happiness can come from small talk and listening to petty asides; and, for better or worse, Mary took off her harness and retired to the world of good books. She read and she dreamed and, quite unsuspected, she looked out the window for *him*.

The man! There is always a man, some man, for every woman who dreams. Rimrock Jones had come once and gone as quickly, but his absence was rainbowed with romance. He was out on the desert, far away to the south, sinking shafts on his claims—their claims. He had discovered a fortune, but, strong as he was, he had had to accept help from her. He would succeed, this fierce, ungovernable desert man; he would win the world's confidence as he had won her faith by his strength and the bold look in his eyes. He would finish his discovery work and record all his claims, and then—well, then he would come back.

So she watched for him furtively, glancing quickly out the window whenever a horseman passed by; and one day, behold, as she looked up from her typing, he was there, riding by on his horse! And as he passed, he looked in, under the shadow of his hat, and touched a bag that was tied behind his saddle. He was more ragged than ever, and one hand had a bandage around it; but he was back, and he would come. She abandoned her typewriting—one of those interminable legal papers that McBain was always leaving on her desk—and stepped out to look down the street.

The air, warm and soft, was spiced with green odors and the resinous tang of the greasewood; the ground dove in his tree seemed swooning with passion as he crooned his throaty *Kwoo, kwooo*. It was the breath of spring, but tropical, sense stealing; it lulled the brain and bade the heart leap and thrill. This vagabond, this rough horseman with his pistol and torn clothing and the round sack of ore lashed behind; who would ever dream that an adventurer like him could make her forget who she was? But he came from the mine she had helped him to save, and the sack might be heavy with gold. So she watched, half concealed, until he stopped at the bank and went striding in with the bag.

As for Rimrock Jones, he rode by the saloon and went direct to L. W., the banker. It was life or death, as far as the Tecolote was concerned, for his four hundred dollars was gone. That had given him the powder to shoot out his holes to the ten feet required by law, and enough actual cash to pay his Mexican locators and make a legal transfer of the claims; but four hundred dollars will not last a lifetime, and Rimrock Jones was broke. He needed more money, and he went perforce to the only man who could give it. It would be a fight, for L. W. was stubborn; but Rimrock was stubborn himself.

"L. W.," he said, when he found the banker in his private office in the rear, "you used to be white, and I want you to listen before you spit out what you've got in your craw. You may have a grievance, and I don't deny it; but, remember, I've got one, too. No, it isn't about my mine—I wouldn't sell you one share in it for your whole little jim-crow bank. I've done my first work, and I've recorded my claims, and I'll offer them—somewheres else. All you know is gold, and before we go any further, just run your eyes over that."

He dumped the contents of his bag on the polished desk, and L. W. blinked as he looked. It was picked gold quartz of the richest kind, with jewelry specimens on top, and as L. W. ran his hand through it his tight mouth relaxed from its bulldog grip on the cigar.

"Where'd you get it?" he grunted, and Rimrock's eyes flashed as he answered shortly:

"My mine."

"How much more you got?"

L. W. asked it suspiciously, but the gold gleam had gone to his heart.

"About two tons of the best, scattered around on the different dumps, and a whole scad more that will ship. I knew you wouldn't lend on anything but gold ore, and I need money to pay off my Mexicans. I've got to have some ore bags to sack that picked rock in, and hire freighters to haul it in. Then there's the freight and the milling, and with one thing and another I need about two thousand dollars."

"Oh! Two thousand dollars. Seems to me," observed L. W., "I've heard that sum mentioned before."

"You have, dad-burn ye, and this time I want it. What's the matter—ain't that ore good for it all?"

"It is, if you've got it, but I've come to the point where I don't place absolute confidence in your word."

"Oh, you have!" said Rimrock sarcastically. "That sounds like some lawyer talk. You might've learned it from Apex McBain when you was associated with him in a deal. I won't say *what* deal, but, refreshing your memory now, ain't my word as good as yours?"

He gazed intently at the hard-visaged L. W., whose face slowly turned brick red.

"Now, to get down to business," went on Rimrock quietly, "I tell you that ore is there. If you'll loan me the money to haul in that rock, I'll pay you back from my check. And I'll give you my note at one per cent a month, compounded monthly and all that. I guess a man that can show title to twenty claims that turn out picked ore like *that* —well, he's entitled, perhaps, to a little more consideration than you boys have been showing me of late."

L. W. sat silent, his burning eyes on the gold, the cigar clutched fiercely in his teeth—then, without a word, he wrote out a check and threw it across the desk.

"Much obliged," said Rimrock, and, without further words, he stepped out and cashed the check. And then Rimrock Jones disappeared.

The last person in Gunsight to hear what had happened was Mary Fortune. She worked at her desk that day in a fever of expectation, now stopping to wonder at the strange madness that possessed her, now pounding the harder to still her tumultuous thoughts. She did not know what it was that she expected, only something great and new and wonderful, something to lift her at last from the drudgery of her work and make her feel young and gay. Something to rouse her up to the wild joy of living and make her forget her misfortunes. To be poor and deaf and alone—all these were new things to Mary Fortune; but she was none of them when he was near. What need had she to hear when she could read in his eyes that instant admiration that a woman values most? And poor? The money that she had given had helped him, perhaps, to gain millions!

She worked late that afternoon, and again in the evening she made an excuse to keep her office lit up. Still he did not come, and she paced up the street, even listened as she passed by the saloons—then, overwhelmed with shame that she had seemed to seek him, she fled to her room and wept. The next day and the next she watched and listened, and at last she overheard the truth. It was Andrew McBain, the hard, fighting Scotchman, who told the dreadful news—and she hated him for it, always.

"Well, I'm glad he's gone," he had replied to L. W., who had beckoned him out to the door. "He's a dangerous man—I've been afraid of him—you're lucky to get off at that."

"Lucky!" yelled L. W., suddenly forgetting his caution. "He touched me for two thousand dollars! Do you call that lucky? And here's the latest—he hasn't got a pound of picked ore! Even took away what he had. And that old, whiskered Mexican says he up and borrowed that from him!"

"That's a criminal act!" exclaimed McBain exultantly, as he signaled L. W. to be calm. "Sh-h-h, not so loud; the girl might hear you. Let him go, and hold it over his head."

"No, I'll kill the dastard!" howled L. W. rebelliously, and slammed the door in a rage.

A swooning sickness came over Mary Fortune as she sat waiting stonily at her deck; but when McBain came back and sat down beside her, she typed on automatically as he spoke. Then she woke at last, as if from a dream, to hear his harsh, discordant voice; and a sudden resentment, a fierce, passionate hatred, swept over her as he shouted in her ear. A hundred times she had informed him politely that she was not deaf when she wore her ear phone, and a hundred times he had listened impatiently and gone on in his sharp, rasping snarl. She drew away, shuddering, as he looked over some papers and cleared his throat for a fresh start; and then, without reason that he could ever divine, she burst into tears and fled.

She came back later, but the moment he began dictating she pushed back her chair and rose up.

"Mr. McBain," she said tremulously, "you don't need to shout at me. I give you notice—I shall leave you on the first."

It was plainly a tantrum, such as he had observed in women, a case, pure and simple, of nerves; but Andrew McBain let it pass. She could spell—a rare quality in typists—and was familiar with legal forms.

"Ah, my dear Miss Fortune," he began propitiatingly, "I hope you will reconsider, I'm sure. It's a habit I have, when dictating a brief, to speak as though addressing the court. Perhaps, under the circumstances, you could take off your instrument, and my voice would be—ahem!—just about right."

"No, it drives me crazy!" she cried, in a passion. "It makes everybody think I'm so deaf."

She broke down at that, and McBain discreetly withdrew and was gone for the rest of the day. It was best, he had learned, when young women became emotional, to absent himself for a time. And the next day, sure enough, she came back smiling cheerfully and said no more of leaving her job. She was, in fact, more obliging than before, and he judged that the tantrum had passed.

With L. W., however, the case was different. He claimed to be an Indian in his hates; and a mining engineer, dropping in from New York, told a story that staggered belief. Rimrock Jones was there, the talk of the town, reputed to be enormously rich. He smoked fifty-cent cigars, wore an enormous black hat, and put up at the Waldorf Hotel. Not only that, but he was in all the papers as associating with the kings of finance. So great was his prestige that the engineer, in fact, had been requested to report on his mine.

"A report!" shouted L. W. "What —a report on the Tecolotes? Well, I can save you a long, dusty trip. In the first place, Rimrock Jones is a thoroughpaced scoundrel, not only a liar, but a crook; and in the second place, these claims are forty miles across the desert, with just two sunk wells on the road. I wouldn't own his mines if you would make me a present of them and a million dollars to boot. I wouldn't take them for a gift if that mountain was pure gold. How's he going to haul the ore to the railroad? Now, listen, my friend, I've known that boy since he stood knee-high to a toad, and of all the liars in Arizona he stands out pre-eminently as the worst."

"You question his veracity, then?" inquired the engineer, as he fumbled for some papers in his coat.

"Question nothing!" raved L. W. "I'm making a statement! He's not only a liar—he's a thief! He robbed me, the dastard; he got two thousand dollars of my money without giving me the scratch of a pen."

"Well, that's curious," broke in the engineer, as he stared at a paper. "He's got your name down here as a reference."

CHAPTER V.

THE PRODIGAL'S RETURN.

It is an engineer's duty, when he is sent out to examine a mine, to make a report on the property, regardless. The fact that the owner is a liar and a thief does not necessarily invalidate his claims; and an all-wise Providence has, on several occasions, allowed such creatures to discover bonanzas. So the engineer hired a team and disappeared on the horizon, and L. W. went off buying cattle.

A month passed by, in which the derelictions of Rimrock were capped by the machinations of a rival cattle buyer, who beat L. W. out of a buy that would have netted him up into the thousands. Disgusted with everything, L. W. boarded the westbound at Bowie Junction and flung himself into a seat in the half-empty smoker without looking to the right or left. He was mad— mad clear through—and the last of his cigars was mashed to a pulp in his vest. He had just made this discovery when another cigar was thrust under his nose and a familiar voice said:

"Try one of mine."

L. W. looked at the cigar, which was undoubtedly expensive, and then glanced hastily across the aisle. There, smiling sociably, was Rimrock Jones.

L. W. squinted his eyes. Yes, Rimrock Jones, in a large black hat, a checked suit, rather loud, and high boots. His legs were crossed, and with an air of elegant enjoyment he was smoking a similar cigar.

"Don't want it!" snarled L. W.; and, rising up in a fury, he moved off toward the far end of the car.

"Oh, all right," observed Rimrock, "I'll smoke it myself, then." And L. W. grunted contemptuously.

They rode on for some hours across a flat, joyless country without either man making a move; but as the train neared Gunsight, Rimrock rose up and went forward to where L. W. sat.

"Well, what're you all bowed up about?" he inquired bluffly. "Has your girl gone back on you, or what?"

"Go on away!" answered L. W. dangerously. "I don't want to talk to you, you thief!"

"Oh, that's what's the matter with you—you're thinking about the money, eh? Well, you always did-hate to lose."

An insulting epithet burst from L. W.'s set lips, but Rimrock let it pass.

"Oh, that's all right," he said. "Never mind my feelings. Say, how much do you figure I owe you?"

"You don't owe me nothing!" cried L. W., half rising. "You *stole* from me, you scoundrel—I can put you in the pen for this!"

"Aw, you wouldn't do that," answered Rimrock easily. "I know you too well for that."

"Say, you go away," panted L. W., in a frenzy, "or I'll throw you out of this car."

"No, you won't, either," said Rimrock truculently. "You'll have to eat some more beans before you can put *me* on my back."

Rimrock squared his great shoulders, and his eyes sparkled dangerously as he faced L. W. in the aisle.

"Now, listen!" he went on, after a tense moment of silence. "What's the use of making a row? I know I lied to you—I had to do it in order to get the money. I just framed that on purpose so I could get back to New York, where a proposition like mine would be appreciated. I was a bum in Gunsight, but back in New York, where they think in millions, they treated me like a king."

"I don't want to talk to you," rumbled L. W., moving off. "You lied once too often, and I've *quit* ye!"

"All right," answered Rimrock, "that suits me, too. All I ask is—what's the damage?"

"Thirty-seven hundred and fifty-five dollars," snapped back L. W. venomously, "and I'd sell out for thirty-seven cents."

"You won't have to," said Rimrock, with business directness, and flashed a great roll of bills.

"There's four thousand," he said, peeling off four bills. "You can keep the change for *pilon.*"

There was one thing about L. W.—he was a poker player of renown, and accustomed to thinking quick. He took one look at that roll of bills and waved the money away.

"Nope! Keep it!" he said. "I don't want your money—just let me in on this deal."

"Huh!" grunted Rimrock. "For four thousand dollars? You must think I've been played for a sucker. No, four hundred thousand dollars wouldn't give you a look-in on the pot that I've opened this trip."

"W'y, you lucky fool!" exclaimed L. W. incredulously, his eyes still glued to the roll. "What's the proposition, Rimmy? Say, you know me, Rim!"

"Yeh! Sure I do!" answered Rimrock dryly, and L. W. turned from bronze to dull red. "I know the whole bunch of you, from the dog robber up, and this time I play my own hand. I was a sucker once, but the only friends I've got now are the ones that stayed with me when I was down."

"But *I* helped you, Rim!" cried L. W. appealingly. "Didn't I lend you money time and again?"

"Yes, and here it is," replied Rimrock indifferently, as he held out the four yellow bills. "You loaned me money, but you treated me like dirt—now take it, or I'll ram it down your throat."

L. W. took the money and stood gnawing his cigar as the train slowed down for Gunsight.

"Say, come over to the bank—I want to speak to you," he said, as they dropped off the train.

"Nope, can't stop," answered Rimrock curtly. "Got to go and see my friends."

He strode off down the street, and

L. W. followed after him, beckoning feverishly to every one he met.

"Say, Rimrock's struck it rich!" he announced behind his hand, and the procession fell in behind.

Straight down the street Rimrock went to the Alamo, where Old Hassayamp stood shading his eyes, and while the crowd gathered around them he took Hassayamp's hand and shook it again and again.

"Here's the best man in town," he began, with great feeling. "An old-time Arizona sport. There never was a time when I was down and out that my word wasn't good for the drinks."

And Hassayamp Hicks, divining some great piece of good fortune, invited him in for one more.

"Here's to Rimrock Jones," he said to the crowd, "the livest boy in this town."

They drank, and then Rimrock drew out his roll and peeled off an impressive yellow bill.

"Just take out what I owe you," he said to Old Hassayamp, "and let the boys drink up the rest."

With that he was gone; and the crowd, scarce believing, stayed behind and drank to his health. Not a word was said by Rimrock or his friends as to the source of this sudden wealth. For once in his life Rimrock Jones was reticent, but the roll of bills spoke for itself. He came out of Woo Chong's restaurant with a broad grin on his face, and looked about for the next man he owed.

"You can talk all you want to," he observed to the onlookers, "but a chink is as white as they make 'em. And any man in this crowd," he added impressively, "that ever loaned me a cent, all he has to do is to step out and say so and he gets his money back—and then some."

The crowd surged about, but no one stepped forward. Strange stories were in the air, resurrected from the past, of Rimrock and the way he paid. When the Gunsight Mine, after many difficulties, began to pay back what it had cost, Rimrock had appeared on the street with a roll. And then, as now, he had announced his willingness to pay any bill, good or bad, that he owed. He stood there, waiting, with the bills in his hand, and he paid every man who applied. He even paid men who slipped in meanly with stories of loans when he was drunk; but he noted them well, and from that day forward they received no favors from him.

"Ah, there's the very man I'm looking for!" exclaimed Rimrock in Spanish, as he spied old Juan in the crowd, and, striding forward, he held out his hand and greeted him ceremoniously. Old Juan it was of whom he had borrowed the gold ore that had coaxed the two thousand dollars from L. W.—and he had never sent the picked rock back.

"How are you, Juan?" he inquired politely, in the formula that all Mexicans love. "And your wife, Rosita? Is she well also? Yes, thank God, I am well myself. Where is Rico now? He is a good boy, truly. Will you do one more thing for me, Juan?"

"*Si, si, señor!*" answered Juan deferentially.

Rimrock smiled as he patted his shoulder. "You are a good man, Juan," he said. "A good friend of mine—I will remember it. Now, get me an ore sack—a strong one—like the one that contained the picked gold."

"*Un momento!*" smiled Juan, hurrying off toward the store, and the Mexicans began to swarm to and fro. Some reward, they knew, was to be given to Juan to compensate him for the loss of his gold. His gold and his labor and all the unpaid debt that was owing to him and his son and the rest. The streets began to clatter with flying hoofs as they rode off to summon *el pueblo,* and by the time old Juan returned with his sack all Mexican town was there.

"*Muy bien*," pronounced Rimrock, as he inspected the ore sack. "Now come with me, amigo."

Amigo Juan went, and all his friends after him, to see what El Patron would do. Something generous and magnificent, they knew very well, for El Patron was a gentleman, *muy caballero*. He led the way to the bank, still inquiring most solicitously about Juan's relations, his children, his burros, and so on; and Juan, sweating like a packed jack under the stress of the excitement, answered courteously, as one should to El Patron, and clung eagerly to his sack. The crowd entered the bank, and as L. W. came out Rimrock placed Juan's sack on the table.

"Bring out new silver dollars, fresh from the mint," he said, "and fill up this sack for Juan."

"*Santa Maria!*" exclaimed Juan fervently, as the cashier came staggering forth with a sack; and Rimrock took the bag containing a thousand bulging dollars and set it down before him. He broke the seal, and as the shining silver burst forth he spilled it in a huge windrow on the table.

"Now fill up your ore sack," he said to Juan, "and all you can stuff into it is yours."

"For a gift?" faltered Juan, and as Rimrock nodded he buried his hands in the coin. The dollars clanged and rattled as they spilled on the table, and a great silence came over the crowd. They gazed at old Juan as if he were an Aladdin, or Ali Baba in his treasure cave. Old, gray-bearded Juan, who hauled wood for a living, or packed cargas on his burros for El Patron! Yes, here he was, with his fists full of dollars, piling them faster and faster into his bag.

"Now shake the bag down," suggested El Patron, "and perhaps you can get in some more."

"Some more?" panted Juan, and, quite mad with great riches, he stuffed the sack to the top.

"Very well," said Rimrock. "Now take them home, and give part of the money to Rosita. Then take what is left in this other bag and give a fiesta to the boys who worked for me."

"Make way!" cried Juan, and as the crowd parted before him he went staggering into the street. A few shiny dollars, heaped high on the top, fell off and were picked up by his friends. They went off together, old Juan and his amigos, and L. W. came over to Rimrock.

"Now listen to me, Henry Jones," he began; but Rimrock waved him away.

"I don't need to," he said. "I know what you'll say—but Juan, there, has been my friend."

"Well, you don't need to spoil him—to break his back with money, when ten dollars will do just as well."

"Yes, I do," said Rimrock. "Didn't I borrow his picked rock? Well, keep out, then; I know my friends. He'll be drunk for a month, and at the end of his fiesta he won't have a dollar to his name, but as long as he lives he can tell the other hombres about that big sack of money he had."

Rimrock laid down one big bill, which paid for all the dollars, and walked out of the bank on air. He was feeling rich —that wealthy feeling that penny pinchers never know—and all the world except L. W. Lockhart seemed responsive to his smile. Men who had shunned him for years now shook his hand and refused to take back what they had lent. They even claimed they had forgotten all about it, or had intended their loans as stakes. With his pockets full of money, it was suddenly impossible for Rimrock to spend a dollar. In the Alamo Saloon, where his friends were all gathered in a determined assault on the bar, his popularity was so intense that the drinks fairly jumped at him, and he slipped out the back way to escape. There was one duty more—both a duty and a pleasure—and he headed for the Gunsight Hotel.

The news of his success, whatever it was, had preceded him hours before. Andrew McBain had hid out, the idle women were all atwitter, but Mary Roget Fortune was calm. She had heard the news from the very first moment, when L. W. had dropped in on McBain; but the more she heard of his riotous prodigality the more it left her cold. His return to town reminded her painfully of that other time when he had come. She had watched for him then, her knight from the desert, worn and ragged, but with his sack full of gold; but he had passed her by without a word, and now she did not care.

She looked up sharply as he came at last, a huge form, half blocking the door; and Rimrock noticed the change. Perhaps his sudden popularity had made him unduly sensitive—he felt instinctively that she did not approve.

"Do you mind my cigar?" he asked, stopping awkwardly halfway to her desk; and he suddenly came to life as she answered:

"Why, yes. Since you ask me, I do."

That was straight enough, and Rimrock cast his fifty-cent cigar like a stogie out of the door. Then he came back toward her with his big head thrust out and a searching look in his eyes. She had greeted him politely, but it was not the manner of the girl he had expected to see. Somehow, without knowing why, he had expected her to meet him with a different look in her eyes. It had been there before, but now it was absent—a look that he liked very much. In fact, he had remembered it, and thought, apropos of nothing, that it was a pity she was so deaf. He looked again, and smiled very slightly. But no; the look had fled.

CHAPTER VI.

RIMROCK PASSES.

In the big moments of life, when we have triumphed over difficulties and quaffed the heady wine of success, there is always something—or the lack of something—to bring us back to earth. Rimrock Jones had returned in a Christmas spirit, and had taken Gunsight by storm. He had rewarded his friends and rebuked his enemies and all those who grind down the poor. He had humbled L. W. and driven McBain into hiding; and now this girl, this deaf, friendless typist, had snatched the cup from his lips. The neatly turned speech—the few well-chosen words in which he had intended to express his appreciation for her help—were effaced from his memory, and in their place there came a doubt, a dim questioning of his own worth. What had he done, or neglected to do, that had taken that look from her eyes? He sank down in a chair and regarded her intently as she sat there, composed and still.

"Well, it's been quite a while," he said at last, "since I've been round to see you."

"Yes, it has," she replied, and the way she said it raised a more poignant question in his mind. Was she miffed, perhaps, because he had failed to call on her that time when he came back to town? He had borrowed her money—she might have been worried that time when he went to New York.

"I just got in a little while ago—been back to New York about my mine. Well, it's doing all right now, and I've come around to see you and pay back that money I owe."

"Oh, that four hundred dollars? Why, I don't want it back. You were to give me a share in your mine."

Rimrock stopped with his roll half out of his pocket and gazed at her like a man struck dumb. A share in his mine! He put the money back and mopped the sudden sweat from his brow.

"Well, now, say," he began, "I've made other arrangements. I've sold a big share already. But I'll give you the money—it'll come to the same thing." He whipped out his roll and smiled at her hopefully, but she drew back and shook her head.

"No," she said, "I don't want your money. I want a share in that mine."

She faced him, determined, and Rimrock went weak, for he remembered that she had his word. He had given his word, and unless she excused him he would have to make it good. And if he did—well, right there he would lose control of his mine.

"Say, now, listen a minute," he began mysteriously, "I'm not telling this on the street——"

"Well, don't tell it here, then," she interrupted hastily; "they're listening most of the time."

She pointed toward the door that led to the hotel lobby, and Rimrock tiptoed toward it. He was just in time, as he snatched it open, to see McBain bounding up the back stairs, and a woman in a rocker, after a guilty stare, rose up and moved hastily away.

"Well, well!" observed Rimrock, as he banged the door. "I don't know which is worse, these women or peeping Andrew McBain. Are you still working for that fellow?" he inquired confidentially, as he sat down and spoke low in her phone; and for the first time that day the smile came back and dwelt for a moment in her eyes.

"Yes," she answered, "I still do his work for him. What's the matter—don't you fully approve?"

Her gaze was a challenge, and he let it pass with a grin and a jerk of the head.

"Just sorry for you," he said. "You'd better take this money and get a job with a man that's half white."

He drew out his roll and counted out four thousand dollars and laid them before her on the desk.

"Now, listen," he began. "That four hundred then was worth four thousand to me now. I had to have it, and I sure appreciate it—now just accept that as a payment in part."

He pushed over the money, but she shook her head and met his gaze with resolute eyes.

"Not much!" she said. "I don't want your money, and, what's more, I won't accept it. I gave you four hundred dollars—all the money I had—to get me a share in that mine, and now I want it. I don't care how much, but I want a share in that mine."

Rimrock shoved back his chair and once more the sweat appeared on his troubled brow. He rose up softly and peeped out the door, then came back and sat very close.

"What's the idea?" he asked. "Has some one been telling you who I've got in with me on this deal? Well, what's the matter, then? Why won't you take the money? I'll give you more than you could get for the stock."

"No, all my life it's been my ambition to own a share in a mine. That's why I gave you the last of my money—I had confidence in your mine from the start."

"Well, what did you think, then," inquired Rimrock sardonically, "when I jumped out of town without seeing you? You'd have sold out cheap if I'd've come to you then, but now everybody knows I've won."

"Never mind what I thought," she answered darkly; "I took a chance, and I won."

"Say, you're strictly business, now ain't you?" observed Rimrock, and muttered under his breath. "How much of a share do you expect me to give you?" he asked, after a long, anxious pause, and her eyes lit up and were veiled.

"Whatever you say," she answered quietly; and then: "I believe you mentioned fifty-fifty—an undivided half."

"My—God!" exclaimed Rimrock, starting wildly to his feet. "You don't —say, you didn't think I meant that?"

"Why, no," she said, with a faint flicker of venom, "I didn't, to tell you the truth. That's why I told you I was talking business. But you said: 'Well, so am I.'"

"Well, holy Jehosophrats!" cursed Rimrock to himself, and turned to look her straight in the eyes.

"Now, let's get down to business," he went on sternly. "What do you want, and where am I at?"

"I want a share in that mine," she answered evenly—"whatever you think is right."

"Oh, that's the deal! You don't want fifty-fifty? You leave what it is to me?"

"That's .what I said from the very first. And as for fifty-fifty—no, certainly I do not."

There were tears, half of anger, gathering back in her eyes, but Rimrock took no thought of that.

"Oh, you don't like my style, eh?" he came back resentfully. "All you want out of me is my money."

"No, I don't!" she retorted. "I don't want your money! I want a share in that mine!"

"Say, who are you, anyway?" burst out Rimrock explosively. "Are you some wise one that's on the inside?"

"That's none of your business," she answered sharply. "You were satisfied when you took all my money."

"That's right," agreed Rimrock, rubbing his jaw reflectively; "that's right, it was no questions asked. Now, say, I'm excited—I ought not to talk that way—I want to explain to you just how I'm fixed. I went back to New York and organized a company and gave one man forty-nine per cent of my stock. He puts up the money, and I put up the mine—and run it, absolutely. If I give you any stock, I lose control of

my mine, so I'm going to ask you to let me off."

He drew out his roll—that banded sheaf of yellow notes that he loved so dearly to flash—and began slowly to count off the bills.

"When you think it's enough," he went on ponderously, "you can say so, but I need all that stock."

He laid out the bills, one after another, and the girl settled back in her chair. "That's ten," he observed— "these are thousand-dollar bills—well, there's twelve, then—I'll make it thirteen." He glanced up expectantly, but she gave no sign, and Rimrock dealt impassively on. "Well, fourteen—lots of money. Say, how much do you want? Fifteen thousand—you only gave me four hundred. Sixteen, seventeen—well, you get the whole roll; but, say, girl, I can't give you that stock."

He threw down the last bill and faced her appealingly, but she answered with a hard little laugh.

"You've got to," she said. "I don't want your money. I want one per cent of your stock."

"What—of what I've got left? Oh, of the whole capital stock! Well, that only leaves me fifty per cent."

"That's one way of looking at it. Now look at it another way. Don't you think I'm entitled to that? Don't you think if I'd said, when I gave you that money: 'All I want is one per cent of your mine'—don't you think, now, honestly, that you'd have said, 'All right!' and agreed to it on the spot?"

She looked at him squarely, and the fair-fighting Rimrock had to agree, though reluctantly, that she was right.

"Well, now that you've won when nobody expected you to, now that you've got money enough to get the whole town drunk, is that any reason why you should come to a poor typist and ask her to give up her rights? I'm putting it frankly, and unless you can answer me I want you to give me that stock."

"Well, all right, I'll do it," answered Rimrock impulsively. "I promised you, and that's enough. But you've got to agree not to sell that stock—and to vote it with me every time."

"Very well," she said, "I'll agree not to sell it—at least not to any one but you. And as far as the voting goes, I think we can arrange that; I'll vote for whatever seems right."

"No, right or wrong!" challenged Rimrock instantly. "I'm not going to be beat out of my mine!"

"What do you mean?" she demanded. "I hope you don't think——"

"Never mind what I think," answered Rimrock grimly. "I got bit once, and that's enough. I lost the old Gunsight just by trusting my friends, and this time I'm not trusting anybody."

"Oh, you're one of these cynics, these worldly-wise fellows that have lost all their faith in mankind? I've seen them before, but it wasn't much trouble to find somebody else that *they'd* wronged!"

She said the words bitterly, with a lash to her tongue that cut Rimrock Jones to the quick. It had always been his boast that there was no man or woman that could claim he had done them a wrong, and he answered back sharply, while the anger was upon him, that he was not, and there was no such thing.

"Well, if that's the case, then," she suggested delicately, but with a touch of malice in her smile, "it seems rather personal to begin now with me, and take away my right to vote. Did this man in New York, when he bought into your company, agree to vote with you, right or wrong? Well, then, why should I? Wasn't my money just as necessary

when I gave it to you as his was when he gave it later?"

"Oh——" Rimrock choked back an oath and then fell back on personalities to refute her maddening logic.

"Say, your father was a judge," he burst out insultingly. "Was he a promoted lawyer, too, or did you learn that line of talk from McBain?"

"Never mind about that. You haven't answered my question. Wasn't my money just as necessary as his? It was! Yes, you know it. Well, then, why should you choose me for the very first person that you ever intentionally wronged?"

"Well, by grab," moaned Rimrock, slumping down in his chair as he saw his last argument gone, "it was a black day for me when I took that four hundred from you. I'd have done a heap better to have held up some Chinaman or made old L. W. come through. And to be trimmed by a woman! Well, gimme your paper, and I'll sign whatever you write."

She drew in her lips and gazed at him resentfully; then, sitting down at her typewriter, she thought for a minute and rattled off a single sentence. Rimrock took the paper and signed it blindly, then stopped and read what it was:

I, Henry (Rimrock) Jones, for value received, hereby agree to give to Mary Roget Fortune one per cent of the total capital stock of the Tecolote Mining Company.

"Yes, all right," he said. "You'll get your stock just as soon as I get it from the East. And now I hope you're satisfied."

"Yes, I am," she answered, and smiled cryptically.

"Well, I pass!" he exploded, and, struggling to his feet, he lurched out upon the street.

TO BE CONTINUED IN THE NOVEMBER 20TH POPULAR.

The Peppercorn Entail

By Frederick Irving Anderson

Author of "Sterling Exchange," "The Mouse Hole," Etc.

Concerning a young master of one hundred millions in securities and one thousand millions in directorates whose immediate object was the restoration of what he conceived to be the piratical gains of his illustrious sires. A story of New York of to-day

A FEW steps off Broadway, and a stone's throw from that part of Fifth Avenue known as the Trough—since the myriad garment workers of the neighborhood have taken to congregating there in tribal units the while they consume their midday meal—stands an unpretentious red brick building of one story and attic, wearing a nicely polished brass plate with the magic legend—"The Aylesworth Estate."

It is a matter of notable surprise, even to the seasoned New Yorker, to encounter this staring yet dignified sign in this by-street, otherwise entirely consumed with the shouts of truck drivers, the rattle and slam of packing cases, the whir of sewing machines from open windows, and the cry of hucksters in many tongues beguiling the noonday throng into unwonted extravagance.

Yet the legend speaks for itself. There is only one Aylesworth family, as has been the case for eight generations—since the first Aylesworth was a gardener on the old Chelsea Road, which has long since been wiped out of existence, almost of tradition. For eight generations the Aylesworth family has passed itself and its fortunes on to an only son; and, its fortunes having grown quite considerable—into "interests," in fact—the Aylesworth name inevitably arrests the eye and challenges speculation. To the casual metropolitan

the name calls up a somber, magnificent yet smoky edifice, somewhat like the Bank of England, in Wall Street, where the reigning Aylesworth has from time immemorial sat in state in his swivel chair and nodded, or turned down his thumbs, as his spirit or his spleen moved him.

At one o'clock in the afternoon, on the eighteenth of August of the present year, a young man, tall and slender and swinging a stick, a little overdressed, the look of the world in his eyes, and a quizzical expression playing about the corners of his mouth, stood on the pavement contemplating, first, the immaculately polished, white marble steps—as prim as a Quaker entry—and, second, the mirrorlike brass sign with its portentous legend. His satirical survey took in the barred windows, the nail-studded door, even the well-scoured bricks, before he deliberately mounted the steps and entered.

In the seclusion of an inner office sat a second young man, before a mahogany desk, engrossed in the consideration of a bowl of brown milk and a tin of patent predigested biscuits. The milk on its silver salver had been brought to this table for this hour at a cost that would sustain any soul among the two hundred thousand nibbling onions, cheese, and dried fish, at the other end of the block, for a week. The biscuits bore the imprint of a well-known manufacturer, who, could he have guessed that his product was the sole solid food served daily to this man, would have spent a year's profits in advertising that fact. For this sallow, puffy, and altogether insignificant individual was none other than Francklyn Aylesworth, eighth of the line, and sole master of a great many millions. His father, recently dead, had been a grim humorist during the greater part of his life; but in nothing had he been so grim as in naming this son his residuary legatee, after the tradition of the Aylesworths.

The second generation usually solves the problem of hoarded wealth by playing ducks and drakes with it; very seldom do millions, constituting a family name, persevere after the third generation. The Aylesworth fortune, distinguished from other great fortunes in many things, differed from them in nothing so much as having persisted intact now to the eighth generation.

The eighth of the line, however, seemed to offer a prospect for the ducks and drakes. Francklyn Aylesworth was not the gilded youth commonly associated with such contingencies. He was quite the reverse. The family lawyers, McWethy, Milson & Hatch, in private diagnosed his weakness as "ingrowing conscience," and, with their fences in repair, were calmly awaiting the catastrophe. Young Mr. Aylesworth, master of one hundred millions in securities, and one thousand millions in directorates, shunned the grimy marble palace downtown; but, instead, at his desk in this by-street, he was contriving the most astounding plans for pulling down the pillars of the temple so carefully reared by his ancestors. His immediate concern was the restoration of what he conceived to be the piratical gains of his illustrious sires. Francklyn the Eighth lacked the humor, even in its grimness, of his predecessors.

The somewhat flamboyant visitor to the outer office found himself con- fronted by a wall of brass wicker, similar in its proportions to the entry to the Tombs—with which he was not unfamiliar. On the opposite side of the window sat a youth at a table. The young man passed in his card with the information that his business was with Mr. Francklyn Aylesworth.

"Concerning what?" asked the youth at the table, without looking up from his task, which was sheet writing for the office baseball pool.

"I wish to know," said the young man, "if by any chance he possesses a lock which will fit this key."

He drew from an inner pocket a metal case, itself notable for an elaborate lock which fastened its two halves together. Opening this, he produced a great key of wrought iron, evidently fashioned at some remote period by a blacksmith with the crude tools of a forge. The youth took the proffered key, and, still without looking up, he called loudly. A second youth appeared.

"James," he said, "can you tell me offhand how many doors Mr. Aylesworth possesses?"

"Thirteen hundred and forty-six," responded James as solemn as an owl, stealing a look at the flashy young man at the wicket. It was the truth; or, at least, approximately so. This little office was the funnel through which filtered the rents of some thirteen hundred domiciles, business and domestic, which constituted a considerable, though not a major, portion of the Aylesworth fortune.

"Please see if this key fits any of the locks," said the sheet writer, passing over the ponderous bit of metal. "The young man will wait."

"Thank you," said the caller on the other side of the wicket, taking off his hat and fanning himself as he looked for a seat. "And, at the same time," he added from a corner where he found graceful repose, "will you please give me a statement of my account in peppercorns, compounded to date."

"Huh?" said the youth at the table, now for the first time looking up and examining the caller. He was impressed. Regardless of his gay attire, the young man challenged attention because of his build—broad and spare at the shoulders, narrow at the hips, with ears laid close to the skull, and tight, curly hair. It was the cut of a light-weight aspirant, which the youth instantly recognized.

"Peppercorns?" he said.

"Peppercorns," repeated the caller from over a morning paper which he was now reading. The youth shoved aside his tally sheets and went over to the head bookkeeper, with whom he held whispered converse, occasionally glancing at the caller and significantly tapping his brow. Together they examined the engraved card.

"Peppercorns!" said the bookkeeper; and he straightway sought out the office manager.

"Peppercorns?" said the office manager, peering out through a crack in the door at the languid figure in the corner. He at length tapped lightly on the door leading to the outer defenses of the young man at that moment sorrowfully sipping his brown milk and nibbling his patent biscuit. Mr. Priestly, secretary to the head of the house, took the card and the key, listened to the whispered explanation, and in turn ejaculated:

"Peppercorns? Peppercorns!"

He, too, tiptoed out for a glimpse of the extraordinary caller, who, to all appearance, was content to await the testing of the key and the compounding of his tally in peppercorns until the crack of doom.

Then, softly, the secretary tapped on the mahogany panels, and at the sound of a soft-spoken "Enter!" admitted himself to the inner shrine. There was no occasion for whispering; yet Priestly whispered, holding the card under the nose of Mr. Francklyn Aylesworth as he confided his message.

Francklyn Aylesworth did not wait for him to finish. He rose with such precipitation as to all but upset his bowl of certified milk, and snatched the key from the hands of his man. His fingers were trembling as he held it up to the light of the window. He took a second key from his office safe and compared the two critically. They were identical—except for one detail: the key which the young man had produced from its elaborate strong box bore the unmistakable signs of age, great age. The ring was all but parted at its outer arc, as though the constant caressing of salty fingers had slowly burned a way through the iron of which it was fashioned. Aylesworth's key had been forged by modern skill and tools, though its design was ancient and a replica of the other. Calmness in the face of great emergencies was the dominant characteristic of eight generations of this house. No Aylesworth had ever before faced an emergency such at this, though in their time they had wrecked railroads and browbeaten kings. Francklyn Aylesworth carefully put away his own key, laid the second at his elbow, and sat down to his biscuits and milk.

"I will see him," he said. "Show him in."

Then, rising with sudden determination: "No; I will bring him myself."

For all his ingrowing conscience, Francklyn Aylesworth was not without guile. He could not have been the son of the mighty seven who had gone before without possessing guile. His unusual procedure in seeking out the caller, instead of awaiting him in his sanctum in state, with his back to the light, was a compromise between his ingrowing conscience and his genetic guile. He strode through the corridors through the brass gate to the corner where the somewhat overdressed young man was still immersed in his paper.

"Mister—ah——" began the head of the house of Aylesworth; and then, as if the name had slipped him—which it had not—he consulted the card. "Mister Stewart Calthorpe?" he inquired.

The young man continued reading to the end of some absorbing bit of news before he turned.

"Yes," he said, "I have sent my card to Mister Francklyn Aylesworth."

"I am Francklyn Aylesworth."

The young man apparently was ill prepared for this announcement. As he surveyed the soft, yellow personage before him, at first as though in surprise, then obviously with a sudden embarrassment, for the moment he continued seated. Then he sprang to his feet and began lamely:

"I beg your pardon! I beg your pardon! I—I—I—— You understand— I think I have never seen your picture. Now—your father——" He ran on, getting better use of his tongue, "now, your father—I was familiar with his face and bearing."

With undisguised impertinence he took stock of this master of millions before him. The recent Francklyn Aylesworth was a great bull of a man, beside whom his son was as so much overweaned veal. The son of the great house saw the look, appraised it, and was not offended. As a matter of fact, he rather took pride in his flabbiness, played on it, in his self-appointed rôle of jesuitical justice. So he reached out and took this young man, who had come with a key seeking peppercorns, by the arm, and led him into the innermost sanctum, and begged him to be seated. They sat for some time, neither speaking, regarding each other; the master of the Aylesworth millions peering out through eyes that glistened earnestly with the call of his conscience; and the claimant of peppercorns waiting with a languorous ease of some confident feline.

"So you are Stewart Calthorpe?"

The caller admitted it with a nod and a smile.

"You are—the—eighth—of the line?"

"The seventh. We have been longer-lived than the Aylesworths."

The assumption of equality was perfect.

"Undoubtedly you have your proofs?"

"That goes without saying," said the other easily. "This is what has delayed me. Otherwise," he smiled, "I should have been here earlier. I had the proofs," he said, lounging deeper into his chair and balancing one elbow on top of his slender cane, "eight months ago. But," and again he smiled oddly, "I studied your father's picture —and I decided it were more prudent to wait."

"For me?"

Stewart Calthorpe nodded.

"Yet we have been waiting for you a long time," said the young master, not insensible to the subtle flattery. "Since —let me see—since 1710."

"1712," corrected the caller.

"Yes, quite true, 1712—two hundred and four years. There have been great changes since that time. You will scarcely recognize the place, I am afraid."

For the first time young Francklyn Aylesworth permitted himself to smile; and his visitor, noting the smile, drew himself together a little closer. They surveyed each other again in silence. Aylesworth's gaze sought a framed map of the island of Manhattan on the wall before him. Calthorpe followed his eyes, and studied the thing attentively. Toward the lower end of the island, enveloping Fourteenth Street north and south, and extending from Union Square well over to the North River, an irregular section had been blocked out in red ink. It consisted, possibly, of four hundred acres, though one seldom thinks of New York real estate in terms of acres, any more than one thinks of cut diamonds in terms of pounds. It was this demesne which had been turned over, some two centuries before, by the notorious pirate Calthorpe, to the keeping of his francklyn, Ayleswythe, for a consideration of twenty peppercorns per annum. Aylesworth turned from his contemplation of this kingdom, on which the fortunes of his house were founded, and took from a drawer a neatly bound bundle of papers.

"You were born the seventeenth of November, 1878," he said, reading.

"The sixteenth of June, 1876," corrected the visitor, still intent on the map.

"Your father was the Reverend Stewart Calthorpe, curate in the village of Wolden, Surrey. He died in 1897 at the age of seventy-two. His son was educated, against his own inclinations, for the church; and in 1896, following a series of escapades, the last one of such a nature as to shock the elder Calthorpe into a stroke of apoplexy, he was withdrawn, and, for several years, nothing was known of his whereabouts. We have another record here, beginning with the Boer War, when Stewart Calthorpe enlisted in the 117th Surrey Yeomanry——"

"Northumberland," corrected the young man.

"And—following some details which I shall not recount—he was listed among the 'missing' at Maegersfontein."

"I deserted, and came scot-free through Johannesburgh."

"Yes, yes, so it appears. This Stewart Calthorpe was five feet ten in his stockings; he weighed one hundred and sixty-five pounds; he had light-blue eyes, brown hair; a scar from a bolo on his left thigh, and a strawberry mark under the hair just forward of his right ear. You see, Mr. Calthorpe, we have pursued some rather diligent inquiries

during the last eight months, seeking a possible heir to the ancestral—ah—freebooter, shall we say?"

"You seem to have acquired a considerable mass of misinformation," said the visitor imperturbably. "The strawberry mark is in front of the left ear —and the bolo wound on the right leg. You put me at a disadvantage, sir."

Francklyn Aylesworth rubbed his hands, and wrinkled his flabby face in another smile; at which the young man in the chair tightened his muscles again imperceptibly.

"And now," said the sole heir and residuary legatee of the leaseholds inclosed in the blood-red square on the map of the city, "I suppose you have come for your peppercorns."

"Yes."

"Only twenty a year, so the—ah—tradition, runs. Compound twenty for two hundred and four years," said Francklyn Aylesworth ruminatively, gazing intently at the bronze ceiling. "Do you know," he said, leaning forward and smiling, "you remind me of the wise man who, when the king sought to reward him for a great service, said, 'Sire, place one grain of wheat on the first square of the chessboard; two on the second; four on the third; and so on through the sixty-four.' We have a big wheat crop this year, Mr. Calthorpe, but it would not have satisfied him. Possibly we can make accounting in some other medium than peppercorns."

He laughed aloud at his own jest.

"Your great-grandfather, fifth removed, sailed for England in 1711. His ship never touched shore."

"Seventeen-twelve," corrected the peppercorn claimant imperturbably. "His ship never touched shore. But he was not lost at sea."

"Indeed! I have spent a great deal of money trying to establish that fact, Mr. Calthorpe."

"I could have saved you the trouble,"

responded the young man; and he took a packet of papers from his pocket and laid them before the young master. "You will find it all there. Those documents, of course, are duplicates," he added, with an almost imperceptible curl of the lip.

"Duplicates, naturally," said the young master, and he pushed the packet into an open drawer "You have no idea how much you interest me."

"He was shipwrecked—touched shore —made one of those horrible journeys across continents, to which sailors of the old days were subject—and he survived long enough to leave a son—and a story of possessions in the New World—the story, which has been handed down from father to son as a tradition, is to the effect that he made a deed of rent in writing, and confided it to the security of a vault on the premises."

"A deed of rent—in writing!" exclaimed Francklyn Aylesworth, suddenly sitting erect. Calthorpe nodded.

"A vault on the premises! It is in a vault on the premises?"

"It was—so the story runs."

Aylesworth let the implication pass. The peppercorn claimant, all his cards face up on the table, was calmly studying the map on the wall.

"You are a very—pardon me—a very ingenuous person, Mr. Calthorpe. We have always had records, of course, of our original ancestor religiously paying twenty peppercorns each year to a rather phantom fund entitled 'Calthorpe.' But we never had a record of a deed of rent being actually in existence, in writing. How does it happen," he went on, with an encouraging smile, "that you have waited until a time when five million people settled around the old plantation, before coming forward?"

"Because," said the young man blandly, "I am the first Calthorpe with wit enough to identify the 'francklyn named Ayleswythe' with Francklyn Aylesworth, the money king of the present day. If I had any doubt, it would have been removed instantly by the discovery that your agents were looking up us Calthorpes in England, lately."

"I feel this is going to be simple," said Francklyn Aylesworth, rising. "We are going to be of great help to each other. You say you are Stewart Calthorpe, the only lineal descendant of this—Sindbad the Sailor. I believe you! I admit I have tested you. The strawberry mark *is* on vour left leg; and the bolo scar is above your right *ear.*"

The peppercorn claimant let this last slip pass, with rather a wry smile.

"Now, I ask you to leave your proofs and give us time—say a week or so. Do you need funds for immediate wants? I am pleased to advance them."

For just the fraction of a second indecision played about the eyes of the caller.

"No; I am prepared for immediate necessities." In another minute he was in the street again, examining the front of the building bearing the sign "The Aylesworth Estate."

"He's *not* 'the safest of the family,' " he was humming to himself, as he strode off down the street, in blissful unconsciousness—or seemingly so—of the fact that two men of the office force of the building he had just quitted had suddenly and innocently found business in the direction he was pursuing.

II.

The whole affair was, of course, grotesque, absurd. Any one who took the pains to inquire could have learned that the Aylesworths did not own the land in the heart of New York, upon which they had paid taxes for two hundred years; that in every pernicious instrument of ground rent negotiated by them in the last century, their name had invariably appeared as "trustee." Still, there are laws of adverse possession, statutes of limitation, and a hundred and one usages in equity, by which time is made a means to destroy obligation.

Yet Francklyn the Eighth, as he dropped two keys in his pocket, adjusted his hard-boiled hat, and left his office, an hour later, was thinking neither of discriminatory laws, nor of the absurdity of the situation. He was thinking that he was very much pleased with himself. In the beginning he had foreseen that his quixotic campaign of restitution, for the sins of his fathers, must needs be prosecuted with secrecy and guile—even with stealth. And he was thinking, sadly, of how the young man, who had come like a ghost out of the past, had insisted that he had been born on the sixteenth of June. And he was also thinking, as he strode along, that he would have to fight all alone in this first battle of the campaign. His lawyers, who regarded him somewhat as an inexplainable runt in an otherwise true litter, would fight him to the death, with commissions in lunacy, if necessary.

A few minutes' brisk walk brought him to the home of his fathers. It still stands, the manor house of the old plantation, in the midst of a neighborhood that crowds grudgingly on all sides, with tall office buildings shoulder to shoulder.

Twenty peppercorns was probably a very fair valuation of the barren plantation itself, in the old days. During the early period, there had come to be a road cut through the alternate ridges of rock and slough cesspools, of this part of the island, connecting the old village of Greenwich with the newer house—hewn in incongruous magnificence out of stone by English artisans who had learned their trade over centuries of building abbeys and castles and machicolated towers—then looked out over a dusty, neighborly highway in-

stead of scrubby fields of grain. The road took a little twist at this stage, so that the fine old house, erected by the original Calthorpe, might face it squarely. But the originators of the present city plan—during the fourth generation of the tenant Aylesworths—were less considerate. In their mania to erase the circuitous cowpaths that had come in time to affect the dignity of streets, they disregarded line fences and ridgepoles. They ran streets east and west, and avenues north and south, just a point or two off the compass; and to effect their purpose they lopped a corner off the mansion, and ran an avenue through the grand saloon on the first floor. This mutilation was accomplished notwithstanding the righteous indignation of the tenant Aylesworths, who straightway turned the key in the lock and deserted the home of their fathers.

It still stands to-day, this dog-eared mansion, viewing the passing city life from an angle of seven degrees west of north; an ugly side wall to show where the desecrating ax fell; a stout picket fence surrounding a dismantled garden upon which stare sullenly four floors of grimy windows each of many and very small panes leaded together.

Aylesworth applied a key to the rusty lock of the gate and admitted himself to the garden. As he picked his way among the paths—once, to judge from the outcroppings, lined with brilliant fragments of quartz and rare shells, now all but lost under the dust of ages—passers-by stopped and peered through the pickets, wondering what ghosts of long ago must be called to life by the clang of the great front door, creaking on its hinges. The key fitted. That, of course, was of little consequence. Any one, in the darkness of night, behind the shrubbery, might fashion a key even for this antiquated lock. Any one, were he so minded, might even sweat the ring all but in twain to simulate the effects of salty fingers caressing it over ages of time. The reverberations were still ringing through the dusty corridors when Francklyn Aylesworth slammed the door behind him, and advanced and peered up the great stair well.

At five o'clock that afternoon, a starved rat—after waiting for ages for a silent figure seemingly asleep in an old chair to show some sign of life—risked a journey across the drawing-room floor. At midnight, the same rat risked a like journey. At six in the morning, when the sun forced a sallow ray through a dirty fanlight in the door, the young master of the house of Aylesworth was still sitting in his chair. At nine he was back in his office in the by-street calling for the old Mayhew map of the island of Manhattan, dated 1803. This map set forth, if Francklyn remembered with accuracy, the fact that a salt-water creek, navigable by a longboat at high tide, once poked its nose into the very heart of the present city of New York. That estuary, if tradition were correct, was a very important item in the original Stewart Calthorpe's traffic in rum and molasses after nightfall. It was very important in the present emergency.

But the map was not in its usual place. Nor did a long search of the office files reveal it.

"It is of no importance," said Francklyn Aylesworth. "If I require it, I can find a copy in Marleybone's Surveys, which will be in the library. Priestly, I am going away for a time—a week—two weeks—I don't know for how long. While I am gone, relax your vigilance over our friend. Say in a day or two. Treat him well. Surfeit him with good things—anything that money can buy. I think he is a very interesting young man, and he will probably be of great service to us if we treat him right. And, Priestly, put those documents in that safe and have the safe people change the combination. Keep the combination in your head till I come back."

So saying, he walked out of the office. At the first corner he paused.

"The only question in my mind," he mused, pleased with the new logical trend of his thoughts in the last few hours, "is as to the confederate. The confederate, as I see it, must be something of an——" He paused and smiled. "Yes, that is it. He must be something of an ass."

He caught sight of his own reflection in a show window, and he smiled again. Francklyn the Eighth was slowly but inevitably acquiring some of the grim humor of his fathers.

III.

On the fifth day following the disappearance—for it was no less than a disappearance, so the legal firm of McWethy, Milson & Hatch anxiously decided—of Francklyn Aylesworth, the young man seeking peppercorns presented himself again at the brass wicket of the little office in the by-street. He was told politely by Mr. Priestly that Mr. Aylesworth was out of town, but that the matter of his account was being pursued vigorously, none the less. Meantime, and that he might not be put to inconvenience by the delay incident to cabling, et cetera, et cetera, an account had been placed to his name in the Aylesworth bank, and he was at liberty to draw to such an extent as his personal requirements necessitated. If he would put aside any objections on the grounds of delicacy in this regard, the young master would regard it as a personal favor.

It was ten days later that Stewart Calthorpe again entered the offices of the Aylesworth estate. His restless spirit had begun to chafe.

"My affairs are beginning to press," he confided to Priestly. "I am afraid I may be forced to put my claim into the hands of attorneys unless something definite develops shortly."

There was a veiled threat in the softly spoken words.

"I was about to suggest that course, myself," said the gracious Priestly. "If you will pick out a firm, we will be very glad to attend to the matter of fees."

Stewart Calthorpe did not nominate a firm. Instead, he strode away, conscious of the fact that the taste in his mouth, which had been bitter for some time now, was growing more bitter. The young man was still at the same hotel. He had moved into more commodious quarters, but his windows still looked out on humdrum city life such as one encounters in the back eddies on either side of the main thoroughfares. One versed in the ways—and the appearances—of the world, would not have set down Stewart Calthorpe as a bookish young man. Yet through these weeks he had devoted himself assiduously to books—though it must be confessed that the reading was not of the weightier sort calculated to improve one's mind. He saw no one, except the occasional haberdashers' representatives from Fifth Avenue, sent by Priestly to urge him to profane extravagances in the way of outfits of apparel. Priestly, in his endeavor to drive the claimant out of his seclusion, had gone the length of assigning one of his "happy-days" men—professional entertainers attached to all great firms. But Calthorpe, though he recognized a fellow craftsman in the glorious youth who called, abstained.

All his bills were mysteriously paid. All his wants were miraculously supplied. If anything could have drawn him forth from his perusal of French novels, the temptations strewn in his path by the artful hand of Priestly should have done so; but they did not. One thing, only one, Calthorpe accepted. That was the use of a racing runabout, from the Aylesworth garage.

It was a low-slung, sportive-looking thing, stripped for action. Calthorpe came out of his hermitage and tested it out. It was like flying. With shrewd eyes that saw, yet seemed to see nothing, he had scurried hither and yon in the popping monster. He was not being watched—so much was plain. No one could follow with such an engine at his command. This removed his last suspicious doubt.

But, as he moved away now from the too-obliging Priestly, every sense was again on the alert. With eyes in the back of his head, but outwardly still bearing his indolent air, he began the slow task of throwing off a possible shadow. He lost himself repeatedly in department-store crowds, doubling and redoubling on his trail. A taxicab took him to Columbus Circle; and from a second cab he emerged at Sixteenth Street and Fifth Avenue, and started at a brisk walk toward the North River. Some distance over he abruptly descended a flight of steps into a basement beer saloon, dignified with the sign "The Funnel." It was an untidy place, with a beery smell in the air, unclean sawdust on the floor, and flies clustering about greasy tables. He took a seat and rapped sharply with a piece of money. The Funnel was not exactly a thriving business center. In fact, even the entry of the lone customer did not arouse the fat German balanced on one elbow on the bar reading a newspaper.

It was not until the customer uttered a sharp command that the host looked up. He immediately gathered together a collection of bottles and set them before the impatient one. Calthorpe looked at him questioningly. The fat German, in the act of depositing change in the center of a wet pool on the table, shook his head as though in answer to some spoken question, and went back to his newspaper.

At length the young man arose. He

went out not by the front door, but by the rear, which let him into a small, inclosed yard, on two sides of which stood the bastionlike walls of loft buildings. On the third side, the rear, stood a high board fence, through the cracks of which was to be had a view of the dismantled garden of the old Aylesworth mansion.

He descended a flight of steps. These steps were interesting in themselves. To descend them, one must first ascend three rising blocks of granite. The steps were arched over with a groin of masonry of unusual proportions; in fact, the shabby old building that housed The Funnel looked like a mere house of straws to the massive foundations on which it rested. At the bottom of the steps the young man paused and examined a rusty padlock on the door minutely. Then he opened the door, not by unlocking the thing, but by the simple expedient of removing a section of the hasp, which came away easily from the rotten wood in which it was sunk. Inside there was the unmistakable smell of salt water, something a thousand years of time cannot eradicate from moldy timber and clay. He stood still for a long time, listening; but no sound came, except from the tenant rats. When he started forward, it was with the aid of a pocket torch to guide him. He came to a pile of rotten timbers in a corner which he began removing. Under the timbers was an old iron grating, and under the grating was a short reach of decaying steps down which he crawled into a subcellar, so foul with damp stenches that he breathed with difficulty. What he sought hung on the wet wall. It was a rusty, iron door held by hinges, and a lock rendered so fragile from the ravages of time that a slight blow would have crumbled them to bits. With the minutest care he examined the door and its fastening. He drew a sigh of disappointment. He threw the light ahead of him. It re-

vealed the fact that the arched vault in which he stood came to an abrupt end an arm's length away, shut in by an irregular wall of stone, bricks, and earth, evidently dumped in from above. If one consulted the old Mayhew map of Manhattan Island, it would have revealed the interesting fact that at one time a subterranean passage connected this spot with the manor house in the adjoining yard. Doubtless the original Calthorpe had uses for such a means of egress, which connected with a water gate by which he might put out to the river in a longboat at high tide.

Five minutes later the peppercorn claimant had replaced the iron grating and the pile of decaying timbers on the cellar floor, and carefully reset the hasp of the unsprung padlock.

The taproom of The Funnel had, in his brief absence, lost its lonesome air. Seated at the tables, or lounging against the bar now, were, perhaps, a dozen porters, men in blue jeans who had been busy trundling trucks in the street when Calthorpe had entered a short time before. They did not appear to be particularly intelligent men, nor curious, either; but it would be just as well not to give them grounds for curiosity. This resolve was strengthened by a movement on the part of the now busy German. He caught sight of the peering face of the young man in the rear door, and he cautiously batted one eye. Two hundred years ago, old Sindbad the Sailor who, for reasons of his own, constructed this retreat, had more than one way out. When he felt honest he could leave by the front door. The peppercorn claimant at the present moment felt honest; and the impetuous young man in another moment had vaulted the rear fence and let himself in to the old mansion fronting on the next street. As he entered the main corridor on the drawing-room floor, he was thrilled by a discovery as momentous to him as must have been the discovery of the footprint by old Robinson Crusoe on·his desert island. For there on the floor, in this old rookery so long tenanted only by rats, lay a scattered heap of empty condensed-milk tins, also a handful of empty biscuit tins.

And, peering cautiously round the door jamb, he was electrified by an even more momentous discovery. A figure, which could be none other than that of young Francklyn Aylesworth, lay at rest in a musty old easy-chair, his hat drawn over his eyes, as though he were asleep.

Stewart Calthorpe was stealthily revolving for flight, on tiptoe, when the well-known voice of Aylesworth broke the silence.

"Well, well!" said the voice. "At last! I had begun to think, Mr. Calthorpe, that this business about a murderer revisiting the scene of his crime was all bosh. Did you find the vault intact, Mr. Calthorpe?"

The person addressed thus languidly by Francklyn Aylesworth, who was stretching and yawning in his chair, stood rooted to the floor, dumb, for a precious second. There was only one way out now. With a bellow of rage and a bound, he was at the side of the· soft young master, pinioning him. The task of overpowering one of Francklyn Aylesworth's physical capacity was child's play for this lightweight aspirant. Aylesworth did not attempt to struggle. Instead, when his assailant, holding him fast, finally came to rest menacingly over him, Francklyn said:

"If you will take the trouble to go to that window, you will see two men in blue jeans, astride a pushcart, outside the gate. Across the street, in front of the cigar store, is a third. There are two more under the porch, whom you cannot see. There are several more at the—ah—the postern gate. They all have instructions to let you in—but not out, Mr. Calthorpe."

The peppercorn claimant released his fierce hold, and stepped to the window. It was true. There were the men in blue jeans, innocent-looking porters. There was no way out, now.

"Well," he said airily, forcing a laugh, "what are you going to do about it?"

"What am I going to do about it? What are you going to do about it, you mean. Calthorpe—or whatever your name is—you can leave this house, alone, if you want to, by either gate. If you do, those men have business with you. If you leave with me, they have instructions to let you go. Sit down, and make yourself at home in the old place."

Distinctly, there was no humor in the situation. The peppercorn claimant continued to glare savagely. If there were only a hole to crawl through, he would cheerfully have turned himself into a worm. Aylesworth resumed his seat and produced a paper from a pocket. Sullenly, Calthorpe sat down.

"Here we have the deed of rent," said the young man, holding the dirty paper at arm's length and surveying it critically. "As an antique, it is admirable. Except for one fact. Old Sindbad, who was shipwrecked and suffered a horrible journey across uninhabited continents before reaching his beloved England, was careless enough to sign his name in Prussian blue ink. Now, maybe you don't know it, Mr. Calthorpe, but Prussian blue precipitate is a comparatively recent invention, for use as ink; and how old Sindbad got hold of it two hundred years ago is more than I can make out."

The recent Stewart Calthorpe squirmed in his chair, but still he said nothing.

"Would you mind telling me, Mr. Calthorpe, how you managed to secrete this paper inside of that musty old vault without removing the hinges. No? You won't tell me. Very well. I will tell you how I took it out without removing the hinges. I dug out the wall, sir, and I hired a mason to put the wall back. The mason made a most remarkable discovery. The wall had been taken out once before, and put back with Portland cement! Very careless of old Sindbad, on the second count. Cement, like Prussian blue ink, is of comparatively recent history on Manhattan Island, and how the old pirate got hold of it before its time is more than I can make out."

Again he placed a quizzical eye on the recent Stewart Calthorpe; the latter muttered something under his breath, and looked out of the window.

"No, Calthorpe, I am sorry to say that you are not constituted temperamentally for the profession you have sought to follow. In the first place," said the young master, spreading out his fingers to keep tally of his points, "you were not born on the sixteenth of June. It was very wrong of you to suggest—insist on it. When you helped yourself to the Calthorpe documents, which I spent so much money to gather, you carelessly got hold of a copy full of clerical errors. Mistake number one. In the second place, in helping yourself to my old 1803 map of Manhattan Island, to locate your deed of rent, you forgot to return it. Mistake number two. Number three is the grade of ink, to which we have already alluded. Number four is your prehistoric use of Portland cement. I ask you, Mr. Calthorpe, if you do not think you have been very careless. You have failed to make allowances for accident, ignorance, and carelessness. There is only one feature in the whole affair on which I can compliment you for astuteness."

He paused expectantly, but the peppercorn claimant had no question to ask.

"You embarrass me," said Francklyn Aylesworth. "I congratulate you on your choice of a confederate."

"Confederate?" The peppercorn claimant looked up, puzzled. "You don't mean old Dutch Louey—the saloon keeper——"

"No, no, not Dutch Louey. Poor old Louey didn't know what you dragged him in for. I refer to the other one."

"The other one?"

In spite of his dilemma, the late Calthorpe could not help being curious.

"Yes; the other one. I refer to the consummate ass you had in mind to help you—the flabby milksop, so obsessed with the idea of justice that he would excavate all Manhattan Island, if he thought he could find a deed o' rent that would disinherit him from his landed possessions. I refer to myself, Mr. Calthorpe."

The prisoner stared at first, unbelieving, at Francklyn Aylesworth. Then he broke into a laugh, in spite of himself.

"I seem to have picked the wrong generation of Aylesworths," he exclaimed, with conviction. He looked at young Francklyn now with different eyes. There was nothing to do but take his medicine. "Well, what's the damage?" he said curtly.

"Damage?" exclaimed Francklyn Aylesworth. "Damage? Why, my dear sir, there is no damage! In fact, quite the reverse! The diversion you provided has been very entertaining—and quite flattering, too, I assure you, to my sense of vanity. I am in your debt. Indeed, yes. Will you take a little stroll with me, sir? We will talk over your prospects. I really believe you are destined for a career of honest endeavors, with my assistance, Mr.—ah—— By the way, what is your name?"

"Stewart—Angus Stewart."

A few minutes later the squadron of carelessly placed guards, disguised as porters, picked up their tools and dispersed, on seeing young Francklyn Aylesworth and Angus Stewart stroll down the steps and up the avenue, chatting in the most friendly fashion.

Pretty Soft

By H. C. Witwer

Author of 'Aw, Let 'Em Vote," "Safety First," Etc.

We have with us to-night Three-Star Warrington, a millionaire and the latest competitor for the heavyweight championship. With the aid of an ice-cream soda and a box of candy he makes a tremendous sensation in the ring. A novelty in prize-fight stories one of the funniest we have had from Witwer

ONE of the quickest ways to get up there with the big leaguers in any pastime from pinochle to politics is to pull *your* act a little different from the other guy. If you're diggin' streets, dig *yours* with the *handle* of the pick—anybody can dig 'em with the other end! Get me? And if you're runnin' a delicatessen bazaar, instead of sellin' butter by the pound, do it up by the yard!

Don't follow the mob, make 'em wait and watch *you* pass! Surprise 'em, show 'em somethin' new! Wear the soup and fish down to breakfast and appear at the opera in a suit of pink pajamas! Grab off the spotlight for yourself in any way you can and make 'em look at you, talk about you, and think about you—and your name will get in the electric signs, the newspapers, and the income-tax list!

Be *different!* Get me?

Pelham Warrington, 3d—that ain't where he finished—that was his complete name—alias "The Millionaire Mauler" followed that line of dope, and, if he'd been on the level, he'd have made the Standard Oil Company look like a bush-league sick-benefit lodge. As it was, he cleaned up enough in less than a year to pay off the Mexican army.

Old Doc Reese claims I'm all wrong about Pel—even though he got took himself. The doc says it was a wallop back of the ear that landed on Pel's Ephus Doffus Loffus, or somethin' like that, and it changed his disposition, character, and ambition.

I'm sittin' in what the agent of the Marlboro Buildin' swears is a spacious, light, and airy office suite, one afternoon —tryin' to kid Young Daniels, one of my ex-meal tickets, out of makin' a touch, when the office boy butts in.

"One of the chorus men from the Winter Garden is outside," he pipes, "and he claims he wants to see you!"

Young Daniels snickers, and I turns on the kid.

"He's probably got the wrong joint," I says. "Did he *say* he was a chorus man?"

"He don't have to!" the kid comes back. "Wait till you give him the up and down! He looks like one of them rough-and-ready guys that poses for the figure and once had four ginger ales at a crack without leavin' the bar! If his name ain't Percival it's probably Algeron. D'ye want a flash at him?"

"Shoo him in!" I tells the kid. "You got me interested!"

The kid goes outside, and in a minute he's back again. I don't see nobody with him right away, so I bawls:

"Well, well—bring on the roughneck! Where is——"

"Pardon me!" says a soft, delicate voice. "I stopped for a moment to admire that painting of the former champion of the heavyweights. It is really a work of art—the execution is perfect!"

"So was *his!*" I says. "What brought *you* here?"

He had eased himself all the way into the room by this time; and, bo, me and Young Daniels had somethin' to gaze upon, as they say! This guy was a good six foot, and he looked like a two-hundred pounder, offhand. He had on a light summer suit of some kind of stuff that looked like silk, and it fit him like they'd poured him in it. Not only that, it's so far ahead of any clothes I ever seen that I guess it's what they'll be wearin' in 1926. He had on white shoes, and you could just get an eyeful of white silk socks with what looked like charlotte russes embroidered on 'em here and there. In one hand he carried a panama hat turned down all the way around so's the rain'll run right off it, and he wore a cane in the other. He also was there with a red tie that would have made a tomato seem pale. His hair is light and wavy, and his face would have made one of them massage creams famous or a chorus girl independent.

He stands there lookin' from me to Young Daniels, and then he says:

"Which of you gentlemen is Mister Burns, the noted boxing impresario?"

"Ha, ha!" pipes Young Daniels to me. "Somebody's been knockin' you!"

"Shut up!" I says. "I don't make that impresario thing," I answers the tall person. "I been called a lot of devilish names but mostly in English! I'm Jack Burns, the fight manager, if that's who you want."

"Quite so!" this handsome dog comes back, flashin' a row of milk-white teeth on me. "May I speak with you alone?"

"Oh, this guy's all right," I says, noddin' to Young Daniels. "If he starts anything rough I'll have the office boy hide his hat. Go ahead—what have you got?"

"I suppose I had better introduce myself first," he begins, lookin' at Daniels like he figgers he's takin' a chance at that. He fusses around in his coat, drags out a little trick silver box, and deals me a card with this on it:

> PELHAM WARRINGTON 3D.
> UNIVERSITY CLUB.

"Is this you?" I says.

He nods his head and smiles some more.

"Pelham Warrington, hey?" I reads off the name. "It sounds like a country home or a Pullman car to me. What's the idea of the 'third?'"

"I am the third of my house bearing the name," he explains, "and as the others are living we differentiate to avoid confusion."

"Oh! That's it, eh?" I says. "I figured it meant you were favored for the show money, or it was like the stars on the sportin' finals. Now——"

"That differentiate thing is what I like!" butts in Young Daniels, with a grin. "The next time I fall off the wagon I'm goin' to have one of them if it kills me!"

The other guy smiles like he knows he's bein' kidded, but what's the difference.

"Lay off!" I tells Daniels. "Anybody would think from you that bein' ignorant was a gift! Mister Three-Star Warrington," I says, "meet Young Daniels."

Daniels gets up and sticks out his hand, but the other guy just bows and passes it up. Daniels grunts and stands in front of him.

"Hey, fellah!" he says, stickin' out his chin. "What's the matter—don't I belong or what?"

Pel smiles and gets off to another start.

"I have been passionately fond of athletics all my life, and——"

In comes Daniels again.

"That's the tip-off!" he sings out, slappin' my desk with his fist and givin' Pel the laugh. "The Athletics couldn't beat a semipro team of seven men! Why, Connie Mack is through, and ——"

I jumps up and stands over him.

."Now, look here, you big boob!" I says, "I ain't goin' to warn you no more! This guy has been here fifteen minutes and can't get no further than showin' his card on account of you. I asked you in a nice way to lay off before—the next time I'm gonna bean you with a stool!"

Daniels growls and looks at Pel like he wished they had somethin' instead of the chair for murder.

"All right, Pel," I says, "that roughneck ain't got no manners—he's just a poor, ignorant ale hound that don't even know how to enter a room. Don't pay no attention to him, you're with me. Go ahead, I got you—you're crazy for the Red Sox or the Athletics, I mean, and——"

"I'm afraid you don't follow me," smiles Pel. "Perhaps this way it would be clearer. I am a comparatively rich man, and——"

Daniels moves over to the door like he can't keep it in no longer.

"Rich is right!" he hollers, with his hand on the knob. "He looks as rich as a custard to *me.*"

And he beats it!

"Who is that quaint character?" asks Pel, after the door banged.

"Young Daniels," I says. "He used to be a pretty good heavy until he turned bar fly and started to fight the brew. He ain't much now, because he can't take 'em in the stomach—it's all gone."

"I see," says Pel, like he's filin' away that dope in his dome. "Well, to continue—I am a wealthy man, and since I graduated from—er—Yale, I've spent a lot of money in the study of one branch of athletics that has always had a fascination for me. I refer to the manly art of self-defense."

"Art?" I says. "That ain't no art—that's a *plea!* Do you mean box fightin'?"

He nods his head and pulls that lovely smile on me again.

I reaches in the desk and extracts a cigar.

"Smoke this one on me, Pel," I says, "and we'll get down to figures."

"No, thanks!" he pushes it away. "I haven't smoked in years. I find it bad for the wind."

The door opens about an inch all of a sudden and Young Daniels sticks his nose in.

"Hey!" he says. "Are you guys playin' checkers on me or what? Gimme that dough and I'll duck!" He shoots a side glance at Pel and laughs. "Ain't cutey a riot, though, eh?" he says.

But Pel goes right on like we're alone on the bridge.

"In short," he says—"in short—I wish to enter the prize ring as a competitor for the heavyweight championship, and I hereby place myself in your charge!"

Wow! It takes me right in the wind and I fall back in the chair. But Young Daniels dashes in the room and lets out a yell.

"Whee!" he hollers. "This bird is a knock-out! He wants to wallop somebody, eh?" (Honest, he's laughin' till the tears is runnin' down his face!) "You git a cream puff," he yells at Pel, "and I'll git a chocolate eclair and we'll whale each other's brains out all over the office! Ha, ha!" he says, "we have with us to-night Kid Marshmallow— the dashin', smashin' ice-cream-sody champion of——"

Pel waves me back and walks over to Young Daniels.

"My man!" he says, in that velvety voice of his, "I have permitted your uncouth pleasantries out of consideration for Mister Burns. If you do not cease instantly, I will be forced to take measures to stop you!"

He lays his hat and cane on a chair and Daniels throws up his arms, winkin' at me.

"Coises on you, Jack Dalton!" he says. "He's goin' to strike muh!"

Pel frowns.

"Have I your permission, Mister Burns?" he says, shootin' a funny look at me.

Now, I didn't want this Pelham guy beat up in my office. I'm funny about them things—know what I mean? And then the agent would probably be around the next mornin' tellin' me to rehearse my gunmen out at the trainin' camp. So I sticks my hand in my pocket and pulls out a five-case note.

"Here!" I says to Young Daniels, "get the air! I can't hold this guy back any longer. He's been drinkin' raw tea or somethin' somewheres, and he's got to get action! You know he can handle himself—he *admits* it and——"

Do you know what this big bonehead does? He grabs up Pel's hat and the trick cane and starts to walk across the floor—liftin' up the tail of his coat like a woman does with her skirt on a rainy day or on a busy corner.

"Chase me, boys!" he says, in a high, female voice, "I'm a nut sundae!"

He turns around as he passes Pel and

Say! I don't know what kind of a wallop it was, because I didn't get to see it—but whatever it was, believe me, it was a *success!* The floor comes right up and smacks Young Daniels in the face, and he lays there as cold as zero.

That was ample for me! I'm up on the top of the desk before Pel can set for another one.

"Fine!" I says. "Great! You don't need to show *me* no more of your work because I seen when you come in what a wallop you packed. Now——"

He starts over to me, wipin' off his hands on a silk handkerchief, and, if the wall paper hadn't been so smooth, I'd have made the ceilin' easy.

"I must apologize," he says, "for being the innocent cause of this brawl in your office. The fellow was so vulgarly insulting that I fear I lost control——"

"I don't see a thing wrong with your control!" I interrupted him. "Not a thing! You got lots of speed and a hop on your fast one, which is a pretty good layout. If you'll promise to keep your hands in your pockets where they can't do me no harm, I won't make no cracks that'll annoy you—and——"

Young Daniels opens his eyes and sits up on the floor.

"So this is heaven, eh?" he says—his voice is still kinda cracked, and he twists around and takes a slant at me. "How did *you* git here?" he says. "I ——"

He sees Pel and shuts up all of a sudden, meanwhile gettin' on his feet. He acts like a guy just comin' out of the ether after the operation—yes, and he looks it, too! He eases himself past Pel very careful, gets around to me, and pulls down my head.

"Hey?" he whispers in my ear. "This guy is stallin'!" He jerks his thumb over at Pel. "Don't let him hand you that bunk about bein' called Pelham whosthis—his name is probably Cyclone McGinnis or One-round Murphy! No guy with a name like he give out here could make *me* take a dive, *you* know that! He's tryin' to slip somethin' over on you with that trick make-up, and I hope you ain't gonna fall for no such coarse work as that!"

"*You* fell for him, didn't you? I says.

He ain't got nothin' ready for that—them lowbrows are always soft for an intelligent feller—and then Pel walks over.

"I trust you feel no ill effects," he says to Daniels, givin' him the old smile.

"I'm off you!" Daniels comes back, edgin' away from him. "I don't want no part of you! Never mind how I feel —you go your way and I'll go mine! I don't like to start nothin' in Jack's office here or I'd bust you one at that— when I get sore I look like a champion from front, and you're gonna know you been to the fights——"

I grabs him and lead him to the door.

"Stop it!" I says. "Stop stealin' this guy's stuff! He can't be knockin' you dead here all afternoon, me and him wants to go into one of them conference things." I opens the door. "You got no kick comin'—you got a long count, and the crowd was with you at the go-in. You don't class with this guy, and the only thing you can start is a fast gallop for the elevator. Good-by and good luck!" I winds up and eases him out in the hall.

An hour later Pel has signed up to battle for me, money and notoriety, during and while the next twelve months is with us. I didn't make him sign for more than a year, because a lot of them guys is champs in the gym and bums in the ring. Carryin' a hick fighter in your stable is about like havin' a bet on the seventh horse at the finish. You don't even get a chance to *cheer* for your money—know what I mean?

The next mornin' I got Pel out at Hawkins' road house where all my athletes train, and in half an hour most of the newspaper bunch is up to look him over and go back and knock. I get 'em together at the bar and let 'em have the works on Pel. When I get all through they look at each other, at me, and at the ceilin', without sayin' a word. One guy blows his nose and another one starts to whistle.

There's a little guy from the *Gazette* there named Higgins. He'd done time in Yale or Harvard or one of them col-

lege joints, and he's one of them birds that figures everything is the bunk. Know what I mean?—you, me, Congress, the corner grocery, and the subway—all wrong, see? He thinks the Civil War was put on for the movies and the Allies has got Germany framed to fight a fast draw. Higgins winks at the rest of the bunch and says to me:

"Lead on, friend Burns! Take us to the safe-deposit vault where you keep this highbrow mauler of yours and give us a slant at him. I heard of these gentleman sluggers before—they usually think Keats' 'Endymion' is a patent medicine, and a pearl-gray derby, tan shoes, and yellow gloves about right for evening wear! If this one don't say 'dese, 'dose,' and 'dem,' and refer to us as 'youse guys,' I'll purchase for the party."

I don't say a word—I just give that guy a *look*, that's all, and then I give 'em the sign to follow me into the gym.

Pel is wallopin' the punchin' bag so fast that it sounds like a steam drill manicurin' rock, and the handlers is standin' around watchin' him very respectful. Away over in the corner, takin' it all in and tryin' to hide behind the medicine ball when he pipes me, is— Young Daniels.

I calls Pel over and introduces him to the newspaper guys, and the way he goes through the thing makes 'em all pay attention.

All except Higgins.

"They tell me you are a scion of an old and aristocratic family," he says to Pel; "a college graduate and a man of wealth. So you will excuse me if I ask you a few easy ones, just to make it look good."

Say!—that little runt puts Pel through a civil-service examination that would make the third degree and the Ellis Island test look like a kids' spellin' bee! He asks him about things that even *I* never heard of, and Pel just stands there smilin'—leadin' and counterin' until he's got Higgins outpointed from here to Chicago. Now and then Higgins tries to sneak one over in Latin that will end the thing, or he'll shoot over a couple of jabs in Greek and French, but Pel ducks and comes back in Spanish or poetry, and at the finish he's got Higgins holdin' on and wavin' for the bell.

He had Pel in a bad way just once. That was when he uppercut with somethin' about a guy called George B. Shaw—but Pel right crosses him with some stuff from a wop named Confucius, and Higgins goes all but out standin' up!

As Pel walks back to the bag, Higgins turns to his gang, which is givin' him the loud and merry giggle.

"Well," he says, tryin' to luck out of it, "he took me, all right—he's there sixty ways!" He turns around and takes another slant at Pel. "I guess he'll turn out to be yellow," he says. "That's probably what it'll be!"

Can you tie that? There had to be somethin' wrong accordin' to that guy's dope!

"Now, boys," I says to the gang, "you all know Young Daniels here. He was a pretty good battler when he was right, and he can still tell a left jab from the announcer. Just keep your seats for a minute, and I'll have the Millionaire Mauler go a round with Young Daniels, so's you can see the latest boxin' sensation has somethin' besides his good looks!"

Young Daniels coughs and tries to give me the wink, but I make out I don't get him. He clears his throat a couple of times and goes, "Psst, psst!" but nothin' doin'—I'm deaf. I know what's the matter—he don't want to fuss with Pel, but there ain't a chance for an out unless he quits cold in front of the reporters. So he lets out a sigh and takes off his coat, reaching up on the wall for a pair of gloves.

Pel is over at the other side of the gym punchin' away at the bag again, and just as I go to call him over he releases a left swing, it hints the bag, and the rope breaks. I remembered at the time it had worn through the day before, and was only tied together in a loose knot.

But what I'm gettin' at is this—that bag just sailed across the gym, whizzes past Daniels' head, and hits the wall just as he turns around. So the picture he gets is Pel standin' there lookin' after the bag which is a good fifty yards away layin' at his feet! He looks at Pel and back at the bag a couple of times, and his mouth falls open like it's on a hinge.

"Some wallop!" says one of the newspaper guys, winkin' at me as Pel starts over.

"You said a handful!" chimes in another, catchin' on and lookin' at Daniels. "Why, he split the wood a foot, and he's got the brass bracket all twisted out of shape!"

"Psst, psst!" goes Daniels, tryin' to catch my eye.

Just then Pel sees him for the first time—standin' there with the gloves on, and, as far as he can see, ready to mix.

"Well, my man!" says Pel, frownin'. "What do you want?"

Daniels backs away, lickin' his lips. He looks at me, at Pel, at the reporters, and back at that bag layin' at his feet. He pulls a sick-lookin' grin and shakes off one glove.

"I'll take a cigar—thanks!" he chirps.

The newspaper bunch goes in hysterics.

"Why, you big ham!" I yells, "are you gonna quit cold on me?"

"I ain't gonna quit, no!" he says, shakin' off the other glove, "I can beat that—I ain't even gonna start! What d'ye think I am, the original fall guy? Ain't this man-killer of yours ever gonna fight nobody but me? Let him circulate around a little, will you?" he says.

"Well," I sneers at him, "all I can say is that you're so yellow you must have come from the Canary Islands, you——"

"I ain't yellah, I'm *careful!*" he grins back, "and there's just two little words that keeps me from takin' a chance, at that!"

"What are they?" asks one of the reporters.

"*Safety first!*" says Daniels—and beats it away from there.

The newspaper bunch goes back to their offices, each with a picture of the Millionaire Mauler in his pocket, and they just let their typewriters run wild.

All but Higgins.

That bird writes that the bag was framed to break and Daniels and Pel were roommates and had probably rehearsed the act.

Say, I'll bet that guy thinks somebody is *pushin'* the water over Niagara Falls!

The first regular brawl Pel has is with a guy called Terrible Teddy Burke. Burke was one of them guys that, havin' nothin' to deliver, figures they can win by makin' ferocious faces at the other guy.

Appearances mean absolutely nothin'. get me? Take a lobster, for instance! D'ye think the first guy that ever saw one wanted to *eat* it?

Well, as it's Pel's initial appearance in the big town, as we say at the hotel, and we're only goin' to get three hundred dollars for our part in the quarrel, I go around to Terrible Teddy's manager, who drives a milk wagon as a side line, and I says:

"Will you fight us for one hundred dollars?"

"Yes!" he chirps. "*Your* man and any other guys you can pick up on the way to the clubhouse!"

"Fine!" I says. "There's just one thing more I want to know. D'ye think Terrible Teddy can take a dive for

fifty dollars more—say in about the third round?"

"Make it seventy-five dollars," he says, "and if he's on his feet when the bell rings for the fourth frame, I'll knock him dead with the bucket!"

I finally fixed it for sixty dollars. What d'ye mean, crooked? This was Pel's first start, wasn't it? Well, a guy's got to have a *little* enouragemant, don't he?

We catch a good crowd for the mill, the society-boxer thing havin' helped a whole lot. I see a sprinklin' of hardboiled shirts in the boxes, and some of them guys has brung their lady friends. Their crowd come to see the highbrow beat the roughneck, and the regulars is there to enjoy the slaughter of the Fifth Avenue hussy by one of their own set.

When Pel climbs through the ropes, I notice he's kinda pale and nervous lookin', but I put it down as stage fright and let it go at that. The guys in the boxes gives him a hand, and he turns around and bows. Terrible Teddy climbs in, and the boys in the gallery lets go all they got. I got Spider Moran and Skinny Yerkes, two of the best handlers that ever swung a towel, in Pel's corner, and I'm right there myself to see that we gets the breaks. While we're waitin' for the announcer, Pel turns to me and whispers:

"I say, old fellow—what is that weird-looking liquid in the bottle there?"

"That's all right!" I says. "We'll give you a shot of that in case you slow up and——"

"Pardon me!" he cuts me off. "Is there a confectioner in the vicinity?"

"I don't make you," I says.

"A candy store," he explains. "I wish to send out for something before this contest begins."

Spider Moran looks at him and laughs. "There's one of them icecream-sody dives on the corner," he says. "I seen a guy stagger out of it on the way over here."

"The very thing," says Pel. "I want you to run over there and get me a chocolate ice-cream soda with plenty of sirup and some whipped cream on the top. Don't forget the straws—and if you see any nice bonbons there, fresh, you know, get a half pound of those."

The Spider like to fell over the bucket laughin'.

"Ain't he a riot, eh?" he says to me. "Always makin' some comical crack and——"

"Come!" says Pel, lookin' at the wrist watch he insisted on wearin' right into the ring, "they will sound the gong in a moment. Hasten!"

"D'ye mean to say you're on the *level* with that stuff?" yells the Spider, lookin' from Pel to me.

"Well, I certainly must have a stimulant of *some* sort before I attack this brute over there!" pipes Pel, very indignant.

Before I can make a crack, a newspaper guy; which is sittin' in the press box and takin' this all in, reaches over and grabs me by the arm.

"Make him get the soda!" he shoots in my ear. "You big bonehead—this guy is wasted on you! If he sits in that corner and drinks the stuff it'll be worth two columns to-morrow mornin'. Get wise to yourself—this fellow is as simple as a fox. He's new, he's *different*, you——"

Say! In ten minutes Pel is sittin' there in his corner drinkin' one of them soda things with a straw and eatin' bonbons from a box with *pink ribbon* on it! The bunch in the gallery and standin' up in the back has gone nutty, and the reporters is writin' like they got to catch an edition with the assassination of the president!

And they had somethin' to write about, believe me!

Can you picture it? A heavyweight sittin' in his corner at a Bowery fight club waitin' for the bell—sippin' an *ice-cream soda,* eatin' *candy,* and wearin' a *wrist watch* on his left arm!

That's the reason I always say, no matter what this guy did afterward, you got to hand it to him—he was *different!*

Terrible Teddy is such an awkward-lookin' bum that he makes Pel look like Jim Corbett. All Teddy ever had was a wallop, and as that is tied up by my money, he was like a guy in a rowboat without any oars.

He dives in the third round—doin' a trick fall that fooled everybody that couldn't get in to see the fight.

The crowd, though, seen somebody go *down,* and, as that was what they paid out their dough for, everybody was happy.

Except Higgins.

"That's gettin' away with *arson!*" he yells up to me. "Who was that—his brother?"

I'll bet that guy believes to this day that Washington *bought* off the English!

While we're gettin' off Pel's gloves and the crowd is millin' toward the exits, Pel whispers in my ear:

"Go to the box office at once and get the remuneration due me for my victory. See that it is in small bills, and hurry back—quick! Don't stop now to ask questions!"

I didn't. This guy is over my head, but he's gettin' the notoriety, and that's all I want to know. But as I come back he walks to the middle of the ring and faces the crowd, which, not bein' able to figure him, stops goin' out and spreads around the ring.

"One moment, gentlemen!" says Pel. "If you will keep your seats for a few seconds—ah!" he pipes me at the ringside and he leans down. "Give me the gold!" he says.

I pass it over. I done like he said about gettin' it small, and it's all in ones, twos, and fives. The crowd is now six deep around the ring, every-body lookin' like they knew somethin' phony was goin' to be pulled, but as long as they're here they might as well stick.

"Gentlemen," Pel goes on again, holdin' up this roll of bills which looks like the fare to Egypt, "I did not enter the prize ring for financial gain, but purely for the love of the sport. There-fore, I could not dream of accepting *money* for merely gratifying a whim." He stops and throws out his hands, "Look alive there!" he yells.

What did he do?

He throwed that whole handful of dough, my bit and all, right over the ropes into the crowd!

Can you imagine it? Three hundred beans, American money, *and he feeds it to the hams out in front!*

And *I* gotta slip Terrible Teddy sixty iron men for layin' down!

Well, for a second we all stand there in a trance. Then a great, big five-dol-lar bill floatin' through the air lands on some guy's hat.

Say, you've seen a lot of riots and football games and the six-o'clock mas-sacre at the Fourteenth Street subway station, ain't you? Well, all them things are friendly arguments along-side of what was had, as they say, around that ring! Them guys went after that dough with one short yell that like to raised the roof, and then the thing settles down to a bitin', snarl-in', knock-'em-down-and-drag-'em-out gang fight. Half a dozen little, *private* quarrels over a five-dollar bill or a two-spot starts here and there, and in lessen five minutes *everybody's* in the game. The referee pipes two bills layin' near one of the ring posts and tries a quick snatch, but somebody got him on the chin and he went over the ropes like a divin' seal. Terrible Teddy's seconds has left him flat, and they're down there on the floor somewheres, doin' their little best. And then Terrible

Teddy, which is hangin' over in his chair, supposed to be unconscious from the awful wallop he didn't get, takes a flash at what's comin' off, and in an-other minute *he's* in there tryin'— shootin' over swings and hooks that would have knocked Pel out of the State if he'd used them a few seconds before!

Me? I'm up against the ropes tryin' to clear my head while these guys is in there battlin' for my money! The last thing I heard was Higgins, going out the door.

"I'll bet that dough is *stage* money!" he's tellin' a friend.

That guy don't believe Lincoln was shot—he thinks he's *hidin'* some-wheres!

The reserves stopped the riot half an hour later. Some of the losers went to the hospital and the others wound up in the night court.

Outside the club, Pel takes out a lit-tle notebook and a pencil and says:

"I say! You know I really couldn't accept that money to-night, old chap. I'm half sorry, though, that I stirred those people to such an extent, but ——."

"Yes!" I butts in, "I got you—I know just how you feel. You figured they'd get together and hold a spellin' bee with the winner takin' all! Now, *I* didn't get in that party back there myself, not bein' invited or nothin'—and I know them guys didn't leave nothin' on the floor, or I'd go back and look for it. What I'm gettin' at is—where do I get mine? The fight game may be the way you get your pleasure, but it's different with me—that's how *I* get my room and board!"

"That's just what I'm marking down here, old fellow," says Pel, smilin' pleasantly. "I'll have my quarterly check within a few days, and I will at once pay you your percentage on to-night's adventure. Meanwhile, I'm afraid I'll have to ask you to advance me a small sum, say a thousand, until my next engagement."

I stops dead and looks at him, but he's as serious as typhoid fever.

"Do you think you can get by on a *thousand?*" I asks him. I gives him a sarcastic look with it, but he only smiles back.

"Oh, yes!" he chirps, "for a week or so, I should say. I don't mind roughing it a bit for a time—the training camp has rather accustomed me to it."

"Well, Pel," I says, "I hate to disappoint you, but I'm afraid I can't quite come through with a thousand. I never carry no small bills with me; it tips you off as a piker when you pull 'em out. But I'll tell you what I'll do —I'll stake you to a two-case note until you get your alimony or whatever it is you're figurin' on."

Say! He laughs and takes me by the arm, and all the way back to the camp he gives me the work. His stuff was the greatest I ever heard! On the level, that guy could have made a bartender vote for prohibition!

What did I do? I slipped him a hundred beans at the door of the gym, and if it had been two blocks farther away he'd have got my scarfpin!

The next mornin' all the sports the papers took any serious notice of was Pel's first start the night before. Them newspaper guys hadn't missed a trick, and most of them throwed in a few acts that didn't come off so's to be sure they got everything covered. One guy had Pel placed as the young millionaire that strangely disappeared after leavin' college, and the amount of dough he throwed away run all the way from three hundred dollars to three thousand, accordin' to what edition you had.

That afternoon I get phone calls and wires from every manager in the world that had anything that *looked* like a heavyweight in their stable. They wanted to fight Pel all the way from

one round to a hundred—they knew the mob that would turn out for a chance at some of the change Pel throwed over the ropes would pay their feed bills for the next couple of years.

I pick out three of the worst hams that ever sat in a corner and signed Pel up with them.

Pel goes to the post with the first one before a crowd that could have elected a socialist president. Our percentage calls for nine hundred dollars, and at the last minute I gets to this guy—and for an extry one hundred and fifty dollars he promises to call it a day in the second round.

Hey? Well, it was only his *second* start, wasn't it? You gotta boost a guy along at first, you know!

But this boob wants to make it look good, as he ain't goin' to be there long, and he cops Pel on the jaw in the first round.

Down goes the Millionaire Mauler like a submarine!

He stays down the legal limit, and, when he comes up, he's got "I'm lookin' for an out" written all over his face!

The other guy's so surprised at the success he's had he come near forgettin' that one hundred and fifty dollars and levelin' 'em all from then on. But Pel stalls through the round, and, durin' the short rest, I get the other guy's eye.

He claims a foul and quits in the next round.

But it was awful close, believe me, and it got me thinkin'. I don't know much about "How to Behave at a Dinner" and stuff like that, but box fightin' is my dish. This guy can't take it, I tells myself, and, what's more, he *won't!*

The crowd has got in close around the ring, and front places is goin' to the guys with the best wallops. I look up from where I'm sittin', and there's the manager of the club climbin'

through the ropes with a roll of bills in
each hand. I tear around the side of
the ring to nail him, but it's too late.
The mob lets out a terrible yell, and I
know what's happened.

Pel is feedin' 'em that nine hundred
beans!

I can't find nobody in the box office
to strangle for givin' Pel that money,
because they're all takin' part in the
battle royal around the ringside!

Well, that's the way it goes for the
next two scraps, both of which is set-
ups for Pel. I can't get a nickel out
of him, and he keeps stallin' me with
that waitin'-for-the-big-check stuff.
He's got me stopped at every play I
make, because I got so much dough
sunk in him already that I'm hangin'
on, hopin' to break even on his next
start. If I let him go, there's a million
guys waitin' to grab him up, because
he's the greatest card that ever hit
Broadway.

Why, every time he fought the house
was sold out the day he signed articles.
Club managers fought with each other
on the street for the honor of havin'
him box at their club. The papers was
full of him every day—he was *the* guy.
He *owned* the town!

It didn't make no difference who,
where, or how he fought—tickets could
be from five to fifty dollars a copy and
everybody sent in.

You know the average guy is a riot
when you study him. These birds
would part with say fifteen dollars to
see Pel fight some bum, because they
figured there was a chance of grabbin' a
ten-spot, maybe a *handful* of 'em, when
he started to throw it away. Never
mind the fact that they were goin'
fifteen in the hole for the privilege of
fightin' for this other money, old Pel
was goin' to heave it away, and you
never could tell *what* you might grab!

But Pel had a new idea—brand-new!
Instead of *him* fightin', he knocks cold

some bum which I'd paid off the day
before, and the crowd that has got into
the rent money to see him perform
puts on the show *themselves* outside the
ring—scrappin' for what was actually
my money!

And then one day Pel comes to me
when I got him signed up to box Terry
Mitchell, another ham, for ten rounds.

"I say!" he says, "I have decided not
to meet this Mitchell person. I have
toyed quite long enough with these sec-
ond-raters, and I think I have demonstrated my worth as a drawing card
par excellence to these coarse, commercial promoters. I am about to grat-
ify my lifelong ambition. In short, I
want you to negotiate with the heavyweight champion of the world for a
finish contest with the title at stake. I
will meet him as soon as he is ready.
And, by the way," he goes on, before
I get my breath, "I should think you
could arrange for a considerable sum
for my percentage—say, fifty thousand
or so!"

I started to laugh—and then I
stopped short.

Pel had remarked a pageful! The
bout would draw everybody that was
this side of the cemetery, and a purse
could be hung up that would stagger
Europe! The chance to see a world's
champion, Pel, and real money flooding
the arena after the scrap would have
guys breakin' out of jails and hospitals
to get there.

Wait—I'm comin' to that. Of
course, I intended to see that Pel's
money-throwin' arm got out of commission in this particular quarrel. This
was the one where it would all get
hurled at *me* in a hotel room somewheres.

But I didn't have to get *my* private
affairs on the billboards advertisin' the
scrap, did I?

I knew we couldn't get fifty thousand
—but there was a great chance of us
grabbin' twenty-five.

I had a flash of Pel bein' advertised to throw away twenty-five thousand iron men to the crowd!

Say, would *you* have come to see that scrap?

I've always been a quick breaker—I don't always cop, but I never get left when the gate goes up! I grab my hat and beat it up to Steve Lorimer, the biggest and gamest promoter in the pastime in them days. I let him have it quick, and he listens very quiet.

"Come around in the mornin'," he says, when I've shot the works, "and I'll let you know."

I did and he did. He offers me twenty-five thousand bones for our end. The fight is to be twenty rounds and for the heavyweight championship of the world. The champion's manager had seen Pel work, and when Lorimer offered him fifty thousand he stopped right on the street where Lorimer was talkin' to him and signed the articles in the doorway of a grocery store.

That fight comes on the Fourth of July, and it was held in the open air, because that was the only place we could get that would hold the crowd that was willin' to commit murder to see it. They tell me that trains come rollin' in for seven hours after it was all over, packed with come-ons that wanted to be among those present.

In the dressin' room I got eighty-four handlers workin' over Pel and tellin' him how to fight the champ. Pel's noddin' his head, but he's got a funny look on his face, like he's thinkin' of some joke he heard last week, and he can't remember how it started off now. He makes me go out and get our twenty-five thousand before he'll start for the ring. He claims he don't want no mix-up when the fight's over and have people, which has come for miles, disappointed.

I get it, and he fusses around and packs it in a satchel which is carried into the ring with him.

The crowd goes crazy when they see him and the dough bag.

After they had got the crowd where they was ready to bite nails in half, by introducin' everybody from the ward leader to a couple of movie stars, the bell rings and the big fight is on. The crowd gives a long-drawn-out sigh of joy and sits back to watch a fast, hard-fought battle.

One second later the fight's all over!

Say, for one of the longest minutes I ever lived there ain't a sound! And then—— Well, I understand a hundred and six guys went *deaf* from the racket!

I never seen nothin' like it in my life! I get somethin' in my eye and *winked*—and when I look up again, Pel is flat on the canvas and the champion is walkin' to his corner!

While the riot is at its height, I hop over the ropes and push through the mob that's standin' over Pel in the middle of the ring. Nobody seen the wallop, nobody knew what hit him—but he's not only out——

As far as I can see, he's *dead!*

Somebody yells to the crowd that Pel has croaked—the cops pour into the ring and start to pinch everybody in sight, and there's an old-fashioned stampede for the gates. The crowd gets out and mills around outside, swearin' and threatenin'.

We throw Pel, still dead to the world, in an auto and rush him out a secret gate to old Doc Reese, about the greatest pill roller in the country.

It's a fifteen-mile run, and we work over Pel all the way, but there's nothin' doin'. I figured the champion must have *stabbed* him in the heart.

Well, we get to the doc's house and by luck grab him in. I guess he was the only guy in the world that wasn't at that fight. The doc has Pel laid on a sofa and chases us out of the room. I grab the bag of dough, and we get back in the car and start for the bank.

With one of the handlers on each side of me, I breeze up to the cashier's window, winded but happy. I got twenty-five thousand beans in that bag, and there ain't nobody can throw *that* away!

Don't let anybody ever tell you you can't live without breathin'—I did, for three minutes!

Wait! There was .twenty-five thousand in that bag, all right—twenty-five thousand *lead slugs!*

We run over more guys on the way back to Doc Reese's house than would have got hit in that town in ten years ordinarily—and we meet the old doc on the steps.

"The poor boy, the poor boy!" he says, as I dashes up.

"Is he *dead?*" I yells.

"No," answers the doc, "that's the remarkable part of it—he's *vanished!*"

I keels over on the steps, all but out cold.

"In some manner," the doc goes on, "he climbed out a window while I had left the room for a moment to melt a tablet for a strychnine injection. I'm afraid he'll wander around and some harm will befall him and——"

"He's probably passin' Sydney, Australia, now!" says a voice.

I look up, and there's that Higgins guy!

Well, we go inside, and the doc finds that when Pel climbed out that window he had everything with him that wasn't nailed.

I tells the doc the whole story then, just like I told it to you, and, when I got all through, he jumps up like he's got the answer, and it was a cinch.

"That's a remarkable story," he says, "marvelous! But I think I have the correct diagnosis. It's quite beyond reason to think that that boy—who so generously gave his every penny to the crowds at the ringside—is crooked——"

"Ha, ha!" says Higgins—"pardon me, doc!"

"The solution is this," goes on the old doc, frownin' at Higgins. "The champion undoubtedly struck that poor boy on the Ephus Doffus Loffus"—that's the way it sounded to me, anyhow—"a nerve back of the ear and directly connected with the brain. The paralyzing of that important nerve accounts for this startling change in his character. There are medical precedents for my presumption."

Higgins gets up, looks at the doc, and yawns.

"I'm sorry, doc," he says, reachin' for his hat, "because you probably went to a lot of trouble dopin' that out. Also it makes a crackajack yarn, and your diagnosis will appear in my paper this afternoon."

He turns around to us with his hand on the doorknob.

"But that gettin' hit on the Ephus Doffus Loffus thing is the *bunk! That guy didn't get hit nowhere!* As the champion pulled back his left for the very first try—the well-known Millionaire Mauler took a *dive!*"

D'ye know, for *once* this guy had me guessin'!

❦

SPEED! SPEED!! SPEED!!!

COLONEL ROBERT M. GATES, of Tennessee, admits that at times a Southern gentleman's thirst for a cooling, but alcoholic, drink becomes great, even colossal.

One day Doctor Peters, a friend of Colonel Gates, was met by an old gentleman on the streets of a Tennessee town.

"How about walking down to my house and having a drink?" the old gentleman politely inquired of Peters.

"Thanks," replied the doctor; "but what's the matter with running?"

Stalemate

By Robert Welles Ritchie

Author of "The Saxons," "Wings of the Wind," Etc.

The first in the best series of detective stories we have had in POPULAR in years. The plots center around Raoul Flack, a French criminal who escapes from the lime pits of a tropical hell, flies to America and gathers about him a band of expert lawbreakers to make war on society.

SAPPHIRES are the primordial stones. They hold in their depths the glint of a glacier's heart, a thousand feet from sunlight; theirs the abysmal blue of that first sea which was before a Fabricator said, "Let there be a firmament in the midst of the waters." The chill of their birth in the dark laboratories of earth stays with them after they have been fashioned for the eye of woman.

Mrs. Edgerton Miles was a lover of sapphires. They were, in fact, her passion. A cold, aloof woman, who climbed the social ladder with ruthless disregard for fingers stepped on, falterers cast down into the darkness of submerged "impossibles," she loved the stone for its matching spirit. The lights in the heart of the sapphire were those in the depths of her eyes—bitter cold, and with a rime of arctic frost. Amid the glitter and gold of the horseshoe at the opera there was no gorgeous, disdainful shadow of frozen color to match that which was clasped about her firm white neck. The incomparable Edgerton Miles sapphire collar was known to have been bought for fifty thousand dollars. Its stones had been gathered by an expert in Antwerp—this one representing the sacrifice of a ruined family to pride; that, once the gift of a prince to a beloved dancer.

Now, these mute relics of tragedy were all gathered together in a glittering wonder, strung on gold mesh and platinum, with diamonds tucked in arabesques of precious metal to act as foils for the more precious blue gems. The whole, put together by a New York jeweler to the élite, represented the sacrifice of an American robber baron upon an altar of chilled affections.

On a day in early November, a week before the opening of the opera season, the Miles electric brougham threaded a way through crowded traffic on Nassau Street, turned into Maiden Lane, and drew up at the curb before a jewel house known to connoisseurs above all the flash and pomp of larger establishments on Fifth Avenue. Mrs. Edgerton Miles stepped out, and into a waiting elevator. A few minutes later, she was slipping her ermine stole from her shoulders in the private office of the head of the firm, and that important gentleman was hovering close, in anticipation of her wishes. Mrs. Miles was a good customer. It was the firm of Sutton & Sutton that had secured and mounted the incomparable sapphire collar.

"Mr. Sutton, my husband insists that I bring down the collar to have you examine the settings." The lady spoke tersely, with proper aloofness.

Mr. Sutton bowed admiration for Mr. Miles' wise precaution.

"Of course, I'll have to have it for 'Thaïs,' next Monday night. You will have it overhauled by that time, I am sure. Mr. Miles will call for it himself. I'd a great deal rather have him bring it home than one of your men, for in case anything should happen——" She left unsaid the terrible weight of responsibility that would fall upon the head of Edgerton Miles in case of disaster.

"I will insure it in my name while it is with us, Mrs. Miles," the head of the firm hastened to assure. "A mere precaution; but the firm does not overlook its responsibility." He put out an eager hand to receive the oblong Russia-leather jewel case, marked in gold, "J. C. M.," which Mrs. Miles brought out from beneath her stole. With a flick of his thumb, the cover popped up, and the full, chill glory of the fifty graded stones smote his eyes. He had not seen them, except about the neck of their owner, in the horseshoe, since they left his establishment, three years before. Just one satisfying peek he allowed himself, then turned toward the vault in the rear of his office.

"Then I will tell Mr. Miles to call for the thing on Monday afternoon next," the collar's owner said, in parting.

"Everything will be finished—tightened up and polished by that time, Mrs. Miles."

Before the door of the brougham had closed behind the possessor of the famous sapphire collar, Mr. Sutton was at his desk, with a telephone receiver at his ear. He called for a number.

"Ah—Mr. Miles? This is Mr. Sutton. I wished to tell you that—er—

you may come over to the office at any time that suits your convenience, and we can talk over that little matter between us. What's that? Oh, yes, she brought it down. She has just left, in fact. Right away? Very well, Mr. Miles."

The senior partner of Sutton & Sutton, jewelers, permitted himself a quiet grin. Mr. Sutton did not object to compounding a felony so long as another man initiated it.

Within fifteen minutes, Edgerton Miles stepped into his office with the live gait of an eager man. Edgerton Miles was the perfect type of the genteel buccaneer—as sweet a pirate as ever scuttled a railroad or cut a dividend. Pink and rosy, tubbed, manicured, barbered, tailored, with a cocksure eye and a booming voice, Edgerton Miles was a walking denial of the catechism theorem of an outward and visible sign being indicative of an inward and spiritual grace. He had no inward and spiritual grace whatever; that didn't go with his business or his moral code.

Mr. Sutton greeted him with the dark smile of a conspirator, closed and locked his office door, and brought out from the vault the small Russia-leather jewel case Mrs. Miles had just left; also a jewel tray, with a blue velvet lining, upon which reposed a small tissue-paper bundle. The bundle he unwrapped, and spilled from it a glittering heap of sapphires—fifty of them, large and small. Then he sprung back the top of the case wherein reposed the sapphire collar.

"Uh-huh!" Miles grunted with satisfaction. "I thought I'd never get my wife to give up that collar business for even a day. Now that you've got it, why——"

"We can go right ahead," Mr. Sutton purred. "Mrs. Miles said you would call for the collar next Monday; this is Tuesday, so we have six full working days ahead."

Miles put out a pink, stubby finger and stirred the loose sapphires gently.

"They're just the same?" he queried.

"Absolutely," the senior partner affirmed. "By the greatest good luck, I've been able to get together what is practically a duplicate of the stones in Mrs. Miles' collar. Now that we have the model to work from, we can turn out a collar that Mrs. Miles herself could not distinguish from her own—and do it in six days, too."

"Well—er—the person who's interested in this business says she won't be satisfied unless it's just the same," Miles mumbled. "You know what women are—what they want they want. But, Sutton, this is way on the low-down, you know. If Mrs. M. should ever get wise—why, good night for E. Miles, esquire!"

"My dear fellow," Mr. Sutton chided, "you do not credit me with much discretion. This little matter of business will be absolutely confidential."

"Well, rush it through." Miles rose, and buttoned his greatcoat about him. "I'll drop in Monday afternoon and deliver them both—in person." He gravely lowered one eyelid and made for the door. The senior partner followed to the elevator to renew a pledge of inviolate secrecy.

When the Wall Street buccaneer had departed, the senior partner seated himself at his desk and summoned by house telephone his expert jewel setter. The artisan, whose name was Henri, entered Sutton's office. He was a squat, stolid Fleming, with the bowed shoulders and squinting, nearsighted eyes that come from much peering through a jeweler's glass over close work; his hands were those of an artist—delicate, sensitive, instinct with the genius of creation. Henri stood blinking before his employer, waiting commands.

"Henri, I have a particularly important and delicate piece of work for you to do," Sutton began, indicating with a sweep of his hand the sapphire collar in its box and the scattered gems on the tray beside it. "Here is a sapphire collar of fifty matched stones; here are fifty loose stones as nearly like the originals in the setting as we can find them. I want you to duplicate this collar—duplicate it down to the last platinum link—and have the job done by next Monday afternoon. Take this collar now for your model. When you are ready for the stones come to me."

The jewel setter tucked the Russia-leather case under his arm and started for the door.

"And, Henri," his employer called, in afterthought, "you will be wise if you say nothing about this job to the other men in the factory." Henri gave a nod of his bullet head and passed out.

Because of his position as chief artisan of the Sutton & Sutton staff, Henri enjoyed the dignity of a working office cut off from the rest of the factory by partitions. There were his bench, his lathe, melting pot, and all the delicate tools of his trade. Alone under the strong light of a dazzling incandescent, Henri screwed his glass into his right eye and carefully examined the exquisite collar of sapphires. The first discovery he made was a triple line of finely engraved script in the gold backing of the three-stone pendant dropping from the front of the collar. Though this was no concern of Henri's—or shouldn't have been—he took a memorandum from his pocket and copied on a page therein what he read on the gold surface:

JULIANA COPE MILES.
13 East -9th N. Y.

The second discovery was not long in coming. As he turned the collar slowly, and stone by stone, under the glass, his lips pursed themselves into a pucker, and he softly whistled. Henri's brain was one peculiarly receptive to matters beyond the province of his trade. Because of that catholicity of interest, he had duly qualified as one of l'Incomparables—a very competent member of Raoul Flack's troupe of expert lawbreakers. Now, with Mrs. Miles' sapphire collar slowly passing under his sensitive eye and fingers, this quality of being able to see beyond the rim of the cup suggested to him certain entertaining and profitable activities to follow upon the two discoveries he had just made.

But as a conscientious workman for Sutton & Sutton, Henri dismissed these pleasing anticipations from his mind and got down to the work in hand. Plaster of Paris became live clay under his deft fingers; a mold of all the infinite tracery of grape leaf and flower twining about the jewels in the collar was baked in the electric oven; then, with platinum and fine gold, his fashioning fingers were busy. To make a duplicate of Mrs. Miles' jeweled collar within six days would require all of Henri's craft and speed.

But Henri did not work at night— not at his bench, that is. After leaving the Maiden Lane jewel establishment, at the close of the day when his arduous task had been set for him, Henri did some telephoning, then took the elevated to Christopher Street. A few minutes' walk from the elevated stairs brought him to the Grape Arbor. Now, the Grape Arbor is one of the relics of Greenwich Village's elder day, before all the world flooded down into that quiet and homy district to disrupt its neighborhood intimacy and fill its quaint streets with alien tongues. Its ancient taproom has not changed a cobweb since the days when sailors—with rings in their ears and barbarous oaths on their tongues—used to swagger up the crooked bypaths of the village from the big clipper ships docked in North River, and pound their pewter mugs on the stained oak of the bar. Faded lithographs of the *Flying Cloud,* the *Star*

of the East, and those other queens of the tea fleet still hang above the porcelain handles of the ale taps, and the tang of the brown liquor that comes from the casks is as sharp as the tongue of the crusty old Glasgie man who is the Grape Arbor's present presiding genius. In all New York there is no more intimate rendezvous.

Henri was seated before his oysters, in the little back room, when Gaspard Detournelles came in. The exquisite had tempered his toilet to the democratic standards of the village; there was nothing about the man to mark him as one more familiar with the Casino at Newport than a tavern in the backwash of the New York docks. When the red-faced Irish miss who is barmaid, cook, and waitress at the Grape Arbor had served the newcomer, and they were alone in the cubby-hole called a dining room, Henri went right to the core of the matter that had prompted the meeting. He brought his memorandum book from his pocket, opened it to the page whereon he had entered a copy of the inscription on the sapphire collar, and thrust it under the other's eyes.

"Know her?" Henri grunted. Detournelles glanced at the name and address.

"Assuredly. I am on her social list," he answered.

"Do you know the jewels she wears?" Henri put the question as a challenge.

"Of a surety."

"A collar of sapphires, worth, say, forty or fifty thousand—you know that?" The exquisite's eyebrows raised ever so slightly.

"No. I have never seen her wear such a gem," Detournelles denied. "I met her only during the summer season—last summer. She was not wearing her major jewels then, of course. But tell me—does she possess such a treasure?" A predatory flash lighted the tired eyes. Henri, ignoring the other's question, put one of his own:

"Your acquaintance with this Miles woman—how intimate?"

"Sufficient." Detournelles gave his shoulders a little shrug, and a wry smile turned down the corners of his mouth —the mouth of a hunting animal. "Last summer she was very gracious. I am listed for the first entertainment she gives *chez elle* at her town house here."

"When is that?" Henri inquired, a little strain of eagerness in his voice.

"Next Monday night—the opening of the opera. A dinner at the home of Madame Miles; then her box in the horseshoe."

Henri almost choked on his ale. He set the mug down, sputtering:

"Next Monday night you will be at the Miles house—of a surety?"

"Come, come, little rabbit! No more mystery between us!" Detournelles attempted to hide his impatience and curiosity under a smile. "What about this sapphire collar of Mrs. Miles?"

"Not a word—not a word!" The little jewel setter's fine hands were fluttering excitedly. "Take me to the Master at once—to Maître Raoul, whom you say you have seen, and whose face will be a benison for me. Only the Master can handle so great and so delicate a situation. Come, come! We go!"

Three hours later, near midnight, three heads were gathered under the grudging light of the student lamp in a dark house on one of Staten Island's forgotten thoroughfares. The great white head of the Phantom—head of an ascetic, an anchorite—nodded sagely at each point in little Henri's narrative of the afternoon's affair in Sutton & Sutton's factory. When the fashioner of jewels was finished, the Phantom spoke:

"Very pretty—a very pretty case for us, my children."

CHAPTER II.

On the Monday set as the time limit for its completion, Henri, the little artificer of jewels, set the finished collar side by side with the model furnished by Mrs. Miles. Studiously he compared the two glittering wonders, detail by detail, then nodded his head. His craftsman's soul was satisfied.

But not that other sly and predatory instinct which dwelt in the same soul chamber, and which, by its activities, had commended Henri to membership in the select circle of the Incomparables, back in Paris, five years before. A very irregular detail of artificing had yet to be accomplished before Henri should turn over the completed collar and the model. So irregular it was, in fact, that his squinting eyes peered like a weasel's around the corner of his office workroom and assured him there were no observers before he undertook it. A half hour later, he trotted into Mr. Sutton's office with two jewel cases— the Russia-leather one, marked "J. C. M." and a plain pigskin casket, such as the firm supplied for outgoing purchases of value.

"A cracking job," was the vehement approval voiced a few hours afterward by Edgerton Miles, when he opened the two cases in Sutton's office and compared the radiant twin jewels. "Comes high, of course, but got to be done." The senior partner, privy to the Wall Street pirate's secret motive for so expensive a deceit, and mildly thrilled in sympathy with his customer's stratagem, received a check for fifty thousand dollars with the air of a fellow conspirator. Edgerton Miles dropped down in the elevator to his limousine, with the two jewel cases, one in each capacious pocket of his greatcoat.

Before he went to his home to deliver to the official lady of his heart her sapphire collar, Edgerton Miles directed his chauffeur to take him elsewhere. In the discreet privacy of soft lamplight, he opened the pigskin case and revealed to a cooing and platonic Helen the fulfillment of a promise more extravagant than any made by perfidious Paris.

Mrs. Edgerton Miles' dinner that evening was the perfection of an astute hostess' entertainment. Six guests sat down to a wonderland of fern, blossoms, damask, and silver, wherein the succession of courses was but incidental magic and the procession of the vintage a lure to visioning. Color there was on the table, but still more brilliant color made an aura of changing lights above the napery; this from jewels about white necks and on slim fingers. Dazzling the diamond luster, and glowing hot the heart of rubies, but from the head of the table, where sat the hostess, the cold blue flames of sapphires outshone them all. Strand on strand about Mrs. Miles' round, firm neck, lay the sapphires of the famous collar, diamonds glinting in thin pin points among the interstices of the supporting chains.

Gaspard Detournelles, Viscount Allaire, who had the place at the hostess' right, and whose attention was frantically bid for by a fluffy-headed near-débutante and title worshiper at the plate beyond, counted that opportunity precious which gave his eyes a feast on the blue glory of the gems just beyond his shoulder. Diplomatically he stood off the débutante with clever verbal fencing, in order the better to bring to bear upon Mrs. Miles the light batteries of his table talk. Detournelles outdid his own clever self in the matter of airy banter and insidious flattery. With consummate grace, he managed to cut out for his own the almost undivided attentions of the lady with the sapphires. Edgerton Miles, from the opposite end of the table, observed with a sardonic eye the success of the graceful Frenchman, and wished him luck.

When it came time to adjourn to the opera, Detournelles was the one to hand Mrs. Miles into her limousine, and was graciously invited to fill the seat beside her. A few minutes later, they were seated, with the rest of the party, in the Miles section of that glittering half circle of puissance, most coveted display space in America—the horseshoe of the Metropolitan. Musky darkness about them and on the great stage; far down in the well of blackness, hot love of Egypt swept to tragedy under nodding palms.

Detournelles had a seat directly behind his hostess. Back of him, the curtains. So close the great stones of the collar that, under fugitive tendrils of hair, he could see their squared surfaces, now blue-black in the dusk of the box.

The opera came to the final intermission before the last act plumbs the depths of tragic dissonances. With Miles and the other gentlemen of the party, Detournelles left the box for the herding place of the Metropolitan's bored masculine contingent—the lounge. As he was passing the foyer, the Frenchman's quick eye leaped for an instant to a face in the crowd and then away. A most unusual and striking face it was: Dead white, under a high, white pompadour of hair, and with a thin white goatee, wire-waxed, shooting out from the heel of the chin; hollowed below the jaw sockets, and with cavernous shadows marking the position of the eyes. With all the evidences of premature age, and even decrepitude, about the features, there was indomitable spirit in the carriage of head and shoulders and the cold, searching gaze from the sunken eyes. A button of the Legion of Honor in the lapel of the black evening coat confirmed the sharp impression of the man's foreign birth.

His eyes met those of Detournelles, as they passed in the foyer; perhaps there was just an instant's swift communication in that sharp glance, but none would have been aware of it save the one for whom the glance was meant. A short smoke, and the gentlemen of the Miles party returned to the box.

When the curtain went up, Detournelles was in his chair behind Mrs. Miles, one arm thrown over the back of the hostess' chair. He had removed the white glove from his right hand.

The sweep of tragedy, with its terrible interpretation by the snarling brasses and wailing flutes, had even the blasé spectators of the horseshoe spellbound—all save Gaspard Detournelles. His eyes were not for the stage, but for the complex trickery of a jeweled collar's hasp. In the light touch of his trained fingers lay art as high as that of Massenet. The burnished surfaces of jewels, now blue, now black, winked invitation.

The final curtain dropped to the noise of a great sigh over all the house. Lights went up. There was the rustle and silken sweep of wraps gathered from near-by chairs. Detournelles, quick to serve, lifted Mrs. Miles' cloak of silk and lace from the back of her chair and threw it over her shoulders. He boggled the job, and murmured apology for his clumsiness; for he had the delicate confection of draper's art turned wrong side out; and, while Mrs. Miles laughed ripplingly at a man's ignorance, the gallant rectified his mistake. Then he stepped out of the box ahead of the others.

The gentleman with the white hair and Legion of Honor button, whom Detournelles had seen in the foyer during the final intermission, stumbled lightly against the latter's shoulder in missing a step to the level behind the boxes. For the fraction of an instant his weight was on the younger man's shoulder; then the white-haired gentleman begged pardon and passed swiftly down the alley toward the grand staircase. Detournelles turned to take

Mrs. Miles' arm. He was murmuring bits of criticism and commendation of the performance just over.

All the gold and jewels of the horseshoe were flowing in a broad stream down the staircase to the foyer, and the bedlam of the carriage starters on the curb beyond, when Mrs. Miles put a gloved hand to her throat and gave a startled cry, half-strangled gasp. The women of her party crowded close about her, questioning. Mutely she pointed to her throat, white, and unadorned.

A little swirl in the foyer, sharp questions passed over heads, hurried exit from the office of the management, press agent, and head detective. Mrs. Miles tried to hurry on to the sidewalk, shaking her head mutely at the interrogations of women crowding about her. But Edgerton Miles would not let her dodge publicity. He seized her arm and brought her up sharply.

"Look-a-here, Juliana! You can't duck home this way!" he chided. "If you've been robbed, you got to stick around a while, and give the house detectives here a description of the thing."

"No, no, Edgerton! It's nothing— nothing, I tell you!" Mrs. Miles' voice shook with nascent hysteria. "I'll explain to you when we get home. Come! The motors are waiting."

"Nothing! A fifty-thousand-dollar collar nothing? You're talking nonsense, Juliana!"

A reporter began to worm his way through the crowd. He put a question, and Mrs. Miles fled for refuge to the dressing room. The feminine contingent of her box party, all at sea, and knowing not what to do in the painful circumstances, followed her into retirement. Miles, his first surprise giving way to hot anger, began, in a loud voice, to give the opera management an appraisement both of the stolen jewels and of the double-riveted son of Sheol who had lifted them. While attendants hurried to search every inch of the Miles box with electric torches, the manager of the house, desirous of soft-pedaling so painful an incident, gently insinuated Miles and his male guests into the office. There they ranged themselves in a fidgety group, each man casting dubious glances at his neighbor, all save Miles suffering acute mortification. As for the evening's host, he raged without let.

The office door opened, and Mrs. Miles, in full possession of her chilling calm, stood there.

"Edgerton, if you'll calm yourself, and conduct our guests out to the motors, I think we need stay here no longer. I have something to say to you which will——"

"There's nothing for you to say at this time, Juliana," the husband snapped. "Take the women home, if you like, but we stay here for a while."

Mrs. Edgerton Miles was not one to make a scene to carry a point—not in public, at least. She turned to Detournelles:

"Viscount, will you be so good as to escort me to my motor?" Detournelles bowed, and stepped toward the door.

"No, you don't!" Miles jumped nimbly between his wife and his guest, facing the man with a nasty snarl on his lips. "No, you don't, Viscount Allaire! Your place is in this room with the rest of us until we clean up this little matter of the robbery."

Mrs. Miles withered her husband with a glance, and closed the door. Detournelles bowed punctiliously toward his host and stepped back to his place. A sense of strain in the green-lit office gripped every man there. It was increased when the attendants returned to report that there was no trace of the missing collar in the box, nor in the alley leading to the stairs.

"Well," Miles began, glowering from face to face of his three guests, "well,

8A P

maybe it's not the proper thing in society, and it may look sort of rough, but there's only one thing to do in a case like this, and that——"

Detournelles was the first to anticipate his meaning. With a quiet smile, he shook himself out of his evening coat, passed it to the head detective, then stood in his waistcoat, arms up, to be searched.

"M'sieur Miles is admirably direct—though quite correct," he murmured. "In this America, fifty thousand dollars excuses—all."

The detective, at a nod from Miles, perfunctorily patted Detournelles' pockets, explored the evening coat and returned it to him. The other two men were similarly treated. When the operation was finished, Miles, vaguely sensing the weight of insult he had forced upon his guests, essayed apology:

"Of course, gentlemen, I may have acted hastily, but you won't hold it against me, I hope."

"My dear M'sieur Miles," Detournelles was quick to take him up, "it is my regret that you did not find the valuable jewel on my person, and so have an end to your very natural distress."

CHAPTER III.

Falling barometer, with violent winds increasing to tornado velocity, would have been a conservative forecast of Edgerton Miles' mental weather the day following the theft of the sapphire collar. The clerks of his office staff, the pert stenographer, and even the juvenile buccaneer who held down the post of office Mercury, all sought their cyclone cellars with perfect unanimity of impulse. Miles, teetering in his swivel chair, before an accumulation of business in his letter basket which he could not bring himself to attack, reviewed a gloomy situation.

First, a fifty-thousand-dollar collar

was gone—the major gear of the whole Miles machine of social flash missing. Secondly, he was in very bad with Mrs. Miles—a more or less constantly recurring situation, but this time aggravated because he knew he had invited punishment by his boorish conduct in the Metropolitan office. His lady wife had not spoken to him since the incident, and there was every promise of an indefinite taboo on conversation between them. The capstone of woe—to throw a crumb of credit to a discreditable citizen—was the reflection that only the day before he had sent the mate to the stolen sapphire collar to a greedy bit of fluff who had made a monkey of him. The fluff had a sapphire collar and Edgerton Miles' wife had none.

The office boy tiptoed into Miles' private growling place and shoved a card under his employer's eye. Miles read the name, and grunted, "Show him in." The boy ushered into the presence Roger Boylan, of Boylan's Confidential Agency.

Now Roger Boylan was known to certain lawyers of high clientele as a detective without any frills. He had no doctor to trail him on cases and ask fool questions, nor did he carry concealed about his person a five-foot instrument for recording the blood pressure of suspects under a "third degree." He always refused to be all that hero detectives are, possibly because he wanted to succeed in his business, which was detecting. No piercing eye nor gaunt, nervous frame was Boylan's. He was well upholstered, had an apple-dumpling face, with no strong points to it whatever, dressed and looked the part of, say, the owner of a hardware store in a town of ten thousand. What he did possess unqualifiedly was a reputation for shrewd work, a reputation established with lawyers who had hired him on delicate tasks. One of these, Miles' own counsel, had recommended

Roger Boylan to Miles over the phone and arranged this meeting.

The grouchy stock manipulator acknowledged Boylan's greeting with scant courtesy and indicated a chair. He plunged to the core of the interview without preliminaries:

"Last night my wife was robbed of a sapphire dewdab worth fifty thousand dollars, between the first act and final curtain, at the Metropolitan. Can you get it back for me?"

"I never make promises," the detective answered, the wrinkles of a smile clustering about the corners of his blue eyes. "Why not tell me the circumstances, then I may be able to judge of the case."

"Well, I haven't told the police, because they'll make a brass-band parade about it," Miles grunted, "and I don't want you to raise a hullabaloo, either—no pictures of yourself or of Mrs. Miles in the papers, and all that sort of stuff. Huh?"

"Don't get me wrong, Mr. Miles," Boylan cut him off. "I may not take the case at all. It depends upon whether I think I can earn my fee. Now, if you don't mind, describe this valuable jewel. Tell me the circumstances of your visit to the Metropolitan, and just when Mrs. Miles missed her sapphires."

Miles, his bluster blunted by the other's hint of indifference, came down to essentials. He gave a description of the collar, glaringly masculine in its inadequacies, enumerated the names and social position of the box guests of the night before, so far as he was able—he knew next to nothing about his wife's friends, as a matter of fact—and recited the incident of the search in the office of the Metropolitan management.

"You saw the collar about Mrs. Miles' throat after you had taken your seat in the box?" the detective inquired.

"Sure!" Miles assented gustily.

"Did any of your guests leave the box before the end of the opera?"

"Huh? Oh, yes, the men and I went down to the lounge for a smoke before the last act."

"When you returned to the box, did you notice whether Mrs. Miles still had her collar?"

"I don't know. I guess the curtain was up when we got back, and I couldn't see."

"Who sat nearest to your wife, if you remember?"

"Why, that French viscount fellow who'd been playing poodle dog to her all evening." Miles made no attempt to hide his dislike for Detournelles, Viscount Allaire. It was the inherent dislike of a social blunderer for a polished squire of dames.

"Tell me something more about this Detournelles," Boylan was saying, when interruption, violent as it was unexpected, burst upon them. First, confusion sounding from the main office beyond the partition, a woman's shrill voice crackling with anger; then the door opened with a catapult suddenness, and a woman—a handsome and furious creature, swathed in furs—flounced into Miles' private office. The evil genius of that office nearly tipped over with his chair at the sight. With a long stride, the invader was at his desk. She slammed down upon it a pigskin jewel case with such violence that the cover jarred open, and indigo lights leaped from a sapphire collar reposing inside.

"I might have known you'd play the cheap skate, Edgerton Miles! I ought to have expected nothing better from a four-flusher like you!" Her voice rasped like a dull saw, and the look in her eyes was deadly.

"Say, look-a-here!" Miles pulled himself back to stability with hands clawing at the edge of his desk. "Who let *you* in? Didn't I tell you never to come down here? What's all this——"

"Do you want to know what this is?" The flushed vixen swept a scornful finger toward the sheaf of blue lights in the jewel case. "Well, I'll tell you, because, of course, you don't know: This is a neat bundle of paste junk—a fancy package of near-sapphires, worth just five hundred and twenty-five dollars in any department store—sign on them, 'Take me home for five hundred and twenty-five dollars.' This is Edgerton Miles' gift to a lady!"

Roger Boylan, who took a vivid interest in this little colloquy, unheeded by both, tried hard to keep his face ironed out to a neutral pattern. Developments in the Miles sapphire robbery were interesting him mightily, however. He saw a purple flush mount to Miles' neck and heavy cheeks, saw him reach out to the jewel case and lift a blue glory therefrom.

"Who told you these were phony stones?" he snapped.

"Oh, the expert up to Tiffany's; but, of course, *he* don't know anything about sapphires!" This with scorching scorn.

"So you went to get the acid test put on 'em, eh?" Miles' face was a thundercloud now.

"Considering the giver, who wouldn't?" A pretty nose was uptilted to an outrageous angle; one slim, booted foot tapped the floor in a menacing tattoo.

"Ya-ah, consider the giver!" Miles mocked, his lips trembling with rage. "Consider the duffer who separated himself from fifty thousand bucks to get a smile from a fancy yellow dandelion with a heart about as big as a two-spot in a cold deck. I guess you and I just about separate on this corner, paste sapphires or no paste sapphires! On your way!"

The vivid blond head under the fur toque wavered on a stiff neck, drooped a little. Swiftly the light of battle sped from round blue eyes, and a languishing softness filled them. Red lips trembled.

"Edgerton, I'm sorry. Perhaps you did get stung, and didn't know it. I was so wrought up——"

"Stung is right!" The man's voice was bitter. "There's a sign over that door, 'This way out'!"

Now complete surrender came, with precipitation on the side. The invader cried copiously into a tiny square of lace. Miles, unheeding, stepped to the door and held it open. One tear-splashed appeal was shot at him through wet lashes, but he was adamant. Suddenly the drooping head snapped back, and a jeweled hand shot out to the pigskin jewel box on the desk.

"I'll take these along, anyway," the lady said, with decision.

"Mistake number two!" Miles snatched up the sapphire collar before she could reach it, and grinned malevolently. "First mistake, bawling me out; second, thinking you can get away with the goods."

"Give me my property!" She stamped her foot, and made a futile snatch at the jeweled collar.

"Your property—huh! You just returned this paste junk to me."

Again tears—genuine article, and backed by whirlwind rage.

"I'll have my lawyer file suit for my property! You'll hear from this! You'll have to tell a court why you robbed me of my property! I—I——"

"File away, little Bright Eyes. Remember I've got a witness—this gentleman here. And good day!"

She was gone in a flurry of fox heads and trailing silk. Miles shut the door and turned to the detective.

"That brings up another point connected with this robbery business," he said, with a weak smile. "I guess I didn't quite explain all the details. We'll now go over and put the screws on that hound Sutton for selling me a phony sapphire collar."

Fifteen minutes later, the door of the private office of Sutton & Sutton, jewelers, closed on the senior partner, Miles, and Boylan. Miles wasted no preliminaries.

"I've come to get back that check for fifty thousand dollars I gave you yesterday," he said, cocking a cigar like a threatening bomb at the jeweler.

"Why—Mr. Miles! Nothing unsatisfactory about the collar, I hope?" Sutton's thin hands fluttered nervously.

"Nothing 'cept the sapphires are paste. Otherwise, it's a pretty little toy."

Sutton fell against the side of his desk, white as the alabastine ceiling.

"Impossible, Mr. Miles! Why, I chose every one of the fifty stones in that collar myself! I'd take my oath on it they're genuine!"

"Take another look at 'em," the broker snorted, tossing the woven chains of gems on the jeweler's desk. With a trembling hand, Sutton fumbled in a drawer for his glass, screwed it in his eye, and picked up the collar. He stepped to the window, where light was strongest, and began turning the ornament slowly under the glass. Boylan, watching him keenly, saw little beads of sweat start above the eyebrows, noted the increased trepidation of the hands.

"Paste!" The admission came with a groan. "Paris paste, every one of them—even the diamond chips!"

"Case of substitution, then?" Boylan put the question tentatively.

"Why, it must be! No other explanation!" the distraught senior partner retorted.

"Look-a-here, Sutton! Did you sell these stones to me for real, or did you know they were paste? No monkey business, now! Straight talk!" Miles launched the question truculently. Flushing to the eyes, Sutton turned upon him.

"You're insulting!" he managed to

ejaculate. "I do not run a pawnshop here!"

The detective, seeing the snarl Miles' bullheadedness was likely to entail, took a hand:

"Mr. Miles has not told me when he purchased this jeweled collar, Mr. Sutton."

"It left the shop yesterday, after it had been constructed in duplicate——" Sutton paused, eying Miles. The latter nodded his head glumly. "After it had been constructed in duplicate of one in the possession of Mrs. Miles."

"Which was stolen at the Metropolitan last night," Miles cut in. The senior partner sat down hard, his jaw falling. "Stolen?" he murmured.

"Who did the work on this duplicate collar?" Boylan continued.

"The best workman in my shop—a Flemish diamond setter I know only as Henri."

"And he had Mrs. Miles' collar to work from all the time?"

"Yes; except, of course, I kept both in the safe at night."

"Could he have had time to make fifty paste sapphires—of this Paris paste, as you call it—and set them in the duplicate collar?"

"I don't see how he could," Sutton answered the detective. "He had only six days in which to do the whole job, and he had to work at top speed to finish in that time."

"Well, couldn't he have picked up these paste stones somewhere among the trade in New York?" the detective insisted. "They're common enough."

"No, he could not have done any such thing," Sutton answered, with a slight touch of asperity. "The stones that went into the duplicate collar were matched, stone for stone, with those in Mrs. Miles' original, or as near matched as I could get them. Some were of uncommon size. Anyway, French paste is not at all common in the trade on this side of the water.

Jewelers here all go in for 'reconstructed' stones, which are quite different things."

"That lets your little lady of the furs out," Boylan said to the stock juggler. The latter, who had followed with difficulty the trend of the detective's questioning, started with an inquiring "Huh?"

"Why, if an expert diamond setter, familiar with the trade, could not duplicate the stones in Mrs. Miles' collar by paste ones in six days, Miss—er—Dandelion couldn't have taken good stones out of her sapphire collar and substituted false ones overnight." Miles slowly turned this over in his mind and nodded assent. That possibility had not occurred to him.

"I think we will have a talk with this Henri, if you please, Mr. Sutton," Boylan addressed the senior partner. The latter quickly stepped to a house telephone and spoke a few words into the transmitter. A knock sounded at the door a few minutes later. Sutton admitted the round-shouldered artisan, who stood in his ticking work apron, squinting curiously from face to face. The detective looked up at him out of his bland little eyes and addressed him softly.

"Henri, Mr. Sutton says you're a good judge of stones. We want your opinion on the value of some sapphires. Look at these"—he handed Henri the collar—"and give us your opinion on their value."

With precise movements, Henri stepped to the window, picked up the jeweler's glass, and, with it in his eye, passed the collar in review, stone by stone. After five minutes he looked up.

"Well, what is your opinion, Henri?" Boylan asked.

"Paste," the diamond setter answered succinctly.

"What kind of paste would you say?"

"Paris paste."

"You recognize this sapphire collar, do you not, Henri?"

"Yes."

"It is one you made just this week, on a rush order."

"No."

Just that monosyllable, but it straightened the backs of three men. Boylan, perilously near losing his poise, batted his cherubic eyes and bored in again:

"You tell us you didn't make this sapphire collar here in Sutton & Sutton's factory?"

"I said that," was Henri's grudging answer.

"Well, who do you suppose made it, then?"

"I don't suppose. I know!" Henri answered, squinting hard at the detective. "Franchon Frères, of Paris, made this collar, and the number is 9001."

"How do you know that?" Boylan wanted to know.

"Here is the name and number, engraved very fine on the back of the clasp," the jewel fashioner returned. "See for yourself." He passed glass and collar to the detective, who found the inscription, as Henri directed, after considerable search. Sutton was on his feet now, and must needs read the manufacturer's name, too. Miles, too bewildered for words, sat fanning himself with a ruler, looking helplessly from Boylan's face to Sutton's. The detective hesitated a minute, then put the question:

"If this isn't the sapphire collar you made, then——"

"It is the one given me to copy from," the stolid Henri finished.

"My wife wear paste sapphires! You say my wife wears phony jewels?" Miles was on his feet with a bound, his face purpling with outrage.

"I don't know you—I don't know your wife," Henri retorted, without heat. "I say this is the paste-jewel collar Mr. Sutton give me to make from it a duplicate of genuine stones."

CHAPTER IV.

For a long minute there was no further word. The sudden twist to the mystery given by Henri's declaration that the collar given him as a model—Mrs. Miles' collar—contained paste jewels left the inquisitors temporarily groping. The nimbler wits of the detective were the first to draw significant deduction from the new fact. That Mrs. Miles should be robbed of a sapphire collar on the very night of its return from the jeweler's was an interesting coincidence; that if substitution of genuine for imitation had not previously been made, the thief would have got paste jewels worth half a thousand dollars instead of real stones valued at fifty thousand, was a still more striking coincidence. Granting as true the jewel setter's assertion that the collar put into his hands to model from was the false one there on Sutton's desk, substitution could have been made in no other place than Sutton & Sutton's factory, unless——

"Mr. Miles"—he turned to the broker, who was still growling to himself over Henri's revelation—"do I understand that you took both collars away from this office at the same time, and delivered them both the same afternoon—yesterday?"

Miles nodded.

"And you did not open either or both of the cases—this pigskin one here, or the one in which you thought Mrs. Miles' collar lay—from the time you left this office until both were delivered?"

Miles answered that he did not. Boylan then turned again to Henri:

"When you had finished with the duplicate collar, what did you do with it?"

"Put it in a pigskin case—one like that," the man answered, indicating the opened casket on the desk, "and took it, along with the original, in here to Mr. Sutton."

"So you didn't make a mistake, and put the original collar, the one with the paste jewels, in this pigskin case?" Boylan pressed.

Henri's eyes blinked owlishly.

"Why should I make a mistake when the collar with the Paris paste sapphires was sitting all the time in a case with the name of the owner marked inside it—the lady's name?"

"The lady's name, eh?" Boylan seemed interested. "What was that name?"

"'Juliana Cope Miles, No. 13 East —9th, New York,'" Henri quoted glibly. "That was the inscription." The detective's eyes twinkled.

"I think, Mr. Sutton, we are through with Henri," he said to the senior partner, and the latter nodded the artificer out of the office. Miles and Sutton looked expectantly into Boylan's bright eyes.

"Well, Henri seems to have cleared himself?" Sutton ventured.

"On the contrary," the detective took him up, "Henri has proved himself one of the crowd that got away with Mrs. Miles' collar—that is, the genuine collar, which was sent by design to Mrs. Miles, in place of her paste collection."

"I don't make you," Miles cut in. "First place, I don't believe for a minute my wife would lose a fifty-thousand-dollar sapphire collar and then try to get away with it by wearing phony stuff. She's not that kind."

"Mr. Sutton, if you'll give me a little acid and a brush, I'd like to try an experiment," Boylan commanded, ignoring the broker's challenge.

The jeweler rummaged for the required articles in a desk drawer. Boylan screwed the jeweler's glass into his right eye, picked up the sapphire collar, and turned it to bring the gold back of the three-stone pendant between his fingers. Then lightly he began to touch the surface with the brush, wet in testing acid. The others watched him curiously. For several minutes the man's round head was bent to his task. Little clucking noises of satisfaction came from his lips.

"I guess that's enough," he said finally, and passed the glass and upturned pendant first to Miles, then to Sutton. What they saw, faint as hair lines against the smeared face of the gold was:

IANA C E M LES
13 E 9th N. Y.

"That should answer all doubt you have about the character of Mrs. Miles' sapphire collar." Boylan turned his boyish smile on Miles. "This was the collar Mrs. Miles gave you to bring down to Mr. Sutton to have the settings tightened. I thought from the first Henri was telling the truth about that. I was positive when he rattled off so easily the inscription, which, as you see, was on the collar, not the case, and which he was careful to blot out before he delivered the two collars to Mr. Sutton yesterday. The full name and address of a person entirely unknown to our little jewel setter would not have stuck in his memory unless he'd had reason to observe it carefully. He was so eager to prove his case that he overplayed just at that point."

"Then this Henri fella made the swap in this shop, so's one of his pals could do the lifting at the Metropolitan," Miles ruminated heavily. Boylan nodded.

"But why swap at all?" the broker continued. "So long as the gang knew Mrs. Miles' sapphires were paste, and the others real, why didn't they let the real ones go—go where I took 'em, and pinch the bunch there?"

"For one thing, Mr. Miles," the detective answered, with a words-in-one-syllable air, "the clever gang of which

Henri is a member had a name and address—the name and address of Mrs. Miles. Without question, the man selected to do the trick of lifting was somebody acquainted with your wife—the gang played in luck there. So, instead of a wild-goose chase after—er—Miss Dandelion—allowing they could trace the real gems to her, they played safe by having Henri make the substitution right here."

"Then the thief was in my box last night, after all!" Miles brought his hand down on his knee with a slap. "By gad, I searched the three men, at least, down to the bone, and didn't find a trace of that collar. As for the women——"

"I think we can discount the women in this thing," Boylan interrupted. "And you overlook the certain fact that when the collar was slipped from Mrs. Miles' neck, the thief passed it to one of his pals, either when you went down to the lounge, at the final intermission, or just as your party was leaving the box. Who was the first man you searched down in the manager's office?"

"Why, that fella Detournelles, the viscount boy! He offered himself to be searched before I got the words out of my mouth."

"What is his address?"

"I don't know, but I could get it over the phone from my wife's social secretary." Miles started for the telephone, but afterthought stopped him.

"Say, look-a-here, Boylan," he began, a sheepish grin slitting his features, "you're such a clever detective, you'll get me in a jam before I know it. Going too fast altogether, that's what you're doing. I don't want anybody arrested—don't want some geezer to get on the witness stand in his own defense and tell the wide world there's two sapphire collars, one phony—which is the wife's—and one genuine—which wasn't intended to be the wife's. Where'd I be if all that came out—me, with one

threatened suit likely to bawl me out, as it is?"

Boylan wiped away a smile with a discreet hand.

"I am not undertaking to arrest anybody, Mr. Miles, though Henri would look in his proper place behind bars. But if you'll get me the address of this Detournelles, I think it will go a long way toward restoring the stolen sapphires."

Miles turned to the telephone, and, after a brief conversation, was able to give the detective the number of Detournelles' smart lodgings in a street off Central Park West.

Sutton spoke up:

"Henri—you don't intend arresting him, then?"

"Not at all," the detective assured. "Henri thinks he's cleared himself. I wouldn't change his opinion right now, for he may come in handy."

Miles was drawing on his gloves, when his eye fell on the collar lying by the side of the pigskin case. He swept his hand toward the false glitter as he addressed the jeweler:

"Here! Keep this junk until everything's straightened out. I don't want it—not now, at least."

Boylan stayed Sutton's hand.

"I think, if you don't mind, Mr. Miles, I'll take care of this collar for a while." His eyes brightened in a shrewd afterthought. "Maybe if I can lay hands on the real stones, you wouldn't care greatly if I had to sacrifice these to do it."

"Go the limit!" Miles boomed; and, as Boylan pocketed the case with the collar in it, the broker playfully pushed him out of the door.

Parting with Miles on Maiden Lane, Boylan took his first step toward tracing the collar stolen in the horseshoe to that as yet unknown and unsuspected third person to whom it had been deftly passed by the actual thief—by Detournelles, as the detective was now reasonably certain. He walked to a telegraph office, the nearest one to the factory of Sutton & Sutton, and consequently the one which the astute Henri would naturally use were he to send a telegram, in emergency, immediately upon finishing his day's work over the bench. There he filed a despatch to "Gaspard Detournelles, No. — West Ninety-first Street," a dispatch containing only a single word, and unsigned.

"Do not forward that until after five o'clock this afternoon," Boylan instructed the clerk.

"Two chances," the round-faced little man assured himself, as he went out into the crowded street. "If our French friend thinks this telegram is from Henri, and acts accordingly, we've got him nailed as an accomplice, and the one who lifted the goods. If he thinks the other fellow—the man who's got the sapphires now—is the sender, why, all we've got to do is to stick to him, and he'll lead us to the pretty blue stones."

CHAPTER V.

On a hidden road in the heart of unknown Staten Island, where stages still ply and the hoot of owls at night breaks the silence of a desert, stands an ancient dwelling whose architecture is of the early fifties—all scrollwork and jigsaw gables over cathedral-pointed windows. Its tottering chimneys are bound to the perpendicular by heavy cables of vines; trees—which were not saplings when Lord Howe went to treat with Benjamin Franklin at Tottenville—screen the decrepit mansion from the road, wrap it in a mantle of shadow day and night. As far from the knowledge of Broadway as any lamasery in Tibet is this country house of some long-dead Manhattan aristocrat.

This was the temporary abiding place of Raoul Flack, once known to the Paris Sûreté as "The Phantom," and thought to be enduring a living death in the French penal colony of New Caledonia. How the Phantom escaped from the lime pits of a tropical hell—made a super hell by the ingenuity of guards; what the incidents of his flight from one spice island to another, through all the Dutch archipelago, of his burrowing into oblivion in the broad expanse of America, and his summoning, through the devious channels of the underworld, the remnant of his old band of l'Incomparables—trite Parisian police cognomen—this is a story which some day may be written. This will be the narrative of a man whose body has been well-nigh broken by society, but whose intellect, sharpened by suffering almost to the absolute of mathematical logic, is dedicated to a single object— the compassing of revenge upon society for five years of torture.

The Phantom had but recently come to make his abode—alone, save for the service of a doddering old housekeeper —in the house on the wilderness road. His appearance at the Metropolitan on the night Mrs. Miles' sapphire collar disappeared had been his first venture abroad; nor would he have dared that had not necessity compelled.

A worm of lights, which was the New York train bound to the end of the island, crawled to a stop at the packing-box station that lay a mile below the Phantom's house on the bayward sweep of the highlands. Detournelles, Viscount Allaire, was the only passenger to step onto the dark platform; but just as the train began to get under way again, a blotch of shadow detached itself from the last car's rear platform, dropped to the tracks, and there crouched in darkness until the hollow footsteps on boards changed to the noise of feet on a frosted turf. Detournelles paused to light a cigar, cast a cautious look behind him, and, seeing nothing but the shadow block of the station, swung into a sharp stride up the road. The noise of his own boots on the road, flinty, and resounding under the amalgam of frost, drowned that other almost inaudible rustle and whisper of broken weeds that kept pace for pace with his stride, behind him in the pitchy maw of the forested thoroughfare. Had he looked back, Detournelles would have seen nothing but the far-off twin sparks of the Highlands Lights and the two walls of the cloven forest that marched with him up the hill. Impalpable as the breath of fog off the marsh by the sea's edge was the trailing shadow.

It was nine o'clock, and the Phantom, seated in the grudging circle of light that fell from an inverted green shade of a student lamp, was engaged in an absorbing task. His back to the only two windows through which unlikely spying could be done, before him the blue-and-gold resplendence of the stolen collar, the master of the Incomparables was absorbed in an appraisement of the jewel, stone by stone. Pencil and paper lay to hand on the table; a strong reading glass was brought to bear on each blue blot in the gold filigree, and the column of estimated values grew with every lowering of the glass. The face of the man, white and cold as the face of one dead, was set in lines of complete absorption.

A knock sounded hollowly. The Phantom leaped to his feet and snatched a black automatic from the hollow of his armchair. Three other knocks came, accurately spaced. He dropped the collar in a pocket of his smoking gown, went to the front door, and admitted Detournelles. Their hands clasped.

"You see, I have come," the younger man said. The other led the way back to the lighted library, without speech. There he turned and challenged with one word:

"Why?"

Surprise registered on the face of the visitor. His eyebrows lifted in puzzled inquiry.

"Your telegram," he answered.

"I have sent no telegram," the Phantom denied, with a flash of impatience. "Telegrams for all the world to read? Bah!" Detournelles reached to his breast pocket, brought out a yellow telegraph form, spread it on the table, and pointed to the typewritten message. There was his name and address, and, below, the single word, "Come." No signature.

"What time did you receive this?" the Phantom demanded.

"It was waiting for me at my rooms, when I returned, at six o'clock this evening," Detournelles answered. He looked closely at the form, studying the lines of hieroglyphics representing the company's receiving frank and station number. "See! This says five-fifteen! That would be after Henri's working hours—when he was able to leave his office. Before five o'clock he could not send a telegram. He would not telegraph, except in necessity. Foolishly, I jumped at the first impulse, and came here, believing you called me."

"If they suspected Henri——" the Phantom began.

"He would not dare telegraph me if there was danger of the telegram being traced, if he was under suspicion."

"Yet, why the telegram?"

"Something we must know, Maître Raoul—that he wishes to tell us at once. You he cannot reach by telegraph. Only through me can Henri get word to you. This message, now, would it not include you as well as myself?" The white-headed one honed his hollow cheek in thought.

"If it were a trick—some detective's work—would he not have signed the name, 'Henri,' or appointed some rendezvous? Assuredly. He would set a trap by naming the hour and place of meeting. You were not followed tonight?"

Detournelles laughed shortly.

"If one followed me, he had a hard time of it. Two taxis and the elevated train between my lodgings and the ferry." The Phantom bent his head in thought for a minute. Then:

"I will accompany you to Henri. It is safe, and may be necessary."

Before he stripped off his smoking gown, he took the jeweled collar from the pocket and laid it on the table. Detournelles pounced upon it eagerly, held it stretched between his fingers, and lovingly fondled with his gaze each soft spot of royal color.

"Yes, a good haul—a very good haul," the Phantom commented, as he slipped his arms into jacket sleeves and next buried himself in the lapping folds of a heavy fur coat. "Come! We will put the little beauty away for the night."

He took the collar, crossed the room to where a heavy bust of Demosthenes looked down with sightless eyes from the high top of a bookcase. The Phantom gripped the bust with one hand while with the other he put torsion on the crown of the head. The plaster skull of the ancient worthy unscrewed just above the fillet binding his brows, and the collar disappeared into a hollow brainpan.

The Phantom was screwing back into place the detached headpiece, when his hand hesitated by ever so little. A sound came to his ears, a sound so faint that Detournelles gave no heed to it. It was the faint scratching of a branch against the glass of one of three windows looking out from the room upon the clotted shapes of trees standing in guarding ranks about the ancient mansion. Just that thin noise of tender wood against a pane, as if a heavy wind were sweeping a bough tip up against the glass. Yet the Phantom knew the night was quiet. There was no wind.

He did not turn his head toward the windows, nor betray by any gesture the germ of suspicion that the squeaking branch had planted. Instead, he carelessly pocketed the automatic he had left lying in a hollow of the armchair, blew out the lamp, and, hand on Detournelles' arm, piloted him to the front door. He closed it with a resounding bang, which threw on a spring lock, and walked with his companion through the jungle of small plants to the gate.

"Do not look around," he cautioned, in a low voice, as they passed out onto the road. "Do not even change your pace. At this first heavy cluster of trees I will leave you and turn back. Continue on to the railroad station alone. No, no! I do not need you! It may be nothing. I will explain later—if need be. Now, au revoir."

The room so lately quitted by the two suddenly was shot through with a chill rush of night air. There was a faint creak of rusty sash pulleys as one of the three windows slowly lifted. A blocky figure, hardly to be distinguished from the surrounding shadow of leaves, slipped from a stout oak branch—to which it had clung—onto the window sill, and thence noiselessly down to the carpeted floor. A faint click, and a round white eye sprang into being. The eye groped and groped about the walls until it looked straight into the dead eyes of Demosthenes on his high perch. An invisible hand brought the bust down; there was a dry, scraping noise as the attic orator's head was halved. The white eye rested for an instant on the blue glory of jewels lifted from the plaster well——

Bang! A vivid red stab of flame from the raised window. Clatter of falling shards of plaster, the trash of a shattered Demosthenes.

Out flicked the white eye. A thump of a heavy body dropping to the floor. A second lighter thud over by the opened window, as of some one lightly vaulting from sill to floor. Then silence.

For a full minute, this silence in the black room, menacing, terrible. Then, from nowhere, a voice strongly accented with the French twist, but dry as rustling leaves:

"You—M'sieur Detective, I have you, of course. You cannot leave this house excépt by the window—through which you came, and I followed. To kill you will be inconvenient; for you to kill me, next to impossible. You follow?"

Roger Boylan, face down on the floor, was too wise to betray his whereabouts by an answer. His eyes roved the darkness, straining, straining——

A chopped laugh sounded.

"It is interesting, yes. But for the noise of the branch against the glass, my dear M'sieur Detective, my folly in leaving curtains up in this so desolate place would have cost me the jewels. Is it not so?"

Boylan's revolver, slowly creeping out of his pocket, struck a button on his jacket. The click sounded loud as the explosion of a thirty-two-centimeter gun.

Bang! A bullet threw lint from the carpet into Boylan's eyes. Swift patter of feet followed.

"I said to kill you would be inconvenient." The disembodied voice was studiously cold. "Do you not accept hints?"

To the detective, glued to the floor, the hopelessness of the situation in this strangling dark was overwhelmingly apparent. To attempt a duel with a man familiar with the big room, its several ambushes and screens of furniture, would be to invite sudden death. Yet to escape with that precious bundle of hard points pressing against his chest was——"

"M'sieur, my ultimatum!" Again that dry, crackling voice. "Crawl to the table—*vraiment*, you are on your knees —do I not know it? Deposit there

your flash light, with the light showing. Deposit in that light the jewels you took from the plaster head, also your weapon; then go out by the window unharmed."

No move by the detective. A chuckle from the darkness.

"Until you make a light, M'sieur Detective, you cannot see my guarantee of honorable intentions. My weapon, two chambers exploded, as you know, will be on the table. If it is not—mark your course accordingly."

Boylan began to hitch himself along the floor, groping with his revolver tip in the dark ahead. The barrel struck a wooden table leg with a sharp rap. The groping figure cautiously raised itself, and, holding the flash light at arm's length, reached up and settled it on the table top. A finger pressed on the light, which went streaming, like some spilled incandescent liquid, across the red cloth cover.

"Now the sapphire collar, dear friend," came instructions from the dark.

With a crisp rustle and click of gold filaments, a glittering heap of yellow and royal blue color spilled under the light and lay sprawling there—an evil toy to incite covetousness, to inspire murder, even.

"A-ha! Now, perfect guarantee of your good faith—your weapon."

Very slowly the blue barrel of Boylan's gun crept into the zone of light. The fingers, reluctantly unclasping from the butt, one by one, seemed alive with caution. Hardly had they loosed the stock when from out of the dark a blunt, ugly automatic clattered down into the plane of radiance, rolled over once, and brought up against the heaped jewels.

"Perfect neutrality, my friend!" The laugh that sounded in Boylan's ears was stripped of all quality save only vitriolic cynicism. "Now the arm of the law departs via the window, with my hope for future rencontre, which—ah—may we say is mutual?"

"Mutual is right," grunted Boylan, breaking silence for the first time in ten minutes which were centuries; and he went out of the window.

On the following night, Edgerton Miles returned from the office to his home with a fine glow about his heart and a sapphire collar in his overcoat pocket. He stood not upon the *status quo ante* of strained relations, but breezed into his wife's boudoir, surprising her in the midst of her dinner toilet. With all the skipping grace of a trained bear, he stepped behind the chair where she was seated before her dressing table, brushed aside the maid who was arranging her hair, and with both hands drew the gorgeous strands of peacock tints about his wife's throat.

"Huh! How about it?" he roared, as he essayed a kiss on the chaste brow.

"I hope you haven't been to any trouble, Edgerton, in getting these paste things back," came the chilling rejoinder. "If you had only listened to reason at the opera, the other night, I could have told you there was no great loss. The real collar is in the safe-deposit box." Miles pursed his lips, and his eyes went wide with surprise. "I haven't worn it once since I picked up this very creditable imitation in Paris, three years ago."

Edgerton Miles tiptoed from Mrs. Miles' boudoir, hastened downstairs to the cellarette, and poured himself four fingers of finest Bourbon.

"Here's to what some of us didn't know—and what some of us don't know yet!" he toasted himself in the panel mirror.

Which cryptic remark might have been taken to cover certain facts. Item:

That the sapphire collar he had just clasped about Mrs. Miles' white throat was the genuine one, worth fifty thousand dollars, which Detective Roger Boylan had brought away from the house of the Phantom, leaving in its stead Mrs. Miles' own imitation stones of Paris paste.

That, through the intervention of some wonderfully astute criminals, a sapphire collar, worth fifty thousand dollars, and designed for a perfectly unworthy, and now quite discredited, Miss Dandelion, was now in the possession of Edgerton Miles' lady wife—a duplicate, but genuine, of another such in her safe-deposit box.

That—and this was the most important fact of the three—the aforesaid lady wife would never know she possessed one hundred thousand dollars' worth of sapphires.

The next story in this series—entitled "His Master's Voice"—will appear in the November 20th POPULAR.

ALWAYS GETTING BETTER

WILLIAM JENNINGS BRYAN had outdone himself in a Chautauqua speech in a Western town. Even the oratory which had won him his first presidential nomination in Chicago had not been more brilliant than what he had just said. His audience was still electrified, loath to leave the meeting place.

"My!" exclaimed one admiring woman. "Bryan is such a wonderful man. He is the true orator, because, as he grows older, he becomes more eloquent—and his facundity is greater."

"Yes," agreed the pale little woman beside her; "he *is* taking on flesh."

A Cheerful Giver

By Henry Rucker

Some people like the story with a "kick." Here's one with three of them. A yarn about a locomotive fireman who wanted to do a good turn to his fellows

I WISH to state thus early in the tragedy that I've got a new job in a line I enjoy, and that I am making forty large, wrinkled dollars a week. Next month I'll be drawing down fifty, and the prospects are lovely for a man who has recently dropped a coal shovel.

These statistics are shoved in here to keep you from feeling sorry for me, because if you don't know how well I'm doing now, you are liable to leave off in the middle of this and sob yourself sick. And, remember, too, that the old job only paid me fifty dollars a month, so you can see where I'm going financially.

Up to some time ago I held that fifty-dollar-a-month job, which was nothing more or less than firing locomotives on the Pomona & Western Railroad, with headquarters in Pomona. During that fevered period I was twenty-three years old, and burdened with the thoughtful intellect you will find among the lower orders of the sand dabs. It was my first job on the coal box of a locomotive, and you can consider yourself at liberty to tell all your friends it will be my last.

The boys on the P. & W. were a congenial, good-natured lot, and I horned into their councils from the beginning. Whenever a social affair was organized in Pomona, Marty Lee had a finger in the pie, and if there was a punch bowl, I was the general manager, with full authority to clean up what punch the guests left unnoticed in the bottom.

There was one thing needed in Pomona at the time. The railway branch of the Y. M. C. A. was growing rapidly, but the boys had no regular home, and what we wanted was a red brick building, with running water and flowerpots. So, some months before the divorce between me and the railroad business, we started to erect the Railroad Men's Y. M. C. A., and everybody was glad.

Like most sensible railroads, the Pomona & Western was pleased to have its employees belong to the Y. M. C. A. There is a reason for that. If a man leans toward Y. M. C. A. customs, and follows what he hears, he isn't so liable to fill his hide full of rum, and try to do something humorous with a loaded passenger train.

Maybe you believe there never was such a thing as a stewed engineer. There are none now, and have been none for many years, but there used to be—long ago. I know. I fired one night on a passenger run between San Pasquale and Pomona with an engineer, now out of the service, who didn't know whether he was running a locomotive or a rowboat. And if you want to be entirely free from the languor of monotony, just try firing a fast train with a pickled gent at the throttle. I have gray hairs clean down my spine that date back to that feverish night.

Well, we started out cheerfully to build the new Y. M. C. A. building, and the townspeople gave us kind words and dollars.

The people of Pomona were generous, but the place is neither a large town nor a wealthy one, and soon we began to see that we were going to run out of citizens and money. Thereupon we went after the big bugs, and, between firing locomotives and trying to collect for the building fund, we stokers were about as busy as the worm-hole borer in an antique-furniture factory.

There was a committee, composed exclusively of firemen, and headed by Alvin Monroe, who was made chairman because he weighs three hundred pounds, and looks like a chairman. I was an active member of that committee. Looking back, I can see that when you called me an active member, you told no lie.

Well, we invented a system which made the contributions more interesting than just writing out a check for the Y. M. C. A. We fixed it up so that the wealthy people of the town issued their contributions in the form of prize checks, and these prizes were hung up for the winners of various competitions, in which the Pomona & Western firemen took part. In other words, we made a game out of it. The result was the same, and in the meantime we kept up interest in the new and moral structure, and brightened the Saturday afternoons for the populace.

We had a five-mile race, the prize being a five-hundred-dollar check, put up by Joe Salisbury, the automobile man, and Rufus Collins won that from a field of about nine firemen. He turned it into the fund, with name attached in honorable mention. Three thousand Pomonans saw that race and cheered the winner. I will state that I was in that contest part of the way, and when I quit you could have hung your overcoat on my tongue. No more road races for Marty Lee. I don't mind five fast miles on a good locomotive, but not on your crotched end.

Martin & Co. came across with a four-hundred-dollar check, and we had a pole vault for that, won by Joe Hackett, he out-pole-vaulting the rest of us by several feet, the reason being that Joe weighs all of ninety pounds in his winter underwear.

Henry Forrester donated a five-hundred-dollar prize for the best hurdler, and Ward Snaiger hurdled himself into prominence. Luke Underhill won another five hundred by throwing a baseball farther than any other coal shoveler on the road, and Luke would also have won, had the contest been for throwing the bull. Any time it's throwing, Luke wins.

So things progressed, and the building fund mounted apace, as you might say. Somebody would offer a new donation to the fund, and the firemen would cheerily go out and compete, whether they felt like it or not. It made the act of giving away money less painful for the gents behind the fountain pens, and I do believe our competitive system loosened up a number of citizens who otherwise would have remained in close juxtaposition to their dough.

In the course of time, we used up most of our prominent and cash-bearing citizens, and our eyes turned toward Simeon Means, who was then, and is yet, King of the Crabs. I have not mentioned Simeon, but I will now state that he was the official town tightwad, and, while I have come across a good many close-fisted and penurious male objects, I have never yet found the equal of Simeon Means. He was the world's champion miser and dollar pincher, and he was skin-tight. I would say offhand he was so tight that when he winked, both his kneecaps moved about an inch.

Every town has its Simeon Means, and he usually looks and acts about the same, whether in Sawtelle Falls or Herkimer, New York. Our Simeon was medium in height, and lean all over.

He looked like what you would expect a mean, penurious man to look like. His face was thin, sour, and wrinkled up with a brownish parchment which, in other people, would be skin. His cheek bones protruded, and his eyes squinted. His legs were long, carelessly mated, and formed the largest part of him. He walked with the quick, nervous stride of a man desirous of quitting the company of a sniffing dog. And if the old wretch owned the Rocky Mountains, he wouldn't give you a free stone bruise.

He foreclosed mortgages whenever he saw one open, and if he failed to commit usury before three o'clock each afternoon, he felt that the day was wasted. A surgical operation might have detached him from a dollar, but he would have charged the surgeon two bucks for experimental services. He had his business headquarters in Pomona's proudest commercial block, and there he sat, day by day, in a second-hand chair, training the dollars so that they would roll into his safe and play dead. You could borrow money from him, but you paid a high rate of interest, and you *did* pay. If you failed, he had it in writing that you left your right leg until the debt was canceled. That, roughly, is the kind of man Simeon Means was.

Well, the Pomona local took to considering Simeon as a possible source of supply, and the ways and means committee, which I graced with my presence, determined to stick the needle into him and see what happened. As I said, Alvin Monroe was the chairman, and, besides myself, there was Barry Mulloy, Otto Mohler, and Rufus Collins, all firemen, and all expert committeemen.

"That old reptile," said Rufus, when we were discussing the situation, "has got money, and lots of it. He made it here in Pomona, every penny. First he sold worthless land to the railroad,

and then he put up those collapsible houses and rented them to us helpless railroaders. Every time we pay a gas or water bill, we put money into his pocket. For years we have been working and turning over part of our income to him, and now it's time for him to do us a favor. I say we ought to walk right into his office."

"Yes," growled Otto, with the innate pessimism of his race, "and let's leave the door open, because we'll be walking right out again. We won't stay in long. That old skunk wouldn't give a dime to watch a nihilist chase the czar up Main Street. Any time it comes to giving away money, Mr. Means is under the chloroform cone."

"All right," I put in hopefully, "but we've got to try."

"And," said Alvin Monroe, "we'll start off with fair words. If we can't induce him with polite conversation, we'll stow away our inducer and give him the rough work."

That being settled, several of the committee took occasion to drop in for a formal call at Mr. Means' office. He welcomed the four of us as though we were smallpox germs.

At this point I had better explain. I was, of course, a member of the committee, but I should have taken that morning off. The night before, I had attended a large and illuminated party, and so interesting were the various events that I wholly neglected to go to bed. About breakfast time I began to feel miserable, so I sneaked into Joe's Place and conciliated my outraged system with three life-savers. Foolish? Sure. But I'm writing now about the time when I was foolish, and cheerfully admit it.

When I joined my solemn-minded committee for the call on Mr. Means, my breath must have smelled like the lot where the circus was yesterday. You could probably have propped up a heavy automobile on my breath, that summer morn, and removed both hind wheels. But nobody paid any attention to me, and I blew into Means' office behind the others.

"Mr. Means," Alvin began, standing near the door, and surrounded by the rest of us, all in uneasy attitudes. "We are the ways and means committee for the Y. M. C. A. building fund. As you know, we are going to erect a building which will be a credit to Pomona and the railroad men, and I feel sure you will not permit this opportunity for doing a fine thing to pass you by."

Our host twisted in his chair and looked at the committee with an icy smile.

"Humph!" he snorted. "I suppose you think you can hold me up, eh?"

"Humph!" Alvin humphed right back at him. "We don't think anything of the kind. We are not in the holdup business, Mr. Means. We are respectable firemen, and we represent the railroad men of Pomona. I am chairman of the ways and means committee, and as such——"

"And you want my money," Simeon snapped, with the cheerful manner of an angry turtle. "You have decided to come sneaking around and see whether you can squeeze old Simeon Means, hey?"

"No," Alvin went on, restraining himself from a violent outbreak. "You don't get us right, and, besides, you are using bad words. We are talking to you politely, and you are trying to insult us. The business men of Pomona, as you are aware, have contributed generously to the new Y. M. C. A. building, because they realize it is a laudable enterprise, which will result in the good of all. The town will profit, and up to this time you are the only citizen of importance who has not contributed."

"And suppose I refuse to be held up?" Simeon demanded, squinting at us. "Suppose I won't be gouged or bullied by a lot of——"

9A P

He went on for a minute, using nothing but offensive words.

I had been hovering about the outskirts of our timid group, examining with some interest a flock of exploding stars, which will sometimes appear in the human eye on the morning after, and I had been paying but little attention to Simeon Means. My reflections had solely to do with whether or not another shot of rum would cheer me up a little—and then, suddenly, it occurred to me that this man was treating us with scant courtesy. I suddenly came to life, brushed the flying comets from my vision, and entered the discussion without preliminaries. Pushing Alvin Monroe to one side, I strode over to Simeon Means' desk, where I could look him in the eye and breathe on him. And right there, as I look back, was where S. Means must have learned about my convivial habits. I thought nothing of it at the time, but I see now my breath was a give-away.

"All right," I said to Mr. Means. "We've been nice and kind with you, old man, but it seems you have to handle tar in a tarry and rough manner. We came over to see you about getting five hundred dollars for the building fund, and we're going to get it. You are the town miser, and your name is a hissing in people's mouths. You have stung and cheated everybody in Pomona, including the widows and orphans, and if you got what was coming to you rightly, some telegraph pole around here would be holding up more than wires. Your money comes from us railroad men, and five hundred dollars is a joke to you, compared with the monthly loot you take away from us. If you don't come across with this donation, we'll take off your hide and hang it on the fence for little boys to write remarks on. You are already unpopular, you old scorpion, but you are going to be more unpopular. Do you get all this?"

You would think, after that general statement of personal views, the time had arrived in my affairs when I would be thrown out bodily by the office force. But no! Mr. Means leaned back in his chair and actually sniggered. My remarks seemed to hit him on the funny bone, and for the first time in man's memory, Simeon Means broke into a series of facial contortions that passed with him as laughter. He continued to look at me. He even leaned a little closer to me, and I tried to hold in my breath, knowing that my bark was, at the moment, a heap worse than my bite.

"Well, boys," he said, after a time, "I suppose you saw your duty, and you did it. You came up here and asked me for my money. You did what you could to gouge me, and now it's about time for you to go away and stop littering up the office. I'm not mad, because I regard firemen as people you have to be tolerant with, the same as young children and idiots. You haven't much intelligence, or you wouldn't be firemen. And, furthermore, I regard the rest of this railroad outfit as a gang of petty grafters. So you can toddle along to the man who gave you the candy to do this, and tell him that S. Means refuses to be bled. Mind the flowerpot on your way out."

We stumbled out into the clear light of day in a dreary silence, after I had added a couple of useless insults to my previous statements, neither of which caused Mr. Means anything but mild amusement. Otto Mohler enlivened the walk back to the roundhouse by reminding us that he had told us so, seeming to derive some comfort from the thought.

For three days Alvin Monroe and the rest of us spent the time in an effort to convince the people of Pomona that Simeon Means should be driven from our midst. What we said about that old varmint would burn holes in a stove lid, yet he went along without giving a sign of suffering. On the fourth day I walked up the street from the yards, with my dinner pail on my arm, and I ran into Simeon Means. It was too late to cross the road, and the little man stopped me.

"Hello!" he said, just as though I hadn't called him anything on our previous meeting. "Do you suppose you could bring your committee around to my office this afternoon?"

"What for?" I demanded.

"I think I can give you some good news."

"You mean——"

"Never mind what I mean. You bring the committee."

He walked away, leaving me to wonder whether he intended to play some new game on us when we got there. I told the gang about it, and in the afternoon the four of us returned, ready for anything, including arrest for defamation of character.

Well, Simeon met us at the door, and I saw at once that he was a changed man. He walked around and shook hands with us all, and then addressed most of his remarks to me, although Alvin Monroe was the chairman.

"Sit down, boys," he began. "I presume you can guess why I've sent for you?"

"No," Alvin answered, "we can't."

"I have decided," Simeon said to me, "to accede to your request about the contribution. I am going to join the other donors to the Y. M. C. A. fund."

"That's mighty nice of you, Mr. Means," I answered, somewhat stunned, because it wasn't what I expected.

"I know that Pomona regards me as a heartless old villain, without a spark of generosity, and I want to show my townspeople that I am as liberal as any one. When you came here before, I was opposed to your enterprise, but I have investigated, and I find that it will be a good thing for the town. So I am going to help."

"The usual five hundred dollars?" I asked encouragingly.

"No," replied Simeon, "I am going to make it a thousand dollars."

Rufus Collins, who had been prowling about uneasily, walked into a door. I suppressed my own feelings, and Otto Mohler opened his mouth in Teutonic unbelief, and kept it open during the rest of the interview.

"Yes," went on the liberal giver, "I feel like being top man in this case. I believe one thousand dollars will be the largest sum contributed, will it not?"

"It will be," I said, "when you hand us your check for one thousand dollars. Until now, six hundred dollars leads."

"What kind of contests have you had so far?" he demanded.

I told him. We had had several ordinary foot races, a pole vault, ball-throwing exhibitions, greased-pole climbs, hurdle races, and jumping contests.

"Well," he said, coming over with the little, brown check, which said one thousand dollars on it, and placing it in my hand, "I've been giving the subject of contests some thought, and I have decided on something new. Races and jumping are all right, but they have nothing to do with firing locomotives. They're outside your profession, which is the care and operation of engines. I've thought up an original contest, and it's logical, because it is part of your daily work."

"What is it?" I asked.

Then he outlined his contest, and I will state, with due admiration for the little runt, it was a bird.

Maybe you don't know anything about railway roundhouses, so I'll tell you. A roundhouse is where the locomotives rest up between runs. It is a sort of locomotive livery stable, with a number of tracks leading in from the turntable, which is located out in the yard. The tracks spread fanwise from the turntable. When an engine comes in from its daily schedule, the engineer gets down and feels around for hot boxes and general trouble, after which he takes a chew of tobacco, and tells his fireman to run her into the house. His work for the day is ended. The fireman finishes up the chores.

He sneaks the locomotive onto the turntable, and a couple of greasy yard men in dirty overalls grab the handle and push him and his engine around, until the pilot points to his regular house track. Then he nudges the engine gently into the house, until the stack is under a smoke hood, whereupon he climbs down and asks the wipers how they feel to-day.

That's all. And it is a matter of vast pride with all decent firemen to be able to drive a locomotive onto a turntable and stop in the exact center, so that the weight balances on the turning pin. One man can shove the table and engine around with a fifty-ton load, if the engine is balanced exactly; but forty men can't budge it if the locomotive weight is on one end. You can figure that out for yourself. Some firemen get so expert that they can hit the exact center almost every time, which means stopping in the space of an inch or two.

Well, Simeon Means wasn't so desperately ignorant of the ways of firemen as you might think. Here's what he doped out for a unique contest, the winner to grab off the thousand-dollar check, and have his name associated with it in the building fund. You know these lanterns switchmen use? They're like the kind you keep down cellar, only heavier, with thicker glass. Simeon's contest was a lantern-smashing exhibition, for firemen only, using locomotives as projectiles.

The lanterns were to hang from nails

inside the roundhouse wall, suspended several inches above the track, and each lantern was to be set exactly between the rails. The contestants were to get up there and drive their engines in from the yard, and, with the steel-shod tip of the pilot, smash the lantern glass, without striking the wall. Get all that? Quite a contest, wasn't it?

You see, to win this, you would have to drive in slowly and stop—Bang! You had only one trial, and the chances were you'd stop short on account of fearing to hit the brick wall. In other words, it was like stopping on the turntable, but with a little added risk.

"That," affirmed Simeon, when he had finished explaining, "is a game calling for skill, nerve, and coördination between brain and hand. The fireman who wins it will be known henceforth to his fellow workers as a cool, capable person, who can handle an engine under delicate conditions."

"Delicate is right," I said to Simeon. "When do you want this to take place?"

"To-day is Thursday. Make it Saturday afternoon."

We let it go at that. I folded Simeon's check into a compact wad and pinned it in my pocket against sudden accidents. We departed, making pretty speeches, and I felt ashamed of my former roughness.

Saturday morning, Simeon Means sent word he wanted to see me personally, and I went around to his office. He began calling me Marty immediately, and it appeared that he liked me.

"I want you to win this contest, Marty," he said, "and I'm going to help you do it. And, just between us, I'm going to slip you a hundred dollars for yourself, if you do win."

"I'm a new fireman," I told him, "but I can run an engine better than most of the boys. Maybe I will win."

"Sure you will," he continued, "if you take my advice. There's one mistake

they will all make. They'll see the lantern hanging there on the wall, and they'll stop their engines too short. They won't hit the lanterns at all, because that's human nature. And you want to be sure to hit your lantern, Marty. You want to make certain you don't stop too short."

And right about then Mr. Means bought me a drink. I mean, he went over to a concealed cupboard and brought to light as nifty a private bar as ever I saw. It had a number of bottles and materials for making mixed concoctions. I brewed myself a fair-sized shot, and put it away, and Simeon talked on. In fact, he continued to talk for a long time, punctuating his remarks by pointing out the desirability of having one while the having was good.

I went to lunch with him, and we frolicked around together like a couple of pals until the middle of the afternoon, and along toward competition time I was pretty thoroughly embalmed. And at intervals Simeon impressed on me the need of hitting the lantern, and not stopping short of it.

"If there's one thing in this world you don't need to worry about," I told him, about the ninth drink, "it's whether I hit that lantern of mine. I'll hit it, all right."

That was my principal thought at two o'clock in the afternoon, when I wandered through the yard, looking for the old mogul I had been firing all these weeks. Engineers and firemen were scattered about, in the roundhouse and out among the tracks, and a couple of wipers had hung up the lanterns. It is needless to state that the officials of the line did not know we were about to play one-old-cat with their roundhouse.

Most of the engines that should have been steaming peacefully under their smoke hoods were sliding up and down the yards, and various firemen were practicing quick stops. Rufus Collins was the first contestant, and he drove in slowly, approached his lantern, and stopped six inches too short. I saw Simeon Means just once that afternoon, and he was moving rapidly toward the street that ran outside the railroad property.

Apparently nobody noticed that I had no right to be fooling with the throttle of a grown-up engine. It occurred to me that I was going to see two lanterns when I drove in, because I was seeing two of everything, including two roundhouses and two locomotives, both numbered 139. I remembered what Simeon had said about not stopping too short, and when I climbed up into the cab, it was my firm intention to avoid stopping before I had hit the lantern, or lanterns.

Somebody called out my name, and I opened my eyes with a start, grabbed the throttle, and started to smash my lantern. About halfway in, I heard a confused shouting, and I noticed men running in various directions. I saw the wall ahead, but no lantern, though I knew where it must be, and presently I realized that I was driving my mogul too fast for the short distance to be covered—say about nineteen times too fast.

All I remember was a loud crash. The end of my engine hit the lantern all right, and that wasn't all. We went right on through the wall, bringing down part of the roof. I shut off steam in a cloud of falling mortar, bricks, girders, chimneys, smoke hoods, and window glass, and found myself in the clear light of day, having passed clean through the roundhouse, and smashed into a passenger coach on the other side. A piece of flying brick caught me over the nose, and about then I decided that I had made a mistake, and might as well go quietly away somewhere and think it all over.

I didn't learn anything more about the main facts that day, because I was principally elsewhere; but the next day I came back to earth, and met the deluge. To begin with, that lantern competition ended abruptly with my effort. Nobody felt like going on with it, and the railroad officials began galloping around in circles. I have never yet been torn limb from limb, and that is only because nobody could find me that afternoon.

Well, I discovered that I had lost all my friends. I had also, it appeared, dragged the Y. M. C. A. into the bog of disrepute, and automatically that organization ceased to have anything to do with me. I was fired off the roster for conduct unbecoming a member, and I deserved to be. Furthermore, the Pomona & Western Railroad decided that it could struggle along without the services of a fireman who gave himself over to battering down roundhouses. Seven engineers were suspended, and nine stokers were up on the carpet for investigation. Everybody who had a hand in the competition was officially censured, but the only one who lost his job was Marty Lee.

And when you figure it out in cold blood, I had it coming. Of course, old man Means shouldn't have led me into temptation and filled me full of rum. That was wrong; but still, it was all up to me. Simeon provided the libations, to be sure, but he didn't force them on me. Remember that. It was all my own fault, and, just to get it into the records, I have never touched liquor since that day of competition and wreckage.

I looked up Simeon Means as soon as things quieted down, intending to give him a reproachful call, but he was out of town, and by and by it occurred to me that I might as well go and be out of town myself. Pomona was no longer a lovely village of the plain. Everybody hated me because I had got a lot of people into trouble, and every time I met a member of the Y. M. C. A. he looked at me as though I had murdered his mother. The division superintendent wrote me a letter, in which he called me a debauchee, and, after looking up what debauchee meant, I decided that a new start in life was necessary. In Pomona, I was all through. My railroad career was finished, and less than a week after the excitement, I started west, alone, unwept and unsung; also, a stern and unyielding member of the prohibition party.

Anyway, I never was intended by nature to be a railroad fireman. I thought a lot of earnest reflections on the way to the coast, and when I reached Los Angeles I had just about determined that the serious time in my life had arrived. Up to now, life had been more or less of a joke. Now it certainly had ceased to be a joke, because I was nearly out of money, and the first necessity was a brand-new job.

I read an advertisement in a newspaper about a week later, and it went on to say that one thousand active men were needed to be the mob in a picture of Babylonian days. You know, Los Angeles is the home of moving pictures. Such citizens as got the jobs would be paid a dollar and a half a day.

"All right," I said to myself. "Let's go and get a job."

The next morning I rode twenty miles on a street car, and later on battled with several hundred infuriated mobites who wanted that one-fifty a day, and wanted it bad enough to commit several minor crimes.

After a while I fought my way into the place, where a man was giving out jobs, and I got mine. I suppose I must have been peculiarly adapted by nature for the place, because the man took one look at me, and then handed me a lot of confused instructions, a pair of scarlet pants, one tin helmet with a

brass cupola on it, and a sleeveless shirt, trimmed with brass.

"You go on over there and dress," said the man. "We're going to have a rehearsal at noon."

He waved his hand in the general direction of a brick wall, and when I got there, I found a row of wire animal wagons and scenery, but no place where a gentleman could change his clothes. There is a certain lack of privacy about a wire animal wagon, if you have ever seen one, so I tagged along undecided, with forty or fifty other wondering souls, all carrying ancient Roman articles of clothing and worried expressions.

Pretty soon I concluded that my gang of helmet carriers and pants bearers didn't know any more about where they were going than a horse knows about harmony, so I wandered off by myself, using my native wit, and still carrying my iron hat and the blushing pants of a bygone era. I clambered over a paper wall and a wooden castle with paper roses on it, and pretty soon I found a doorway that looked dark and dismal enough for my simple purposes. I sneaked in and found myself in a sort of subdued light, where I could trip over chairs and unseen objects with great freedom.

I fumbled around in the half light, feeling for something to sit on, and before I could change into the borrowed and barbaric habiliments of a bygone age, I heard a number of voices talking, and then came the sharp, familiar pur you always hear in a moving-picture theater, when the operator begins to tune up.

That's where I was—in a sort of moving-picture theater, though not a regular one, where the public is admitted. This was one of these private theaters or dark rooms, where they show off the new pictures before the various officials, and make changes in them, before shooting them at the great unwashed at a nickel a throw.

I dropped my Babylonian trousers on the floor, and, while I was scurrying around in the darkness, they began spraying a picture on the screen, and the men started talking about it. Somebody with a loud voice was evidently the boss, because he kept saying this was rotten and that was rotten, and it looked like the whole blasted thing would have to be done over.

I will now state that it was a mighty interesting picture to me, because I'm not an expert on such things, like these officials were. Somebody would say, "Joe, that's terrible," and all the time it looked fine to me. I temporarily forgot about my dollar-and-a-half job, and the gladiator business went to pot while I sat there and watched the picture.

Every now and then the boss would speak to Joe, and I gathered that Joe had taken the picture, or dictated it, or whatever they call it. Then Joe would answer in an irritated way, and say that hell could freeze over, but, so far as he was concerned, there would be no retakes on that film.

"It was no good to start with," the boss said. "It was always bad, and I was against the thing from the start. Besides that, it's cost four times what it should."

"That's on account of the wreck stuff," Joe answered. "That's all right, you'll admit. There's nothing the matter with that, is there? Wait till that comes, boys. Just watch that wreck! Ain't it a bird, Dave?"

Dave admitted it was a bird, and I went on sitting there, with a shoe in one hand and a feeling that I was prying into other people's affairs. Still, the picture wasn't bad. It was named "The Fireman's Sweetheart," and that interested me, because all the firemen I knew were married men. The story was about an honest young fireman who

was in love with the daughter of a prominent railway official, and she loved him, too, though there was no sensible explanation of why that was. I know a lot about the railroad business, and I never heard of any prominent official's daughter being in love with a fireman. Anyway, she loved the lad, who was too handsome for the firing business, and there was also a vicious young devil in the picture named Montmorency, who loved the girl, and this guy had a strong drag with the high-up officials.

Montmorency, seeing how things were going, spent all his time trying to put the fireman on the bum, and finally, having failed to separate him from his rich sweetheart by ordinary deviltry, he grew desperate, and hired a confederate. He had the confederate kidnap the rich girl, tie her up in her father's private car, which he thoughtfully arranged so it would be smashed, and then he fixed it so the Limited would run into the private car and kill everybody. The joke was that the honest young fireman was on the Limited, so thus the villain had the lover kill his own sweetheart. He was a grand little villain. He left nothing undone that might contribute to anybody's discomfort.

The star scene was where the Limited comes along through the night and kills the girl, only it didn't kill her. The picture fluttered along down to that scene, with Dave saying it was rotten, and Joe defending it. Then came the line: "A Fiendish Vengeance." Right after that you saw the wreck, and as a wreck it left nothing to be desired. It was considerable wreck.

"Boys, watch this!" I heard Joe exclaim.

Then it came. The huge locomotive sped down the track. It got beyond control of the honest fireman, and the next time you saw him, both man and engine were headed for destruction.

The engine came crashing head on through a brick wall, and boiled into the president's private car, where the beautiful heroine was bound hand and foot. And at this point I dropped my iron hat on the floor with a clatter and stood up.

"Suffering Spinoza!" I remarked, to nobody in particular.

I saw myself!

I saw my old engine, No. 139, Pomona & Western, heavy type.

I saw the Pomona roundhouse, and Railroad Street in front of it. And bang! There I came through the old roundhouse, on the day of the lantern-smashing contest, and into the passenger coach, which was on the outside track. I saw myself lifted out of the cab, covered with mortar and profanity, and that was the first time I knew how I got out of that wreck. Then the camera slowed down, and I could hear the men talking. I stood there, trying to make my brain work, but it wouldn't.

"That," said Joe, the director, "saves the whole picture. That's the greatest wreck scene ever put on the screen. There's a real wreck, boys; no built-up stuff."

"It certainly is one stirring scene," said another voice. "It will make them sit up and take notice."

"It ought to," Joe growled. "It cost us three thousand dollars."

"You mean for that one scene?"

"Three thousand bones for that one scene," Joe continued. "And it's worth it, because it saves the picture. That's a real roundhouse. That's the roundhouse of the Pomona & Western Railroad, at Pomona. The passenger coach we dragged in where it would get caught in the ruins when the engine came through. And we never paid a cent for the passenger coach at that."

"How did you get it?" still another man asked.

"Funny story," Joe went on. "We built the whole drama about that one scene. An old guy comes in here one day with an offer. Says he can provide us with a high-grade wreck for three thousand dollars, and will deliver the wreck before he takes a cent. I don't know the details of his scheme, but part of it had to do with a stewed fireman, who certainly carried out his part, if it consisted of getting stewed. I took the old man up. We hid our camera men in his livery stable, which is across the street from the rear of the Pomona roundhouse. He pulled off his stunt on schedule time, and there you see the result. One of the finest wrecks in the known world."

At this point I noticed that my mouth had been wide open in astonishment, so I closed it. Besides stars, I began to see the real depth of Simeon Means, and to understand what he meant by having a lantern contest, and by urging me to convivial extremes.

"The funny part is," Joe said, laughing heartily, "the joke is on the railroad. After smashing up their pet roundhouse, the old scoundrel went right in and got the contract for rebuilding it. Ain't that great?"

Somebody laughed, but it wasn't me.

"You know," I heard Joe say, "I could use that fireman—the stewed boy who did all this. If he ever has any sober moments, I certainly could use him."

"That's what I contend, exactly," Dave, the boss, put in emphatically. "As it stands, the picture is no good, with the exception of the wreck. And why? Because the fireman we see all the way through, up to the wreck, is a handsome devil, and he ain't the same fireman we see lifted out of the busted cab. Any audience in the world will give that the hoot. They'll know you're using two different men. Don't you realize that?"

"I do," Joe answered, with mild sarcasm, "and I suppose you expect me to go back to Pomona and hunt through the hospitals till I find the alcoholic maniac who ran the engine. Not me. They have a large and chilly jail in Pomona, and I'm going to stay away. If the railroad people ever find out the truth——"

At this point some sucker turned on the regular lights, disclosing a surprised outsider standing there in a grievous state of undress. About nine men in their shirt sleeves stared at me. The fattest one came over to me and looked at the scarlet pants and the iron hat.

"Who are you?" he asked, using some private adjectives of his own.

"Well," I said, "my name's Marty. I'm the fireman in that wreck scene, and I've been listening—accidentally, of course—to what you said about how nice it would be if you could get hold of that fireman. If it's of any interest to you, I'm all through firing on the P. & W. They saw to that, right after the wreck."

Joe looked at me and then laughed. The other men gathered around and asked questions. They also laughed.

"Are you the stewed fireman!" Joe asked.

"I *was* the stewed fireman," I answered. "Put a lot of accent on that past tense, because I've quit liquor."

Joe turned and talked to Dave, the boss.

"This is what I call a piece of luck," he said.

"Luck is not the name," retorted Dave. "This is a modern miracle."

"I like to hear you gentlemen so enthusiastic about it," I said, picking up the scarlet pants. "Those are nice words, but if you can use this fireman, what's the salary?"

"Twenty a week, if you drink," Joe answered.

"I drink nothing but water," I told him.

"Then forty a week, if you're telling me the truth. I've made actors out of worse things than coal shovelers. And there's a bunch around this studio that ought to be shoveling coal right now."

"Forty dollars a week suits me," I told the director. "When do I start?"

"What's your name?" he asked.

"Marty Lee."

"All right, Marty," Joe continued. "You probably can't act at all, but even then, you haven't got anything on a lot of other heroes in the movies. Put on your pants and come along with me. You're an actor now."

And that about winds it up, except that you ought to go see that picture.

The whole thing goes to show that no bunch of immature firemen can rush up and squeeze blood out of a turnip— Simeon Means being the turnip. Think of that sucker dragging down three thousand dollars! And we thought we were financial sharps.

Some day I'm going back to Pomona and thank the old reptile for what he did for me.

🙠

LACKAYE DELIVERS ANOTHER JAB

AS the boy with the limber fang and the ready stingaree, not to mention the acrobatic tormentor and the trusty snickersnee, Wilton Lackaye, the actor, is at the head of his class.

One evening he met Percy Hammond, the Chicago dramatic critic, who had said unpleasant things about a play in which Mr. Lackaye was appearing.

"I suffer so unnecessarily," sighed the actor to Hammond. "Here I am, compelled to encounter you, who were created just when the heavenly powers had a passing liking for caricatures."

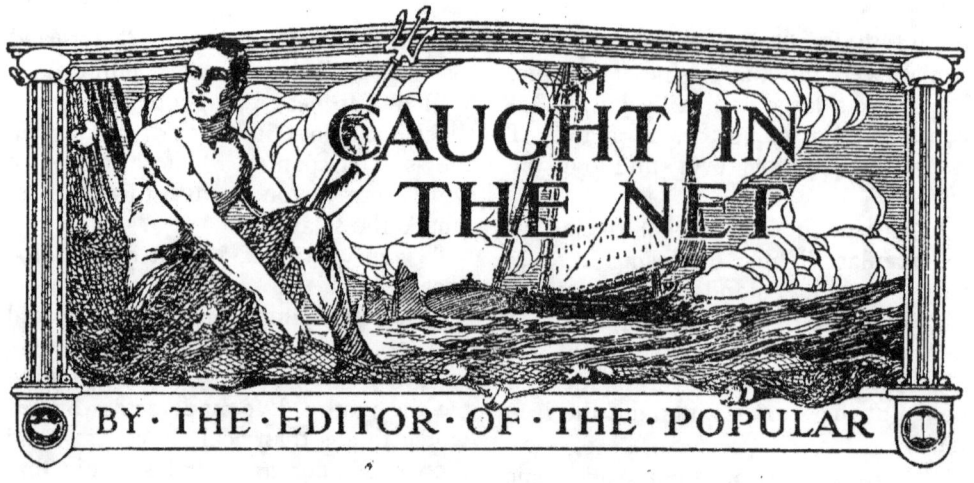

THE PRESIDENCY

QUADRENNIALLY, in November, there is waged our great battle of ballots, which involves between fourteen and sixteen million voters of these United States—an expression of popular political sentiment that is without parallel in its influence upon the nation, and affects even remote republics and kingdoms. It is an extraordinary occasion, at which every citizen, whether he live in a tiny hamlet or a big city, on prairie or mountain, may lend his voice to the selection of a head for this government, and give into the hands of an individual greater power than is exercised by most of the rulers of the world. Lifted to his high office by virtue of public acclamation, this man becomes spokesman for a hundred million people, his every word and act analyzed and weighed and recorded indelibly by a vast multitude of minds, and set down in journals of every sort and tongue.

Selection of the president has with the passing of time come more and more under the direct control of the people. Originally, as specified by the Constitution, the people were not given any direct voice in the election of their chief magistrate, it being held sufficient that they control by popular vote the election of the members of the House of Representatives. To the State legislatures was given the power to appoint presidential electors, who, in turn, chose the nation's chief. But beginning with the year 1800, the political organizations became too complex and powerful to permit of the foregoing plan, and party nominations were instituted by which congressional caucuses chose presidential electors. Until 1824 this scheme served, then there arose vigorous protest against it, the reformers laying claim to the people's right to choose their own electors to cast the final vote for the president. Another plan was thereupon adopted of mass conventions and State legislatures deciding the momentous choice, but it was found cumbersome and impracticable. However, by 1832, the groping for the proper political machinery resulted in the rise of the national convention, the national committee, and the national platform, and by 1844 all of the presidential conventions had accepted the present principles of party government; but not until 1876 had the modern political campaign, as we know it, put in its appearance, with its large financing and skillful publicity.

Self-government is exemplified in its highest development in the United

States, maintained by means of political machinery unlike that of any other government, and requires a force of about half a million men and women to keep it working smoothly and effectively. Its master mind is that of the president, who must supervise the expenditure of a billion dollars annually, who must give his time and attention to the appointment of petty officers as well as to foreign relations that involve grave issues, who must execute the laws of the land and guard the interests of the people, and who must be open to all citizens desiring to write or see him. These duties give us only a glimpse of his herculean task. Like most other positions of the present day, the presidency has grown exacting, and demands of the incumbent almost incredible performances. More is expected of the president than of any other man in public life on earth. There is no other governmental head under such lenses of burning criticism. Human he must be, yet something beside, for we are an incurably idealistic nation, with belief in the powers of man beyond any experience to justify it, perhaps. For this reason alone the presidency is one of the most difficult conceivable jobs to undertake, embodying responsibility of the first magnitude. Increasingly, politics are coming to express the moral purpose of the country, and the people are above all else placing a faith in their chosen leader that he possess and hold that vision without which a nation perishes.

On the whole, we can be justifiably proud of the men that the presidency has called forth from the ranks of the commonalty, and their fitness for such high destiny has been one of the supreme and inviolable proofs of the value and permanency of our form of popular government. Men who had been lawyers, soldiers, tailors, farmers, and tradesmen have been selected for this great office, and whether intellectual or not, they have proven men of illuminating character and unimpeachable integrity. Whichever may be the candidate chosen as our twenty-ninth president, this election, we are sure he will not fall far short of the expectations we entertain, of the ideals we cherish.

MONUMENTS TO LONELINESS

CONSIDER the sheep-herder. With us, loneliness is a thing that comes now and then, like the headache, or the nerves. With him, it is a part of his daily existence. A lowly, little-known atom of a world's life he is, a piece of humanity stuck far out upon the sagy stretches of Wyoming and Montana, or Colorado and Utah; an atom who cares for the wool supply of the United States, but whose main job is to be lonely.

There is no one to whom the sheep-herder may talk. There is no place for him to go, except a deadly repetition of the sand-strewn, sagebrushed stretches which lie all about him. Now and then, one of them becomes mad from the horror of it all, and his bones are found months later, where he has died by a shot rather than endure the society of only himself. But those are the weaklings, the men who do not understand that companionship does not necessarily mean the company of humans. The sheep-herder—that is, the true one—has solved the problem of loneliness by making the whole world, animate or otherwise, his companion.

The sky is his friend, for he can lie on his back and watch the clouds by day, or try to count the stars by night. Every insect that crawls or flies or squirms is an intimate acquaintance—for many a day has been passed away just in watching an ant hill, and trying to figure out what all the activity's about. Even the dangerous rattlesnake is almost out of the enemy class.

Out there, when you ride the plains, you see towering piles of stones atop the sandy hills, stretching high into the sky. Great bowlders form their bases, bowlders that required struggling strength, and the work of days to move into place. Sometimes the stones themselves have been carried for half a mile, across smooth sand and rutty gully, finally to be placed upon the stack with the rest. Monuments they are, great, towering monuments, that have cost the labor and time of weeks, sometimes months, to build. And yet, when you ask whose grave they cover, what battle they commemorate, you learn that they were built by sheep-herders for no other purpose than to pass the time away. To pass the time away, by sweat of the brow and work that would be called hard labor under any other circumstances—to pass the time away in building great, high-reaching monuments to the God of Loneliness! And yet we, who live where there are things to see and persons to talk to, we sometimes whine against the world and say there is nothing to do, that we are lonely!

INVESTING CREDIT

CREDIT is a man's best capital. It may last through the loss of a half dozen fortunes, and enable him to succeed the seventh time. It is useless to advise men to stay out of debt. It is also foolish, for, on our present basis, a majority of men cannot do business without credit.

However, it is imperative that a man knows the sort of debt he is making. To use one's credit in his business may be a wise investment. But it is always dangerous to live on one's credit—to eat it up and wear it away. Credit merely consumed leaves a deficit that is a fearful handicap. A man should live some way on what he earns; and invest his credit only when careful investigation and his best judgment convince him that it will be safe and yield a profit.

A tightwad is not a lovely creature; but even he is to be preferred to a dead beat; and a man who persists in spending more than he has or makes, must inevitably become a dead beat. It is folly to squander money one will need for real expenses; it is worse than folly to be a spendthrift with other people's money.

The only intelligent, self-respecting plan is to spend no more at most than one earns; and to use one's credit solely as a business asset; a capital, to be invested only when returns are reasonably sure.

SINGLE TRACK

WHEN all is said and done, it would seem that dogged persistence is the greatest single factor in success. It enters largely into the make-up of the schoolboy who stands at the head of his class. It is a main characteristic of the business man who wins out over his competitors. It is the lifting force that puts a man on the level where large achievements are possible. Success is sustained interest; failure is the lack of it. No one can be kept out of his inheritance who is able to seize upon his object and hold it for examination and knowledge. There is a large place in the world for the man who can inclose a thing in a circle and focus his mind upon it with sustained attention, inhibiting everything else that does not relate itself to that thing.

The habit of focalization is one of the greatest helps in securing an honorable position in life. Nobody cares to be associated with a scatterbrain. No job that is worth having can be held long by a man whose mind wanders over a score of things when it should be fixed upon one. The power of attention—the single-track mind—will make for clearness of thought, retentiveness of memory, saneness of imagination. It will help you to your share of all good things.

STATES OF OPPORTUNITY

VI.—A Western Banking State

WHEN the Federal board came to locate the twelve national-reserve banks authorized for the whole United States, they put two of the banks in one State—and the State was not New York nor Pennsylvania—but Missouri.

Missouri is an old State, and very conservative. It is now preparing to celebrate its hundredth anniversary of statehood. It has a daily newspaper over one hundred years old; and there still stands many a house built in the days of Daniel Boone and James Fenimore Cooper.

Perhaps no other State is so hard to classify. Whether it is a Northern, Southern, or Western State is always open to argument. It is a part of all three, with a great deal of the East mixed in. It is a large State, both in size and population—and very wealthy. In a national convention it casts thirty-six votes. It has two very large growing cities—St. Louis and Kansas City; and four other cities larger than the biggest city in many a State—St. Joseph, Springfield, Joplin, Hannibal. It has a big university of high standing, and almost a dozen good colleges scattered about the State.

And yet, there are many people in America who imagine Missouri is a raw, wild-West State of Indians and bank robbers. Following the Civil War, a gang of desperate and rather picturesque bandits won for themselves and the State a great deal of notoriety. But it should be remembered that the James boys had gone out of business in Missouri even before Tweed's gang evacuated New York. For more than thirty years, Missouri has been conservatively, even technically, and almost painfully law-abiding.

Although Missouri has been settled a long time, and is in a pretty high state of development, it is full of opportunities of every conceivable sort. There is plenty of room, an abundance of raw material, and exceptional railroad and river facilities for shipping.

Land is not yet as high-priced as the same sort east of the Mississippi. To the man of small means the Ozark Mountains, in the south part of the State, offer great chances for fruit growing and stock raising. Thousands of acres of land may be had for ten to twenty dollars an acre, and although broken and rocky, the soil is good, and is excellent for pasturage and fruit growing. The climate is almost ideal, and the apples, peaches, and strawberries of this section are famous throughout America.

Instead of robbing the newcomer, Missouri offers him the best banking facilities, and a way to make something to put in the bank.

Indigo Pete, Adjuster

By Henry Herbert Knibbs

Author of "The Amazing Tenderfoot," "Sunny Mateel," Etc.

A holdup story that is "different." A brief but exciting bit of action from the West, in which a tenderfoot figures as the victim and a holdup man is the hero. A well-drawn character, the "adjuster." You'll want to hear more of his adventures

THE sun was close to the rim of the desert when the tenderfoot reached the top of the range. Below him a white dot shimmered and wavered in the oncoming shadows. The dot was the tent, and the tenderfoot wished with all his heart that he had heeded his friend Yeabo's advice—Yeabo was not a tenderfoot—and allowed the latter to make the journey to town for supplies. Turning and looking the other way, the tenderfoot saw a dot of light, then another and another. Malachite was beginning to wake up. It was almost as far to the town as it was to the tent. Still—the tenderfoot sighed and tugged at the lead rope of the burro. Down the trail they clattered. The tenderfoot whistled bravely. Somehow or other the Romance of the Desert had vanished; dissolved in the sunset, leaving a creeping chill of unpleasant anticipation.

Halfway down the range the tenderfoot turned. The noise behind him was that of a horse slipping and catching itself among the loose rocks of the trail. Then came a whole-souled curse and the jingle of bridle reins. The tenderfoot naturally wondered who it was. Presently the sound of shod hoofs on rock came nearer, and a voice, low-pitched and tinged with an inexpressible melancholy, quavered into song:

"Oh, I had a girl in San Antone,
  She had a beau lived down that way,
I met up with him one night alone——

"Stand on your feet, you glass-eyed lizard, you! That's what's your feet's for."

Then came the "chuck" of spurs and a grunt:

"I met up with him one night alone,
  And that's why I'm skinnin' mules to-day."

The tenderfoot grinned despite his fatigue and fear. He enjoyed the lyric. But a tense silence followed, broken only by the soft slither of rolling pebbles. Just then the tenderfoot sneezed.

"Put 'em up!" called the unknown, and he was obeyed.

With the heavy breathing of the horse and the creak of saddle leather came the dim outline of a tall individual, huge in the gloom and loosely alert. "Stand right where you be. Don't move!" And a hand jerked his pistol from its holster. "Now, shell, and don't waste time thinkin' about it."

The tenderfoot "shelled." A watch, twenty-five dollars and some odd cents, a pocketknife, a collapsible drinking cup, a silver cigarette case, a bunch of keys——

"*And* that there ring," signified the gaunt intruder.

The tenderfoot demurred. The ring was graven with a college class emblem and precious to its owner.

"What's the idea?" queried the tenderfoot. "The ring isn't worth much."

"The idea's mine," said the horseman.

Slowly the tenderfoot drew the ring from his finger and handed it to the other.

"All right. Now, get a-goin'."

"But the burro—the—supplies—I'm camped with a friend down below. Surely——"

"Surely is right. I'm just needin' a burro and a pack of grub myself. Get a-goin'."

"If you'll put down that gun and stand up like a man——" began the tenderfoot.

The other laughed. "I sure hate work," he said, "and it would take some right smart work to down you, I reckon. You size up square."

"That's more than I can say of you, sir!"

"It's kind of dark to see, ain't it?" queried the other.

The tenderfoot realized that discretion had its uses and gave over the lead rope grudgingly. "If I were in your business, I'd hold up something worth while and not go about pilfering," he said scornfully.

"You don't reckon yourself worth much, then?"

"I do. But your—er—pilfering hasn't got you much."

"That's right, pardner. I ought to got you afore you bought them canned goods. But I'm wastin' time. Get a-goin'."

"No hurry, is there?' came from the brush just back of the outlaw.

The tenderfoot felt his heart jump and stop and then pump hard.

The outlaw stood stiff in his tracks. Slowly his hands went up. The tenderfoot could see the dull gleam of his pistol in the dusk. The unexpected arrival pushed through the brush and neatly secured the gun.

"He's got another—mine," said the tenderfoot.

"Thanks," said the third member of the coterie. "I'll see to that."

"I'm mighty grateful to you," said the tenderfoot, addressing his apparent rescuer.

To this the other paid no attention, but peered through the gloom. "Oh, it's you!" he said suddenly. "Well, as you was just sayin' to this here hombre, 'get a-goin'.'"

The outlaw grumbled and swung to the saddle.

"And go on down—not up," said the third member.

Past them he rode, slouching in the saddle; clattering down the steep trail. From below came the echo of a range ditty about San Antone. "It's Rasp Harper," said the rescuer. Then he got busy.

"Just set down," he said. "You need a rest, anyhow. Now, what's the pile amount to?"

"It's all on that rock there," said the tenderfoot.

"Well, keep a-settin'." And he struck a match and surveyed the little pile of money and trinkets. "Huh! Rasp must 'a' been hard up. Was he aimin' to take the burro and all?"

"He was."

"Huh! You camped near here?"

"Down below, with Yeabo. He's prospecting."

"Uh-uh! He's like to know me. I'm Indigo Pete, adjuster."

"Adjuster?"

"Uh-uh! Kind of settlin' things."

"Well, I'm mighty glad you happened along."

"So'm I. If I hadn't, who would, eh?"

The tenderfoot laughed. "That's one way of looking at it. Well, I think I'll be jogging along."

"I wouldn't."

"Why not?"

" 'Cause I says so. I ain't adjusted this here business yet."

"I'm grateful. I thank you——"

"Don't! I got feelin's, same as you. Wait till I git through."

"Why, there's nothing——"

"Yep. Lots. Listen. That there Rasp he's just a plain, low-down horse thief. He ain't got no principles. Now, I'm different. When I set out to do a job I do her big. Sabe? Uh-uh! Well, listen: I'm a-goin' to tell your fortune. As I was sayin', I'm Indigo Pete. Some knows me and some don't want to. Cards is my failin'. Bein' short on looks and long on sand, I takes to cards, when they ain't a chance for a big haul and a easy get-away. Bein' a adjuster, it's kind of up to me to furnish referances like. Well, I been bronchobuster, puncher, stage driver, pony-express rider, and married. Them bein' what you might call my side lines mostly. Now, mebby you think it don't do a man good to talk himself out to some fella what kin listen and understand. Goin' around like a coyote and thinkin' too much is bad for a man. I been doin' that recent; ever since the Limited was held up over to Cut-Bank Station. Yes, I seen you stiffen up. I was in it, but she panned out bad. Two of us got ours, and I got away. That's me, Pete. So, nacherally, I'm honin' for comp'ny and a leetle rest. I'm afoot. Run my hoss down day afore yesterday—plumb played out and nothin' I could get a string on. Well, as the preacher says, 'Worms will turn.' So I sure turned. Here I be stickin' you up, and you a plumb gentle tenderfoot, for the price of a hide-out with the Mexican folks over the range till the pot quits boilin'. So I turned; me, Pete. I turned agin' old Rasp and took the goods right out of his war bag, which is agin' the rules of the game. He seen you first. Course, him bein' nothin' but a low-down, chicken-lifter kind of a holdup, it ain't so bad. He'd ought to be discouraged in his work. He ought to be skinnin' mules or somethin' what don't take brains. Anyhow——"

The tenderfoot made as if to stand up, but Pete's gun swung round. "Set still, pardner. I ain't half through."

"But do you mean to say that you deliberately held up a—er—fellow outlaw and that you intend——"

"You said it all. I sure do. I need the money."

"But, man alive——"

"And goin' to keep alive a spell yet, yes. Me, Pete. But don't work into the collar to gall yourself any. Listen: I'm a adjuster. Now, here's the layout. Rasp stuck you up and shelled you. I sticks up Rasp and shells him. Who be I takin' the stuff from?"

"That's logic, but it's wrong just the same."

"Nope. It's as dead right as the law—only different, because you call it stealin'. Listen: Rasp takes your pile. I take Rasp's pile. I sure don't touch you for anything, eh?"

"But the money and things weren't his."

"So? Well, from what I seen when I rambled along in, they looked like they was his."

"I mean, not legally. He was a thief."

"You're right there. So am I. But I'm stealin' from him. Listen: If they was a judge and jury right handy, and you could prove this here stuff was yourn—and it's hard to prove cash is yourn—why, you'd get it back and Rasp'd get sent over. Me? Why, I'd come in as the fella that had the goods on me, but you'd have to swear Rasp took 'em. Settin' reputation aside, I'd stand a good chance of gettin' off easy. But they ain't no court of law 'cept me and this here gun. *Law* ain't what things ought to be, but what things is. Sabe?"

"I understand that I've fallen out of the frying pan into the fire—that's all."

"Hold on, pardner. It's a plumb disgrace to get stuck up by a four-flusher like Rasp; but when you tells folks Indigo Pete rolled you off'n your wealth, why, that there's somethin' to talk about! But I ain't goin' to. I'm goin' to adjust this here thing right. You ain't got enough dough to make me go after it hard. But I'm sure settin' on the rocks this trip, and I need help. Listen: I gives you your burro and pack and them things—all of 'em. *But* I charges twenty-five bones for adjustin' this business. Sabe?"

The tenderfoot grinned despite himself. He felt that he was well out of it at the price. "Yes, it's another way of taking it, that's all."

"You make me mournful—talkin' like that, pardner. Kin you tell me what's to hender me takin' the whole works?"

"No, I cannot."

"Correct and short. You're gettin' wise. As I was sayin', I'm afoot. You're afoot. Listen: You're camped down yonder with old man Yeabo. He's furnishin' the talk and doin' the cookin', and you're furnishin' the grub while he goes peckin' round lookin' for color in these here hills. Uh-uh! I knowed it. Well, if I thought this here was Yeabo's stuff I wouldn't tetch it. He's a old-timer. But you ain't. We're afoot and the night is fine. Now, what do you say to a little pasear over to Malachite?"

"But I just came from there! I——Yeabo'll be expecting me."

"He'll let you do the worryin' about that. Listen: I got a hunch. You're lucky——"

"Yes. Looks like it!"

"Wait! Ever buck faro?"

"No."

"Good! This is the proposition: We fan it for town. The game will be runnin' high about time we git in. You takes the little, ole twenty-five and plays her—anywhere, on the deuce, tray, jack, king, or the floor. You're sure a winner if you never touched the cards before. Course, I'll hang round

10A P

and watch out that you don't forget I'm there. Sheriff is over to Hawley lookin' for me, so it'll be easy-goin'. You needn't to worry about gettin' hurt, 'cause they knows me—over to Malachite. I got friends; anyhow, it won't be our outfit that'll get hurt; it'll be the other side if somebody starts somethin'. Are you game?"

"Why, what about the burro?"

"Good gosh, but that is like a tenderfoot! The burro kin feed all night or fan it down to camp—which he'll most likely do. Burros don't count with me right now. I got to make a stake."

The tenderfoot, who was in reality a rather husky young chap and only "tender" in that he was new to the West, nodded. "I'll go," he said and rose.

Indigo Pete sighed and holstered his gun. "I'm feelin' better. Ain't talked so much since I tried to explain to my second wife that the first one didn't come a-lookin' me up because I asked her to. Jest step ahead and we'll try our luck."

Smoke eddied through the swinging doors as Pete pushed into the room. The tenderfoot followed. "Have somethin'?" queried Pete.

The other shook his head.

"Correc'. We'll wait."

For an appreciable second a tense hush fell over the crowded room as Pete pushed back his battered sombrero and nodded to this one and that one. Then began the hum of low-voiced conversation. The ball spun in the wheel, and the monotonous voice of the dealer beat upon the undercurrent of talk. Straight to the faro layout marched Pete. The tenderfoot pulled a handful of gold and silver from his pocket and placed it at random. Pete edged close to the table. Again came the hush—then a voice. The tenderfoot smiled nervously, gathered in his winnings, and turned to Pete. A bystander sneered and murmured, "quitter!"

Pete swung on his heel, reached in his pocket, and, with tobacco and papers, rolled a cigarette. His eyes narrowed. "Gents," he said slowly, "this here gent is a friend of mine. Any objections?"

There were no objections.

Out in the glimmer of stars the tenderfoot turned to Pete: "I counted one hundred and seventy-five dollars. Here's one hundred and fifty."

"Nope, I'm a adjuster. Listen: There's different kinds of ways of playin' square. Half for me and half for you goes. I ain't got time to talk. They's one fella in there that I don't know, and such is takin' chances. I'm gone. So long. They'll be pokin' around your camp to-morrow lookin' for somethin' they won't find. If they ask if you seen me, tell 'em 'sure thing.' If they ask where I be, tell 'em to ask me. That's all."

The tenderfoot turned and started up the street to face the long journey back to camp. He had passed the corner when he heard the clatter of a horse's feet, a shout, and a shot. He turned. Pete dove under a pony that was hitched to the rail in front of the saloon, whipped the tie rope loose, and swung to the saddle. Across the street came a man, running. Figures surged in the doorway glare of the saloon. Pete tore past the tenderfoot, bending low in the saddle. "S' long, kid! 'Nother adjuster just lit in town. I reckon"—and he turned and shouted the final words—"he'll be wantin' to talk to you."

A horse or two flicked past in pursuit of Indigo Pete. The tenderfoot turned at the pressure of a hand on his shoulder.

The situation was a difficult one to explain away. "And so some holdup shells you—then Pete shells both of you—huh! And you got the face to tell me you come peaceful with Pete and jolt the faro layout for a hundred and seventy-five—and you a tenderfoot! Think up somethin' that'll slip down easier."

The tenderfoot smiled. "That's all there is to it, sheriff. I'm not used to lying."

"Well—mebby—— Say, where you from, anyhow?"

"Utica, New York."

"Oh, sure, yes! But I mean recent."

"I'm camped with Yeabo Jones, the prospector—over the range."

"Yeabo, eh? And he lets you run loose like this?"

"See here, you're an officer, and I'm bound to respect the law, but I want to tell you right now that you won't gain anything by that style of talk. I'll answer any decent question, and I'll answer it straight. I'm a tenderfoot—that's settled. And I'm where you can have a heap of fun with me—perhaps. Pardon me if I suggest that you'd look better on a horse after Pete than trying to josh me."

"Good! Now, I know you're all right. I knew the minute you begun to git mad that you were tellin' a straight story. Just my way of findin' out, young fella."

The tenderfoot smiled again. "That's all right. I didn't appreciate your system, that's all. I suppose I can go now?"

"Sure! But it's a long drill over the range, and it's gettin' late. Better turn in at the hotel. I'll lend you a hoss in the morning."

"Thanks. I think that's a good idea."

With the crisp dawn the tenderfoot was astir. A few dusty and weary riders loped in and dismounted. They had lost Pete's trail somewhere up in the hills. Moreover, their ponies were not fresh, having been used the previous day in trailing Indigo Pete to Hawley. The tenderfoot had breakfast, mounted the borrowed horse, and ambled toward the hills. He had come West in search of local color, and he felt saturated with it, for the time being.

Up the range he plodded, and down the range he drifted, sitting back and marveling at the ease and sureness with which the little pony kept its feet on the ragged trail. At the place where he had experienced his first real "thrill" —all thrills of fiction were decidedly secondary now—he reined up. The burro was gone. Had he been alive to the trail, he would have seen burro tracks and pony tracks zigzagging on down the steep toward the white dot on the flat far below. He wondered what Yeabo would say. Probably the old prospector would enjoy the joke, for there was much humor in the recent circumstance despite its promise of trouble. The tenderfoot had been robbed—twice—and had his belongings restored, with interest to boot. The trail became steeper, and he centered his attention on the pony—a most unnecessary but natural proceeding.

As he drew near the little tent he heard voices. Evidently some one had made an early-morning call. And some one had.

The tenderfoot swung from the saddle and hailed the camp. From the tent emerged Yeabo, his white beard fluttering in the breeze. Then he disappeared into the tent. "It's all right," he heard Yeabo say, and Indigo Pete pushed back the flap and stood grinning in the sunlight. "Yep, it's me. Welcome to our city. Yeabo'll rastle some grub, and I'll picket that hoss of yourn. Come on in! You found the right place."

"B-but they're after you."

"Sure as a cat with kittens. But they ain't got me."

The tenderfoot failed to grasp the subtlety of Pete's plan. The last place on earth that a sheriff would search would be the camp of the man who had been robbed. Indigo Pete was as safe in Yeabo Jones' camp—safer, indeed—than out in the brush. And Pete had said he knew Yeabo. Evidently he did, for the two old-timers were deep in a discussion of placer mining when the tenderfoot finally got himself together and entered the tent. The tenderfoot felt that he was, for the nonce, about as noticeable to them as the fly which crawled lazily along the ridge of the tent. When you are in Rome—an alien—be silent. So he thought and instinctively refrained from talking. There were questions he wanted to ask. All in good time they were answered without his having asked.

"I ain't much stuck on work," Indigo was saying, "but they's times when it's necessary. If you think you got something good, Yeabo, why me and the boy here'll dig in and try her out. I need a rest, anyhow. Course, I reckon to leave right sudden if I see the time comin'. If you want to make a handshake on it, here's mine."

Yeabo mumbled his cud of tobacco and spat. Then he extended his knotted, brown hand. "She goes," he said, and turned to getting breakfast.

"Me and him's rid together—in the ole days," said Pete, addressing the tenderfoot. "Yeabo thinks he's got a strike up in the cañon yonder. Somethin' to keep a fella from thinkin' of his past life—workin' a claim, eh? Well, we'll work her, and let the county pay for hoss feed and ammunition a spell. Course, you got a say in it. What do you say?"

"Oh, nothing. I'm satisfied. Only I think you're taking a big risk."

"Ever see a fly on a hoss' nose? Yep. Well, that fly was sure safe's long as he stayed on that hoss' nose, eh? What could the bronc do? Jest r'ar and stomp and run—and the fly gits a free ride, sabe? That's me. I'm settin' on the hoss' nose—which is this here

Malachite County. And the county will be r'arin' and stompin' around tryin' to git me—while I'm restin'."

"Your idea of resting strikes me as peculiar. You're the most active 'rester' I've ever seen."

"Course! Did you know it rests a bronc to lope after he's been walkin' Same's it rests a bronc to walk after he's been lopin', and I been lopin' some, boy; lopin' some!"

"But the horse you—er—borrowed?"

"Course! Turned him loose this mornin'. He'll jest nacherally stray back to Malachite. Where'd he light from? says the posse. And nobody knows, eh?"

"But as you said last night, you're afoot. Isn't that rather against your principles?"

"You're whistlin', boy! It sure is. But the bunch over to Malachite knows me, and they won't be lookin' for me afoot. They's more to this here game than you sabe, I reckon. She's a humdinger to play right."

"Come and get it!" called Yeabo, and the hungry ones came.

Several days later, while panning "color" in the cañon, Pete approached the tenderfoot who was tasting the first and keen tang of getting gold from the earth. "You need a rest," said Pete, squatting and rolling a cigarette. "Why don't you ramble over to Malachite and take a look around? Mebby you could pick up a hoss—you was sayin' you expected to buy a good saddle hoss right soon. Me and Yeabo can wash all the dust we can git out of this nickel-a-pan deal."

"But I thought it was a good find."

"S-sh! Don't talk so loud, or you'll make ole Yeabo feel bad. Anything that looks like gold tickles him to death. He's dreamin' right now that this here wildcat deal of his will make him rich. All prospectors does—and the ole-timers is the worst. It's goin' to play

out afore long. I know the looks of it. But it keeps him happy—so don't say nothin'."

"Oh, I see! Well, I won't."

"That's right. Yeabo's got feelin's, same as you and me."

"He's great!" exclaimed the tenderfoot.

Indigo Pete smiled slowly. "Yes—to you he is. He's filled you up with all kinds of yarns about the West. Sure he has moseyed around some; but his life's been like Sunday-school teachin' alongside of me. Why, I could tell you—but, say, you goin' over to Malachite?"

"Well, perhaps. I don't exactly see the necessity just now."

"Course. But I does. I'd kind of like to know who is talkin' over there these days. Sabe?"

"All right. I'll run over in the morning."

"Say, boy, I wouldn't. Walk; you'll finish stronger."

That evening, round the tiny fire, they talked of various things. Deftly Pete led the conversation round to horses. He touched the subject lightly at first, having a plan in mind. Then he elaborated, and the tenderfoot absorbed some actually valuable information about the points of a Western cayuse. When Pete had finished his talk, the tenderfoot thanked him. "You have told me more about horses than I ever knew could be told," he said.

Pete smiled to himself. "I sure want you to get a good one," he said, and the tenderfoot wondered why old Yeabo's beard twitched, and why that rugged old rascal passed his hand over his face as though brushing away a—smile, perchance?

The evening following the tenderfoot rode in to camp astride a short-coupled buckskin that stepped briskly and displayed considerable good-natured action. The tenderfoot was a bit astonished that Pete manifested so little interest in the horse. Yeabo Jones inspected the pony and approved of him. Still, the tenderfoot was not so overwhelmed with enthusiasm that he did not notice Yeabo's expression of worry —Yeabo who was usually as placid as the hills. Could there be something wrong with the horse?

"How much?" queried Pete presently.

"Only a hundred. Isn't he a beauty? Now I'll be able to go anywhere. I needed a horse."

"Uh-uh! He's fair. Where'd you get that saddle?"

"With the horse—all in one lump—for a hundred."

"Uh-uh! Center fire. Ole Visalia tree. Easy to ride."

"I'm glad you like it. Gee, but I'm hungry!"

The pony was picketed. They had supper and gathered about the night fire as usual. Yeabo seemed unusually silent. The tenderfoot mentioned that the townfolk of Malachite had seemed to have almost forgotten the recent and brief advent of Indigo, and the ripple of excitement following. Indigo coughed and rolled another cigarette. The tenderfoot was tired. He drowsed, sitting before the fire with head drooping. Indigo beckoned to Yeabo Jones, who immediately got up and followed him to the tent. There was a whispered argument—a terse word or two from Pete, and Yeabo came out and took his seat by the fire. Several minutes later Indigo also appeared, nodded to Yeabo, and passed back of the tent and disappeared.

Yeabo's eternal "Come and get it!" summoned the sleeping tenderfoot to consciousness and eventually to the fireside. He ate heartily, and then proposed to inspect his new pony. Yeabo busied himself with the dishes. The tenderfoot rose and stretched, grabbed up his hat, and strode toward the flat where the pony was picketed. Yeabo was wiping a tin plate when the tenderfoot came back on the run. "Where's my horse? Where's Indigo Pete?" he shouted.

"I was wonderin' you didn't miss him at grub," said Yeabo.

"Thought he might have had breakfast and gone to the stream," said the tenderfoot.

"Well, he's gone."

"Gone! You mean——"

"Uh-uh!"

"But why didn't he say something? Great Scott—and he took my pony?"

"Reckon he did. Pete takes 'most anything he needs."

"But I thought he was going to stay here! Said he was safer here——"

"Yep! But he got to thinkin' last night. When you said the folks over to Malachite had quit wonderin' where he was he got a hunch. Things acts that way sometimes. If they'd been talkin' about him lots he'd 'a' stayed longer. He's a wise one—that Indigo."

"I thought he was—er—at least half decent in his way," said the tenderfoot.

"I reckon he is—to some. Now, I got these here dishes put by, I'll give you his letter." And old Yeabo plodded to the tent and returned with a scrawled sheet of soiled paper. The tenderfoot seized it and read:

The hoss is a good hoss and I needed one so I took him. You sure was lucky in gettin a stayer for I am goin to make the long ride. It is time to make the ride for I got the right hunch. Hunches is worth more than money if you listen to them. Yeabo was ornery about lendin me the money to pay for him but I am honust at times when I feel like it. This one of them times. You are not the worst I met. They is lots worse. Mebby some day you and me will meet up again. You say the hoss was one hundred. I only had about eighty from that good play you made in Malakite. I stuck up Yeabo for the twenty to make it a hundred him actin bronk but it was no good. He knows me. Not trustin him too mutch I leaves the hundred under that rock by the stream where you

set when you git tired of pannin gold. You kin find it there. Yeabo would lied to you if I give it to him for you. Now to fix this thing up. You got the price of your hoss back again and I borrows twenty from Yeabo. You kin pay Yeabo the twenty and make it all square. I allus was trew to my friends as my enemys knows. You are my friend if I do say so. Yeabo is a ole fool but he canot help it. If you ever need a frend and I am around just holler.   INDIGO PETE
ADJUSTER.

The tenderfoot reread the scrawl and turned to Yeabo: "Did he borrow twenty dollars from you?"

"He did—with a gun in my stummick."

The tenderfoot smiled. Then he got up and hastened to the rock. There he found a roll of bills and some loose silver—a hundred dollars in all. Slowly he returned to camp, stripped two tens from the roll, and presented them to Yeabo. The old prospector glanced up in surprise. "That squares us—all around," said the tenderfoot.

"Did Pete leave the dough—for you!"

"It seems so. But we won't discuss it further. I—here is his letter."

Yeabo took the scrawl and held it upside down pretending to read it. The tenderfoot had had no idea that Yeabo could not read. Carefully the tenderfoot folded the letter when Yeabo had completed his bluff at reading. "I can't understand just why Pete left us," he said.

"Thar's why," said Yeabo, pointing toward the range.

Silhouetted against the morning sky line were four riders. They stood gazing into the valley—then reined round and rode on down toward the little tent on the flat.

"Leave it to Pete," said Yeabo. "He's got twelve hours' start."

JUSTIFIABLE FAMILIARITY

JUDGE WILLIAM H. MOORE, formerly of Chicago, but now a New Yorker, exhibited on one occasion a very fine mare in the roadster class at a spring horse show. Much to his surprise and the disappointment of his friends, the entry took third honors. Meeting his groom, "Chip," after the event, he asked him for an opinion on the failure.

"It was your bad driving," was the groom's terse reply.

Judge Moore made no comment, and passed out of the grounds. A friend who accompanied him, much surprised by the groom's gruffness, turned to the owner and said:

"Moore, why do you let your groom talk to you like that?"

Moore smiled.

"You won't wonder," he answered, "when I tell you a bit of personal history. A number of years ago in Chicago, when I was operating in New York Biscuit and Diamond Match stocks, they got me. I was sold out to pay the claims against me. On the morning after the sale, as I came down the steps of my home, I saw my pet driving pair standing at the curb, and Chip was holding the reins.

" 'Why, Chip, what are you doing here with those horses?' I asked.

" 'I'll tell you, judge,' was his quiet reply. 'I've been driving for you a long time, and I don't like the idea of driving for anybody else. I've been saving money the last twenty years, so I bought this team. It will be here waiting for you every morning, and it will be down at your office every afternoon waiting for you when you are ready to go home.' "

The Third Phase

By Francis Metcalfe

Author of "The Tower of Terror," "When Sullivan Was Mpret," Etc.

SYNOPSIS OF PART ONE

In the collection of Tommy Williams is a sword said to be the cherished possession of generations of Japanese noblemen. Baron Moto Takimura, a man thoroughly imbued with the traditions and customs of the vanquished samurais of the old Japanese feudal system, recognizes the sword as the one used by his father for the sacred rite of hara-kiri. Tommy refuses a fabulous sum which the baron offers for it. Inspector Arkell, of the secret service, calls upon Tommy Williams and his companion, who narrates the story. In connection with the Mexican situation, in which he is interested, Arkell cites three phases: the commercial, the Teutonic, and the newest, and possibly fully as menacing —the one Arkell thinks is directed by Baron Moto. Arkell is also of the opinion that the supposed Baroness Takimura—O Yucha San—is La Duvalief, a Russian thought to be an international spy in the German pay. This opinion is confirmed the following day when the baron and the "baroness" consult Tommy about a proposed portrait of O Yucha San. Before leaving Tommy's studio, the baron receives Tommy's consent to pocket the key to the cabinet in which the coveted sword is kept, in order to prevent its being defiled by rough handling. Later that day Arkell brings news of a Villista outbreak in Mexico, and makes known his intention of taking a midnight train to the seat of the trouble. Promising surprises, Tommy invites Arkell to a dinner party just prior to his departure. Arkell attends; another guest is La Duvalief, without her Japanese disguise. A scheme to steal the sword, participated in by the pseudo baroness, is thwarted by Tommy. With the sword in his possession, Tommy accompanies Arkell to the railroad terminal. Before leaving La Duvalief, Tommy accepts her challenge to penetrate her mask and to reproduce her true self on canvas, and, in this connection, he promises the secret-service man some interesting information upon his return.

(In Two Parts—Part Two)

CHAPTER IX.

WE were at the station a half hour ahead of train time; but Baron Moto was already there, and, unobserved, we watched him as he walked up and down the platform beside the train, smoking and keeping a watchful eye upon the gate from the waiting room. Arkell, who did not care to have him know that he was traveling on the same train with him to the border, kept in the background, arranging with Tommy for a method of communication during his absence.

"I'll send back orders for Morrison

and Ferros to give you any assistance you may require; they're good men, accustomed to working together, and you're liable to need help if you keep on fussing with that Russian Indian," he concluded. "I wish you were going with me, Tommy; I expect I'm going to find some tough riddles to guess down there."

"I expect to find a good share of the answers right here in New York, or at least a straight tip as to where to go to locate them," answered Tommy confidently. "I have a hunch that it will be the latter, and that we'll meet again and by comparing notes clear the whole

This story began in the October 20th issue.

thing up. Now get under cover, for I'm going to make your task easier by rousing the feudal daimio so thoroughly in our Japanese friend that he won't be able to get his 'Made-in-Germany' strategic machine working smoothly for another week!"

The baron caught sight of us as we passed through the gate, but he manifested no surprise and advanced eagerly to meet us.

"This is an unexpected pleasure; are we to be fellow voyagers?" he asked cordially.

"No, I have things to do in New York just now; among others a portrait of La Duvalief, which will partially console me for my disappointment in losing the commission to do the baroness," answered Tommy. "But we did come here to see you, baron; we have had rather a curious experience in my studio. While we were at dinner in the adjoining room, the cabinet containing the sword you are so much interested in was opened."

The baron gave an exclamation of surprise, and his hand went to his pocket with a suddenness which startled me; but he withdrew it, grasping nothing more threatening than the cabinet key.

"But, Mr. Williams, this has never for an instant been out of my possession!" he exclaimed. "I hope that you do not suspect that I was concerned in this—I confess that you might be justified, knowing how ardently I desire to obtain possession of that weapon of my ancestors—which, by the way, I sincerely trust has come to no harm."

"No, I know that key did not open the cabinet; the one which did was left in the door. As for the weapon, that is still safe and in my keeping, as you can see for yourself." He opened the cloth, exposing to view the lacquered box; but for a man who had been so passionately interested the baron looked at it with a strange indifference.

"Ah, my dear sir, I am inexpressibly relieved, for one day I hope to prevail upon you to permit me to purchase that weapon from you," he said, after satisfying himself that the silken cord was still fastened with the same curious knot which only Japanese fingers fashioned. "I am even more relieved that you will have no reason to suspect me. I am carried away most unexpectedly, and had the attempted theft been successful, you would have been quite justified in reading a plausible connection between it and a departure so sudden that it would suggest flight."

"Yes, such a thing might have been possible; but, as the thief was unsuccessful——" With a quick movement he unfastened the knot and opened the cover. The hand which the baron had extended in a fruitless effort to restrain him fell to his side, and an involuntary exclamation came from his lips as he gazed like a man hypnotized at the sword still resting upon the padded silken cushion. Ignoring the exclamation and the sudden change in his manner, Tommy finished his sentence as unconcernedly as if there had been no interruption: "——and, as I prevented his escape by temporarily disabling him with a bullet, there was no reason to connect you with the attempted theft."

For just a moment I didn't know whether the baron intended to start a fight or make an attempt to bolt; neither would have surprised me, for he looked like a cornered rat; but, with a most unexpected ease, he recovered his self-possession and met Tommy on his own ground. In spite of the absence of a direct accusation, Tommy's actions and explanation demonstrated plainly enough that he had not been hoodwinked, and the baron tacitly admitted at least a most profound interest in the affair.

"Temporarily disabled, but he still lives?" he demanded, and Tommy nodded.

"Yes, he was still unconscious when I left the studio to come here; but the wound was only trivial; it was the shock of concussion which knocked him out," he explained. "I expect that he will have left when we return, as he was the only one who sustained any damage. I have no wish to make this thing public."

The baron looked at him curiously. There was nothing of gratitude in his expression; he seemed to appreciate that Tommy was willing to match wits without taking advantage of the opportunity to enlist outside assistance.

"And this woman, La Duvalief, she was there when this happened?"

"Rather; she was dining with us and making herself so fascinating that, except for an accident, the trick would have been turned without our knowing anything of it," answered Tommy, and I am sure that even the keen scrutiny of the baron discovered no trace of suspicion in his voice or expression. "She is charming, baron; I am indebted to you for the introduction, and I trust that the near-tragedy in which she was unwittingly involved will not deter her from returning for her portrait. I shall try to guard against a repetition by depositing this in a safe place."

The baron could not conceal the covetousness in the eyes which watched Tommy's hands replace the cover on the box.

"Mr. Williams, I trust that you will guard and preserve it carefully until I return," he said gravely, his face again curiously like the daimio portrait which Tommy had painted. "There is much which you cannot understand; but one day I hope that I can tell you enough to win your consent to part with it."

There was a grim smile on Tommy's lips as he finished wrapping it up in the cloth, and to my surprise he extended his hand to the baron when that task was accomplished.

"I'll promise you this much, Baron Moto," he said quietly: "I'll do my best to prevent it from passing to any one else—and also to bring things about which in the old feudal days of Japan would have made you doubly anxious to get it into your possession."

The baron made no pretense of ignoring the challenge, and he smiled as he accepted the proffered hand.

"I understand; I thank you for your generosity. Your first victory; but I will again quote the proverb, 'To-day to thee, to-morrow to me!'" he said confidently.

"Safety first; that's my motto!" exclaimed Tommy, with a grin, when I asked him, as we rode back to the studio, what had induced him to take the trouble to look the baron up. "That was one beautiful little scheme which he had framed up, and our lives wouldn't have been worth a canceled postage stamp if he had gotten away with it. The full beauty of it didn't dawn on me until I noticed his indifference when I exhibited the box to him in the station. Just remember this: according to his lights, he was doing nothing dishonorable in trying to cop out that sword. I suppose that as a matter of fact it was stolen from his family; the mikado's adherents were doing everything possible to destroy the feudal traditions and the power of the shoguns, and most of their possessions were looted. But he must have done some remarkably quick thinking this morning in the studio, for his plan was made right there. He put the cover on the box, and you may have noticed the peculiar knot of the silk cord which fastened it; the fashioning of that knot is just as scrupulously regulated by custom as every other detail of the old feudal life. The secretary, Sheygio—as thoroughly imbued with the old traditions as his hereditary chief—would tie it in exactly the same way, almost automatically. That knot was the one thing which the baron examined with the slightest interest when I showed him the box at the station, and it was mainly to make that test and convince myself that I took the trouble to go there."

"I don't get you; it seemed to me that he didn't betray any particular interest until you opened the box—or started to."

"That last qualification gives me a little hope for you!" exclaimed Tommy impatiently. "If you live long enough and travel with me, you may learn to observe such trifles. In the first place, when I unwrapped the cloth, the baron had every reason to suppose that we had simply discovered that the cabinet had been opened; at that time I had told him nothing of the interruption of the theft. He probably supposed that only a part of the scheme had miscarried; that, after removing the sword, his agent had neglected to lock the door. That is why he started to prevent me from opening the box; he didn't believe the sword was in it, and he didn't want me to discover that it was missing. Here is just what I had figured out: The sword itself, the real thing that he was after, was formerly in full view through the glass, because I purposely left the box uncovered. Now, a good deal of his talk about screening it from the view of profaning eyes was pure bunk, a part of his scheme. When he asked my permission to carry away the key, he believed that it would prevent me from opening the cabinet until he returned it; but he undoubtedly gave me credit for an observation keen enough to make me notice the peculiarity of that knot through the glass. Now, had things gone off just as he planned, La Duvalief would have kept us so interested and absorbed at the table that we should not have noticed anything going on in the studio. His soft-footed clansman would have slipped in, removed the sword from the

case, retied that peculiar knot so that I would never suspect it had been tampered with, and made his get-away with the real goods without arousing our suspicions. That unsuspected burglar alarm upset everything—and fortunately the strong electric shock so disturbed Sheygio's aim that he missed me. That is the way I doped it out, and the test I just finished with the baron convinces me that I was exactly right. He expected Sheygio to join him at the station with the sword in his possession."

"But, Tommy, that sort of figuring seems to me to be about as profitless as crying over spilled milk!" I protested. "You had the main facts, and you couldn't have doubted for a minute that Baron Moto was behind the whole scheme. What's the use of——"

"I wanted to satisfy myself of just what we are up against, of just how far that medieval Jap was capable of going—and I've satisfied myself that he'll go the limit to get this!" interrupted Tommy grimly, the grip of his hands instinctively tightening on the package. "If everything had turned out just as he had planned, he could have counted safely on at least twenty-four hours' freedom from suspicion; it would probably have been at least that before my curiosity would have led me to force the cabinet lock. That would have been ample time for his Japanese household here to disappear. Now, fond as we are of the diggings we have so long occupied, you'll acknowledge that they are so isolated that almost anything might happen there without attracting attention, and that ramshackle old building is notoriously a fire trap. It's my guess that if he had pulled off the first part there would have been a second which would have prevented a discovery of the theft; before we became suspicious, the whole place would have been destroyed."

"By Jove, Tommy, that's going pretty

far; but I believe you are right!" I ac- knowledged. "La Duvalief even con- fessed that she would be willing to burn the place to get that confounded thing!"

"Exactly; it was that casual remark which first suggested it to me," agreed Tommy. "You must always remember one thing, old chap: try as hard as we may, we can never fully realize what a tremendous appeal this weapon makes to the clansmen of the Moto Takimuras, for it appeals to traits and sentiments which our race has forgotten for a thousand years. To them this weapon is a sacred thing; in trying to recover it they are actuated by the same spirit which sent the Knights of the Round Table over the face of the earth in search of the Holy Grail and stimulated the Christian kings of Europe to forget their quarrels and unite in a crusade to wrest the holy sepulcher from the possession of infidels. They didn't hesi- tate to sack and burn towns which stood in their way, and I don't believe these Japs would consider it anything but a legitimate move if they were forced to commit murder and arson to get this back. That's why I told 'em to turn that delegate, Sheygio, loose; making a charge of burglary against him would have been a little too much like having Sir Galahad pinched for breaking the speed limit when he was chasing the Grail."

We had reached the studio entrance as he made the whimsical conclusion to his explanation, and I laid a restrain- ing hand upon his arm.

"Just the same, Tommy, it won't make much difference to us whether we are bowled out by a common bur- glar or a fanatic, and if you'll take my tip you'll drive to the Day and Night Bank and leave that thing until you can put it in a safe-deposit box. Then in the morning you will recall your invi- tation to La Duvalief to sit for her portrait. She isn't swayed by any of these motives of barbaric chivalry, but she's out for the goods, and from what we've seen of her she isn't too finicky in her methods. She was ready to shoot me this morning; she did her best to poison you, and if Arkell hadn't ducked she would have shot him across the table—and I don't see that we need that kind of a visitor in the apartment." Tommy shook himself free and stepped to the sidewalk, and his face was very grave as he turned to me in the door- way.

"My boy, if I can inveigle her into coming there regularly, we can get some sort of a line on what she is up to—and in these troublous times that's a useful line to know about," he said seriously. "You are entirely right; she isn't actu- ated by any of the motives which make the Japs unscrupulous as to methods to get this weapon, but she would be even more unscrupulous than they if she could accomplish the same result. Just remember that Arkell divided this Mex- ican situation into two phases: the first of them the commercial, which is over with; the second the Teutonic, which concerned itself simply with Mexican internal affairs. But there is a third phase developing beneath the surface, a phase which for the first time dis- tinctly threatens us, and from what we know we have every reason to believe that the hand of Baron Moto is pull- ing the strings. Now, just what motive inspires La Duvalief to aid him I don't know; but I am convinced that it is a powerful one, and I'm going to find out. So long as I have this sword in my possession, that Jap isn't going to lose track of me; and it's the one best bet that La Duvalief will be the agent he employs to spy upon me. He doesn't know that we discovered the imposture of O Yucha San, and thinks that his introduction was taken at its face value as a simple courtesy. And then, above all, there is another reason."

He hesitated, looking at me with a

strange expression of embarrassment in his eyes.

"Confound it, I suppose that you'll think that I'm an erratic fool, carried away by a sentimental chivalry, but I can't help it!" he went on quickly. "La Duvalief is no innocent little schoolgirl, but she's white. Now, I can't get it out of my head—call it a hunch if you like—that she's in the power of that yellow schemer; that she is in deathly fear of him; and I've got just enough of the Caucasian prejudice against the tinted races to make that a pill which I can't swallow. If she is mixed up in any scheme, Teutonic or Japanese, which will lead to attack upon the United States, I'll do my best to beat her; but that's a different matter from standing by and seeing a white woman obeying a yellow-skinned man through fear."

He turned abruptly, and in silence I followed him up the interminable stairs. I knew that argument would be useless, for he had expressed in words only a tenth part of the aversion which was one of his pets; but I hoped that a night's reflection would convince him that his scruples were quixotic. He paused at the studio door and turned to me with a finger on his lips.

"That's strange; I thought they would have cleared out before this!" he whispered.

I listened, and, muffled by the thick oak of the door, a subdued chanting was audible from the studio. Tommy carefully inserted his pass-key and opened the door. The studio was brightly illuminated, and contained the same human occupants as when we left; but there was a marked and amazing change in their grouping.

On the divan, where we had left him stretched unconscious, Sheygio sat upon his heels as only a Jap can. Perhaps six feet from him, on either side, the secret-service men stood, watching him closely; while La Duvalief, her eyes alert, her face white, and her lips set, watched them. She was standing close to the door, so close that Tommy had to motion to her to move before he could open it fully. The Japanese was swaying his body gently forward and back from the hips in time with the curious rhythm of the weird chant which came from between lips which barely moved. It was that strange tune which we had heard, and, while our entrance did not interrupt it, its character quickly changed as his curious, inscrutable eyes caught sight of us. Before, it had seemed a simple narrative; but, rising to a shrill falsetto, it became an unmistakable defiance or pæan of victory. No word of it was intelligible to me, and I knew that Tommy knew no more of Japanese than I; but in the situation he read a significance which I missed.

"Grab him, quick!" he shouted to the two officers, and even before they could make a move he jumped for the man on the divan himself, only to fall sprawling, tripped by the dainty foot and ankle which La Duvalief shot out in front of him. She was evidently too resourceful to depend twice on the same tactics, and when I, too, jumped forward I was stopped by her full weight fairly catapulted against me, while my arms were pinioned to my sides in an embrace which for a moment I found it impossible to break. And just that moment was enough, for over her shoulder I saw Sheygio draw from beneath his coat a sword which in size and design was almost the counterpart of the one he had come to steal. And then, before the startled officers could reach him, he plunged the keen blade into his abdomen and gave the long handle a wrench sideways which must have made the blade half sever his spinal column.

With the cry of defiance suddenly stilled, he sat for a moment bolt upright, and then the soul of Moto Ito fled to the Shinto Valhalla to proclaim to the shades of his samurai ancestors that, strong in the faith of his fathers, he had chanted the death song of the Moto Takimuras and paid for his failure in the mission on which his chief had sent him according to the ancient and honorable rite of hara-kiri. His body pitched forward, and Tommy, his expression strangely reverent, helped to replace it on the couch before turning on the woman who met defiantly his sternly accusing eyes.

CHAPTER X.

"Mademoiselle, that man's death is as much on your head as if your hands had driven the sword home!" said Tommy, his voice dangerously steady, his manner ominously restrained. "You speak Japanese; you knew that he chanted the samurai death song, and your intimate knowledge of the people must have told you that chant is always the preliminary to suicide."

La Duvalief shrugged her shoulders and seated herself comfortably before answering. To all outward appearances, she was the least moved and shocked of any of us by that sudden tragedy.

"Your attitude savors of the judicial; but I have your own word for it that decisions in the sort of game *we* are playing are rarely rendered in a court of law," she said, her voice as steady as his own. "That being agreed upon, I will make admissions which might otherwise be damaging.. Yes, I knew that he chanted the death song, but it did not need that to tell me that he would resort to hara-kiri. From the moment I recognized him after he was wounded, I realized that that would inevitably follow. Perhaps I might have delayed it, but it would only have been a matter of hours; he would never have let the sun rise upon his dishonor. Mr. Williams, you are saddling me with the

responsibility for the whole code which it took the samurais generations to perfect, when you should be thanking me for saving your life. If I had not tripped you and prevented you from reaching him, you would have received that sword through your heart. The electric current which your ingenuity devised disturbed the aim of his pistol and saved you; but Moto Ito was the most expert of his clan in the use of the ancient samurai weapons. Perhaps it was fortunate for you that I do understand Japanese, for the death chant which your entrance interrupted changed suddenly to the Moto Takimura war cry of victory—and I let him sacrifice himself to save you."

There was a suggestion of tremor about her lips, a softening of her voice as she made that last admission; and Tommy, evidently finding it difficult to meet the eyes in which defiance had given way to an expression which he found embarrassing, turned impatiently to the secret-service men.

"Perhaps you fellows have something to say which will explain this; you were slow enough to act when I hollered at you," he grumbled.

Morrison shook his head. "You can't pass the buck to us, Mr. Williams," he answered. "That chap came around within a few minutes after you left, but the concussion seemed to have knocked everything but Japanese out of his head. As soon as he straightened up, he made a break for that cabinet, and when we tackled him to hold him back, he gave us both a jujutsu toss that stood us on our heads—it was the slickest trick I ever saw turned. We were ready to tackle him again, but this lady said a few words to him in his own lingo. It seemed to knock all the fight out of him, but it didn't make him feel any happier. He squatted there on the couch and commenced that spiel. We weren't wise as to what it was about; we thought he was just plain nutty, and so long as he wasn't doing any damage we didn't want to start anything before you came back. You bet we were wary about jumping for him; that poor little cuss was all live wire and spring steel, and we were looking for an opening to get a strangle hold on him. I'm mighty sorry, but if you had seen the way he put it over us before, you'd have looked for an even break before jumping at him, too."

Ferros curtly corroborated his side partner's story.

"Mademoiselle, may I ask just what you said to this poor fellow?" asked Tommy, after locking the sword away in a drawer of his desk.

"Certainly, for I said only a few words which prevented him from killing needlessly," answered La Duvalief frankly. "If you had not taken that sword with you, he would still have accomplished what he came for as soon as he regained consciousness. Had he found it there, he would have killed both of these officers before they could have regained their feet. I saved them when I told him that the sword had been taken away while he was unconscious and that he had been recognized by their superior officer, Inspector Arkell. Unfortunately I could not make him believe that your promise of immunity would be respected; in the game he has learned there is no room for mercy, and he undoubtedly believed that he would be treated as a common criminal. I am sorry, Mr. Williams, for more reasons than one. He died without suspicion that you had penetrated my disguise; had he lived to see Baron Moto, his report would have been so favorable to me that I should have been far advanced in his chief's confidence. It was no small sacrifice which I made when I had to choose, on the spur of the moment, between your life and the success of his mission; for had I not tripped you, the man who lies there would have left this studio in triumph with the object of his quest. I should have accompanied him—and behind us we should have left four dead men." She spoke of that possible solution with a callousness and indifference which sent a cold shiver down my spine, and Tommy's eyelids narrowed as he watched her.

"I fear that your triumph would have been short-lived, mademoiselle; you forget that Arkell would have read the true significance of that evidence—and your wrists would soon have known again the touch of his manacles." I guessed that he had purposely reminded her of that humiliation, for his voice was cuttingly sarcastic. If he had intended to anger her, he was successful, as the flush which darkened her cheeks testified.

"Clever as your friend may be, he could hardly read the significance of evidence which had ceased to exist!" she retorted. "And, wise as you think yourself, you have small conception of what these people whom you despise are capable."

Tommy could not resist the temptation to shoot a glance of triumph at me.

"Perhaps I can guess that even better than you can, mademoiselle," he answered. "For instance, I believe that they would have been quite capable of destroying evidence by burning this building and cremating our mortal remains to cinders—if the white man's blood which you have inherited had not made you revolt against the unholy alliance which you have made, when you were put to the crucial test." The involuntary start which she could not conceal betrayed how closely he had arrived at the truth, and the flush which deepened on her cheeks was eloquent of humiliation. "In so far as it lay in my power, I paid in advance for your service to me; I talked with Baron Moto at the station, I did my best to advance you in his confidence. When he returns, I have no doubt that you will be able to resume your interrupted relationship and——"

"Stop!" she exclaimed passionately, as she rose to her feet. "It is not fair for you to judge me so harshly, for in your eyes I read even a greater scorn than your cruel words imply. Yes, you are absolutely right; it was part of the plan to destroy evidence by burning this building, but evidence of a theft only. Cannot you understand that I came here to prevent the possibility of violence? I knew of the plan to remove that sword from its lacquer box, surreptitiously if possible. But, knowing those men and the mania to possess it which obsessed them, I realized that if by any chance their plan went wrong they would not hesitate to amend it by murder. That was one reason that I volunteered to become an accomplice in the theft. What does the possible loss of that trinket mean to you? Nothing! I hoped that they would succeed, but I came here determined to prevent violence. That is why I attempted to drug you, Mr. Williams. That concoction was harmless; its effects would have disappeared within a couple of hours; but you were safer asleep than alert to guard your property when those fanatics came for it."

Tommy's smile was plainly incredulous as he turned and picked up the automatic which Arkell had knocked from her hand.

"And this pretty little toy—I notice that the clip contains a dozen soft-nosed bullets; it is a curiously deadly weapon for a peacemaker to carry," he said.

"With that pretty little toy I could obliterate the pips on the ten of diamonds across this great studio in twenty seconds!" she answered impatiently. "That it is loaded with soft-nosed bullets should make it tell its own story; a fanatic takes a lot of killing. I carried that as a last precaution, sir; when I came here I believed that it was Baron Moto himself who would make the attempt. You do not know—it is not probable that you ever will know—the price I should have to pay for my weakness; but had the circumstance required it, I should have sent the first of those bullets through his head, the second through my own heart. I can't tell you why; I do not know myself. God knows that in my life I have experienced little to prove to me that the quality of mercy exists; certainly nothing to teach me to practice it. As O Yucha San, I came to this studio this morning prepared to do anything which would further the one cause for which I have uncomplainingly suffered —a cause which I could further only by serving Baron Moto. But the moment I stepped inside of that door I was conscious that I had entered an atmosphere which I had never before known, and it affected me most curiously. Never before have I played that part so perfectly; but that was because I did it automatically—and I was playing the part of an automaton. I did not know that you even suspected the imposture; but when by your infernal cunning you roused in him that ancient spirit which he has so successfully concealed from all the world, my very soul revolted; I dared not make open proclamation that I was masquerading, but had my life been forfeited by it I could not have refrained from dropping the mask long enough to deny to *you* that I was kin to that demon you had raised."

The two secret-service men listened, open-mouthed. She was evidently oblivious to them, to the body stiffening in rigor mortis on the divan, to everything except her passionate effort to vindicate herself in Tommy's estimation. And, curiously enough, I realized that in her appeal there was nothing of sex save its method of presentation, which was purely feminine in its inconsistency. There was no suggestion of sentimentality, but I was conscious that from some motive too subtle for me to fathom she was desperately anxious to obtain at least a lenient judgment from Tommy and to establish herself in his good graces without renouncing her alliance with those against whom he had pitted his wits.

And when she turned to me, with true feminine irrelevancy interrupting her attack on Tommy's susceptibilities, and frankly admitted that while she had literally held my life in the hollow of her hand when I had Moto covered with my pistol, she could never have brought herself to the point of killing me, my predisposition in her favor was strengthened. Never until then had I discovered anything beautiful in her face; but there was an irresistible appeal in her eyes, a fascinating attraction in her smile.

"Of course I could never have let you shoot him—you would understand that if you knew how important it is to me that he should live," she continued, with a bewitching artlessness. "I am an expert with that weapon, and even through the kimono sleeve I could have shot that pistol from your hand. Perhaps I might have grazed a finger, but you have ten of them. The baron has but one life, which is most precious to me, and you looked so fierce and stern that I knew your bullet would find its billet if you pulled the trigger."

A very Mephistophelean grin came to Tommy's lips as I mumbled an acknowledgment of my belief in the innocence of her intentions; but he curtly cut her short when, after flashing me a smile of gratitude, she again turned to him.

"We'll take it for granted that in spite of appearances you came here with only the milk of human kindness toward us flowing in your veins, and that at a pinch you were prepared to be our guardian angel," he said dryly. "That, however, does not imply that you are innocent of complicity in a plot to rob us; a plot which has culminated in the very embarrassing situation that we have a dead Japanese to get rid of or account for. You chaps will have to take care of that part of it," he continued, turning to Morrison and Ferros. "You know enough of what is going on to appreciate that we don't want any publicity. Can you manage it?"

"I think that our department has enough drag for that, unless his friends carry the thing to the newspapers," answered Morrison confidently. "Is there any chance that the embassy will start anything?"

"Not the ghost of a chance. They would probably deny that he was even a Japanese," said Tommy grimly. "That needn't worry you. And his immediate boss is on the way to the Mexican border, under the watchful eyes of yours, so——"

"Mr. Williams, you have little conception of the demon you have aroused or created with your black magic, if you believe that!" interrupted La Duvalief hurriedly. "No matter how urgently the business of the mikado might call to the Baron Moto, the Daimio Moto Takimura would never go far from where the hara-kiri sword of his ancestors rested in the keeping of strangers. Give it to me, Mr. Williams. So long as you keep it, you will find it only a menace; with it I could gain my heart's desire and accomplish my mission in life; and I promise you that the Baron Moto will never again cross your path."

Tommy looked at her intently for a moment and shook his head.

"No, not yet, at any rate," he answered. "If keeping it will make him stay away from the border, that will be enough for the present. Arkell is clever in his line, but he hasn't just the quality of brains to fight that Jap's schemes, and——"

A tapping at the door interrupted him, and he bowed low to her after reading the telegram which I took from the panting messenger boy.

"I think I must give you right, mademoiselle," he said quietly. "Arkell was able to secure the drawing-room, after all; for Baron Moto, for whom it was reserved, changed his mind at the last moment and remained in New York."

Her expression suddenly changed; her face became masklike, inscrutable, as the door which I had inadvertently left ajar swung open and Tommy, alert for every sign of danger, wheeled about to face the Baron Moto.

"I believe I heard my name. I hope you were saying something good of me," he said quietly, as he stepped into the studio.

CHAPTER XI.

It was, of course, her voice which had given La Duvalief high place in the world of art; but had she played behind the footlights the various rôles which she assumed in our old studio apartment, the most exacting critics would have ranked her dramatic ability with that of Duse and the divine Sarah. Surely never was an actress on the mimic stage confronted with such a difficult part as circumstance assigned to her when Baron Moto made his startling and unexpected appearance in the studio doorway; but he had not advanced three paces into the room before she had assumed it on the spur of the moment as convincingly as if she were letter-perfect from long rehearsal.

The body of Moto Ito, stiffening on the divan, was a grim reminder that she was playing in a game of life and death. The calm, stern face of Baron Moto, from which inscrutable eyes watched her without the slightest betrayal of the thoughts behind them, testified that the slightest slip would bring the fabric of hope, which she had erected in serving him, tumbling about her in ruins. It

IIA P

was a part within a part; for to retain his confidence it was necessary to hoodwink him, to convince him absolutely of her fidelity to his interests, and that we had no suspicion that she had previously visited the studio as O Yucha San, or that she had the slightest connection with or knowledge of the plot which had culminated in the hara-kiri of Moto Ito.

Never for an instant did she over or underplay that part, although she must have been conscious that a single word from any one of the American spectators would spoil her effort. She was the experienced woman of the world, unwittingly and innocently involved in a sudden and unexpected tragedy, and she behaved exactly as the average man would expect an experienced woman of the world to behave in such an emergency. It was perhaps fortunate that Tommy's remark at the station had predisposed the baron to the opinion that we suspected nothing; it was certainly an advantage to have Tommy distract and monopolize his attention, which he eventually did, but not until La Duvalief had been forced to use her dramatic powers to the utmost.

"Baron, your coming here is as much of a surprise to me as I dare say my visit to the station was to you; but I can assure you that you are welcome," he said quietly, interrupting the convincingly excited and incoherent relation which poured from her lips. "As you can see, the result of the attempted theft has been a tragedy; I assume that appearances will speak for themselves, that you will need little explanation."

The baron walked to the divan, gently closed the lids over the glazed eyeballs, and reverently covered the dead face with a handkerchief of the finest habutai, the conventionalized lotus flower, the badge of his clan, embroidered in its center. There was not the slightest sign of sorrow on his face, nor was there any betrayal of emotion in his voice or expression when he turned to answer.

"No, to a Japanese familiar with the old traditions of his race this hardly needs an explanation," he said simply. "You suspect that he came here bent upon robbery; he is past telling whether or not that was the motive for his visit, but his act testifies that whatever it may have been, his mission failed. May I ask you for the particulars of just what happened?"

"Certainly. He was unconscious when I left here, baron, and I requested Mademoiselle Duvalief to aid in caring for him until he was so far recovered that these gentlemen, who are government officials, could put him in a cab and take him back to the hotel," answered Tommy; and then he proceeded to tell what had happened after our arrival, omitting only the significant detail that La Duvalief had tripped him. "Of course, baron, we are still anxious to avoid any publicity in this matter. It would serve no good purpose, and it might cause embarrassment. We were discussing methods to avoid that just before you entered," he concluded.

The baron cast an inquiring glance at the secret-service men.

"That is a piece of generosity which I might have expected from your honorable courtesy," he said gravely. "If these gentlemen will be good enough to lend me slight assistance, I can relieve you of that embarrassment. You know, Mr. Williams, that this unfortunate man was associated with me; you recognized him as my secretary?"

Tommy bowed assent; and the baron, checking verbal reply with a gesture, drew himself up proudly, and, taking place beside the divan, faced us defiantly, in bearing and expression no longer the Prussianized product of Western civilization, but the daimio of the days of the shoguns.

"Yes, you recognized him as Sheygio,

the secretary of the Baron Moto," he said, a curious intonation in his voice recalling the death chant which we had heard through the studio door. "But he was more than that; he was Moto Ito, a noble of the honorable clan of the Moto Takimura of which I, whom you have known as the Baron Moto, by right of birth and succession, am the unworthy daimio. He was bone of my bone, flesh of my flesh, and blood of my blood, my faithful kinsman and retainer. My quarrel was his quarrel, my honor was his honor. The death which he died I glory in; the task in which he failed shall be mine to complete; should I, too, fail, that duty will pass from man to man, from father to son, so long as the humblest descendant of the great and honorable Hideoyshi, from whom the Moto Takimuras sprang, shall live to glorify and reverence the traditions of their fathers!"

Quite unconsciously and as if oblivious to our presence, he broke into his native language, his voice rising to that falsetto which seems the common tone of all Orientals in expressing strong emotion. La Duvalief, the only one of us to whom his words conveyed a meaning, carefully avoided meeting our eyes; but, clever as she was in dissimulation, she could not entirely disguise her intense and eager interest in them. In fact, had he not been so strongly under the influence of his emotions that in chanting those words of the past he had forgotten for the moment the present, she might have betrayed herself; for La Duvalief, the Russian singer, was not supposed to number the Japanese language among her accomplishments. But she quickly recovered herself, and her face was as eloquent of bewilderment as was my own when the baron broke off abruptly, and, passing his slender, brown hand over his forehead, looked confusedly about the studio.

"I must crave your pardon!" he said

to Tommy. "I fear that I have forgotten myself, Mr. Williams; there must be something about this wonderful room which rouses strange passions and memories."

Tommy shrugged his shoulders.

"Baron, there are getting to be too many tragic associations with it to please me," he said grimly, as he noted that the eyes of the Japanese wandered to the cabinet where the sword had rested. "But, as I am rather attached to it, and don't wish to move, I'm going to do my best to prevent the accumulation of any more. For that reason, perhaps, it would be wise to tell you that the object which your eyes are seeking will not be kept here any longer; for the present I shall put it in a place of safety. And now, if you will kindly tell these gentlemen how they can assist you——"

There was a flash of disappointment in the baron's eyes.

"You do not mean—you cannot mean that you would part with that sword to another!" he interrupted. "You, the one alien whom I have ever known who had a sympathetic understanding of what such an object would mean to me."

Tommy shook his head. "Not for gold and precious stones would I dispose of it to you or to any one else," he answered. "At one time or another in my life I've taken big chances, but there's a limit beyond which even the rashest fool will not go, and I should call having something which all the descendants of Hideoyshi want to get hold of lying casually around just about a million miles beyond that limit. It isn't going to leave New York, baron; it won't go more than a mile away from this studio, but it will be surrounded by greater safeguards than the simple little electrical device which preserved it the first time. I hope that one day it will become your property, but for the

moment I can't see my way clear to part with it. But I can't have it about here, and I am fearful that its possession has already brought me disaster, for I can hardly believe that after the painful things which have happened because of it I can induce Mademoiselle Duvalief to keep her promise to return here for a portrait."

It was fortunate for Baron Moto that turning to face the Russian hid his face from Tommy's observation, for in the eyes which he fixed on her there was a menace and a threat which even she found it difficult to meet. His voice, however, was suave and courteous as he answered for her before she had an opportunity to speak for herself.

"I am quite sure that mademoiselle, whose friendship it has been for a long time my privilege to enjoy, will not let this unfortunate occurrence influence her unduly," he said. "Only I must warn mademoiselle that if she has secrets to conceal she must guard them most jealously, for there is some mysterious influence here which destroys pretense."

Whether it was skillful acting or grim and pitiful reality I could not determine; but La Duvalief seemed suddenly possessed of a paralyzing fear as she shrank back under his threatening eyes.

Tommy started visibly as he noted that expression and the hysterical quality in the laugh of protest which came from lips suddenly blanched and tremulous.

"Baron Moto, I can assure you that mademoiselle need have no fear that her confidence will be forced!" he exclaimed, coming to her rescue. "I take it for granted that you intended no offense in that warning, for it is inconceivable that an American gentleman would take unfair advantage of a woman's fears. Mademoiselle may come here in perfect peace and security. You are not the first man who has insinuated that this studio is a temple of truth, and its walls have listened to many strange revelations and confessions, but no man——"

The baron wheeled suddenly to face him; and La Duvalief, freed from the observation of those eyes which had dominated her, quickly regained her self-possession.

"Mr. Williams, I certainly meant no offense!" protested the baron. "Nor do I read any in your reply. But remember that the customs and ethics of the West have but recently been adopted in our land. Circumstances have required that we accept and practice many things which would not have been tolerated under the old régime; to survive and progress in the world competition which was forced upon us when our protecting isolation was destroyed, we have been obliged to accept them unquestioningly and to practice them most vigorously. Two of them are so much a part of your recognized code of morals that they are taught to your children in the schools as copybook maxims—'Necessity knows no law,' and 'All's fair in love and war.' "

Tommy's smile was suddenly Mephistophelean, and he looked at the Japanese through eyelids narrowed to slits.

"Baron, you can prove pretty much anything by copybook maxims, and there's one of 'em that I've seen verified time and again in this very studio," he said dryly. "It's the one we try to steer by without even a mental reservation, and that is, 'Honesty is the best policy.' There is still another, and I believe that the spirit of it was a part of the code of your ancestors. It is, 'Noblesse oblige.' "

A flush came to the baron's face, and for the first time he found difficulty in meeting Tommy's gaze. For an instant La Duvalief disregarded him, and in that instant I knew that she was playing no part; for in the eyes which she

turned gratefully on Tommy I read the confidence and fearlessness of a trustful child.

CHAPTER XII.

Morrison and Ferros demonstrated the ability which Arkell had claimed for them in preventing publicity concerning the manner of Moto Ito's death, a sensation which would have made a front-page story for every New York paper. The body was removed to the Hotel Blitz, the necessary formalities were complied with, and the whole matter arranged without anything more than a simple announcement that Captain Sheygio, a near relative of Baron Moto, had died suddenly, appearing in print. That announcement, following close upon the heels of the statement that the baroness was confined to her apartment by a severe illness, was sufficient to account for the abandonment of the social program which had been arranged; and, greatly to the disappointment of the secret-service agents, led to the cancellation of Mrs. Padelford's engagement as social secretary.

In fact, it was only from La Duvalief and the reports of the secret-service men, who maintained a constant watch upon their movements, that we knew of the continued presence of that curious Japanese delegation in New York; for the baron's visits to the studio ceased, and we learned that he and all of his party kept themselves secluded in their apartments. La Duvalief, however, came to the studio every day, and, considering the manner of her introduction and the strenuous and tragic incidents in which she had taken part there, her relationship was curiously commonplace.

"Mr. Williams, I have come here on order, but I obey that order because I wish to," she said simply, when she appeared the day following the tragedy. "I am taking you at your word that you would take no advantage of a woman's fear to force her confidence. You gave me the clew to the reason this studio atmosphere is so grateful to me; it is because I felt instinctively that you two gentlemen practiced always all that is implied by that very indefinite 'Noblesse oblige.' And it is just because of that that I shall, if you permit me, make the task which you set for yourself easy; I should value the privilege of coming here and of being within these walls that I never dare to be in the great world outside— the real Nelka Duvalief."

From Tommy's expression I knew that he received her statement as the absolute verity. She, too, was conscious of that; her eyes expressed her gratitude, and, taking his assent for granted, she went on quickly before he could speak.

"And so there must be no false pretense!" she exclaimed. "I am still nominally the agent—the spy, if you wish to be harsh—of Baron Moto; but, as I have received nothing of his confidence, there is nothing which I can betray. The mythical O Yucha San is still in his apartment; I, as La Duvalief, do not enter there, and have no knowledge of what is going on inside the doors. I believe that for the moment he has abandoned the plan in which he thought my services would be of value; in the instructions I received this morning there was no suggestion of it, only the order to come here regularly and to find out, if possible, the disposition you have made of that sword."

"I will make that simple for you; I give you my word that it is in the strongest safe-deposit vault in this city," answered Tommy. "As for the rest, I think I understand—and now for the portrait!"

And with that simple understanding, in spite of all that had gone before, commenced that succession of days in which this strange and mysterious woman posed faithfully and steadily every morning, often remaining with us for luncheon, and occasionally dining with us at a restaurant.

In many ways that portrait was the best thing which Tommy ever produced; but probably no one of the thousands of people who had seen her across the footlights would have recognized it as the likeness of the great singer, and certainly none of the hundreds who had been more or less intimately associated with her in the other phases of her many-sided career would have discovered in it the traits with which they were familiar. It was, above all, the face of a good woman; but not of a woman ignorant of the knowledge of evil. One felt instinctively that the wonderful eyes had gazed far into the depths of human depravity, but in them there was no hint of viciousness. It was the face of a young girl, but by some subtle trick of brush and color he had made it the face of youth prematurely aged by suffering and misery. There was nobility in it, a claim for that pride and purity of purpose which produces the rare woman capable of knowing all evil while practicing none of it.

And I knew that in painting that curiously contradictory portrait Tommy was absolutely honest and sincere in putting on the canvas only what he believed he read in the study of her face. It was not to impress her; for, in spite of her teasing and pleading, from the time when he first outlined her face in charcoal on the white canvas, he never permitted her to get a glimpse of his work. Nor would he discuss it with me, even when we were alone together. And during the many hours which we spent lingering about the luncheon table I was almost convinced that his conception of her was the true one; for she revealed, on closer acquaintance, a most unexpected human sympathy, a broad-minded judgment of men and affairs, and a habit of thought curiously free from cynicism and bitterness in a woman who had observed at close range so much of the seamy side of life.

Even exceeding the strict letter of their tacit agreement, we carefully avoided discussion of her most recent associations and associates; but from the mutual acquaintances, we discovered it was evident that rumor had not wronged her in whispering that she was an old hand in the game of underground diplomacy, for most of them were intimately connected with that vast web of espionage in which we had more than once been involved during our long European residence.

But if La Duvalief did her best to make us forget that, and ignored the spread of that web of conspiracy to this continent, Arkell certainly did his best to keep it constantly before our minds. Not a day passed without a long communication from him, usually sent in code to the New York office and forwarded in plain language from there by the hands of Morrison or Ferros. From all that he was able to discover after his arrival at the border, it appeared that Tommy's first conjecture was right; there was nothing to show that the massacre of the seventeen Americans was anything but a piece of wanton savagery committed by the followers of Villa; but on the other hand, that wholesale murder was quickly followed by disquieting and suspicious developments.

Now, owing to the most elaborate system devised by the secret service during the long period of watchful waiting, there was hardly a rifle, a box of cartridges, a case of munitions, or a pound of explosives which entered Mexico without their knowledge, and in almost every instance they knew the source of origin and the eventual destination. There is nothing partisan about the secret service; for many years it has been exactly what its name implies, and it has always proved en-

tirely adequate to the duties required of it, duties so varied that their scope is not even suspected by the general public which it so efficiently protects and serves. The preservation of neutrality during the European war, and the gathering of accurate information along the Mexican border and in Mexico itself were among those newer duties, and under Arkell's direction they were conscientiously and skillfully performed; but he was quick to realize and sufficiently generous to acknowledge that even in that service Tommy's very peculiar abilities were of the greatest value to him. And so day by day he sent those full reports which told of the mysterious and puzzling events below the Rio Grande, of the growing animosity against Americans, of the increasing arrogance of the ragged revolutionists, of the common bond which seemed to be making them forget their jealousies of each other.

Arkell was unable to obtain absolute and definite proof of his suspicions, but day after day he unearthed evidence which strengthened them. One day it would be the discovery of Japanese officers turning bands of tatterdemalion bandits into disciplined regiments of effective soldiers; the next, it might be the sudden reconciliation of two rival leaders following visits from the slant-eyed Orientals who for months had been investigating the possibilities of the silkworm culture. At Guaymas and the other ports on the Gulf of California, the Japanese fishing schooners arrived in ever-increasing numbers, carrying hundreds of passengers who disappeared mysteriously into the Yaqui Indian country; and at Manzanillo a succession of tramp steamers flying the Japanese flag discharged curious cargoes which were entered at the customhouse as agricultural and mining machinery. In southern California the Japanese colonies were very much depleted; by twos and threes the men—

most of them veterans of the Russian war—slipped away, most of them leaving San Diego to cross the border—to be lost to sight the minute they passed the little frontier village of Tijuana.

But there was one thing which Arkell's reports particularly emphasized: The arms shipments which had characterized what he called the second phase of the situation had steadily diminished from a stream to a trickle, and even that entirely ceased from the moment Villa's bandits crossed the border to raid Columbus. Save for small driblets smuggled across by pack mule and rowboat, not a rifle or cartridge was entering Mexico from the United States or through the Atlantic ports; but still the scattered revolutionists, whose numbers were steadily increased, were readily supplied with equipment, and the soldiers of the de-facto government suffered from no lack of ammunition or arms.

The entrance of Pershing's force into Mexico tremendously increased the difficulty of obtaining information; but still Arkell managed to get a lot, and to me it was most disquieting, for it told of ever-increasing efficiency of the Mexicans; of the quiet concentration of large bodies of troops at points where they could cut the slender line of communication with the base in a dozen places. Tommy shook his head when I voiced my fears.

"If our information is correct, there is no immediate danger," he said grimly. "Morrison assures me positively that the baron and his entire party are still at the Blitz. No one has seen them; they keep themselves absolutely secluded; but he has a cordon of shadowers about the place which they can't elude. Even Nelka has not seen the baron; but every day she makes her report that the sword is still in the safe-deposit vault, and every day she receives renewed instructions in his own handwriting to watch most carefully for

it. He's there, safe enough, and so long as he is, and neglecting his manifest duty to the mikado which calls him to Mexico, nothing is going to happen. He is fairly deluged with telegrams; the secret service has managed to decode a few of them. Each of those has urged that he come immediately; whatever the action he had planned there, it evidently can't start without his personal supervision—and it's the one best bet that Colonel Moto will not go down there until the Daimio Moto Takimura gets what he's after in New York."

He laughed at my protest that the baron might elude the cleverest shadowers, and that La Duvalief, in spite of the good qualities to which his unfinished portrait testified, was still possessed of a past which did not recommend her as absolutely trustworthy.

"I never trust any one too far, and it's about time to stimulate the samurai spirit again, anyway," he said. "If you'll look in the cabinet, you'll see that the sword is there; I brought it from the vault this morning—and I might mention that a Jap who had trailed me from the studio to the bank started on the keen jump in the direction of the Hotel Blitz when he saw me come out with the box under my arm. I asked Nelka to come an hour later than usual this morning; she's just about due, and when——"

Of course it was La Duvalief whom I admitted in response to a nervously insistent knocking; Tommy's eyes always seemed to be able to see through that heavy oaken door. Without stopping to greet us, she ran to the cabinet and an indescribable cry came from her lips as she saw the sword in its customary resting place.

"What is this—the meaning of it—are you as mad as this thing has made Baron Moto and his people?" she demanded, fright and bewilderment mingled in her expression. "Don't you know that you are inviting danger by having this thing here? It needed the evidence of my own eyes to make me believe that he was not mistaken when he told me that you had removed it from the vault and brought it back."

"Don't get excited about a little thing like that, Nelka," said Tommy quietly. "Is there any reason why you should not tell us just what has happened to arouse you so?"

Before answering she tiptoed to the door, opened it suddenly, and, after peering out on the landing, closed it and secured it by lock and chain.

"You knew that you were spied upon, that you were seen to take it from the bank?" she asked, in a voice little above a whisper.

"Certainly. I'm only an amateur at this sort of thing, but I've learned enough to keep my eyes open," answered Tommy. "You needn't be afraid to speak out; there's nobody about but Duck Sing. You have seen Baron Moto with your own eyes."

She gave a little start and looked at him curiously, her eyes troubled, her face unusually pale.

"Tommy, what have you done? There is no longer a Baron Moto!" she said, for the first time calling him by his first name. "But what your black magic has made of him and his followers I have seen, and"—she hesitated, passing her hand, with its delicately manicured nails, across her eyes—"it is incredible, unbelievable; I cannot credit it!"

"Suppose that you tell us about it; we are not easily surprised, and it is impossible to shock us," suggested Tommy soothingly. "You were permitted to enter the apartment to-day?"

"Yes, for the first time since the death of Moto Ito," she answered, her voice so low that we were forced to listen most attentively to catch her words. For days she had been so simple and natural in her bearing that I had almost forgotten the great dramatic powers of which she had proved herself to be possessed; but I was suddenly conscious of them, for there was much that was suggestive of the theater in the furtive wandering of her gaze to the corners of the studio, the tightly clenched hands pressed firmly to her breast, the tenseness of her whole attitude and expression. It was so suggestive that my half-allayed suspicions returned redoubled, and I was more than doubtful of her sincerity.

"Yes, for the first time since Moto Ito's death I entered that anteroom where, as Sheygio, he had performed his labors as the Baron Moto's private and confidential secretary," she continued. "It was as I had seen it last, save that the desk at which he worked was piled high with unopened letters and telegrams, and the air was heavy with the perfume of burning incense. Adjoining it was the large salon where it was originally planned that I, in the character of O Yucha San, was to entertain the people of whom the baron expected to make use. Those entertainments were to have been Japanese in character; he had already made arrangements to have his countrymen here make the decorations and furnishings typically in keeping, and my two *musmes,* both of them perfectly trained geishas, were to serve tea, and, when occasion demanded, press the insidious, tongue-loosing sake upon youngsters by whose indiscreet revelations he might profit." She interrupted her recital, and, with finger on lips, tiptoed to the door, listening for a moment for the slightest sound which might betray listeners upon the outer side.

"I was prepared, therefore, to find it changed when little O Kin San opened the door and beckoned me to enter; but nothing had prepared me for such a transformation as I actually found," she continued, still in that same subdued voice. "I had expected the dainty trappings of a high-caste Japanese lady's boudoir; I stepped from Sheygio's workroom, equipped with every twentieth-century, modern convenience for secretarial work, into the council chamber of the Moto Takimuras of medieval Nippon. The walls were hung with priceless antique embroideries and tapestries, each depicting some incident of the life of the great Hideoyshi from which the clan claims direct descent, and the heroic deeds of the Forty-seven Ronins. On a shrine of exquisite lacquer, heavily decorated with the golden lotus flower in high relief, rested the great, two-handed fighting sword of Hideoyshi, the companion weapon to that hara-kiri dagger in your cabinet."

Tommy could not restrain an exclamation of astonishment as she paused and pointed to it.

"Great Scott! Can that be possible?" he exclaimed. "Is this the weapon of Hideoyshi, the Japanese Sir Launcelot, and Bertrand du Guesclin rolled into one popular hero?"

"No less a treasure would have tempted the Baron Moto, the most trusted officer of the Japanese general staff, to forget all that he has learned of Western civilization and the fealty he has sworn to the mikado in his mad desire to regain possession of it," she answered.

She had forgotten her fears as she spoke; her beautifully modulated voice came in natural volume from the lips to which the color had returned.

"And the reason for admitting you to the chamber?" said Tommy, as she paused. Never for a moment had his eyes left her face, but there was nothing of suspicion in them. He watched her as a scientific investigator might watch the development of a delicate experiment in a chemical laboratory, alert for the first indication that a fresh reagent must be added to get the desired result. And as I in turn watched his

face, I realized that never had an alchemist waited more eagerly to see base metal transmuted to gold in his crucible than Tommy Williams watched to find in this curious feminine bundle of contradictions a confirmation of, and a justification for, the qualities which his brush had so subtly indicated on the canvas which was shrouded by the covering cloth on his easel.

She hesitated long before answering to his suggestion, unable, in spite of her natural talent and long training, entirely to conceal the inward conflict which her face betrayed. Gradually she slipped back into that La Duvalief we had first known, and Tommy's eyes hardened as he watched her expression change.

"Mr. Williams, you must employ that cleverness which you claimed to guess the real reason for that," she answered, the formal address emphasizing the hint of defiance which had unconsciously crept into her voice. "You must remember that Baron Moto has not the slightest suspicion that you discovered the imposture when I came here as O Yucha San; that he believes that you are not suspicious that as La Duvalief I am coming here as his spy. He thinks that I am absolutely faithful to his interests; not because he trusts me, for he trusts no one who is not of his race; but because he knows how prohibitive to me would be the cost of betrayal. I do not yet know his plan; perhaps if he had confided it to me I should not have warned you of the danger of having that weapon here. Because he has not trusted me fully I can tell you this much: he sent for me to give me my orders. I was to come here as usual and verify by my own eyes the fact that you had brought the sword here. If possible I was to find out if you intended to keep it here. I am to report to him and then again assume the character of O Yucha San. She is to make such a quick and unexpected recovery that Baron Moto will ask the privilege of escorting her here this evening, ostensibly to make his apologies for what has happened and to make amends by arranging for you to paint her portrait just as you wished. That is all." The determined set of her lips as she finished confirmed that curt finale; she would volunteer nothing further. But Tommy's expression warned me that he would not let it stop there.

"He'll be granted that privilege, all right; but in spite of his samurai highbinders he's not going to get that knife until I'm ready to hand it to him!" he said, a grim smile on his lips as he turned to me. "See here, old chap; I want you to do me a favor. Go down to headquarters and ask Morrison to detail a strong-arm squad of his men to watch this place; men who are not afraid to take a chance with jujutsu, and who will keep their mouths shut. They are to let Baron Moto and his wife enter unchallenged, but after that they are to hold up everything which looks like a Jap which comes within a block of the entrance—slam 'em into taxis and keep 'em driving around the park until daylight. That'll be about all; I reckon we can attend to things here in the studio."

Again I saw the betrayal of an inward struggle in La Duvalief's eyes as she listened, and when I reluctantly started to carry out Tommy's instructions she motioned me to wait.

"Are you sure of that, Mr. Williams?" she asked. "Remember that I have told you that it means the accomplishment of the mission to which I have devoted my life if Baron Moto's plans succeed. As O Yucha San, I shall come here to further them—as his accomplice, to be brutally frank—and you know that I am capable of doing desperate things."

"Mademoiselle, since you've started being brutally frank, I'll take my cue from you," answered Tommy, turning suddenly to face her; and, consummate actress as La Duvalief had demonstrated herself to be, I realized that my versatile friend was beating her at her own game. The formal "mademoiselle" in place of the familiar "Nelka" which he had used for days, the curl of his lip, the biting sarcasm of his voice combined to express a contempt before which she shrank back as if threatened by a whip, and brought to her eyes a moisture which perhaps prevented her from reading in his that in adopting brutality he was playing a part. I read it there; for, in spite of his harshness, he was still the investigator, the alchemist.

"You prated about the refreshing atmosphere of noblesse oblige which you found so grateful in this studio; but, according to your own confession, you're not the kind of a woman who would recognize that atmosphere if it was strong enough to asphyxiate you!" he went on contemptuously. "Just the same, that does exist here, and I shall be true to the promise I have made— even to the woman you have shown yourself to be. I shall take no advantage of your fears to force your confidence; the confidences of such an inveterate liar would be of no value to any one. Come here to-night, prepared and primed to do any desperate thing your yellow master may command; I do not fear him, I do not fear you. I'm still confident that as a white man I'm more than a match for any Oriental, even one who holds the lash over a white woman who has so far forgotten the traditions of her blood that she lowers herself to serve him. If that sacred mission to which you whine that you have consecrated yourself depends upon his success, you're doomed to as great a disappointment as he is, for I'm going to smash his plans so flat that he'll think a steam roller ran over 'em."

At first she fairly cringed before him, but as the tirade continued it roused a fury within her, and at its conclusion she faced him erect and defiant, her hands clenched, her dark eyes blazing in a face livid with passion.

"You! You for whom I have sacrificed so much, for whom I have risked losing all that I have lived for when it is almost within my grasp; you dare to say these things to me!" she exclaimed furiously. "That much of it is true takes away none of the bitterness of it coming from your lips. I scorn to justify myself to one who knows no gratitude; but what has my life been but a lie, and who has forced me to live it? I do not *prate* of noblesse oblige; it is you who do not know the meaning of it. Nor do I *whine* about my mission; I glory in it. I shall be true to it, even if to accomplish it I must work beneath the lash of a yellow man and trample out the lives of his white antagonists to win!"

Tommy's gaze had never faltered; but, as her defiance terminated with a suspicious tremor in her voice, the mask of contempt dropped from his face. He watched her steadily as he walked over to the easel and placed his hand on the cloth covering the portrait which she had never seen.

"You will pardon me if I repeat that you are an inveterate liar," he said quietly; but the smile on his lips and the kindliness in his eyes drew the sting from the accusation. "The most dangerous kind of a liar, for you are so skillful at it that you deceive yourself. I suppose that you believe implicitly right now that you will be able to carry out the rash threats you have just made; but I know—perhaps through that same black magic which you accuse me of having practiced on Moto Takimura—that you never can; I know it, at any rate, from what I have discovered of the real Nelka Duvalief beneath that lying exterior, the Nelka Duvalief whom Serge Ivanof loved and for whom he suffered, the Nelka Duvalief—my

Nelka Duvalief—whom my brush has imprisoned on this canvas!"

Her face was a study in bewilderment as she listened; no color returned to it, but the fury died in her eyes under his kindliness. And when, as he concluded, he whisked the covering cloth from the portrait, she had ocular proof that he was sincere, a cry of relief and gratitude came from her lips. For a moment she gazed at it, spellbound, and when she turned away from it to look at him, her own face had grown curiously like that one which Tommy had idealized on the canvas.

"You mean that, Tommy, after the life I have led all these years, the deceit I have practiced until it is second nature, the hot plowshares on which I have walked, you can still find that Nelka Duvalief in me?" she asked piteously, as if fearing that she was the victim of a grim joke.

"I mean that absolutely, Nelka; I never force my brush to lie," he answered quickly. "All that you see there I have found in your face; even your art could not hide from me the real Nelka Duvalief. That is why I do not fear you, for I know that when the test comes that real Nelka will be too strong for the La Duvalief; that no fear would be strong enough to overcome the traditions of the white man's civilization at the behest of an Oriental barbarian." With a little cry she turned and came toward me with outstretched hands.

"Go! Go! Go!" she exclaimed hysterically, pushing me toward the door. "I shall betray myself, but there must be no witness—go!" A quick nod from Tommy enforced obedience, and, releasing me, she threw herself on the divan, burying her face in her hands, her body shaken with her convulsive sobbing. And as I looked back from the doorway I saw on Tommy's face, as he watched her, the expression of triumph of the alchemist who has seen worthless dross transmuted to purest gold.

CHAPTER XIII.

When I hurried back to the studio after completing the arrangements for the secret-service operators, La Duvalief had gone. There was an air of elation in Tommy's manner which testified that he believed that he had been successful in his experiment, but I received small satisfaction when I questioned him.

"I can't tell you just what happened; it would be too much like betraying the secrets of the confessional," he protested. "Perhaps you guessed pretty nearly the truth; at any rate, you'll not be very long in suspense, for things seem to be moving toward a quick climax. You have attended to what I asked you to do?"

"Yes, and I was tempted to go farther and ask Morrison to send a couple of men inside," I grumbled. "Perhaps that Russian wept out something after I left that convinced you that you can trust her, but she's played too many parts here to let her come it over me. I'm still not so certain of her that I'd trust her much farther than I could see her."

"Then that will make your part all the easier to play this evening, for you may have to put a bullet through her before the entertainment to which Moto has invited himself is over," answered Tommy, grinning, as he glanced at a note lying on the table. "So far it's come off according to program; the note which she predicted arrived, and I sent back word that I should be delighted to see them—which is gospel truth."

"I'll be hanged if I shall be!" I protested. "I tell you I don't trust that woman; I thought it all over while I was out, and——"

"You won't have to think at all this evening," interrupted Tommy impatiently. "Neither will you have to dissemble your suspicions; for I want you to get the drop on O Yucha San the moment she enters the door. Don't make any bones about it, either; let her see that you've got it, and don't hesitate much longer than it takes a rattlesnake to strike about shooting at the first bad move. If you do, or if you don't shoot to kill, you'll be the central figure at the resulting coroner's inquest. I don't believe it will come to that if you show from the start that you're not bluffing, for within five minutes after they get here I'll have that reincarnated samurai so tame that he'll eat out of my hand and stand without hitching. That will be all the time I need, and I'm trusting to you to keep that bear cat bluffed; but don't be afraid to make your bluff good if she attempts to call it —you know I shouldn't ask you to do anything I would balk at myself."

It was not an alluring prospect, but I knew that I should have to obey, trust him implicitly, or get out. He smiled his gratitude when I mumbled a reluctant promise.

"It's essential that I get the baron here," he continued. "I've been going over Arkell's reports, those you have seen and one which came while you were out, and I'm sure that things are getting about ready to crack. If that Jap should come out of his trance and get back on the job he was busy with before he caught sight of that sword, he might start something in ten minutes which it would take all the might and majesty of the United States a good many years to finish. Now, before he leaves here to-night, I intend to see that he does start something; but it's going to finish along about where I dictate— which is approximately the point where his original plan called for the commencement. Hold on. I'm not trying to mystify you; you'll get what I mean when I tell you that we'll be leaving for southern California to-morrow."

"No, I don't get you at all," I protested, and he grinned as he pointed to the file of Arkell's reports.

"If you analyze those, you'll find one reason," he said. "Pretty much all they contain has, since we received them, been published in the newspapers, and the attention of the public, the government, and the war department is pretty well concentrated on the border from El Paso to Columbus—owing to the pernicious activity of Pancho Villa. Now, I haven't the honor of his acquaintance, but we have a pretty good line on him from the descriptions of trained and accurate observers. They are unanimous in describing him as illiterate, brutal, and bloodthirsty, without moral sense, devoid of conscience, and the incarnation of bestial lust; he is altogether unfitted to be a Salvation Army officer, but he has demonstrated his ability to recruit, discipline, and lead an army of Mexican bandits. He has been accused of pretty much every crime in the calendar, but no one has ever impugned his personal bravery nor accused him of being a fool. Now, so long as Mexico's troubles were confined to her own borders, or if the various factions combined to fight the United States, he would be General Francisco Villa, the leader of a recognized army. But as a result of that massacre and that mad raid across the border, he is Pancho Villa, the outlaw and bandit, with pretty much the whole American army chasing him, and his own people afraid to give him open support."

"I still fail to get you; there seems to be justification for the belief that he's dead—Arkell had positive proof that he was badly wounded, and——"

"It doesn't make any difference whether he's dead or alive—now," interrupted Tommy. "The important thing is the true significance of that massacre and the subsequent raid. Now, admitting that Villa is not a fool, why should he have gratuitously slapped the face of the United States? It's my guess that he is to-day a skulking bandit instead of a Mexican general, because

he failed to receive the support of which he felt assured, and that support failed him because Moto Takimura happened to discover the hara-kiri sword of his ancestors in this studio. You'll notice that up to a certain point everything went like clockwork; Villa's affront was so outrageous that we had to act, and that action meant stripping every army post in the United States to get enough men to chase him and guard the Texas border. There has been no suspicious Mexican activity in Lower California; our attention has been riveted to the other portion of the border; and even the coast artillery, with insufficient men to serve the guns when they are all where they belong, has been called upon to help out. You remember, of course, the opening of the Japanese-Russian war; the Japs virtually won it before it was officially declared by a surprise attack which crippled the Russian fleet and gave them a free sea over which they transported their troops. That's their conception of strategy—and they had also taken the precaution to plant a good many thousand colonists, who were transformed overnight into organized battalions, in the ports they intended to use as bases. Now, Arkell's reports show that the Mexicans are doing enough marching and countermarching to keep our forces concentrated on the Texas border; but the Japs, who are quietly pouring in through the Gulf of California, vanish into the Yaqui country, a district that even Porfirio Diaz was wise enough to leave severely alone. Incidentally, that territory happens to be within easy striking distance of southern California, so that's why we are leaving for there to-morrow."

"To stem, single-handed, the threatening yellow peril?" I jeered, and Tommy shook his head.

"No, hardly that; I've wired Arkell to be there and to have a dozen of his men with him," he answered seriously.

"I expect a very pleasant little reunion out there, and, unless I am mistaken in my guess, among those present will be the Baron Moto. We'll have plenty of time to talk it all out on the train, so now I would suggest that you make the necessary preparations for the prologue here this evening."

I had half suspected that Tommy was joking in his directions, but the care which he took in his own part of the preparations convinced me that he was in deadly earnest. He rearranged the electric lights so that they were concentrated with dazzling brilliancy upon the entrance, and moved several pieces of furniture so that they virtually formed a barrier which would prevent a quick rush from the door to the spot in the shadows where he directed me to stand to receive our expected visitors.

"I'm strong for preparedness," he said grimly, as he surveyed the results of his labors. "I'll leave the door ajar, and the only light will be that one illuminating the cabinet. The minute they come in, I'll switch on the others, and, as I shall have my hands full with the baron, it's up to you to take care of O Yucha San."

Through long association with Tommy I had learned that it was useless to question him when he was preparing one of those dramatic surprises which he delighted in; but I had also learned that he never overestimated the risks. I was, therefore, keyed up to the top notch of expectancy when the door opened that evening; and when the lights were switched on, I was convinced that in this particular instance he had, if anything, rather underestimated them.

There were only two people in the doorway. One of them was the baron; but the other, in spite of the feminine costume, was certainly not La Duvalief masquerading as O Yucha San. At the very moment of the illumination, the kimono fell from a pair of broad, masculine shoulders, the towering wig was impatiently shaken off, and over the barrel of my leveled pistol I looked into a pair of fierce, murderous eyes in the grim face of a samurai. There was no mistaking their intention, for each of them carried a short, stabbing sword, that weapon which the Japanese used with such deadly effect at close quarters at Port Arthur, and I knew that the first of Tommy's predictions was verified; they had come prepared to profit by the strategy of surprise. They were literally stripped for action, especially the baron's companion, who had passed the secret-service cordon in the feminine disguise; for when the kimono fell to the floor it revealed his wiry, muscular torso stripped to the waist, his brown skin glistening with the oil which would have made him as slippery as an eel.

The baron, who found himself facing the muzzle of Tommy's automatic, had worn beneath the overcoat which he had discarded in the hallway only a single Japanese garment of the flimsiest silk, which would have torn like tissue paper in an adversary's grasp; and on his feet were rubber-soled shoes which would have given him secure footing on the polished floor. They were so thoroughly keyed up for attack that I believe in spite of our most unexpected preparedness his companion would have taken a chance; but the baron was quick to see that the odds against them made such an attempt absolutely hopeless, and he checked him with a sharp command.

"That's wise, baron; you can appreciate that it is still my day," said Tommy quietly. "Now, see here, it is quite within our rights to shoot you both down where you stand, and I give you my word that we shall not hesitate to do it if you don't behave. As a first step, kindly drop those weapons."

They obeyed, the baron without the slightest hesitation, his companion only after a repetition of the order from him. "Now, baron, I'm not treating you chaps as common criminals; I realize that your motive in coming here prepared to commit murder, if necessary, justifies you in your own eyes," continued Tommy. "I'm going to make it easy for you, but first I want you to impress upon your friend, there, that he is to remain as passive as a bronze Buddha—or get a bullet in his head. Then, when you have done that, you are at perfect liberty to advance alone and remove from that cabinet anything which happens to suit your fancy."

The baron stared at him for a moment in speechless amazement, apparently more surprised by that unexpected generosity than by the trap into which he had walked. But, familiar from long association with every subtle intonation of Tommy's voice, I knew that he had not yet reached the climax he had planned for, and even after a few stern words in Japanese had stiffened my opponent to the rigidity of a graven image, I still kept him covered with my pistol. With his eyes fixed on the cabinet, which was illuminated strongly, the baron stepped quickly into the studio, threading his way through the disarranged furniture as a somnambulist instinctively avoids obstacles. Without lowering his pistol, Tommy quietly shifted his own position so that a broad table would be between them.

A sibilant hiss came from the baron's lips as he stood before the cabinet and started a reverent kotow before stretching out his hands to grasp that weapon of his ancestors which had made him forget his Western tutoring and his duty as a modern soldier; but it changed to a falsetto cry of disappointment and rage as he gazed through the glass and then, with the quickness of a cat, wheeled about. It was fortunate that Tommy had changed his position, for the Japanese was crouched for a spring which would have meant death to one or both of them; but in just that second

which it required for him to locate Tommy in the shadows he regained a portion of his self-control. He was still laboring under strong emotion, however, and the first words of a tirade, uttered in that shrill falsetto, were so incoherent that they were unintelligible. It spoke well for the discipline in which he held his retainers that the man I held covered never for an instant forgot his original command, and retained a passivity which I knew from the eyes which looked defiantly into mine was not dictated by fear of my pistol.

"Yes, baron, I have tricked you; the day is still to me!" exclaimed Tommy triumphantly from the shadows, cutting short that ear-piercing protest of the Oriental. "You'll have to amend that proverb which you learned from your Mexican friends, for I intend to claim several more of them. That isn't the hara-kiri sword of Hideoyshi, but an imitation of it in papier-mâché and tin which I had made by one of our theatrical property makers. I may tell you that the original has been sent by safe hands to the Pacific coast, and if anything happens to my friend or myself at Japanese hands, no Moto Takimura will ever see it again. That being the case, you will appreciate that you have everything to lose and nothing to gain by violence, so I would suggest that we put away our weapons and try to be nice and clubby as we talk things over."

For a minute or two, possibly because the baron's emotion made it difficult for him to comprehend English, it was touch and go; but as Tommy watched him in silence, he evidently concluded that he had won, for, without waiting for verbal assent, he lowered his hand and slipped his pistol into his pocket. I followed his example, but not until a few words in Japanese caused the half-naked man in the doorway to bow his defiant head and hiss a sibilant assent as he turned to gather up the garments which they had discarded in the hallway. Tommy had restored the studio to its normal condition by the time he had finished, and closed the door after entering.

It was not until then that I had a fair opportunity to study the baron's face, and I realized that La Duvalief had told the truth in describing the change in him which it reflected. He was no longer the suave, impassive, inscrutable soldier whom Tommy had painted in a modern uniform, but the fierce, imperious warrior, daimio, whose word was law to the clan of Moto Takimura. The change was accentuated by his return to the prohibited samurai fashion of hairdressing: the scalp at the sides closely shaven, the long hair at the back woven into a thin, tight braid which was brought forward along the center and fastened to a lock in the front, giving it a grotesque resemblance to a cock's comb. The wisp of mustache had been sacrificed, and the face, set in grim, hard lines, was devoid of hair save for the thin lines of eyebrows which had been distorted until they accentuated the obliquity of the slanting eyes. It was just such a face as the ancient Japanese artists depicted looking through the visors of the medieval lacquered helmets, the likeness which Tommy had approximated in his fanciful portrait. His long days of seclusion in that transplanted atmosphere of the past had carried him so far along the road to yesterday that to all outward appearance he might have been his famous ancestor, Hideoyshi, who made so large a part of the history of medieval Japan. Tommy was quick to appreciate that, and, as it apparently suited his book to prevent a return to modern methods of thought, he curtly interrupted the mumbled attempt at an apology coming from reluctant lips.

"Baron Moto, there is no need for an apology, and we neither of us have cause for complaint against the other," he said. "It is just a difference in standards. I'm sufficiently broadminded to appreciate yours, and under the circumstances you will have to accept mine. Now, I have figured out to my own satisfaction the reason why you originally came here; it was on the tip from the Russian secret service that it would be wise for you to keep track of me while your plans in the south were developing. It would have been a good tip, too, except for the peculiar coincidence that you discovered that sword in my possession. Now, right here let me say that there is only one way in which you can regain that sword, and that is by making absolute and unconditional surrender and doing exactly what I tell you to do."

The baron started, and a fierce scowl came to his face; but Tommy met it in kind and checked his protest with an imperative gesture for silence.

"I'm not arguing; I'm telling you exactly where you get off," he said sternly. "First, I'll make it easier for you to listen by giving you my word that the sword of Hideoyshi will be returned to you in all honor if you do exactly what I tell you and make your followers do the same. I also warn you that unless you do, it will be devoted to uses which will so defile it that the meanest beggar ever spurned by the foot of a Moto Takimura samurai would draw back from it in loathing—and in both these promises I mean exactly what I say. Now get that, please, for I always keep my word." He paused for a moment, and I knew that the baron did get it and that he was convinced of Tommy's sincerity; for he turned to his clansman, who was squatting on his heels near the entrance, and signed to him to be quiet.

"That's right; now we'll get along better," said Tommy approvingly. "I might just mention that in any event you can't count on outside assistance, for I took the precaution to have the secret-service men ready to bag any of your countrymen who might follow you here. No, don't get excited; they will only be detained until you leave, for I'm so sure that I hold the whip hand that I'm not worrying. Now, baron, from reports I have received from below the border I'm convinced that your devotion to the recovery of that sword has caused your carefully made plans down there to get wabbly at the joints. The watching of that part of it is in competent hands, but I have made a promise of sorts that there will not be any complications from this end; so you and your staff will continue to keep hands off, remain deaf to the appeals for assistance from both the Cientificos and the bush bandits. And, just for your own information, I will tell you that as I suspect the success of those plans might cause the United States considerable embarrassment, the secret service will make it its business to see that you carry out my instructions in this part of it. I am not asking you to deliver your code books or do anything active, but the attempt on your part or that of your followers to send a single telegram or letter will be sufficient indication that you are not playing on the level, and will lead to trouble. So much for that. Now we shall come to the more personal part."

Tommy opened a drawer of the table and took out a paper, which he handed to the baron.

"You will kindly have that translated into your very best Japanese and send it to Tokyo by cable," he said. But the baron interrupted him with an exclamation of anger after glancing at the contents.

"I was right to distrust that Russian she-devil!" he exclaimed.

"No, but you were wrong to employ the methods you did; worse than that, you were foolish," answered Tommy, a new and harsher note in his voice. "For what you were planning to do in Mexico I hold no grudge; I know that you

were simply carrying out the policies of your superior officers. For the methods you have employed in trying to recover this sword, in so far as they have threatened us, I freely forgive you; I realize that you were swayed by traditions too strong for you to resist. But when you listened to the teaching of the Russian Third Section, and, following their suggestion, did things which neither the samurai code nor the best of your adopted civilization would sanction, you have made my heart harder than Pharaoh's. Now listen well, Moto Takimura, and know that I mean exactly what I say. Two weeks from to-day you will meet me in San Diego; I know that you can command the services of a cruiser which will carry out the instructions, and with sufficient speed to anchor off Tijuana by that date. On my word of honor, if you have faithfully carried out my instructions, the sword which you covet will be delivered into your hands, and you and your staff will be permitted to depart in safety. But if you fail to keep that appointment, or if you by word or deed violate the spirit or letter of those orders, I pledge you my word that the weapon which safeguarded the honor of your ancestors and preserved that of your father will be given to a Chinese pig butcher to use in slaughtering swine! Not a word! I have said the last one until we meet in San Diego. Now go!"

CHAPTER XIV.

It lacked but a day of the stipulated fortnight when, with Nelka Duvalief as our traveling companion, we arrived in San Diego after a leisurely journey. Tommy had been in constant telegraphic communication with Arkell, and the skirmish at Carrizal, followed by that diplomatic note which would have been an insult demanding an immediate declaration of war if it had not been so childish, indicated that the pot of Mexican troubles was still bubbling. We rarely discussed anything connected with it, for, in spite of the repression and self-control which the girl had learned to exercise in a hard school, it was evident that she was under an intense nervous strain, and we confined our conversation to commonplaces.

Arkell met us in that beautiful southern Californian city, his expression as triumphant as Tommy's was confident as they greeted each other.

"Tommy, I'm a million miles from knowing all there is to know, but we've discovered enough to draw the sting of the Japanese hornet!" he exclaimed. "I don't know just what you've been up to, but the greasers are all in the air; the good old Cientificos are sore because the graft seems to have been cut off, and the revolutionary leaders are sulking in their side-door Pullmans because the pay for their men and the promised arms and ammunition are not coming across. And, best of all, that Carrizal thing and the sassy note has wakened up Washington. You know that the entire militia has been ordered to mobilize, and I've been given a free hand. The only string to it is the order to keep everything as quiet as possible. I am empowered to call on the army or navy for assistance; but I think I can handle it all through our own department. I've located three big caches of stuff, enough to transform the colonies of peaceful yellow agriculturists into a well-equipped army corps, and they are surrounded by enough of my men to seize them. Also, I've got enough on your friend, Baron Moto, to warrant me in clapping the cuffs on him and his whole bunch; I've only held off on your say-so. But I've got the little Jap tea house down the coast, where they are putting up, surrounded."

"Arkell, you're going to have a disappointment there, and as usual the secret service is going to justify its name and reputation and do a great big duty well without publicity," answered Tommy gravely. "Do you know if Moto has received a wireless within the last day or two?"

"I'm holding up one which came for him this morning, a message from the captain of the Jap cruiser *Nikko*, saying that he would anchor off Tijuana to-morrow at daybreak. I'm not stuck on his knowing that; one of the biggest caches of ammunition is on the Coronados Islands, just off that port. The particular island is supposed to be uninhabited, but I've got a dozen men over there with orders to set fire to the stuff if an attempt is made to land; but that wouldn't save them."

"My dear Arkell, they are not in the slightest danger, and you can let that message through, together with one which I wish to send to the baron asking him to meet us at Tijuana to-morrow at nine," answered Tommy, and for the first time in days that aggravating, Mephistophelean smile appeared on his face. "Then we'll sit down and work up the stage directions for a little stunt I wish to pull off. And, old chap, I wish that you would take Nelka out for a sight-seeing trip while we are working. Don't strain your eyes looking out across the Pacific, young woman—it's too big to see across. But I promise you that it's bearing your ship safely to port."

Promptly at nine o'clock the following morning, our automobile rolled into the tiny plaza of the squalid Mexican town just across the border. Save that the precious sword, in its lacquer box, lay across Tommy's knees, there was nothing to suggest that we were armed.

I had no definite knowledge of just what Tommy expected to do; but the expression on his face convinced me that he was preparing a dénouement which would give him the center of the stage; and the sight of Baron Moto, grim of face, sitting in another car, told me that he was cast for the part of the goat. Far out on the blue water, a cruiser flying the ensign of Japan lay at anchor; and as we all got out of our cars, greeting the Japanese with the formality of duelists in the middle of the plaza, a surfboat shot away from her side and headed toward the harbor. Tommy looked at it for a moment through powerful glasses, and then turned and placed the sword in Nelka's hands. We were out of earshot of the plaza loungers when he faced the baron.

"Baron Moto, so far as I can see, you have been wise enough to play the latter part of this game according to my directions," he said quietly. "As your communications have been cut for some time by the secret service, it is only fair to tell you that the plans which you laid have been knocked out. The arms shipments, thanks to the decoding of the cipher messages sent to you by your agents, have been intercepted. The accumulations of stores, artillery, and equipment which you have been gathering for months in preparation for the invasion of California and the arming of your countrymen here have been discovered, and, to prevent the publicity which might arise from their seizure, secret-service agents have been ordered to destroy them by fires which at this moment are being kindled."

The baron nodded indifferently; his face was still that of the fanatic, his eyes were riveted upon the box in La Duvalief's slender hands, and only left it to shoot a glance of venomous hatred at her face. Tommy noted that, and there was nothing of courtesy in his voice when he continued.

"That part, then, we may regard as a closed incident—and there is the proof!" he said, pointing dramatically out over the bay to a low island from which a column of black smoke was rising. "But there is something else which is not, and that is the vindication of Nelka Duvalief. Baron, for every

other thing you have done I can find justification; for your cruelty to her I loathe you. Gentlemen"—he turned to us, markedly excluding the baron from that address—"you have all heard stories discreditable to this girl, for, in spite of her years, she is nothing more. Perhaps I have repeated them, for until I knew her I gave credit to common gossip concerning her which said that she was a traitor to the land of her birth—and she will tell you that the gossip was justified and confirmed by appearances. They told of her having betrayed Russia to Germany because her lover was murdered in a Russian dungeon. That is a lie. Nelka Duvalief has done secret-service work of the vilest kind, but it was always for her own country, and it was done under the lash of the most infamous organization in the world, the Russian Third Section. That lash was not held over her shoulders, but above the scarred back of her lover, Serge Ivanof. He did not die; he has been held a prisoner in Russian penal settlements, and it is for love of him that Nelka Duvalief has saved him from the unmentionable tortures which those fiends know how to inflict by obeying their commands. It has made of her a consummate actress, for she has been obliged to hoodwink the German general staff, the shrewdest spy catchers in the world, into the belief that she was betraying Russia to them. But, heartless as were her own people to her, the Baron Moto proved even a worse taskmaster when chance placed her in his power. You remember that after the Russian war the island of Saghalien, the worst of the Russian penal settlements, fell to the Japanese. In the most loathsome of its dungeons they found Serge Ivanof, forgotten when the other political prisoners and convicts were removed. In all confidence he babbled out to Colonel Moto the story of what he had suffered and of what Nelka had been forced to suffer for him, believing that from the yellow man he would receive that mercy which had been denied to him by the white."

For the first time Moto started to speak; but Tommy was not yielding his place in the spotlight, and he motioned to him to be silent.

"But Colonel Moto was not throwing away the chance which had so fortuitously been thrown into his hands, the chance to command the services of a skillful and beautiful woman in his own espionage system to dictate through fear such obedience as no yellow man can ever exact in any other way from a white woman. Serge Ivanof was retained in captivity, and to save him Nelka entered a service more loathsome to her than the one she quitted."

We had been so intent upon his recital that we had not noticed the arrival of the surfboat at the neighboring jetty, but, turning quickly, Tommy indicated it with a dramatic sweep of his arm. The Japanese sailors tossed their oars smartly, and the little lieutenant and the coxswain helped to the landing a passenger in civilian clothes who had been crouched in the stern sheets.

He was a tall, rawboned man; but the broad shoulders were pitifully stooped, and in spite of his long legs he walked with the short, jerky steps of a man whose ankles had long known the restriction of fetters. His hair, which, judging from the light-blue, lackluster eyes and the white skin, must have originally been blond, was as white as snow, and his face was furrowed with those deep lines which come only from intense physical pain and mental anguish. He shambled ungracefully toward us, docilely following the directions of the naval officer who had been his escort; but there was not the slightest sign of interest on his vacant, stupid face. But when Nelka, with such

a cry of joy as few men are ever privileged to hear from a woman's lips, sprang forward to meet him, there was something in her face which was that of a young girl which banished the years of pain and misery.

He straightened back the stooped shoulders, the drooping head was suddenly raised, and the seamed face was radiant; in the pale eyes was that light which never was on land or sea as he crushed her to his breast with arms which mercifully for her were weak from the years of confinement in the manacles which had left deep scars on the wrists. Those scars were the last things I saw distinctly for a moment, for I confess that my vision was blurred with moisture. Tommy, who was beaming on the happy results of his handiwork, was recalled to earth by a sharp exclamation from Arkell; for the baron, unobserved for a moment, was scuttling toward the boat, the sword of his ancestors clasped convulsively to his breast. Tommy knocked the pistol which Arkell had drawn, from his hand.

"Let him go. We can use his car to get back to San Diego, and after all these years of separation those Russian turtledoves are entitled to drive back alone!" he exclaimed, and he chuckled as in his haste the baron made such a mad leap for the boat that he fell in a heap in the cockpit. "You couldn't pinch him without causing just the publicity you wish to avoid. You haven't any kick coming, Arkell. All you've lost is the chance to clap handcuffs on him; but he's carrying off a valuable piece of my property. I'm satisfied if you are," he concluded, with a significant glance at the reunited lovers, still clasped in each other's arms. "That's cheap at the price, and between us I reckon we've managed at least to put a crimp into the third phase of this Mexican business."

THE END.

Sea Plunder

By Henry De Vere Stacpoole
Author of "The Gold Trail," "Stories of the Legion," Etc.

The adventures of Captain Blood, a skipper who had lost several ships and several small fortunes but had never lost a friend; who had run guns and run gin, and had his name coupled with the word "barratry." In earlier times privateering and grand smuggling would have claimed him and held him by their charms. In these flat times he was just a free lance.

I.—THE CAPTAIN GETS A SHIP

CAPTAIN BLOOD was an Irishman of the black-haired, blue-eyed type, a presentable man and a great favorite with the ladies, with scarcely a trace of the Irish accent, but a voice that would soothe the devil to sleep, and a temper that when roused carried all before it. This gentleman had lost several ships, he had lost several small fortunes gotten more or less illegitimately, he had lost caste in several ports of the world, but somehow or another he had never lost a friend. He had run guns, and he had run gin, his name had been whispered coupled with the word "barratry." In earlier and freer times, privateering and grand smuggling would, without any manner of doubt, have claimed him and held him by their charms. In these flat times he was just a free lance.

After the *Penguin* job, he and Billy Harman, that simple sailorman, had come back to Frisco, the very port of all others one might fancy they would have avoided, but Billy had been a power in Frisco, and, reckoning on his power, he had taken the captain back with him.

"There's no call to be afraid," said Billy; "there was more in that job than the likes of us. Why, they'd pay us money to tuck us away. Whatser use freezin' round N' York or Boston? There's nothin' to be done on the Eastern side. Frisco's warm."

"Damn warm!" put in the captain.

"Maybe; but there's ropes there I can pull an' make bells ring. Clancy and Rafferty and all that crowd are with me, and we've done nothin'. Why, we're plaster saints to the chaps that are walkin' round in Frisco with cable watch chains across their weskits."

They came back, and Billy Harman proved to be right. No one molested them. San Francisco was heaving in the throes of an election, and people had no time to bother about such small fry as the captain and his companion, while, owing to the good offices of the Clancys and Raffertys, Billy managed to pick up a little money here and there and to assist his friend in doing likewise.

Then things began to get slack, and to-day, as bright a morning as ever broke on the Pacific coast, the captain, down on his luck and without even the price of a drink, was hanging about a wharf near the China docks waiting for his companion.

He took his seat on a mooring bitt, and, lighting a pipe, began to review the situation. Gulls were flitting across the blue water, whipped by the westerly wind blowing in from the Golden Gate, a Chinese shrimp boat with huge lugsail bellying to the breeze was blundering along for the upper bay, crossing the bows of a Stockton river boat and threatening it with destruction; pleasure yachts, burly tugs, and a great four-master just coming in with the salt of Cape Horn on her sun-blistered sides— all these made a picture bright and moving as the morning.

It depressed the captain.

Business and pleasure have little appeal to a man who has no business and no money for pleasure. We all have our haunting terrors, and the captain, who feared nothing in an ordinary way, had his. When in extremely low water, he was always haunted by the dread of dying without a penny in his pocket. To be found dead with empty pockets was the last indignity. His Irish pride revolted at the thought, and he was turning it over in his mind now as he sat watching the shipping.

Then he caught a glimpse of a figure advancing toward him along the quay side.

It was Mr. Harman.

Billy Harman was an innocent-looking sailorman, with an open, weather-beaten face and blue eyes that gazed at you direct. A copy-book moralist would have made nothing of Billy, for he was full of guile and yet possessed of a strange sort of innocence. His morals would have shocked a Sunday school, yet he would have been the life and soul of a Sunday-school treat had he ever been invited to one. This gentleman, who could scarcely read and who managed with difficulty to write the words "Billy Harman," had yet been endowed by nature with a mind active as a squirrel. Ward politicians knew Mr. Harman as a useful man, and used him occasionally. Crimps knew him, and tavern keepers. Had he been more of a scamp and less of a dreamer, he might have risen high in life. His dream was of a big fortune to be "got sudden and easy," and this dream, stimulated at times by alcohol, managed somehow to keep him poor.

"So there you are," said he, as he drew up to the captain. "I been lookin' for you all along the wharf."

"Any news?" asked the captain.

Mr. Harman took a pipe from his pocket, and explored the empty bowl with his little finger; then, leaning against the mooring bitt, he cut some tobacco up, filled the pipe, and lit it.

Only when the pipe was alight did he seem to hear the captain's question.

"That depends," said he. "I don't know how you're feelin', but my feelin' is to get out of here, and get out quick."

"There's not much news in that," said Blood. "I've had it in my head for days. What's the use of talking? There's only one way out of Frisco for you or me, and that's by way of a fo'c's'le, and that's a way I'm not going to take."

"Maybe," said Harman, "you'll let me say my say before putting your hoof in my mouth. News—I should think I had news. Now, by any chance did you ever sight the Channel Islands down the coast there lying off Santa Barbara? First you come to the San Lucas Islands, then you come to Santa Catalina, a big brute of an island she is, same longitude as Los Angeles; then away out from Santa Catalina you have San Nicolas."

"No, I've never struck them," replied Blood. "What's the matter with them?"

"The Chinese go there huntin' for

abalone shells," went on Harman, disregarding the question. "I'm aimin' at a teeny yellow bit of an island away to the north of the San Lucas, a place you could cover with your hat, a place no one ever goes to."

"Well?"

"Well, there's twenty thousand dollars in gold coin lyin' there ready to be took away. Only this morning news came in that one of the See-Yup-See liners—you know them rotten old tubs, China owned, out of Canton, in the chow an' coffin trade—well, one of them things is gone ashore on San Juan, that's the name of the island. Swept clean, she was, and hove on the rocks, and every man drowned but two Chinee who got away on a raf'. I had the news from Clancy. The wreck's to be sold, and Clancy says the opinion is she's not worth two dollars, seein' the chances are the sea's broke her up by this. Well, now look here, I know San Juan, intimate, and I know a vessel, once ashore there, won't break up to the sea in a hurry by the nature of the coast. There's some coasts will spew a wreck off in ten minutes, and some'll stick to their goods till there's nuthin' left but the starnpost and the ribs. It's shelvin' water there and rocks that hold like sharks' teeth. The *Yan-Shan*—that's her name—will hold till the last trumpet if she's hove up proper, which, by all accounts, she is, and there's twenty thousand dollars aboard her."

"Well?" said Blood.

"Well, if we could crawl down there —you an' me—we'd put our claws on that twenty thousand."

"How in the nation are you going to rig out a wrecking expedition on two cents, and suppose you could buy the wreck for two dollars—where's your two dollars?"

"I'm not goin' to buy no wrecks," replied Harman, "nor fit out no wreckin' expeditions. What I want is something small and easy handled—no steam, get her out and blow down on the northwest trades, raise San Juan and the *Yan-Shan*, lift the dollars, and blow off with them. Why, it's as easy as walkin' about in your slippers!"

The captain sighed.

"As easy as getting into the penitentiary," said he. "First of all, you'd have to steal a boat, and Frisco is no port to steal boats in; second, there's such things as telegraphs and cables. *You* ought to know that after the *Penguin* job. Then if we were caught, as we would be, you'd have the old *Penguin* rising like a hurricane on us. She's forgotten now, I know, but once a chap gets in trouble everything that's forgotten wakes up and shouts."

"Maybe," said Harman, "and maybe I'd be such a fool as to go stealin' boats. I'm not goin' to steal no boats. But I'm goin' to do this thing *somehow*, and once I set my mind on a job I does it. You mark me. I'm fair drove crazy to get out of here and be after somethin' with money on the end of it, and once I'm like that and sets my think tank boilin', there's fish to fry. You leave it to me. I ain't no fool to be gettin' into penitentiaries. Well, let's get a move on; there's nothin' like movin' about to keep one's ideas jumpin'."

They walked along the wharf, stepping over mooring hawsers, and pausing now and then to inspect the shipping. There is no port in the world to equal San Francisco in variety and charm. Here, above all other places, the truth is borne in on one that trade, that much abused and seemingly prosaic word, is in reality another name for romance. Here at Frisco all the winds of the world blow in ships whose voyages are stories. Freighters with China mud still clinging to their anchor flukes, junks calling up the lights and gongs of the Canton River, schooners from the islands, whalers from the sulphur-bottom grounds, grain ships from half the world away, the spirit of trade hauls them all in through the Golden Gate, and, over and beyond these, the bay itself has its romance in the ships that never leave it—junks and shrimp boats, the boats of Greek fishermen, yachts, and all sorts of steam craft engaged on a hundred businesses from Suisun Bay to the Guadeloupe River.

Wandering along, Blood and his companion came to Rafferty's Wharf. Rafferty's Wharf is a bit of the past, a mooring place for old ships condemned and waiting the breaking yards. It has escaped harbor boards and fires and earthquakes, healthy trade never comes there, and very strange deals have been completed in its dubious precincts over ships passed as seaworthy yet held together, as Harman was explaining now to Blood, "by the pitch in their seams mostly."

As they came along a man who was crossing the gangway from the tank saw Harman and hailed him.

"It's Jack Bone," said Harman to Blood. "Walk along and I'll meet you in a minute."

Blood did as he was directed, and Harman halted at the gangway.

"You're the man I want," said Bone. "Who's your friend?"

"Oh, just a chap," replied Harman. "What's up now?"

Bone took him by the arm, and led him along in an opposite direction to that in which Blood was going. Bone was the landlord of the Fore and Aft Tavern, half tavern, half sailors' boarding house, situated right on Rafferty's Wharf and with a stairway down to the water from the back premises. His face, to use Harman's description of it, was one grog blossom, and what he did not know of wicked wharfside ways could scarcely be called knowledge.

"Ginnell is layin' about, lookin' for two hands," said Bone. "He's due out this evenin', and it's five dollars apiece for you if you can lay your claws on what he wants. Whites, they must be whites; you know Ginnell."

Harman did.

Ginnell owned a fifty-foot schooner engaged sometimes in the shark-fishing trade, sometimes in other businesses of a more shady description. He had a Chinese crew, and, though the custom-house laws of San Francisco demanded only one white officer on a Chinese-manned boat, Ginnell always made a point of carrying two men of his own color with him.

Being known as a hard man all along the wharfside, he sometimes found a difficulty in supplying himself with hands.

"Yes, I know Ginnell," replied Harman. "Him and his old shark boat by repitation. I've stood near the chap in bars now and again, but I don't call to mind speakin' to him. His repitation is pretty noisy."

"Well, I can't help that," said Bone. "I didn't make the chap nor his repitation; if he had a better one, I guess ten dollars wouldn't be lyin' your way."

"Nor twenty dollars yours," laughed Harman.

"That's my business," said Bone. "The question is, do you take on the job? I'd do it all myself only there's such a want of sailormen on the front. It's those durned Bands of Hope and Sailors' Rests that sucks 'em in, fills 'em with bilge in the way of tracks and ginger beer, and turns 'em out onfit for any job onless it's got a silver-plated handle to it. Mouth organs an' the New Jerusalem is all they cares for onct them wharf missionaries gets a holt on them. I tell you, Billy Harman, if they don't get up some by-law to stop these chaps propagatin' their gospels and spoilin' trade, the likes of me and you will be ruined—that's a fac'. Well, what do you say?"

All the time Mr. Bone was holding

forth, Harman, who had struck an idea, was deep in meditation. The question roused him.

"If Ginnell wants two chaps," said he, "I believe I can fit him with them. Anyhow, where's he to be found?"

"He'll be at my place at three o'clock," said Bone, "and I've promised to find the goods for him by that."

"Well, I'll tell you," said Harman, "I'll find the chaps and have them at your place haff past three or so; you can leave it safe in my hands."

"You speak as if you was certain."

"And certain I am. I've got the chaps you want."

"Now look here," said Bone, "don't you take on the job unless you're more than sure. Ginnell isn't no boob to play up and down with; he'd set in, mostlike, to wreck the bar if he thought I was playin' cross with him."

"Don't fret," said Harman. "I'll be there, and now fork out a dollar advance, for I'll have some treatin' to do."

Bone produced the money. It changed hands, and he departed, while Harman pursued his way along the wharf toward his friend.

Blood was sitting on an empty crate.

"Well," said he, as the other drew up, "what business?"

Harman told every word of his conversation with Bone, and, without any addition to it, waited for the other to speak.

"Well, you've got the dollar," said Blood at last, "and there's some satisfaction in that. I'm not the chap to take five cents off a chap by false pretenses same's you've done with Bone, but Bone's not a man by all accounts; he's a crimp in man's clothes, and if all the old whalemen he's filled with balloon juice and sent to perdition could rise up and shout, I reckon his name'd be known in two hemispheres."

"I beg your pardon," said Harman. "What was that you were saying about

false pretenses? I haven't used no false pretenses. They ain't things I'm in the habit of usin' between man and man."

"Well, what have you been using? You told me a moment ago you'd agreed to furnish two hands to this chap's order for five dollars apiece and a dollar advance."

"So I have."

"And where's your hands?"

"I've got them."

"In your pocket?"

"Oh, close up!" said Harman. "I never did see such a chap as you for wearin' blinkers; can't you see the end of your nose in front of you? Well, if you can't, I can. However, I'll tell you the whole of the business later when I've turned it round some more in my head. What I'm after now is grub. Here's a dollar, and I'm off to Billy Sheehan's; you come along with me—a dollar's enough for two—and you can raise your objections after you've got a beefsteak inside of you. Maybe you'll see clearer then."

The captain said no more, but followed Harman. Far better educated than the latter, he had come to recognize that Harman, despite his real and childlike simplicity in various ways, had a mind quicker than most men's. He would often have gone without a meal during that wandering partnership which had lasted for nearly a year but for Harman's ingenuity and power of resource.

At Sheehan's they had good beefsteak and real coffee.

"Now," said Harman, when they had finished, "if you're ready to listen to reason, I'll tell you the lay I'm on. Ginnell wants two hands. I'm goin' to offer myself for one, and you are goin' to be the other."

"I beg your pardon," said Blood. "You mean to say I'm to sign on in that chap's shark boat. Is that your meaning?"

"I said nuthin' about signin' on in shark boats. I said we two has got to get out of here in Ginnell's tub. Once outside the Gate we're all right."

"I see," said Blood. "We're to scupper Ginnell and take the boat—and how about the penitentiary?"

"I'm blest if you haven't got penitentiaries on the brain," said Harman. "If you leave this thing to me, I'll fix it so that there'll be no penitentiaries in the business. Of course if we were to go into such a fool's job as you're thinkin' about, we'd lay ourselves under the law right smart. No, the game I'm after is deeper than that, and it's Ginnell I'm goin' to lay under the law. Now I've got to run about and do things an' see people. I'll leave you here, and here's a quarter, and don't you spend it till the time comes. Now you listen to me. Wait about till haff past three, and at haff past three punctual you turn into the Fore and Aft and walk up to the bar and lay your quarter down and call for a drink. You'll see me there, and if I nod to you, you just nod to me. Then I'll have a word in private with you."

"Is that all?" said the captain.

"That's all for the present," said Harman, rising up. "You'll be there?"

"Yes, I'll be there," said Blood, "though I'm blest if I can see your meaning."

"You will soon," replied the other, and, paying the score, off he went.

He turned from the wharves up an alley, and then into a fairly respectable street of small houses. Pausing before one of these, he knocked at the door, which was opened almost immediately by a big, blue-eyed, sunburned, good-natured-looking man some thirty years of age and attired as to the upper part of him in a blue woolen jersey.

This was Captain Mike, of the Fish Patrol.

"Billy Harman!" said Captain Mike. "Come in."

"No time," said Harman. "I've just called to say a word. I wants you to do me a favor."

"And what's the favor?" asked the captain.

"Oh, nothin' much. D'you know Ginnell?"

"Bob Ginnell?"

"That's him."

"Well, I should think I did know the swab. Why, he's in with all the Greeks, and there's not a dog's trick played in the bay he hasn't his thumb in. Him and his old shark boat. Whatcher want me to do with him?"

"Nothin'," replied Harman, "and maybe a lot. I want you just to drop into the Fore and Aft and sit and smoke your pipe at haff past three. Then when I give you the wink you'll pretend to fall asleep. I just wants you as a witness."

"What's the game?" asked Captain Mike.

Harman told.

Had you been watching the two men from a distance, you might have fancied that there was a great joke between them from the laughter of Captain Mike and the way in which Harman was slapping his thigh. Then the door closed, and Harman went off, steering north through a maze of streets till he reached his lodgings.

Here he packed a few things in a bundle and had an interview with his landlady, a motherly woman whose income was derived from a washtub and two furnished bedrooms.

Among the other belongings which he took with him was a box of quinine tabloids. These he placed in the pocket of his coat, and, with the bundle under his arm, departed.

It was five minutes past three when he entered the dirty doggery misnamed the Fore and Aft, and there before the bar behind which Bone was serving drinks stood Ginnell.

Pat Ginnell, to give him his full

name, was an Irishman of the sure-fwhat type, who might have been a bricklayer but for his decent clothes and sea air and the big blue anchor tattooed on the back of his left hand. There was no one else in the bar.

"Here's the gentleman," said Bone, when he sighted Harman. "Up to time and with the goods to deliver, I dare say. Harman, this is the captain; where's the hands?"

"Well," said Harman, leaning his elbow on the bar, "I believe I've got them. One of them's meself."

"D'you mean to say you're up to sign on with me?" asked Ginnell.

"That's my meanin'," said Harman. Ginnell looked at Bone. Then he spoke.

"It won't do," said he. "I know you be name, Mr. Harman; you're in with Clancy and that crowd, and my boat's too rough for the likes of you."

"You needn't fear about that," said Harman. "I've done with Clancy. What I've got to do is get out of Frisco and get out quick. The cops are after me; there you have it. I've got to get out of here before night—do you take me—and I'm so pressed to get out sudden I'll take your word for ten dollars a month without any signin'."

Ginnell's brow cleared.

"What are you havin'?" said he.

"I'll take a drink of whisky," replied Harman.

The bargain was concluded.

"And now," said Ginnell, "what about the other chap?"

Harman wiped his mouth with the back of his hand.

"I've made an arrangement with a chap to meet me here," said he. "He'll be in in a minute."

"What's he like?" asked Ginnell.

"Like? Why, I'll tell you what he's like; he wouldn't sign on in your tub for a hundred dollars a month."

"Faith and you're a nice sort of chap," said Ginnell. "Is it playin' the fool with me you are?"

By way of reply Harman took the box of quinine tabloids from his pocket, opened it, showed the contents, and winked.

Bone and Ginnell understood at once.

"One of those in his drink will lay him out for an hour," said Harman, "without hurtin' him. Put one in your weskit pocket, Bone—and how about your boat?"

"She's down below at the stairs," replied the landlord, putting the tabloid in his waistcoat pocket. "I'll go and call Jim to get her ready—a moment, gentlemen." He vanished into a back room, and they heard him shouting orders to Jim; then he returned, and as he passed behind the bar who should enter but Captain Mike!

The captain walked to the bar, called for a drink, and without as much as a glance at the others took it to a seat in a far corner, where he lit a pipe. Several wharf habitués loafed in, and soon the place became hazy with tobacco smoke and horrible with the smell of rank cigars.

"Well," said Ginnell, "where's your man? I'm thinkin' he's given you the slip, and be the powers, Mr. Harman, if he has, it'll be the worst for you."

The brute in Ginnell spoke in his growl, and Harman was turning over in his mind the fate of any unfortunate who had Ginnell for boss when the swing door opened and Blood appeared.

"That's him," said Harman. "You leave him to me."

Blood was not the sort of man to frequent a hole like the Fore and Aft, and he frankly spat when he came in. He was in a temper, or rather the beginning of a temper, and Harman seemed to have some difficulty in soothing him. They had a confabulation together near the corner where Captain Mike, his glass and pipe on the table before him, was sitting, evidently asleep, and then, Blood, seeming to agree with some matter under discussion, allowed himself to be led to the bar.

"This is me friend, Captain Ginnell," said Harman. "Captain, this is me friend, Michael Blood. Looking for a ship he is."

"I can't offer him a ship," said Ginnell, "but I can offer him a drink. What are you takin', sir?"

Blood called for a whisky.

The quinine tabloid popped into the bottom of the glass by Bone dissolved almost immediately, nor did Blood show that he detected the presence in his drink. He loathed quinine, and this forced dose added to the flood of his steadily rising temper without, however, interfering with his powers of self-control.

He was a good actor, and the way he clutched at the bar ledge shortly after he had finished his drink left nothing to be desired.

"Let him lay down," said Harman.

"I can't leave the bar," said Bone, "but if the gentleman cares to lay down in my back room he's welcome."

Blood, allowing himself to be conducted to this resting place, Ginnell followed without drawing the attention of the others in the bar.

Arrived in the back room, Blood collapsed on an old couch by the window, and, lying there with his eyes shut, he heard the rest.

He heard the whispered consultation between Harman and the other, the trapdoor being opened, Jim, the boatman, being called. And then he felt a hand on his shoulder and Ginnell's voice adjuring him to rouse up a bit and come along for a sail.

Helped on either side by the conspirators, he allowed himself to be led to the trapdoor.

"We'll never get him down them steps," said Harman, alluding to the stairs leading down to where the boat was swaying on the green water that was swishing and swashing against the rotten piles of the wharf.

"This is the way it's done," said Ginnell, and, twitching Blood's feet from under him, he sent him down the stairway like a bag of meal to where Jim was waiting to receive him.

At half past six o'clock that day the *Heart of Ireland*—that was the name of Ginnell's boat—passed the tumble of the bar and took the swell of the Pacific like a duck.

Ginnell, giving the wheel over to one of the Chinese crew, glanced to windward, glanced back at the coast, where Tamalpais stood cloud-wrapped and gilded by the evening sun, and then turned to the companionway leading down to the hole of a cabin where they had deposited their shanghaied man.

"I'm goin' to rouse that swab up," he said; "he ought to be recovered by this."

"Go easy with him," said Harman.

"I'll be as gentle with him as a mother," replied the skipper of the *Heart of Ireland,* with a ferocious grin.

Harman watched the unfortunate man descending. He had got shoulder deep down the ladder when he suddenly vanished as if snatched below, and his shout of astonishment and the crash of his fall came up simultaneously to the listener at the hatch.

Then came the sounds of the fight. Harman had seen Blood fighting once, and he had no fear at all for him. If he feared for any one, it was Ginnell, who was crying now for mercy and apparently receiving none. Then of a sudden came silence, and Harman slipped down the ladder.

Blood, during his incarceration, had ransacked the cabin and secured the captain's revolver. He was seated now, revolver in hand, on Ginnell's chest, and Ginnell was lying on the cabin floor without a kick or an ounce of fight in him.

"You haven't killed him?" asked Harman.

"I don't know," replied Blood. "Speak up, you swab, and answer! Are you dead or not?"

"Faith, I don't know," groaned the unfortunate. "I'm near done. What are you up to? What game is this you're playin' on me? Is it murder or what?"

"Let me talk to him," said Harman. "Bob Ginnell, you've doped and shanghaied a man—meanin' my friend, Captain Blood—and I've got all the evidence and witnesses. Captain Mike, of the Fish Patrol, is one; he came to the Fore and Aft be request and saw the whole game. That means the penitentiary for you if we split. You'll say I provided the dope. Who's to prove it? When I told you the cops were after me I told a lie. Who's to prove it? I wanted you and your old tub, and I've got 'em. Say a word against me and see what Clancy will do to you. You shanghaied me friend, and now you're shanghaied yourself in your own ship, and you'll never dare to have the law on us because, d'you see, we've got the law on you. The captain there has got your revolver, the coolies on deck don't care, they never even turned a hair when they heard you shoutin'. Now my question is, do you intend to take it quiet, or would you sooner be hove overboard?"

"Faith and there's no use in kicking," replied the owner of the *Heart of Ireland*. "I gives in."

"Then up on your feet!" said Blood, rising and putting the revolver in his pocket. "And up on deck with you! You're one of the hands now, and if you ever want to see Frisco again, you'll take my orders and take them smart. You'll berth aft with us, but your rating is cabin boy, and your pay. Up with you!"

Ginnell went up the ladder, and the others followed.

Ginnell showed to the light of day two black eyes and the marks on his chin of the frightful uppercut that had closed the fight.

He looked like a beaten dog as Blood called the crew, in order to pick watches with Harman.

"I take the chap that's steering," said Blood.

"And I takes Bob Ginnell," said Harman.

They finished the business, and dismissed the hands, who seemed to see nothing strange in the recent occurrence among the whites, and who were thronging now to the fo'c's'le for their supper, their faces all wearing the same Chinese expression, the expression of men who know everything, of men who know nothing.

Then, having set a course for the San Lucas Islands, and while Ginnell was washing himself below, Blood, with his companion, leaned on the rail and looked at the far-away coast dying out in the dusk.

"Seems strange it was only this mornin' I projected gettin' out like this," said Harman, "and here we are out, with twenty thousand dollars ahead of us, if the *Yan-Shan* hasn't broke up, which she hasn't. 'Pears to me it was worth a dose of quinine to do the job so neat with no bones broke and no fear of the law at the end of it."

"Maybe," said the captain.

He whistled softly to the accompaniment of the slashing of the bow wash, looking over toward the almost vanished coast, above which, in the pansy blue of the evening sky, stars were now showing like points of silver.

Another story of the Captain in the November 20th POPULAR.

Get Your Man

By B. M. Bower and Buck Connor
Authors of "Five Hundred Head for a Ranger," Etc.

Like the man without a country is the man in this story who was dismissed from the Texas Rangers after a love affair that blinded him to duty. To get back into the service becomes an obsession with him. There is a terrific fight between two men in the tale—one fighting for his life, and the other for what makes life worth while

IN the gray of a windy afternoon, when the leaden clouds were more sand than vapor, Captain Oakes, of the Texas Ranger force, jerked open the door of his office and looked out just as Bill Gillis was passing.

"Tell Marshall to report to me at once," the captain hailed Bill, and turned back as though the thing was done.

"Marshall ain't here." Bill grabbed for his hat, which the wind had all but swooped from his head, and blinked into the wind and sand while he faced his captain.

"Ain't here? Where is he?" The captain pulled the door shut because the wind was stirring up the papers on his desk, and turned a sharp glance toward the corral and stable.

"Went to town, a little while ago," Bill said reluctantly, torn between Ranger discipline and his personal sense of loyalty to Marshall.

"You go after him." The captain went in, and the wind slammed the door shut. Bill, hanging to his big-four Stetson with both hands, went staggering down to the stable, cursing his vile luck for bringing him past the door at the moment when the captain opened it. Why couldn't it have been Vaughan or Kent or Charlie Horn?

Going after King Marshall did not sound very difficult, since there was only a mile or so to ride; but Bill would gladly have exchanged that errand for a fifty-mile trip in some other direction, nevertheless. Still, when the captain says "Go," there is nothing to be gained by loitering, so within five minutes Bill was mounted on the horse that day assigned to his use, and was leaning into the wind and riding with his eyes two-thirds closed, so that his lashes might strain the dust that half blinded him.

"It's shore a ticklish job, dragging a fellow away from his girl—and that right after you've told him plain and forcible that he'd better cut out running with her," Bill mused uncomfortably. "King's liable to forget who he's speaking to, and tell me to mind my own business; and then," Bill finished, with a quirk of his lips, "the dust'll shore be stirred up along the trouble trail, 'cause I won't take anything like that off'n King Marshall, or no other man."

On the chance that King had met an acquaintance and had loitered in the post office for a few minutes, Bill swung off his horse at the platform, and went in, spitting grit as he went. Perhaps he was secretly postponing his disagreeable errand—but that could not be for long, because the captain wanted King, and the captain was not one to wait patiently when he had called a man to report for duty. At any rate,

King was not in the post office; and Bill, glancing through the glass front of lock box No. 200, saw that he had not been there. Bill opened the box and took out the mail, and returned to his horse.

On the extreme edge of the town lived the girl. Half Mexican in blood, and the traditions of women born to be petted, full American in speech and in a certain careless freedom of the restraining conventions of the better class across the border, Lisa Gonzales had lovers in plenty—yet not so many but she resented fiercely any influence that would take one from her. Bill Gillis she recognized—trust a woman for sensing antagonism a mile off!—as such an influence.

Bill was in no mood for subterfuge or diplomacy. Since he must get King to the captain, he meant to do it as soon as possible. So he rode straight to the flat-roofed adobe house where Lisa lived with her father and a half-grown sister, and struck his knuckles imperatively against the blue-painted door panels.

Lisa herself opened the door six inches, and looked out at him with unreadable, unfriendly black eyes.

Bill tilted his hat in a perfunctory salute—since he recognized and returned in full the antagonism—and wasted no words in preamble. "I'd like to speak to King Marshall," he said straightforwardly.

"You would?" Lisa smiled guilefully. "Well, I'll tell him so—when he comes." And she added, by way of apology, perhaps, "Oh, it is so *windy* to-day!" and pressed the door shut in the face of Bill Gillis and the swirling clouds of dust.

Bill hesitated, glaring at the blank, light-blue panels so affected by Mexicans. He believed that King was in there, beyond that door—but he wanted to be absolutely sure of it before he forced an entrance. What ailed the man, anyway? he thought angrily, as he swung up into the saddle. He turned his horse and stared for another minute at the house.

He did not go back into the town; instead, he went straight to the little adobe shed where Lisa's father sheltered a cow and a meager little pony when the winds were too piercing outside. Without leaving the saddle, Bill rode close to the sagging door, reached out, and pulled it open so that he could look within. There, resting on three legs, half asleep under the saddle, stood the horse King had ridden to town.

"The lyin' little hussy!" Bill snorted unchivalrously. "And I knew she lied, too."

He rode back to the house, swung off his horse on the sheltered side, where the wall was unbroken by windows, and went around to the back door. He did not know for sure, but he suspected that Lisa had been sharp-witted enough to lock the front door when she shut it in his face. At any rate, he did not intend to expose himself to the humiliation of trying to open a door that was locked against him.

He opened the back door deliberately, as though he had a perfect right to walk in where he pleased to go. He went into the kitchen—and faced King Marshall, seated at a table spread with a red-and-blue-checked cloth and filled with savory Mexican dishes. The arms of Lisa were just drawing away from King's shoulders when Bill went in; her black eyes spat hate at him over King's brown head. Bill paid her no attention whatever; he looked full at King, and he tried to keep his face free of all emotion.

"Captain wants you right away, King," he announced casually. "He sent me in to tell you."

"What does he want?" snapped King, lowering a forkful of frijoles to his plate. "I'm not on duty——"

"A Ranger's *always* on duty, King," Bill corrected mildly. He did not so much blame King—a woman's spell can work an unbelievable change in a man.

"Well—you can tell him I'll be along after a little." The soft fingers of Lisa were tapping, tapping on King's shoulders. His left hand went up defiantly, and prisoned them in his palm. "And, Bill, you're kinda butting in on another man's private affairs, don't yuh think?"

"Captain sent me after you, King. You'd better come." Bill stood just inside the door, with his hat pushed back on his head—ignoring, in the face of bigger things, the little courtesy of removing it in Lisa's presence—and his voice stopped just short of being apologetic. He hated this situation into which he had been forced—hated it worse than did those two across the table—but it never occurred to him to shirk his duty.

King Marshall flushed. It was Lisa, however, who answered Bill with a spiteful little smile and a barbed meaning that made the blood beat in the temples of the two men.

"You just want to take him from me!" she cried, her arms slipping around King's neck. "You're mad because—*I* know why—if I wanted to tell! You followed him here, and you want to get him away. Bah! *I* know how much the captain wants him! You can't fool nobody—but yourself," was what she said.

Now, every one knows that a man violently in love is in an abnormal state where truth looks trivial, and the things that are false look true and fine and big. King Marshall was suffering from the infatuation which sometimes seizes a strong man who does not know women very well; and the moment Lisa put the lie into speech, punctuated by little, caressing movements, King, who was in a highly abnormal condition, believed she spoke the truth.

"You keep your hands off my affairs, Bill," he said harshly, forgetting how they two had been friends when Lisa was an untidy schoolgirl in short dresses and long braids. "I've had enough of this spying and interfering in my business. I'll go when I get good and ready!"

"You'll go now, King. The captain told me to bring you." Bill's voice was still soft, but his eyes were not. He wanted to tear those clinging arms from King's neck; perhaps without their insidious influence King would have sense enough to see that he must come when the captain called.

"You've delivered your message—and that lets you out," King parried, reaching with ostentatious ease for the flat, little tortillas Lisa had baked for him. He did not look at Bill—perhaps, in spite of the perverse spirit that rode him hard, he was ashamed of himself. "I'll settle with the captain," he added, lifting his forkful of frijoles again to his mouth. "Lisa, where's that good coffee I smell?"

"Right now I bring it!" Lisa cried eagerly, and sent Bill Gillis a triumphant glance. Duty pitted against love's desire—and love had won, just as it always does win if it is greater than a man's soul. She hurried back to stand close behind King Marshall after she had filled his cup. Her fingers returned to their little, caressing taps on his shoulders. "The beans, are they are plenty full of chili?"

"King, you've got to come now!" Bill, feeling dimly that this was not the real King Marshall, who sat there openly mutinous, was patient even when he wanted to tear those two apart by force.

"Aw, clear out, Bill! You give me a pain. *I'll* settle with the captain, I told you once." King sent him an ugly look. "You're about as welcome here right now as——"

"Get up from there, and come with

me!" Bill's patience snapped all at once. King was no longer a fellow Ranger who was out of his mind with love of a girl, but a man whom the captain had told Bill to bring to headquarters. Putting it on that basis, Bill knew exactly what to do, and how to do it. He had brought reluctant men to headquarters before now.

King looked up into the muzzle of Bill's six-shooter, and caught his breath in sheer amazement. "Why, you——"

"I'll take you to the captain, by gosh, if I have to take you in irons!" snapped Bill. "You lunatic—to let a little snip of a fool girl ruin you with the force like that! For half an hour longer to spoon with her, you'd refuse to obey an order, would you? Well, I'm not built that way myself. Captain told me to bring you—and you'll *go!*"

Bill Gillis was little, as height went —but at that minute he towered above King at the table. Also, the gun in his hand was an argument not to be overlooked even by a love-crazed man. King got up because he knew he must, if he wanted to live any longer. Never for one second did he doubt that Bill would shoot him if he refused. He could not doubt—because he knew.

"Lisa, you go in that next room, and shut the door behind you!"

Whimpering, her chin drawn down, and her shoulders drawn up like a child waiting for a blow, Lisa went.

"Turn your back!"

King did it sullenly.

Bill took King's six-shooter from its holster at his hip and slipped it into his own. Knowing King's habits, he reached into King's coat pocket and got the small automatic which King always carried there against emergencies.

"Go on out!" Bill ordered; and, when they were outside, he made King turn his back while Bill mounted, and then Bill followed King to the shed and watched him grimly while he led out

.13A P

his own horse and mounted. "Lead out," he said, when King settled into the saddle, "and do some going. Captain's waited too long as it is."

King, the color wiped from his face with the rage that held him because he was so helpless, looked at Bill furiously and swore by all the gods men use to cover the puny ineffectiveness of their oaths, how he would get even with Bill Gillis for this.

Bill did not make any reply whatever. As they galloped before the wind, that howled and sent clouds of dust after them, Bill's anger against King cooled to a half-amused sympathy.

When they neared the corral, Bill rode alongside, and held out King's two guns to him. "Here," he said whimsically. "I'm sorry the play came up like it did, but I had to do it, King. Captain said to bring you—and you know what a fool I am about obeying orders. But I want to tell yuh right now, King, that I consider I've done you a big kindness—and I don't care a cuss how you look at it. Far as I'm concerned, this thing ends right here. I'm your friend." He rode on and dismounted at the corral gate.

King looked at him with his lips turned down at the corners, gave his horse a kick, and went on to the office, sour and sore and feeling that his world was against him. Which was, of course, merely one phase of his abnormal condition. He went in and stood, with the stiff back that expressed a dogged defiance of censure, just inside the door. It did not help his mood any that Captain Oakes looked up at him over his reading glasses for a minute-long inspection before he spoke.

"Marshall, you're taking altogether too many liberties around here lately," the captain said, at last, with the cold terseness that his men always dreaded. "Hereafter you will ask permission before you ride off to town—since you have formed the habit of forgetting to tell me that you are going, and why. You should have been started an hour ago on the job I have assigned you. In the Ranger service an hour may measure the difference between success and failure.

"Go up to Tobin and look into this horse stealing, that seems to be an epidemic in that country. Here are all the details that have been sent in. Get started as soon as you can—and try and make up the time that has been wasted in getting hold of you. Take the horse you rode to town. You'll be close to the branch line all the way, and you probably won't need a pack horse. That's all."

Many a time King Marshall had gone off whistling on harder, longer trips than this one promised to be—but to-day he passed Vaughan with a scowl, and did not answer the cheerful hail of Charlie Horne. Under the friendliness he imagined an ironical gloating over him.

He took his carbine and hung it under his right-leg fender, and mounted his horse and rode away, glowering at the familiar, wind-buffeted little adobe buildings that formed the Ranger headquarters. The captain's reprimand repeated itself over and over in his mind, and bit deeper with every repetition, as an acid eats into a sore. From being a mere reprimand because of a small breach of discipline, it became an unjust accusation, wholly undeserved; then an insult which no man should bear in silence. So that he neared Ysleta in the mood for further revolt.

His eyes went toward the adobe where Lisa lived. It would be no more than an act of common kindness to stop and tell her where he was going, and when she might expect him back—and to comfort her with a kiss before he rode on. It was very easy for King to persuade himself that his loyalty to Lisa was a bigger, finer thing than

obeying to the letter his captain's command that he make all possible haste to Tobin. He swung toward the adobe, and, careless whether he were seen stopping there, dropped reins before the door, and went in.

He really meant to stay but a minute. He had no intention of loitering there. But, with Lisa's arms around his neck, and with her cheek pressed against his shoulder, while her big, black eyes looked up into his gray ones, minutes were not easily reckoned. Lisa was telling him what a brute Bill Gillis had proven himself; what a thankless task it was to be a Ranger—a dog of the law, to be harried here and there, and never a word of approval for the risks he took, the hardships he endured.

He stopped her tirade with kisses. Under the delirium of his infatuation there still held firm the ingrained loyalty of the man for his chosen calling. Too long had he been proud to wear the Ranger star, too often had he fought to maintain its integrity, to hear it spoken of slightingly now. When Lisa's fingers twitched petulantly at the star, he laid his hand over hers and pulled her fingers gently away, vaguely hurt because she hated his profession and said so.

"It's a good old star, little girl, and it takes a good man to wear it," he told her lightly. "Kiss me now, so I can go. I'll be back just as soon as ever I can——"

She struck the star with her fist. "I hate it!" she cried, with the fierceness of her father's blood. "It takes you away from me always, just when I have almost made up my mind to promise ——" She looked up at him, tempting him with her lips and her eyes. "Give me the star—and I'll promise—what you want me to promise," she whispered in his ear, standing on her toes and leaning against him. "I think that old tin thing means more to you than

I do! You let it take you away from me—and there are plenty of others to go, if you didn't. Give me the star, King—king of my heart!" She began fumbling it again, tentatively pressing the pin out of its fastening.

King's hand closed over her fingers again arrestingly. "Don't do that, sweetheart," he muttered reprovingly, impelled by a glimmer of sanity. "Kiss me now—I must go."

It was just at that moment that Captain Oakes opened the door and walked in, his face gray with anger. The reason for his being there was simple enough, though King's jaw dropped with astonishment. He had started for town soon after King had left headquarters, and his sharp eyes had seen and recognized King's horse standing tail to the wind before this place. The rest was inevitable, since Captain Oakes knew who lived there and what errand it was that took King there.

"Marshall, you needn't trouble to make that trip to Tobin," he said sternly, standing just within the room. "Ranger business is too important to trust to a lovesick calf like you. You may take your choice, here and now; you may resign from the service, or I shall dismiss you." He looked at King with narrowed eyes, and added grimly: "It will look better for both of us on the records if you resign."

"I reckon I can thank Bill Gillis for this," King blurted hotly. "It's easy to guess he told you I'd be here. And I'll sure settle with *him!*" he finished savagely.

"Marshall, you act and talk like a crazy man. I strongly suspect Gillis of straining a point more than once to shield you. If he knows of your frequenting this place, he has never hinted it to me. Your horse, out there, is plain-enough evidence to any one but a blind man."

" 'Frequenting this place!' " Lisa re-peated the phrase shrewishly. "You talk like this was a—saloon!"

"I'd rather find Marshall in a saloon than here! I'd have more hope of him!" snapped the captain. As though that placed the limit on his staying longer in the house, he pulled open the door. "I shall expect to receive your written resignation before dark," he said to King, "so I can enter it on record and report a vacancy."

He went out with his neck stiff and his back very straight—but he rode back to headquarters without attending to the errand which had brought him out in the wind, and he rode with his shoulders drooped and his eyes bent moodily upon the ground. Discipline sometimes is as hard for the master as it is for the men he commands.

II.

A shock sometimes does more for a man than months of reasoning. King went to the post office, stood before the ink-spattered desk, chose a sputtering stub pen, curled his lip contemptuously, and began to write his resignation from the Texas Ranger force. Two lines down from the top he stopped and cursed the pen for dropping a blot on the words "Unavoidable circum-stances." That is how he was going to put it, and he hoped that the captain would get the inner meaning of the phrase and feel ashamed of his pica-yunish interpretation of discipline. The captain had known well enough that King would go to Tobin—and bring back his man or men if it were humanly possible to do so. Five minutes to say good-by to Lisa—fiddlesticks! That wasn't it; the captain had it in for him, and took this as an excuse to get rid of him. King understood that very well; and, without bawling out the captain or any one else, he meant to word that resignation so that the captain would read his real meaning between the lines.

Kicked out of the service—that was what it practically amounted to. A woman—even the sweetest little girl in the world, he made haste to pay mental tribute—surely does play hob with a man's life. If she would marry him, he'd take her away. What did it amount to, after all, if she were half "greaser?" There wasn't a girl in Texas to compare with her in looks —— He was going to say disposition, also, but his natural honesty stopped him. Her disposition, he had to confess, was no milder than the chili which she ground for the frijoles.

King borrowed another sheet of paper, took the other pen off the desk, and started again. This time he did not write "unavoidable circumstances" at all, and he did not curl his lip. Instead, his eyebrows were pinched together and his nostrils were white, and when he signed his name at the bottom, the letters were quavery as though an old man had written them. It was a hard document to write.

At headquarters, whither he rode in haste to present his resignation and have it over with before the captain could accuse him of reluctance, he packed his few belongings, presented his resignation to the captain without a salute and with no speech on the subject, and left while the captain was still leaning forward to pick up the letter from the corner of the desk where King had dropped it. The boys, scenting trouble in his return and guessing shrewdly what it was, tactfully avoided meeting him. King set that down to ostracism, and resented it—just as he would have resented their friendliness had they been stupid enough to show any.

For the first time since she had smiled invitingly with a droopy-lashed, sidelong glance that tingled his blood, King went without eagerness to see Lisa that evening. He was going away somewhere—anywhere. To stay in Ysleta, and meet the boys and the curious looks of the townspeople was not to be considered at all; not even to be near Lisa would he stay—and that morning he had believed that no power on earth was strong enough to drive him from her!

Her viperish denunciation of Bill Gillis and Captain Oakes and the whole Ranger force grated upon him. Her arms around his neck were more clinging than sweet, and, when she wept, with her face against his breast, he noticed that weeping made her eyelids red. She had wept before now, and he had comforted her without ever seeing the disfigurement of red lids.

"I'm all outa sorts, little girl," he said finally, puzzled because her presence could not soothe his hurt; puzzled, also, because his tongue would not say what he had intended to say to her; would not ask her to marry him on the morrow, and go away with him somewhere. "I guess this upheaval has upset me, somehow. I hate to inflict such a mood on you—so I'll go and cuss it off, and then we'll talk things over. Good night, sweetheart—I'll see you to-morrow, early."

She did not want him to go, and she pouted and cried a few more tears. But King went, just the same, which should have been more enlightening to him than it was. He did not realize that Lisa was already beginning to lose her spell over him.

The next day the perverse mood still held him to a degree. He had not slept at all, though he went early to his room in the little hotel where he had left his "war bag." All through the night memory had ridden him hard. Trails he had taken with his fellow Rangers—nights when he had crouched on guard, straining his eyes into the blackness, not daring to move lest some little noise betray his presence there and bring a questing bullet that way; summer scenes, wherein laughter had mingled with the smoke of many cigarettes, and life had seemed clean and good and worth the living.

King did not know what ailed him that he must remember all these things just when he least wanted to recall them. He would rather think of Lisa —but his mind kept drifting away from her. He would picture her in some desireful pose—and, the first he knew, her image would fade like a "dissolve" scene in motion pictures, and the face of Bill Gillis or Kent or little Charlie Horne would look out at him. So he had lain until daybreak.

He drew his savings from the bank. He even made a purposeless trip to El Paso before he went to see Lisa; that is, it proved purposeless. He went to buy Lisa a ring, but he got no farther with the buying than a half-hearted inspection of a jeweler's window. None of the rings on display seemed to hit his fancy, so he turned away, without looking farther.

Because he had no ring, in the last minutes of good-by, when his infatuation flamed up again while he held her in his arms and muttered promises and love words in her ear, King took from his watch chain the charm he had worn ever since he joined the service, and pressed it into her little, warm palm for a keepsake. It was not of much value, but she had often taken it in her fingers and admired the queer streakings of red in the dull-green stone inclosed in a horseshoe band of gold.

"When I come back," said King dully, "I'll bring you something else. Will you go with me when I come back after you, sweetheart?"

"When will that be?" Lisa was turning the trinket in her hand and staring, as she had stared so many times, at the tiny initials, K. A. M., which King had filed in the edge of the horseshoe band. She did not look up at him.

"When I've got a place fixed for you. I don't know when that will be, but it will be just as quick as I can make it. I'm going to leave town to-day. I hate the place."

"You hate it—and I will be here all the while?" Lisa showed a dimple. "You men say the craziest things——"

The gawky, half-grown sister interrupted them then, and in a few minutes King left. Lisa had not said in so many words that she would go with him, but at the door, as he was leaving, she lifted the watch charm to her lips and looked at him with deep, tragic eyes. That last glimpse of her stayed vividly with King, and did a great deal toward fusing the hot, passing emotion he called love into the deep, lasting attachment which is love's real self.

After that, King wandered here and there for a while. He worked for the Tijana China outfit on their beef round-up, thrashed a man who had been so unwise as to refer banteringly to King as "the famous ex-Ranger," and took his saddle and rifle and bedding roll elsewhere. King was extremely touchy on the subject of Texas Rangers.

He bought a horse and a burro and went down into the wilderness of Brewster County, wandering alone in the hills on the pretense that he was prospecting—not for gold, but for a piece of fertile land, where he could get water on the soil and build a ranch for Lisa and himself. He clung with a persistence that was almost dogged to the idea of making a home for Lisa.

He could have gone back to see her, but the desire for her presence was not too great to be borne with fortitude; not half as great, for instance, as the nagging hunger that filled him for "the boys"—Bill and Vaughan and Kent and Charlie Horne.

He used to sit by his camp fire in the hills, and smoke and stare into the shadows, and relive his days and nights with them. Sometimes he dreamed of Lisa, but not as often as you might think. Primarily King Marshall was a man's man. The image of Lisa grew hazy, and the thought of her more a sense of responsibility for her future than a poignant longing for her immediate presence; whereas the thought of the boys became a growing hunger to have speech with them.

When the nights grew frosty, he drifted into Chico, which is a little "brush town," a day's ride from the railroad. He had no particular reason for stopping there, but he was so dismally adrift and without any definite purpose that he stayed.

"Why don't you buy me out, King, so I can quit this dang place?" the dissatisfied owner of the one little livery stable suggested to him one day, when King was sunning himself apathetically on the bench by the stable door. Without consciously deciding to change his name, he had given it as King when he arrived, and let the Marshall slide into oblivion.

"What you got against me, Murphy?" King retorted, grinning.

"Not a thing. You could have worse things wished on yuh than this here livery business. Ain't nothing the matter with it—not a thing. But I don't want it no longer. I want to go to Californy and live." Murphy nursed his knees and stared down the street as far as the first crook. "I'd sell it cheap," he added wistfully.

"How cheap—just as she stands?" It occurred to King that Lisa, being half Mexican, would probably not object to Chico. But he had no great enthusiasm for the idea—or for anything else, for that matter.

"Just as she stands? King, I'll put on my coat and walk out uh here fer four hundred and fifty dollars. And I own the stable and the house and ground as far back as the crick. You know the horses I've got—nothin' fancy, but they make me a livin'—the burros and the rigs I'll make yuh a present of. Four hundred and fifty cash—that's how bad I want to leave!"

A gift, almost. King said he would take it. He would have fifty dollars or so left—enough to send for Lisa. And the stable was earning a little money every day in the year. The stage that came three times a week from the railroad kept a team here always, which was a steady income, even though it was small. King paid Murphy the money that day, and that is how he came to settle down in Chico.

It was on the very next mail day, when the little store post office was crowded, that King received his second shock. He had a letter from Lisa —forwarded from Marfa, where she had written her last; a tender, misspelled affair with six crosses after her name to signify that she sent him six kisses. King's heart warmed toward her when he read the letter, and he made up his mind that he would send a letter back on the stage next day, with fifty dollars for her fare, and ask her to come at once and take charge of the tidy little place which Murphy's wife was leaving so eagerly.

Beside him a big, fat-cheeked Mexican was reading a letter avidly, with little exclamations of delight now and then. King glanced at him carelessly, and caught the Ysleta postmark on the envelope which the Mexican—one Pancho Mazon—held face out in one hand while he read his letter. King glanced again, to make sure, for the envelope looked very much like the one he had stuffed in his own pocket. Just then Pancho looked up, showing his teeth in a broad smile.

"Look, fellows!—what I gets for my birthday!" he cried jubilantly. "My little sweetheart, she sends." He held up the gift for all to see—he seemed a jovial fellow who must share his joys and his griefs with all his world.

King looked and chilled with the curious sensation that comes when one has felt the treachery of a friend.

A watch charm with a quaintly marked cornelian set in a horseshoe band of plain gold—he knew it as he knew the look of his two hands. He knew—and yet he reached out and took the dangling trinket from the amazed Pancho, turned it over, and saw the tiny initials he had painstakingly filed there during one bored afternoon when he had been left in charge of the Ranger office.

He laughed—because there seemed nothing in the world to say—gave the charm back to Pancho, and walked out, tearing Lisa's letter into little bits and scattering the pieces for the wind to play with. By sheer coincidence, he unconsciously quoted Bill Gillis in the only sentence he spoke. "The lyin' little hussy!" he said, and that was all.

He went back to his livery stable. He took a basin and a sponge and began bathing the saddle galls on one of his horses, and, whenever he thought of Lisa Gonzales, and her six cross kisses at the bottom of the letter she had written him, he called her the name he had called her before—the name Bill Gillis had called her. He tried not to think of her, however; and, after a while, he succeeded.

But there he was, settled in Chico— which he did not like as a town—with a livery stable he did not want on his hands. Had he been free of it, he would have drifted God knows where. But he was not free. No one else seemed to hanker for the livery business, especially now that winter was with them.

III.

One day in late spring the stage came in from the railroad, loaded with passengers and camp outfit, and stopped at King's stable to dump three sacked saddles off there. King was used to that sort of thing, and he did not leave his work in the dim-lighted stall at the far end when he heard the arrival in front. Juan, his stableboy, was out there and would see to things, and if any one wanted the boss, why, Juan had but to lift his voice a little. King had fallen into a passive kind of devotion to his horses, and in the same ratio he had come to feel no interest whatever in men. If a man came to hire a horse, King would look at him, make a swift appraisement, and choose the horse according to his opinion of the man. Beyond that and collecting payment, his interest did not go.

Juan did not call him, so King went on trimming the mane of a horse he had just bought. Even when he heard footsteps coming down the stable, he did not leave the stall to see who was coming—because no inkling of the immediate future did fate permit him.

"He's back, some*where*—I dunno; you will find, all righ'," he heard Juan's voice announcing cheerfully near the door.

King frowned a little, and moved down to the horse's rump—saw who was coming, and retreated precipitately into the shadow. He was not quite quick enough; for Bill Gillis, coming toward him, glimpsed his face and his hat above it, and knew him at the first glance. Bill dove into the stall and grabbed King by the shoulders and shook him a little, and laughed.

"Dog-gone you, King, I'm so tickled I can't say 'howdy!'" Bill said, and laughed again. "I kinda wondered if the King that owns this stable was you —don't know what gave me the notion, but I just naturally had to hunt you up to make sure. How are yuh, anyway? Darn it, are yuh dumb?"

"Just about," King confessed, in a queer, shaky voice, and bit his under lip sharply. He laid one arm over Bill's shoulder and looked out over his head and winked very fast for a minute.

"You popped in on me kinda sudden, Bill," he remarked, when he was sure of his voice. "Give a feller time to get used to the notion." His hand tightened on Bill's shoulder, and he pushed him back a little and looked down at him avidly. "You blamed little, sawed-off runt, I sure am glad to see yuh," he added, in the tone that Bill knew of old. "Down here alone?"

"Captain and Vaughan are here," Bill said, still grinning for the simple reason that his face refused to do anything else just then. "We came down to ride the big pastures—and I guess I might as well start pickin' out the horses we'll want from you, King."

"Fly at it," King agreed absently, trying to adjust himself to this unexpected turn; trying, also, to decide whether he really was glad or sorry to have Bill there, for sometimes it is better not to have a happier past recalled. "I've got some good ones, Bill—and you're dead welcome to the best I got."

Bill covertly eyed King, while he chose what horses they would need, and told as much of the Ysleta news as was tactful. He did not, for instance, say anything about Lisa Gonzales marrying a Mexican—one Pancho Mazon, who had started a new cantina, that had already acquired a reputation of its own. He thought of it, and wondered how King would take the news if he were to tell him.

King stood in the wide doorway, with his hands in his pockets, and watched Bill go off up the street in search of the captain and Vaughan. He watched Bill, and his eyes were wistful and his mouth had a twist of bitterness. He saw the captain, broad-shouldered, straight, and purposeful in his movements, come out of the post office, with Vaughan at his heels. He saw Bill hurrying to meet them—and King turned back into the stable and took down his saddle from its rusty spike.

"Clean up Mouse and Faro and Come Again," he called to Juan. "And clean 'em good, or I'll just about break yuh in two. They're for them three that come in on the stage." He slapped the saddle on his big black, Noches, cinched it hurriedly, and dropped the stirrups into place. "If anybody asks for me," he told Juan, as he led the horse to the doorway, "just say I'll be back *muy pronto.*"

It would have been unjust to accuse King of running away from the Rangers. As a matter of fact, he was attempting something a great deal more foolish than that, for he was trying to run away from himself. He rode out into the hills until they were piled high all around him, and then he let the reins lie loose on Noches' neck, and wandered aimlessly, not caring where the horse took him, so he headed into further wildness.

He returned after dark, and his black horse showed dust-colored streaks where the sweat had dried on his hips and legs, and his neck shone wet to show that his homeward pace had not been slow. Supper time was past, but King waved Juan's solicitous anxiety to help, and himself rubbed down Noches and loosened the hay in his manger and kicked the bedding into a softer pile.

The little man who had come on the stage, Juan informed King deprecatingly, had come with two others, and asked for King. They had waited a little, and gone off to their camping place by the high bank next the arroyo where was the little spring. At sundown the little man had come again, and had waited on the bench. He had gone not ten minutes ago. He left word that the three horses be brought to their camp at sunrise.

"All right. You go to bed. I'll lock up," King told him shortly, and stood in the doorway, rolling a cigarette, while he watched Juan disappear up the crooked street that lay quiet and dark under the starlight. He sat down on the bench and stared at the bluffs beyond the town. After a while he got up and went to the corner of the stable nearest the arroyo, and stood there, leaning one shoulder against the adobe wall, while he stared hard at the glow on the opposite bank from a camp fire. In his eyes there was again a great hunger, and his lips had a twist of bitterness.

He walked slowly down toward the glow. When he was close enough to see the little, licking flames, and could hear the cheerful snapping, he stopped and stood hesitating over whether he should go on. Forms in the firelight he did not see—since this was a Ranger camp, and since Rangers are rather particular about revealing themselves unnecessarily in the light of their camp fires. He waited for a minute and went back and sat hunched together on the bench beside the stable door.

He was very quiet, and very, very bitter toward life.

When Juan came swiftly down the street, just before daylight, to feed the horses that were ordered for sunrise, he found them munching contentedly, heads buried to the eyes in fresh piles of secate. Also they were sleek from long brushing, and King was settling the saddle of Captain Oakes upon the back of Come Again, the best horse in the stable barring King's own private horse, Noches. Whereupon Juan immediately became abjectly apologetic for being so late—though he really had come early.

When King himself led the horses out and swung into Vaughan's saddle with the lead ropes of the other two in his hand, Juan felt that he trembled—literally—upon the brink of dismissal. Señor King must be very mad, indeed, when he would not let Juan take the horses to camp. He looked after King, and got no encouragement from the gloomy face of his master. Something was very wrong—and yet in his heart Juan knew that he had come early enough.

King rode slowly down the arroyo to where the Rangers had made camp. Every step that the horses took, King cursed himself for coming. Yet his eyes went searching eagerly for the camp and for sight of the men who had for three years and more been his close comrades. When he saw them, however, he sat a little stiffer in the saddle; and when he reached their breakfast fire, and dismounted just outside its zone of heat, his manner was carefully neutral, as though he were delivering the horses to strangers. Bill was down at the little stream.

"Why, hello, King!" Vaughan hurried forward and took his hand and pumped it up and down. "You old sun of a gun, you're lookin' fine!"

"Howdy, King," the captain greeted him easily—with a warmth in his manner that King had never expected to see again. "Good horses you've brought us," he added, while he shook hands, his keen little eyes taking in line by line the trimness of the mount King had chosen for his use. "You haven't forgotten my fancy for a long-legged animal under me, I see. I rode a burro once for two hundred miles—since then I want to know that my feet aren't going to drag on the ground every time I straighten my legs."

"He's a good horse," King said simply, turning to pat the hard-muscled neck and to hide a sudden mistiness in his eyes. "He'll carry you all day and all night, and then some. I've named him Come Again. After you've rode him, you'll know why."

"What's the pedigree uh that there critter under my saddle?" Vaughan looked up from the skillet of sputtering eggs to demand. "What's his name?"

"Him? Faro—and you don't go up against any brace game when you crawl in his middle, either." King had himself in hand now, and he faced Vaughan with a smile that reached his eyes. "He's a right true little caballo —and he's a cat for climbing, if you want to know. He'll take yuh anywhere you point him, Vaughan. Bill picked 'em out of a dozen or so I've got down there."

The captain, rubbing the nose of Come Again, gave King a keen glance. "So you've branched out into the livery business," he remarked. "Doing pretty well?" Casual as the question was on its surface, King felt an underlying anxiety for his welfare; knew, too, that Vaughan had looked up and was waiting for the answer.

"Oh—all right, I guess," he said indifferently. "Making money, far as that goes."

Then Bill came and slapped King on the back just as he used to do in the old days. King stayed and ate breakfast with them, and was afterward surprised to remember how matter of course it had seemed.

Having lived for several months in that part of the country, and being engaged in a business that brought him into contact with the riders thereof, King knew a good deal about the fence troubles and the gossip of altered brands and the like. What he knew he told them freely, just as though it was his business to help them. He advised them as to short cuts through the hills, and he offered to keep an eye on the camp while the three were out riding.

Juan was astonished to hear his master come whistling back to the stable that morning.

The cheerfulness, however, fluctuated a good deal in the next three days. Mixed with King's pleasure in renewing old friendships was the bitterness of knowing that he was, after all, an outsider; that when the captain assigned certain tasks to his men, he must sit apart and never be ordered anywhere because he had forfeited his right to wear the Ranger star. He did not feel like whistling when that fact was forced coldly in upon his consciousness.

Then, one evening Come Again came hobbling painfully to the stable, with Captain Oakes riding slack in the saddle, hurt so badly that King had to steady him to the bench beside the stable door. Juan produced a bottle of whisky from somewhere, and, with the temporary strength lent by a swallow or two, the captain got to his camp bed and let King bathe his bruised leg and the strained tendons of his knee, and afterward make him a comforting cup of coffee.

Accident had befallen Come Again, the best "rope horse" in that part of the country. The captain had wanted to inspect more closely a doubtful brand on a particularly wild steer, and had roped it. But the ground was broken into treacherous, small ridges and water-deepened ruts, and when the steer bolted around Come Again, the horse was jerked backward into a ditch, and thrown, and the captain had not been able to jump free because of the rope. The wonder was, he admitted to King, that neither had broken a bone or two.

The next day King spent with the captain, leaving Juan to tend the stable and doctor Come Again. That is why King was in camp when a Mexican brought Captain Oakes a message which had been sent from El Paso, and was permitted by fate to have another chance at the thing he wanted most in his life.

In effect, the telegram said that one Bull Dawson, who had been an outlaw so long that he had almost become an institution in southwestern Texas, had murdered and robbed two men under peculiarly brutal circumstances—even for Bull Dawson. He was somewhere in Brewster County, according to last reports. And, while a sheriff and posse were scouring the northern part, the Rangers were asked to head him off if he got as far down as the hills around Chico.

"I don't see how we can do anything about it," Captain Oakes grumbled, handing the telegram to King—so nearly had the gap between them been bridged. "I can't call Gillis and Vaughan off their work, and I can't go out after him myself, crippled like this. Bull's the kind of man it takes a Gatlin' gun to make any impression on. He's been shot so often he don't think anything of a bullet or two under his skin."

King flicked the ashes thoughtfully off his cigarette. "What kinda lookin' fellow is he?" he wanted to know. He had heard of Bull Dawson often enough, but always in a general way— the name standing for the ultimate depths of depravity and the ultimate heights of strength and ferocity and animal cunning.

"Big—over six foot. Weighs about two hundred. He's a fighter, of course —but he'd just as soon shoot a man in the back. Had a black beard last time his description came in to the office, and hair streaked with gray. Eyes are black, too—the snaky kind."

King got up and stood looking across the arroyo. His fingers kept flicking absently at the end of his cigarette, which was cold by now. "I—if you'd let me do it, I'd like to go after him," he said, while the red rose steadily from his collar to the hair line on his forehead. "Uh course, if yuh don't feel like——"

The captain gave a grunt and heaved himself stiffly up on his good leg, steadying himself against a rock. He looked at King a minute.

"Marshall, I was pretty hard on you last fall," he said. "You made a fool of yourself—but I was pretty hard on

you. If you really want to take this special job——"

"Want to!" King's voice shook a little. "You know well enough—you know I'd give anything I've got in the world to wipe out last fall and be back in the service!"

The captain cleared his throat. "If you feel that way about it, Marshall, here's your chance. There happens to be a vacancy right now; Barrett resigned. I'll swear you in for special duty, to go after Bull Dawson. Here's my star—I'll lend it to you for the trip. And, Marshall, if you get your man you can keep that star. I'll reënlist you to fill Barret's place. Hold up your right hand."

Trembling a little, King raised his hand and took the oath. He drew a long breath when his hand dropped slowly from pinning the star on the lining of his coat.

"I'll send Juan up to look after you," he said. "He's a good boy, and you can trust him as far as you would any outsider. I'm going to get out on the trail. And, captain—I'm going to get him!"

IV.

Once last fall when King was riding through the country, half-heartedly looking for a likable location for a ranch, he had come upon a place that looked very much like a permanent camp. A deep, hidden depression in a sandstone ledge, where the sun shone in during the morning, had been fitted up with a crude stove, made of rocks, and a flattened coal-oil can for a top. In a dark corner a small roll of blankets was suspended from the roof with a piece of wire, and beside it hung a bag with brown beans and a square of salt pork and a little corn meal.

There were no signs, however, of recent occupation. It may have been a month or two, perhaps longer, since the cave had been used. But there was dry wood piled in a corner where beating storms never reached, and King judged that whoever had camped there meant at some time to return, and had provided food and fire and a bed for himself when he did come.

Now, as it happened, while he had been riding at random through the hills, trying to fight off the black mood of vain regrets which the sight of Bill Gillis had brought him, he had met, just before dusk, a horseman riding on a narrow trail which led farther into the hills; a man bigger than the average, judging by the length of his stirrups and the breadth of his shoulders; a man with a black stubble of a beard that had lately been cut short and afterward neglected, and with little, black eyes of the kind called snaky. King had turned out to let the man pass, and had nodded to him in the cursory greeting which men of the open give each passing stranger. The man had nodded in reply, and had ridden on— but King, having the trick of seeing things behind him without turning his head, caught the stranger watching him with his head turned over his shoulder.

Now, however, his Ranger training carried his mind to those two isolated incidents—impelled, perhaps, by the captain's description of Bull Dawson. The man he had met that night might not be Dawson, and he might not have been on his way to that snug little camp hidden away under the sandstone ledge, but there was no reason why it could not have been he. The description tallied well enough, and the man had certainly been traveling into the hills, in the direction of that camp, although it is true that he was a day's ride away from it. He had been traveling light, with just a blanket roll and a slicker tied behind the saddle, which proved that he must have grub within riding distance.

King considered his guess as good as any he could make, and he took a blanket and his rifle and a little flour and bacon and coffee, and ground feed for his horse, and started out with Noches. He knew the country, and he rode straight toward the camp under the ledge. Ten miles out, he camped until morning. He meant to ride by daylight, so that he could pick up the trail of the man he believed was Bull Dawson.

He was so confident of finding the cave camp occupied that he left Noches hidden in a thicket at dusk, and traveled the last two miles on foot. Bull Dawson was noted for his animal-like cunning, and like an animal King hunted him. He did not approach the place by the most direct route up the cañon that held it. Instead, he climbed the ridge at the cañon's mouth, and followed the top until he knew he must be above the place where the camp lay. He had noticed, last fall, that just beyond the camp the ledge ended in a bank of earth, scattered over with scrubby little bushes, such as make shift somehow to live in barren soil, and, by the light of the stars, he watched for the upper rim of that bank.

He found it without much trouble, and, pushing his six-shooter forward, so that his hand could drop to it easily, he began to climb down; slowly, bush by bush, feeling with his feet for soft soil that would take his weight without sound. Bull Dawson, if he were in camp, would watch the cañon; the bluff above him must give forth some sound of footsteps, some sign of movement, before it would draw his attention from the easier approach below. So King reasoned, and took his time.

It took him a long time, but he reached the base where the bank joined the wide shelf at the bottom of the ledge, and he had not made a sound that could have been heard above the faint rustling of the little night breeze that brushed the cañon sides. Nor had he heard a sound under the ledge. He sniffed the air for the smell of smoke, but the wind was in the wrong direction, and he could not tell. He felt in his coat pocket for the handcuffs the captain had given him, so that there should be no slip-up if his man was there. Bull Dawson meant so much to him that King stood there and thought of every little contingency, as an anxious, unaccustomed traveler feels for ticket and baggage checks, purse, and parcels.

Like a cougar stalking a deer, he crept inch by inch along the ledge to where the cavelike opening showed black at the rim. His hand was gripping his six-shooter now; he did not mean to take any chances at all. He reached the opening and stopped there, peering into the blackness. It was like looking into a great blot of ink—he might as well have shut his eyes, for all he could see. But that instinct we cannot name told him that something was in there; something alive, be it man or beast. He strained his ears—and it may have been breathing that he heard, or it may have been a throbbing of the blood in his own veins.

He drew back his head, fearing that he might be seen against the clear starlight. And at that instant a gun roared deafeningly. King remembered afterward that he had felt the bullet fan his face as it hurtled past. At that moment, however, he was grappling and fighting a huge body, that launched itself full at him from the black cave mouth, and trying to keep big, hardknuckled fingers from gripping his throat.

Like two great dogs they fought and rolled before the cave. They did not speak—they needed their breath for something more vital than words. There was no question of motive or object; each man fought for something precious—for one man fought for his life and the other fought for what made life worth while.

Gripping and twisting bodies and interlocked legs, they toppled over the edge of the shelf and began to roll and slide down the steep slope to the bottom of the cañon. As they went, King heard something clink in his pocket, and set his mind and all his energy toward accomplishing one certain thing. Just one thing—let him do that one thing.

They landed with a jolt, and, by the mercy of fate, it was King who lay for one stunned minute on top. One arm, his left one, was pinned under the man, but his right arm was free. He slipped his hand into his pocket as instinctively as one raises an elbow to ward off a blow, and got the handcuffs. The man beneath him heaved himself up, but King caught his right arm and snapped on one iron, jerked his own left arm from under the man, and ironed that one also.

The man sat up dazedly and stared down at their two arms locked together with steel bands that shone bright in the starlight. King was feeling the other's body with quick, practiced movements for weapons. A knife he found and sent spinning away among the bushes. A six-shooter hidden inside the fellow's shirt he sent after the knife. The other one, that had been fired at King from the cave mouth, was back there, somewhere on the shelf.

"Get up, Bull Dawson!" King commanded, with an exultant note in his voice. "I'm a Ranger—and you know the rest."

"You're a ——!" Several things which were the worst he could think of the prisoner spat out venomously.

"It's a long way to camp, Bull," King remarked cheerfully. "We better be starting—'cause we'll have to walk."

"I got a horse." Bull whined, as he stumbled along. "That damn' fall hurt my leg. Why'n't you iron both my hands, an' let me ride? I ain't able to walk—what yuh 'fraid of?"

What King was afraid of he kept to himself. He was hurt—he thought he must have broken a rib or two. There was a salty taste in his mouth that he knew for blood, and, when he turned his head, there was a grinding pain at the top of his shoulder. But he had his man—had him fast to him, so that where one went the other must go. The tug at his wrist whenever Bull Dawson stumbled sent a thrill over King keen as a pain and delicious as the kiss of a loved woman.

"Afraid? Why, Bull, I just want to walk with yuh, that's all. We can stroll along comfortable enough——"

Bull Dawson whirled suddenly, his left hand doubled to a fist, and shooting out to get King under the ear. King ducked his head forward, and saw stars with the blow that glanced off his skull. He poked the barrel of his six-shooter into Bull's side suggestively, and Bull wilted into meek plodding again.

"I thought you'd try that, Bull—but it won't work. Now, let this sink into your mind: Every low-down trick you think of, I've thought of it first. And there's another thing I don't believe has come into your mind yet, so I'm going to plant it there. If you try any of the tricks you think of, I'm going to shoot your left wrist so I'll break both bones. Figure for yourself how dangerous you'll be then!"

In the dark Bull Dawson gulped and turned a sallow shade. "You wouldn't do a thing like that?" he protested nervously. "Why—why, that would be plain brutal! Why, I wouldn't do a thing like——"

King laughed. "All the difference between us is, you'd do it first, if you could, before I had a chance to try anything; or maybe you'd do worse. I'll give you a chance to come along like a white man."

Bull walked along for a time, and said nothing. He did not attempt any further treachery—indeed, he seemed inclined to steady King over rough places, and to lend the help of his greater strength. He seemed to take King's statement as truth beyond argument. King walked steadily, but the pain in his side grew worse. He no longer had the salty taste in his mouth, however, and he took courage from that. But his neck was getting stiff and sore—terribly stiff and sore. He could not take a long breath at all, and resorted to a quick, shallow breathing to supply his lungs with air.

They came to where Noches was tied, and King compelled Bull Dawson to slip the bridle off the horse and hang it on the saddle horn. He was tempted to cuff Dawson's two hands together and make him walk ahead, while King rode behind; that would be safe enough ordinarily. But King was afraid of that pain in his side, that grew constantly a little worse. What if he could not bear the jolt of riding? What if he should faint?

Noches, free to go where he would, chose to follow docilely at his master's heels, until King drove him ahead and urged him with his voice to a shuffling trot. And the two men, walking side by side when the trail was wide enough, King an awkward step behind when they could not go abreast, plodded on through the night.

When daylight came, King left the trail and struck off on a short cut that was not quite passable for a horse because of one ledge along a cañon wall. A man going carefully afoot could negotiate it safely enough, and thereby save several miles of travel. King figured that if he took that short cut they might, with steady walking, reach Chico by sundown.

"We're coming to a kinda ticklish spot, Bull," he announced, when they entered the cañon. "You're remembering what I said when we started out, I hope, and you'll watch where you set your feet. I hope guns don't make you nervous, Bull—you're going to travel quite a piece now with mine cuddlin' your ribs."

"Aw, can't ye see I ain't goin' to try nothin'?" Bull expostulated grievedly. "I was mad when I started out—— I hit out without thinkin'. But I ain't a fool. You've got me, and I know it. And," he finished virtuously, "whatever else they tell on me, they can't say 't Bull Dawson cain't take his medicine."

"Fine," King approved colorlessly, and pushed Bull out along the ledge. "I'm sure glad I can—trust you, Bull."

Midway across, where they had a jagged-edged shelf of a rock a foot wide to walk on, King stumbled. A dizziness had caught him unawares when he glanced down at the thread of water in the arroyo below. Bull, looking over his shoulder, stopped and eyed King intently.

"Sick, ain't yuh?" he asked, in what he meant to be a sympathetic tone. "This here's a little too much for ye, mebby. Jest——"

"Remember what I said about your left wrist, Bull?" King pulled himself together and looked back steadily into Bull's wolfishly greedy eyes.

Bull grunted, and went on, stepping carefully. King, with his lips pressed tightly together, edged carefully after.

When they reached safer footing—a loose, sandy slope that led down to a wider gulch, where they could walk side by side, King stopped suddenly and looked back at the ledge, and down, away down, to the thread of water they could not reach by any means at hand. He grinned a little, and, with a flip of an outward heave, he sent his gun spinning down the cliff. The effort made him catch his breath sharply.

"I—don't need the darn thing," he said, with another little gasp. "I can trust you."

Bull Dawson smiled a great, gashlike smile, that parted his black stubble of beard unpleasantly. "Why, shore you kin trust me!" he cried eagerly. "That's what I bin tellin' ye all along. Shore ye kin!"

"Over she goes," King said cheerfully—too cheerfully, and flung his arm outward again melodramatically. "Didn't need the darned thing—just so much weight to pack. I know I can bank on you."

"Shore ye kin! Say what they will, they cain't say Bull Dawson ain't t' be trusted." His tone was fawningly friendly.

"Come on," said King. "We'll pike along, and get this over with."

"Shore! Git it over with is what I says." Bull smiled again, and then fell silent.

Down that steep bluff they went, Bull Dawson limping a little, King with his lips shut tight and taking little, quick breaths through his nose. Instead of turning his head now, he rolled his eyes when he wanted to look sidewise. And the pain in his side was a consuming fire, that burned and licked along the nerves to his shoulder and down to his thigh.

They went down that gulch, turned into another, and followed that also. They came to a tiny stream of tepid water, and the two knelt together and drank, scooping up the water in their free hands—King with his right hand, Bull with his left. They laved their bruised faces, they sopped water on their hair because the sun was hot and high above them; but they did not talk much.

When King gave the signal to rise, Bull lurched heavily against him, and bore him to the ground. His little, snaky eyes sought here and there, while his body pinned King down, helpless. He leaned and picked up a rock that was all his left hand could lift, and poised it, grinning venomously, over King's head.

"I'm goin' to smash your brains out,"

he stated gleefully. "I guess you wisht now you'd broke my wrist 'fore I thought uh this here little trick, hey?"

King looked up at him, grinning sardonically. "I thought you'd try it," he said, speaking jerkily because of the pain in his side. "That's why I throwed the handcuff key after my six-gun. Go ahead—you'll sure have one sweet time of it—shackled to a dead man!"

Bull's jaw dropped. Also, he lowered the rock to the ground, though he kept his hand upon it.

"You lie!" he screamed. "You never throwed away the key! You lie! You never throwed it away!"

"I did, too. I knew you'd try something like this, and I blocked your play five miles back. You better be sure of that key, Bull, before you go caving my head in!"

Bull looked, swearing horribly while he turned King's pockets wrongside out, hunting in every crease and every wrinkle of King's clothing. He sat back on his haunches finally, and stared at King like a beaten animal in a cage —snarling, lustful to kill, but shaking with fear.

"Ironed to a dead man! Keep that in your mind, Bull, when you want to try something else. And there's no grub in camp, remember, and no gun and no knife—nothing, you swine, but our two legs to get us out of here. And if you don't help me get out, you're here to stay—with a dead man hobbled to you. Help me up, Bull. My side's a fright, and we've got to get to Chico to-night."

Bull called down curses to wither the earth with their blasphemy, had they carried farther than his bellowing voice. Tears of rage rolled down his lined, grimy cheeks into the stubble of his beard. He raised the rock again, quailed before that mirthless grin on the lips of King Marshall, and threw the rock as far away as his strength would send it. With his free hand he worried King's boots off his feet, thinking the key might have been hidden there. He searched King's pockets again. He tugged and pulled and twisted at King's wrist, trying to free it of the steel band that held those two together.

King fainted with the pain of that last performance. He looked so like a dead man lying there that Bull Dawson was scared into acceptance of his defeat. Without food or weapons there in the wilderness, shackled to a dead man—Bull Dawson was baffled, beaten to a stark terror lest his anger had brought upon him that horrid fate which King had named.

He scooped up water, and bathed King's face, watching anxiously for some sign of returning life. He eased the strained wrist as much as he could, and, when King finally opened his eyes, Bull Dawson shielded him with his own big body from the glare of the sun until King was able to stagger to his feet and go on.

At dusk that night, just when the firelight was beginning to cast a dancing glow upon the bank beyond the spring, these two staggered into the Ranger camp. King's face was like a dead man, except that all his intrepid soul looked dauntlessly out from his hollow eyes. He moved slowly, helped along by Bull Dawson, who limped and gazed furtively this way and that as he came.

"What the devil—Marshall, is that you?" Captain Oakes, for once in his life, was startled out of his self-contained dignity.

King's knees bent under him, and he sagged down to the ground just as his hand went weakly up to salute. His lips stretched in a grin that was startling, in that drawn face of his.

"Captain—I—got my man!" he said, and fainted.

A Chat With You

LOTS of nonsense is circulated in this world as real information because no one takes the trouble to think seriously about it or deny it. One of the fool remarks especially irritating to us is the one to the effect that if you want to really get people interested you must tell them a simple love story. We could easily fill these pages with proofs to the opposite. We have read hundreds of love stories, and the only ones that have ever stuck in our memories have been those that had a whole lot to them besides plain and simple love. So far as the great masterpieces have been concerned, from Shakespeare to Stevenson, the stories have been interesting for something beside the love story. We suppose the best love story in the world is that of Romeo and Juliet, but what would the play be without the gallant and whimsical Mercutio, who is not in love at all, and who is twice the man that Romeo is? The next most powerful love story is perhaps that mystical and sinister Celtic tragedy that Wagner chose for the framework of his Tristan and Isolde—and if you were to take the music away from his drama we doubt if many would go to see it.

❡ ❡

AS a matter of fact, falling in love is only a part of a man's life. Byron informs us that "'Tis woman's whole existence," but if he had met some of the women in the United States he might have modified his opinion. If a man's love affair is not complicated with a lot of other things, it is likely to be too sweet for average consumption. It is because of this that we have never leaned very heavily toward love stories.

Some writers, however, have the ability to give the love affair its proper proportion, to make it interesting in a masculine rather than a mawkish sense, and to make us see the woman's side of it as well.

❡ ❡

THE particular writer we are thinking of now is Bertrand W. Sinclair. You remember "North of Fifty-three," and "The Rest of the Story," and that other great novel of his we published last spring, "The Way of the North." They all had real live men in them, and, what is more, they had real live women. They are all considerably wider in scope than mere stories of adventure. As Solomon remarked, the way of a man with a maid is a curious thing. So is the way of a maid with a man. Sinclair's latest novel is called "Landlubber's Luck." It will appear complete in the issue of THE POPULAR out two weeks from to-day. It isn't a love story at all, but there is a love story in it. It is a big, stirring tale of the halibut fisheries; it is a story of big business as well as of physical adventure. Furthermore, it is the story of a girl who, on account of her family, married the wrong man, and afterward lost herself from the world that knew her. There is real, outdoor excitement in it, and the bracing tale of a man who works his way up from nothing to a fortune. Running parallel with his story is that of the girl, who has own her own troubles, her own adventures, her own achievement as a breadwinner. If you were to classify this story, you would undoubtedly say that it was a man's story. At the same time, if you happen to know any woman who wonders why you are so attached to THE POPULAR, and says that she cannot get interested in stories of adventure, get her to read "Landlubber's Luck." She'll understand after that.

◢ ◢

SPEAKING of women, we also want to call your attention to the girl in "Rimrock Jones," by Dane Coolidge. You have read the first installment by this time, but as yet you can have formed no idea of what a broad and human story it is. Rimrock himself is worth a whole book as an example of a stubborn, masterful, thoroughly masculine human, but the girl is just as much a character in her own way. Too many writers of tales of action and adventure have failed in their delineation of women. Beautiful dolls with no savor of humanity mince through the pages of many a book otherwise good. The girl Rimrock is interested in is just as real and vital and unexpected in her way as Rimrock himself. She has a will of her own, and the conflict of the two wills is so fascinating and powerful a drama that the story will be remembered for a long time, and ultimately win a place as one of the biggest novels of the year. You'll hear plenty of people talking about it later on, when it comes out in book form. You are just so much ahead in getting it now.

◢ ◢

THERE are two other Western stories in the next issue of THE POPULAR. One is called "Vanity of Men," and is by J. Frank Davis, who wrote "Garland: Ranger Service," and of whom you will hear a great deal in the future. The other is a short, complete novel, called "The Killer," and is the work of B. M. Bower and Buck Connor. B. M. Bower needs no introduction. Buck Connor is, however, a less familiar name to the readers of this magazine, although it is well enough known in Texas. He is a Texas Ranger, now acting under the direct personal advice of General Scott himself. From his old Captain Hughes of the Rangers he has already secured material that no other writer could possibly have access to. In the guise of POPULAR fiction you have already learned a lot of true things about the Northwest Mounted Police. The Texas Rangers are a body of men of the same stamp. The history of the organization is every bit as thrilling and interesting, but until we started giving it space in THE POPULAR very few knew anything about it. This magazine is the first that ever published real baseball stories taken from the life of the Big League; it was first in the field with stories of the Northwest; it is now doing the same thing with the Southwest. You can read stories elsewhere purporting to give the real life and atmosphere of the Rangers, but we doubt if any magazine save this can give you the real thing. "The Killer" is really a wonderful story, taken from life itself, grim, holding, and tense in its atmosphere. We call special attention to it as an evidence that the magazine is still growing and striking into new and untrodden fields for its fiction.

◢ ◢

BESIDE these things there is a sea story by Stacpoole, a detective story by Ritchie, a funny fight story by Witwer, and a tale of the Northwest by Hendryx, in the next issue of the magazine. There is also a football story by Williams, and a moving-picture story by Ullman. There is a story of the U. S. army by Captain Evans, who knows what he is writing about—and this is by no means all. If there is any choice between this number and the next—the next is a little better.

The Boss is Sizing You Up

Whether you know it or not, he's on the lookout all the time for men he can *promote*. He's ready and anxious to give you bigger work and bigger pay once you prove you can handle it. But your chance for promotion depends entirely on yourself.

If you're *satisfied* just to hang on where you are, rest assured that's as far as you'll ever get. But if you *want* to get ahead, if you want to *be* somebody, to climb into a position of responsibility and good money—

Get Ready—Your Chance Will Surely Come

Choose the position you want in the work you like best—then train for it. You can do it in spare time in your own home without losing a day or a dollar from your present occupation—through the International Correspondence Schools. More than 100,000 men *right now* are putting themselves in line for promotion through the study of I. C. S. Courses. Last year nearly 5,000 men reported advancement and increased earnings as the result of their I. C. S. training. What the I. C. S. have done for others they can surely do for you.

No matter where you live, if you can be reached by the mails, the I. C. S. will come to you. No matter how humble or important your present position, I. C. S. training will help you go higher. No matter what your chosen work may be, some one of the 280 practical I. C. S. home-study courses will just suit your needs.

Choose Your Career

Do you like advertising? Many of the foremost advertising managers in this country were I. C. S. trained. Salesmanship? Thousands of I. C. S. trained men are winning success in the selling game. Accounting? Commerical Law? All over America accountants, bookkeepers, office managers, private secretaries, are reaping the rewards of training gained in I. C. S. spare-time study of these subjects. Engineering? Architecture? Electricity? Hundreds of thousands of men have climbed into big jobs in the technical professions through I. C. S. help.

The boss is sizing you up. If you want a big job that carries responsibility and good money, *get ready for it*. There is an I. C. S. way to do it and all the I. C. S. ask is the chance to show you what it is. The way to find out is to mark and mail this coupon. Do it *now*. It will be the first step upward.

INTERNATIONAL CORRESPONDENCE SCHOOLS
Box 3274, Scranton, Pa.

—and what the Reviewers say about them

—The Powder—	—The Stick—	— The Cream —
"Rapid action throughout, leading to a wholly satisfactory solution of the problem involved." *Tom Beard in The Daily Task* "An everyday problem, treated as a real man likes it." *Professor Barber*	"Clean cut and smooth—no hack work here. All the stubborn characters are mollified and gracefully removed at the end." *Dick Knoburn in The Morning Blade* "Unordinary in its treatment of an ordinary subject." *Editor of Amer. Jrl. of Shavelore*	"Flows smoothly on to a delightful conclusion—leaving a sensation of genuine satisfaction." *Harry Tonsor in Everyday* "Plenty of quick action at the start, well sustained throughout and ending smoothly." *Hon. Every Mann*

It speaks volumes for superior quality—the fact that so many men find complete satisfaction and comfort in the use of

COLGATE'S
SHAVING LATHER
STICK - POWDER - CREAM

Whichever method you prefer the result is the same—a rich, quick, plentiful lather that stays moist and leaves the face without smart or burn. Colgate's needs no mussy "rubbing in" with the fingers. It softens the beard as you work up the lather on the face with the brush.

Sold everywhere, or a trial size of any one sent for 4c in stamps

COLGATE & CO., Established 1806, Dept. B, 199 Fulton Street, New York

Makers of Cashmere Bouquet Soap—luxurious, lasting, refined. A new size at 10c a cake

After the shave, Colgate's Lilac Imperial Toilet Water—refreshing and delightful

Please mention this magazine when answering advertisements.

Please mention this magazine when answering advertisements.

THE UP-TO-DATE MAN

The readers of the magazine may write to this department about any problem of dress. Every question will be promptly answered, provided that a stamped, self-addressed envelope is inclosed.

EVENING dress may be termed the civilian's uniform, since its cut is military in inspiration, and some of its details, as the stripe on trousers, are borrowed from the kit of the soldier.

In its cyclic swing from the knee breeches and buckled slippers of the bygone beau, evening dress has never been so bereft of the ghost of a thrill as this year. There's hardly even a new sugar coating to the old pills.

A very smart fashion here, though it is two years old abroad, is an evening topcoat of bright navy blue with a black velvet collar. It is slightly drawn in at the waistline, and has free-draping skirts, that ripple around the edges.

This coat, worn by a distinguished foreigner, has been widely copied, but its characteristic cut seems to be mastered by only a handful of tailors.

The knitted-silk evening waistcoat will come as a surprise to many, but this, too, is an oft-told tale abroad. The mesh is just like that of a muffler, a fine, soft, figure-flexing fabric, which is far lighter than woven materials.

The evening Inverness, or cape overcoat, is "the last cry" and all that sort of thing, but it takes the irreproachably turned-out man to carry it off. Height,

figure, air, and that sixth-sense gift of smartness, which can't be put into print, are the things that count.

One meets many types of the Inverness coat this season. A totally new one is the 'alf-and-'alf coat, with the cape extending from the back seam to the front. You have the conventional cape front, together with a straight, loose box back.

Alike at the Metropolitan, New York, and Covent Garden, London, the Inverness is now accepted by fashionables as the preferred evening coat "for occasion." It is both the youngster's and an oldster's coat, befitting each, if he have the spare, tallish, well-set-up figure to go with it.

Another smart coat for evening wear this season is the "paletot" or frock overcoat, having skirts split from the waist down. However, the black or dark-gray Chesterfield coat, with a velvet collar, is just as proper and not so extreme.

In dress, as in all the fine arts, it's the little mind that scorns the little things. You can toss a biscuit across the narrow gap that divides the thoroughbred from the underbred.

Legion is the name of the men who

Neōlin Comforts
Neōlin Lasts

Child alike of man's imagination and of his synthetic genius — Neōlin today is acclaimed by the modern man for the modern achievement which it IS. Born but a year ago, its coming marked the decline of the leather sole.

FOR Neōlin—the natural tread—is as superior to leather as is electricity to gas. Neōlin is better in every way that sole-leather is *good*. And good when sole-leather is not. Neōlin costs far less than leather because it wears far longer, and saves not shoe-bills alone but doctors' bills as well.

Indeed, hundreds of thousands are grateful to Neōlin for its absolute water-tight tread and for the foot-muscles it develops through Neōlin flexibility. And Neōlin looks as good as it feels! It comes in one certain dependable grade — Goodyear grade — indicated by the mark "Neōlin." Mark that mark — stamp it on your memory. Dealers or shoe-repairers have Neōlin — or can get it at no added cost to you.

Every Genuine Neōlin Sole Bears the Brand Ꮑeōlin

— the trade symbol for a quality-product of

The Goodyear Tire & Rubber Company
Akron, Ohio

---

mismate top hat with topcoat. The opera or crush hat, in its rightful place, should accompany the Inverness (cape) overgarment.

With the Chesterfield or paletot (frock) greatcoats, only the shiny top-

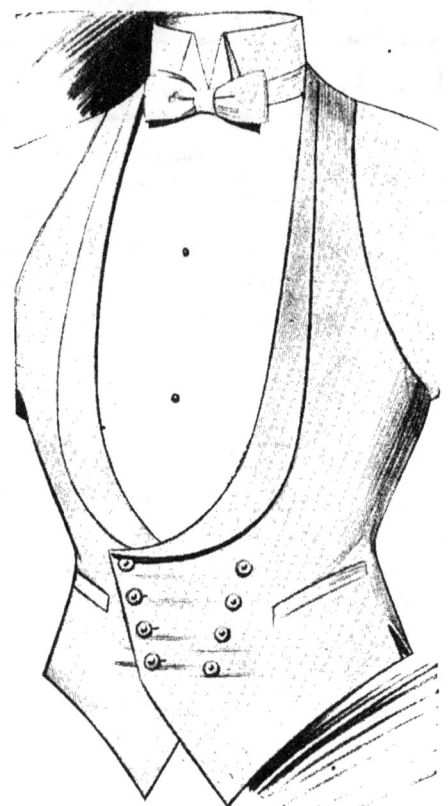

The Formal Evening Waistcoat and Proper Accessories.

per should be worn, for the opera is a theater hat, and nothing more.

Years ago it was worn at random at every sort of gathering, from the small "at home" to the crush, but our new-born, selective instinct distinguishes now as sharply between affairs by night as by day.

The ultrasmart opera hat of 1916 follows precisely the form of the conventional top hat. It has a crown

rather belled and a brim slightly bowed upward, or a brim with a decided outswing and an abrupt edge curl.

You must be full of face and plenteous of chin to carry off the last-mentioned style, as it is a shade extreme, and becoming only to the odd man.

With both types of hats, the poke collar, rather than the wing, is fashionable this season.

Those of us with whom the possession of a motor car amounts to an obsession, may sit warmly in the cold, and pur with contentment.

For touch-and-go winter sports like skating, skiing, tobogganing, and motoring, a new cap is tiptop. It has a drop back, which is pulled down to guard one's ears and neck against the gnawing chill.

First-rate caps of this type are Shetland wool, with an extra-deep visor. The cheaper sort is made of worsteds and tweeds in greens, browns, grays, and mixtures.

Perhaps the best cap for motoring in the thick of winter is genuine sealskin, with a movable visor that may be flipped up or down. For touring, the back unfolds and is drawn snugly over ears and neck.

Sealskin gloves to tally with the cap have leather palms and roomy gauntlet wrists, which, serving as a wind shield for the arms, keep out whipping breezes.

Striped Angora jackets for cold-weather golf are shown with mufflers of the same stuff and pattern, as well as with plain wool stockings, having turned-down tops to match the stripes of both jacket and muffler.

BEAUNASH.

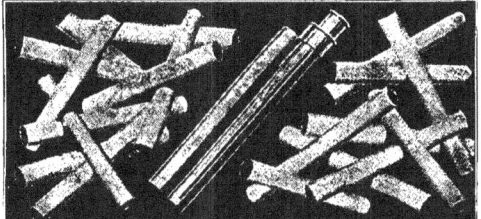
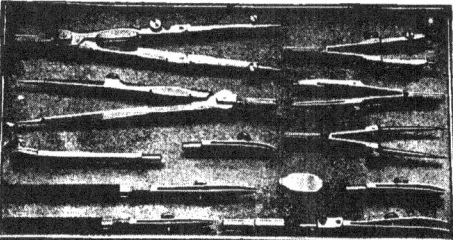

Statement of the Ownership, Management, etc., required by the Act of Congress of August 24, 1912, of THE POPULAR MAGAZINE, published semi-monthly, at New York, N. Y., for October 1, 1916:

State of New York, County of New York, (ss.)

Before me, a Notary Public, in and for the State and county aforesaid, personally appeared George C. Smith, who, having been duly sworn according to law, deposes and says that he is one of the publishers of THE POPULAR MAGAZINE, and that the following is, to the best of his knowledge and belief, a true statement of the ownership, management, etc., of the aforesaid publication for the date shown in the above caption, required by the Act of August 24, 1912, embodied in section 443, Postal Laws and Regulations, to wit:

1. That the names and addresses of the publisher, editor, managing editor, and business managers are: *Publishers,* Street & Smith, 79-89 Seventh Avenue, New York, N. Y.; *editor,* Charles A. MacLean, 79 Seventh Avenue, New York, N. Y.; *managing editors,* Street & Smith, 79-89 Seventh Avenue, New York, N. Y.; *business managers,* Street & Smith, 79-89 Seventh Avenue, New York, N. Y.

2. That the owners are: Street & Smith, 79-89 Seventh Avenue, New York, N. Y., a firm, composed of Ormond G. Smith, 89 Seventh Avenue, New York, N. Y.; George C. Smith, 89 Seventh Avenue, New York, N. Y.

3. That the known bondholders, mortgagees, and other security holders owning or holding 1 per cent or more of total amount of bonds, mortgages, or other securities are: None.

4. That the two paragraphs next above, giving the names of the owners, stockholders, and security holders, if any, contain not only the list of stockholders and security holders as they appear upon the books of the company but also, in cases where the stockholder or security holder appears upon the books of the company as trustee or in any other fiduciary relation, the name of the person or corporation for whom such trustee is acting, is given; also that the said two paragraphs contain statements embracing affiant's full knowledge and belief as to the circumstances and conditions under which stockholders and security holders who do not appear upon the books of the company as trustees, hold stock and securities in a capacity other than that of a bona fide owner; and this affiant has no reason to believe that any other person, association, or corporation has any interest direct or indirect in the said stock, bonds, or other securities than as so stated by him.

GEORGE C. SMITH,
of the firm of Street & Smith, publisher.

Sworn to and subscribed before me this 27th day of September, 1916, Charles W. Ostertag, Notary Public, No. 29, New York County. (My commission expires March 30, 1917.)

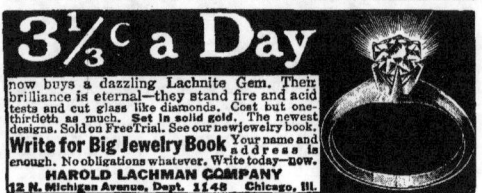

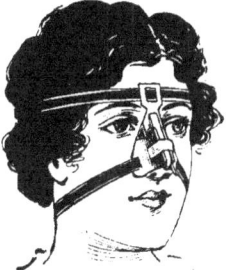

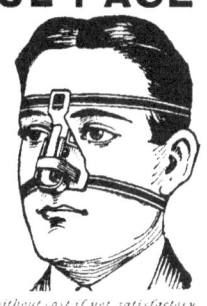

Please mention this magazine when answering advertisements.

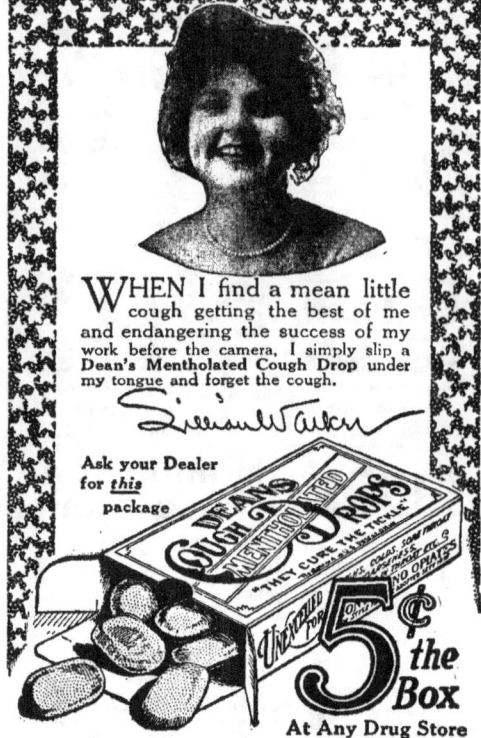

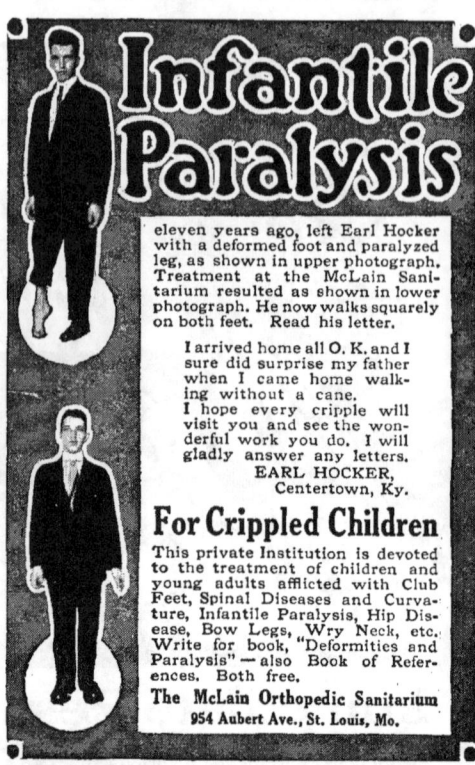

Just Out!
21-Jewel Burlington

All sizes for both men and women.

The newest ideas in gold strata cases.

The new Burlington is ready—just out—and distributed for the first time—on an astounding offer. The superb new model far surpassing everything of the past. 21 jewels, adjusted to positions, temperature and isochronism. Runs almost two days on one winding. Sold on an iron-clad guarantee. New thin design—and all the newest ideas in gold strata cases to choose from. Send coupon today.

Special Offer Now

And—we will send you this master watch without a cent down. If you decide to buy it—you pay *only* the rock-bottom price—the same price than even wholesale jewelers must pay.

$2⁵⁰ a Month!

Just think of it! $2.50 a month —less than ten cents a day will pay, at the rock-bottom price, for the New 21-Jewel Burlington—the master watch. This perfect time-piece will be sent to you, prepaid, without a cent deposit so that you can see and examine it for yourself. When you hold it in your hand you will realize what a gigantic value it is — and you will know how the Burlington brought the highest watch values within the reach of all. Send coupon now.

Write for Introductory Offer

Write today for our new catalog and the introductory offer. Read about this gigantic watch value. Learn about watch movements and why 21 jewels are the number prescribed by watch experts. Read what makes a watch movement perfect—and how the Burlington is adjusted to the very second. The watch book is free. Write for it today and get posted on watches and watch values. Send the coupon.

Burlington Watch Company
Dept. 1149, 19th Street and California Avenue, Chicago

Burlington Watch Co.
19th St. and Marshall Blvd.
Dept. 1149   Chicago, Ill.
Please send me, without obligation (and prepaid), your free book on watches, with full explanation of your cash or $2.50 a month offer on the Burlington Watch.

Name..

Address...

....

The Taste of "PIPER" Is Unique

In no other tobacco can you get the refreshing, tasty, fruity flavor that a chew of "PIPER" gives you. "PIPER" is the world's greatest chewing tobacco—wholesome, appetizing and delightfully satisfying.

PIPER Heidsieck
CHEWING TOBACCO

The ripe white Burley leaf of which "PIPER" is made is unequalled for chewing, and this rare leaf is made still more delicious by blending through it the famous "PIPER" flavor. Chew "PIPER" once — and you'll never again be satisfied with any other tobacco.

5c and 10c cuts, foil-wrapped, in slide boxes. Also 10c cuts, foil-wrapped, in metal boxes. Sold everywhere.

THE AMERICAN TOBACCO COMPANY

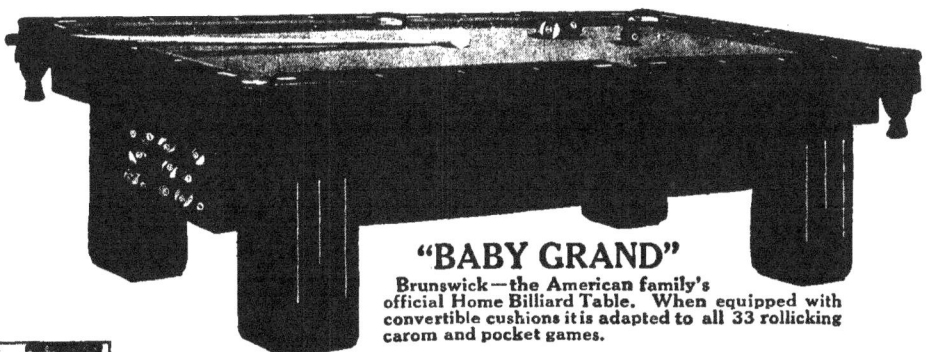